D0107295

THE

Message
in a BOTTLE

ROMANCE COLLECTION

Hope Reaches Across the Centuries Through One
Single Bottle, Inspiring Five Romances

THE
Message
in a BOTTLE

ROMANCE COLLECTION

Joanne Bischof,
Amanda Dykes, Heather Day Gilbert,
Jocelyn Green, Maureen Lang

BARBOUR BOOKS
An Imprint of Barbour Publishing, Inc.

Prologue ©2017 by Amanda Dykes
The Distant Tide ©2017 by Heather Day Gilbert
A Song in the Night ©2017 by Amanda Dykes
The Forgotten Hope ©2017 by Maureen Lang
A River between Us ©2017 by Jocelyn Green
The Swelling Sea ©2017 by Joanne Bischof
Epilogue ©2017 by Joanne Bischof

Print ISBN 978-1-68322-091-6

eBook Editions:
Adobe Digital Edition (.epub) 978-1-68322-093-0
Kindle and MobiPocket Edition (.prc) 978-1-68322-092-3

All rights reserved. No part of this publication may be reproduced or transmitted for commercial purposes, except for brief quotations in printed reviews, without written permission of the publisher.

All scripture quotations, unless otherwise noted, are taken from the King James Version of the Bible.

Scripture quotations marked NIV are taken from the HOLY BIBLE, NEW INTERNATIONAL VERSION®. NIV®. Copyright © 1973, 1978, 1984, 2011 by Biblica, Inc.™ Used by permission. All rights reserved worldwide.

This book is a work of fiction. Names, characters, places, and incidents are either products of the author's imagination or used fictitiously. Any similarity to actual people, organizations, and/or events is purely coincidental.

Published by Barbour Books, an imprint of Barbour Publishing, Inc., P.O. Box 719, Uhrichsville, Ohio 44683, www.barbourbooks.com

Our mission is to publish and distribute inspirational products offering exceptional value and biblical encouragement to the masses.

 Member of the
Evangelical Christian
Publishers Association

Printed in Canada.

Contents

Prologue

"You will surely forget your trouble, recalling it only as waters gone by."
JOB 11:16 NIV

Ballyfír Monastery, the North of Ireland
834 AD

Flames lapped at the monk's robes. He raced down corridors that crackled with the collision of dampness and heat, dodging fire-lit debris. So this was to be the end, then. The night the stones of Ballyfír Monastery would tell their last tale.

Voices ricocheted. Quick into an alcove he pressed himself, wincing against the sharp, foreign echoes. One man barked out heavy words, only to be cut off by another. How many were there? Five in the cross path, by the sounds of it. Maybe more. Perhaps there was yet hope, if their number was small. Another, more distant voice summoned them away, and they thundered in the direction of the cellarium.

Good, he thought. *Let them take the food. If they will but leave the words...*

The monk released his breath then pulled in ash-thick air only to sputter it back out in a fit of coughing. Turning, he flung open the latched window and gasped for clean air. He was too far from the round tower where the finished manuscripts were stored, but he might reach the scriptorium before the fire did. The Living Word must endure.

But as he filled his lungs afresh, he saw them: three ships curled against the night in stark silhouette, horrible dragon mouths agape upon each prow. Torchlights running to and fro on board, on the beach, winding their way up the hill to the monastery like one great serpent, ready to swallow them whole.

"Please, Father." His whispered prayer was raspy. "If we perish, may hope yet live."

Slipping into the empty corridor, the prayer released a thousand leaden weights that had anchored him: the sight of the abbot moments before, slain in the refectory; the desperation that washed over him at the thought of those confined to the infirmary, unable to escape; and the subsequent realization that *none* of his brothers could flee—not far enough, on this island. Tonight Ballyfír—*the place of truth*—would give its life for truth. For hope.

Suddenly the yelling, the crashing debris, the pounding footsteps, and shrieks of a raid faded until all he could hear was his own heartbeat carrying him swiftly to what he sought. In the darkness of the scriptorium he grabbed for something—anything—to protect the words. He laid hold of a vessel, hand-forged by one of the metalworking brothers, its cold bronze inscribed with braided intricacies and a Latin word encircling its neck. He pitched the quills it held and capped it. The bottle was a messenger, now. A guardian.

He gripped it and ran to snatch the parchments from the table. With full arms he lingered but a moment, torn: Should he flee back into the fiery mayhem, where destruction would surely consume the pages? The room seemed smaller and smaller, and so did he, until his eyes fell on the small wooden door in the corner—only waist-high, created to retrieve candles from the cupboard shared with the kitchen. He dashed to it, flung open the door, tossed the cupboard's contents out, and burrowed through to the other side.

A door scraped open behind him. They'd breached the scriptorium. Pulse rushing in his ears, he scrambled into the kitchen and through its door to the outside, where the night cloaked him long enough to reach the cliff-side tower. Wind lashed his face and plucked the parchment leaves from his arms until he held fast to what remained: one solitary sheet in a swirling dance of wind-borne pages. Despair threatened to cripple him, but truth was truth whether one page or fifty. The tower door creaked open to his push, and he took the steps up, up, up two at a time until he burst into the tower chamber—home to the perpetual flame that guided weary visitors to them. The monk shivered, realizing it was the work of his own hand that had guided the Vikings here—for he'd tended the flame just hours ago. Was it such a short time? It seemed an eternity, and now he stood on the brink of just that.

With a mighty heave, he pushed open the window latch overlooking the surf. Time stood still as he rolled the solitary parchment up, glimpsing its ornately illuminated words as he did. He slipped the scroll inside the bottle. This, then, would be their legacy to the world. He would set it free to be carried somewhere, to safety if it pleased God.

Windows in every direction, he turned to take in the sight of his earthly home one last time, clutching the vessel to his chest.

Behind him, he glimpsed the far end of the monastery, where the open-air cloister walled in a handful of candles flickering amid the firestorm encroaching around them. Those who still lived must have gathered there. He could hear their harmonies rising on the wind, a haunting and sweeping steadiness carried with each interlaced note, wrapping him with the peace of his God. Peace that made no sense. Peace that could only be from its very Author.

Beside him, the steady stream of torches grew closer.

And before him, the midnight sea waited to swallow the precious words. Through cracked lips, the monk prayed the waves would not bury them, but carry them until they could speak life into another soul.

Perhaps even the souls of their attackers.

"Father, forgive them. . . ."

He lifted the candle and dripped its wax around the bottle's mouth to seal it before securing the lid. By the light of the single flame, he read the word etched upon the bronze with such care: SPERO.

He stretched his arm out through the window and, gathering every bit of strength left within him, hurled it outward. It arced, briefly catching the moonlight, then dropped into the dark water below.

It was finished.

The monk dropped to his knees, hands clasped, and joined his voice with his brothers in a song of life, even as Viking shouts overpowered them.

The stones of Ballyfír told their last tale that night...but it was just the beginning.

The Distant Tide

by Heather Day Gilbert

Chapter One

Ciar's Kingdom, Ireland
1170 AD

The skies were as unsettled as her own future.

Swirling mountain breezes billowed through Britta's narrow castle window, carrying with them the unmistakable tang of a storm. The sunshine of the morning had given way to glowering clouds this evening. Springtime in Ireland could be fickle.

She swiped at another errant tear. Refocusing on her favorite book, her finger traced the Latin words on the ancient vellum page.

A sharp rap sounded, and her nursemaid, Florie, entered her room in her usual way, without waiting for permission. She bustled toward Britta's chair, her brass-blond hair escaping her kerchief. Her round face was flushed from walking up the tight circular stairs.

"I've been shoutin' for you, Princess. There's no one to come and fetch you, since your father took my servants with him on his journey to see the high king. It's time for our evening meal."

Florie was bolder than any other servant in the castle, but for good reason. After Britta's mother had died young from the fever, Florie had stepped in to care for the toddler princess. Britta couldn't recall one day when her loyal Florie hadn't come rushing when she needed her.

The woman leaned closer, the smell of cooked meat wafting from her clothing. She cupped Britta's quivering chin with her rough hand then pushed black strands of hair off Britta's face. "You've been crying. What worries could be weighing on you, safe and healthy as you are?"

That was just the problem. She was perfectly safe here in the castle—so comfortable, she never had to leave this place. And the largest part of her didn't want to leave. Generations ago, the O'Shea family had settled in this lush pocket of Ireland. This beloved castle and land held her close, as tightly as if she were shackled.

She tried to explain. "You know I've always wanted to share my faith with those who have never heard of Christ, and even to those who still hold to druidry."

Florie nodded, thoughtful. A smile broke across her face. "Perhaps your father will make your dream possible with this journey. You are of marriageable age now,

15

and I have heard the high king has four handsome sons—"

Britta gasped at the suggestion. Surely her father had traveled to discuss kingdom business with the high king, as he did every year. "I can't leave you, Florie. Nor could I leave Father, although he might not miss the opinions I so freely offer him."

"True, I shouldn't like to see you leave, Princess. I doubt your father would, either." Florie's light eyes crinkled. "Perhaps God has another suitor for you, closer to home."

Britta sighed. She didn't want to think about suitors yet. She wanted to understand how to use her talents for God—whatever those talents were. She was a proficient reader. She also enjoyed talking to Father about decisions for the kingdom, but every time she shared her thoughts, it was as though she was talking into the wind. Father listened to his right-hand man, Ronan. Not to her.

The psalmist said she should ask for the desires of her heart, but the two strongest desires were irreconcilable. There was no way to spread the Word without leaving the kingdom she cared so deeply about.

Florie patted her hand. "Come on down to eat. You'll feel better with something in your stomach, and then I can prepare a bath for you." She rustled down the stairs without waiting for Britta's response.

Not even vaguely mollified, Britta glanced out the window. The low gray clouds obscured her view of the nearby mountain. Because its crowning rock formation was shaped like a crow's beak, many viewed the monument as an annoyance, an obstruction to the clean line of rolling green hills that swept to the ocean. But to her, it felt like a protective ally, solid and reliable. Even though it was simply called Crow Mountain, she liked to imagine more poetic names for it, like Eagle Aerie or Piney Bluff.

If only God would make His plans for her as obvious as that mountain.

When Britta reluctantly trailed downstairs, she caught Ronan and Florie attempting to move the tabletop onto the trestle in the great hall. To save space, the table was always taken apart after meals and moved into a corner.

The tabletop was a dense plank of cherrywood, and it would be impossible for two people to manage it, even given Ronan's considerable strength. The guards her father had left behind were already camped at their posts for the evening.

"Let me help." She grabbed a beveled corner, ignoring their black looks. They didn't want the princess to sully her hands with menial labor. But she *was* the princess, wasn't she? Even though Ronan had been left in charge, she could still do as she pleased.

After considerable effort, they successfully maneuvered the tabletop into position. Cringing to think of repeating the task before each meal, Britta declared, "We will leave the tabletop where it is for the duration of my father's absence."

Florie murmured her approval of this plan then scurried off to the kitchen to retrieve the food.

Ronan, too, nodded in agreement. He removed his mace from his belt and propped it against the wall, near his shield and sword.

As always, Britta felt a wave of thanks that her father had left his best warrior behind to protect her. Ronan's family had lived near the castle all her life, and he had battled alongside her father many times. His loyalty was unquestionable.

Glancing at his mace, a shudder passed from head to toe as she imagined the damage the heavy spiked weapon could inflict. A nervous giggle escaped as she tried to picture such a gentle-spirited man wielding such a deadly weapon, although his build was undeniably powerful and she knew he would not hesitate to protect her life with his own.

He glanced up, his dark eyes softening. "Is something amusing?"

Before she could explain, Florie emerged with a large pot of onion soup. She served it up, accompanied by a hunk of white cheese and slightly scorched oatcakes. Finally, she took her seat, waiting for a look from Britta.

Nodding, Britta sipped her soup, the cue that others could eat. She took an oatcake from the pewter dish then cast a furtive look down the table.

Florie started to wipe her mouth on her sleeve then instead used her linen napkin. "Pray tell, what d'you need, Princess?"

"Have you any of the bog butter? I find it gives my oatcakes incomparable flavor."

"I surely do, and I don't know how I forgot to set it out." Florie hastened into the larder, returning with a greeny-black butter ball.

"Thank you. I know Father says it's uncouth, but I've found nothing matches its taste."

As she finished slathering a thick layer of butter on the oatcake, Ronan spoke. "I shall be riding over to Brennan's castle to trade horses in the morning. Would you care to accompany me?"

It seemed a careless question, a discussion to pass the time, until Britta raised her eyes and met Ronan's dark ones. His completely unguarded gaze struck her like the lightning that had finally loosed outside.

She took in his intense look, his half-quirked smile. He was so expectant, so. . . *fixed* on what she would answer. Realization dawned. Ronan found her desirable. Had her giggling led him to think she was admiring him?

Or had he felt this ardor for some time? If so, how had she missed it?

An embarrassed flush covered her cheeks. She tried to invent an excuse. "My stomach. . .perhaps I need to. . ." Unable to continue, she stood and rushed from the great hall. She heard Ronan shove his chair back to stand, and Florie's anxious voice trailed after her, but she could not stop.

Bolting into her room, she threw herself on her bed, thoughts fluttering about like doves' wings.

How long had Ronan found her attractive? For so many years, they had wandered the land together, discussing everything from hawks to laws to books. Had the storm-charged air, coupled with her father's absence, released his hidden feelings?

A sudden thought wormed its way to the forefront. What if this unexpected option was the simple solution to her future, a way to ensure that she could stay in her castle for life? Surely her father would be pleased if she married his right-hand man—the one he would doubtless leave his castle to, since he had no male heirs.

This time, no books could assuage the pounding of her heart. Outside, thunder pounded and rain swept across the moors, spraying mist into her open windows. She jumped from her bed, slamming the shutters together and drawing the iron bar across them for good measure. She wished she could lock her thoughts away so easily, but it was impossible now that Ronan's face had betrayed his true feelings. Was this an answer to her prayers?

This would be a surprise attack. Ari Thorvaldsson cast a lingering glance at his family's chain-mail shirt, which he would leave behind to enable more stealth. His closest friend, Sigfrid, gave him a meaningful stare with his one functioning eye.

"What was the real purpose of this voyage, Ari?"

What sort of question was that? The entire crew understood his motivation to avenge his brother's blood, spilled in this deceptively green place—Ireland, some called it. The clan responsible for Egil's death must feel the wrath of the Northmen, as had so many others on this fair isle.

Feeling weighted by the heavy, humid air, Ari chose his weapon carefully and did not answer. He was most comfortable with his sword, its name carved in the blade: *Peacebreaker.* Surely it was an apt name, since peace had been stolen from him with Egil's untimely death. His brother had only been sixteen when he fell in a raid on this very castle.

Sigfrid pressed him again. "Are you certain you want to attack?"

A sudden twinge of doubt reared its head. He had only been ten himself when his brother was slain. His father forced him to stay with his mother on the longship, waiting for the outcome of the struggle. Although he could barely remember the castle his family had raided, he could still close his eyes and smell the pungent blood that had spread across Egil's chest that day.

His eyes fixed on the odd mountain backing this castle, its point similar to the beak of one of Odin's ravens. Strange that he could not recall it from his youth.

Sigfrid had not been with his family during that raid, so he could not confirm Ari's memory. But he had followed the course his father had mentioned, and the lines of the castle looked so familiar. This was the one.

Blond strands of hair escaped their leather binding as Ari nodded forcefully. "Of course we must attack. We did not sail here to trade or explore. We came for vengeance."

Sigfrid nodded. "Then take care as you scout for us."

Thunder boomed, and he sheathed Peacebreaker, taking his shorter knife in hand. This sharp angled *seax* would serve him well in close quarters. He hoped to gain access to the castle grounds before anyone could send up an alarm.

The men had set up camp last night and would soon lose the benefit of surprise. Ari knew they were still exhausted from the long voyage to this Irish inlet. He had to move now that twilight was falling.

He gave a nod to his men. No words were necessary. If they heard his battle cry, no force on earth could stop them, no matter how exhausted they were. Like a wave of heat and hatred, Vikings would sweep the offensive castle clean.

The rain moved in heavy sheets, forming deep puddles and loosening Ari's footing. Creeping cautiously among the wet tangle of berry vines inside the walled garden, he hoped the tightly stitched seams of his leather boots would keep his feet dry. There was nothing he hated more than cold, soaked feet. At home, when he checked traps in the deep snows, there had been several times he'd feared frostbite would take his toes.

He glanced back at the circuitous route he'd taken to creep up to the rear of the castle. Clambering the stone wall hadn't been easy in the near dark, but it was surprisingly low. Perhaps the Irish were prepared for shorter invaders, or perhaps they anticipated attacks only on the castle gate in the front. He had spied but a single guard stationed there.

It was possible that he had timed his attack well, when the castle wasn't fully manned. And the crashing storm had provided effortless concealment. It was a sign: the gods smiled upon this raid.

He clenched his jaw. Who was he fooling? The gods hadn't protected his brother. They hadn't given him any happiness in the years he had tried to please his father, stepping into the position of heir. They had never even brought him a woman interesting enough to marry.

He fingered the ancient bronze bottle he kept belted inside his tunic. It was unwieldy, but it was his heritage, and he didn't want to die without it. It was a trophy from his ancestor, who had bravely sailed west, to this very country, and plundered the holy men who lived here. This bottle and its story had passed to each Thorvaldsson heir. Ari stomached the thought that Egil should have inherited it and pushed on.

Candlelight flickered in the window then disappeared. This was his chance. He gripped his seax, ready to slash at anyone inside. *For Egil*, he told himself. For Egil he would bring this castle to its knees.

Chapter Two

Spinning her mother's amber ring on her finger, Britta closed her eyes, picturing Ronan's intense gaze and how his sleek dark hair matched his neatly trimmed beard. Why had she never thought of him as a suitor? He was surely handsome, turning women's heads wherever he went.

Maybe it was because he talked to her as a friend—almost as one of the men. When he spoke with her father about taking animals to trade or building onto the castle, he had a way of pulling her into the conversation. Ronan took her opinions seriously; she was sure of that.

Florie rapped and opened the door, once again interrupting her musings. She stood just inside the room, awkwardly shifting on her feet. "Apologies if the oatcakes did not please."

Britta walked to her side, pulling her into a hug. She could never be angry with such a loyal friend.

"The oatcakes were tasty. Perhaps I used too much butter. My stomach has settled considerably."

Florie brightened.

Britta continued. "I wondered—has Ronan ever spoken to you about me?"

The nursemaid's freckled cheeks flooded with sudden color. "Well, now. I am not certain what you mean."

She was blunt. "Does he care for me, as more than just a friend?"

Florie hedged. "To be sure, he's never said a peep to me along those lines." She shot her a shrewd look. "But I've noticed he lets you win at the table games, which is contrary to his competitive nature. He also dashes outside the moment you announce you're taking a walk. And you remember the spring festival? There were so many eligible clansmen there, practically swarmin' around you. Ronan stayed right by your side, do you recall?"

She did. She had thought nothing of it at the time, because Ronan knew she was uncomfortable in large crowds and she'd assumed he was trying to set her at ease. Yet the way Florie described it, he had been protecting her from the advances of other men.

Abruptly, Florie moved toward the clattering shutters, giving a futile tug at the iron bar, which was already secure. "Listen to that driving rain! I'd better feed the guards now. They'll be soaked to the bone." She hurried from the room.

Florie's observations and her nervous behavior confirmed Britta's suspicions. Ronan did care for her. And what was wrong with that? He could read Latin. He loved God, as she did. He was well regarded by her father. Indeed, life with Ronan would be comfortable. But was it a comfortable life that God had called her to?

Stooping, Ari silently rushed the side entry door. The dimming light of an oil lamp on the scullery wall indicated that someone had been here recently. He crept forward, thankful he hadn't worn the clinking chain mail.

A sense of echoing spaciousness met him as he passed through the next door. Embers died in a square hearth by the wall, casting long shadows. This must be the great hall. But where were the residents?

He sensed a movement to his right, but before he could turn to see if someone was there, a dull thud slammed into his stomach. A muffled cry jolted from his lips. Furious, Ari stabbed into the dark, in the direction of the attacker. Another blow fell, this time crushing his foot. Even as he tried to plunge farther, hot pain stabbed at his toes, driving him to the stone floor.

Not far away, a woman gave a horrified shout, filling the vaulted space. Ari tried to drag himself back to the doorway, but his long, large limbs would not respond. It was as if his crushed foot pinned his entire body to the ground.

Candles and lights surged toward him. He could make out the sturdy form of the woman who had screamed. She babbled in her native tongue, waving her hands like birds' wings. Three men drew closer, their lights forming a circle around him. A dark-haired man stooped to retrieve an object from the floor. Ari felt sick when he recognized the bronze spikes attached to a thick stick. He had been attacked with a mace. It was a wonder he had survived.

The man seemed to reprimand the older woman, who continued gesturing to the mace. She must have been the one who had flailed it at Ari, with all the ineptitude of a child wielding his first wooden sword. The bronze head of the mace was too heavy for her to handle, and she must have dropped it right on his foot. He realized the family bottle, tucked in his tunic, had deflected her first ill-placed blow to his chest. Otherwise his insides would have been mangled.

The dark-haired man was in charge, and he seemed to be pondering how to dispose of Ari in the most efficient manner. But the man's attentions were diverted when a single flickering candle moved down the stairs.

The golden light barely outlined a distinctly female form. As the woman approached, Ari sensed the power shifting from the dark-haired man to her. The circle of onlookers opened and she stepped forward, her black eyebrows raised in concern.

Slowly, she knelt by his side. Her feet crushed the lavender and rosemary strewn on the floor, releasing their scent afresh. The dark-haired man took her by the elbow and pulled her back to a standing position.

The older woman launched into her narrative again, only this time, she spoke slowly enough that Ari understood some of the words. His father owned Irish slaves, and he had listened closely and learned their language so he could converse with them. The woman seemed to be repeating the words *Northman* and *giant*. He grinned.

At this, the young woman with the tumbling black hair leaned in, holding the candle over Ari's chest. A hot drop of wax spattered onto his tunic, but he did not flinch, even as it burned his stomach.

The dark-haired man noted Ari's reaction, his face hardening.

As pain seared through his foot again, Ari curled up tighter, trying to relieve the pressure. He inwardly cursed himself for being reduced to such a position. Why didn't the man just run him through with his sword? Perhaps these Irish were torturers.

When he opened his eyes, a milk-white face hovered close. Fjord-blue eyes met his.

She spoke only one word, but it was a word he knew.

Healing.

Britta could not tear her eyes from the Northman. Even curled into a ball, it took all three guards and Ronan to move him to a pallet in her father's chamber upstairs. She had never seen a man so tall and large, saving perhaps Crim, son of the swineherd. And Crim was as filthy as his swine most of the time.

It was puzzling: She had been told that the Vikings were dirty, crawling with bugs and reeking like the corpses of their victims. This man's clothing was not unkempt, and his skin and hair were not foul. Only the faint scent of smoke clung to him.

The hulking blond man had remained mostly quiet until one of the guard's hands accidentally slipped from his shin to his bloody foot. He unleashed a roar that nearly made the guards drop him, and she could not restrain her gasp.

Ronan's eyes were steely as he deposited the Viking, none too gently, on the pallet. He had not approved of her suggestion to rehabilitate the man before her father returned to execute judgment. She had to admit, Ronan's idea of a swift death might be the better plan. The Viking's eyes flashed with unconcealed hatred, and she knew he brought an unprecedented threat to their peaceful inlet.

Yet when his pale, blue-silver eyes paused on hers, his candid gaze spoke louder than words. He longed for certainty, as she did. Perhaps even some kind of redemption. This man had a soul, no matter how brutal his culture was.

Thankfully, Florie knew much about healing, not only because she had nursed many injured clansmen over the years, but because her own husband was an invalid. She would do as Britta asked, despite her fear of the Viking.

Britta grimaced, imagining Florie swinging Ronan's mace blindly in the dark. How had she managed to maim the intruder enough to halt his attack? God must have guided her hands.

The guards nodded at Britta as they took their leave. Ronan walked toward her, placing a light hand on her shoulder and fixing his eyes on hers. She couldn't be sure if they blazed with desire or fierce protectiveness.

"You're certain you want to keep him alive? He seems a beast."

"Yes. Father will want to know if there are more Vikings coming to our shores. Perhaps we can find a way to communicate with him."

After considering, Ronan finally gave a half nod, as if this were a sound reason. "A guard will stand at his door for the duration of his stay."

She knew this would leave them short a guard at the castle gate. She summoned false courage. "I have my own knife, and so does Florie. We will require no extra protection."

Ronan laughed softly. "After seeing how Florie handled my mace, I shudder to think what she would do with a knife. Clancy will be posted outside his door."

The Viking groaned, his body curled toward the wall. Florie would soon arrive with the herbs and cloths to wrap his foot. Perhaps they could offer him warm broth, if he understood they meant well.

But if he did not understand. . . Britta shivered.

Chapter Three

It was only a matter of time before his men would come looking. Ari could not decide which would be better: if his crew stormed the castle or if Sigfrid came alone. If they attacked the castle, his mission would be fulfilled because these murdering Irishmen would be dead.

But his thoughts lurched unwillingly to the beautiful goddess who had devoted herself to his care. The raven-haired, plush-lipped maiden had not ceased trying to coax words from him. Did she suspect how well he understood her language? He had determined to feign ignorance, to be the heathen wild man they seemed to think him. He would not become attached in any way to the family who killed Egil.

Yet the young woman—*Britta* is what they called her—would sit and read aloud to him after the nursemaid changed the herbal wraps on his foot. He supposed she was trying to distract him from his continued pain.

Three days had passed, and his swollen foot had shifted from a deep red to shades of purple and green. The barbed spikes of the mace had left open wounds, but they had begun to heal. The deeper throbbing was what tested his fortitude. But the tea the nursemaid brought regularly—it tasted of willow bark—seemed to ease the pressure.

Ari finally determined that the book Britta read from was her holy book. She treated the thick leather binding, with its numerous vellum pages, with utmost care. He had heard there was a holy book like this not far from his home in Norway, displayed in a newly built Christian church. He had not seen it, because his family would not approve if he went there. They spat upon the ways of Jesus Christ, determined to cling to Odin, Thor, Freyja, and so many others.

Even as Britta devoted hours to his care, the dark-haired man—he seemed to be called *Ronan*—spent most of his time pinning him with blazing looks. There was no doubt the Irishman wanted him dead. Ari closely watched Ronan's movements and moods. Perhaps he was the one who had killed his brother. Ari could probably overpower him, once he was able to walk.

Today, Ronan swept into the room, shooing the guard from the door and leaning over Britta as she read. He spoke so rapidly to her, Ari could only decipher one word: *Viking.* The book she cradled dropped to her lap. She looked at Ari, then back at Ronan.

What had the heartless troll told her?

Ronan's words tumbled out, unharnessed and unsoftened. "A Viking horde camps by the mouth of our inlet. I have watched them as they sit about, sharpening horrible axes and knives. . .gleaming swords like the one this fellow had. They are heavily armed, and with so many, they could take this castle in just a few moments. We must either send this man back, kill him, or send an emissary of goodwill."

The Bible dropped into her lap with a thud, but Britta barely felt it. So many Vikings already encamped. Ronan had been wrong to trust her judgment. She had failed her O'Shea name. And what now? Would her father even be able to return home with those savages encamped so close by?

Yet a glance at the Viking told her he was not as savage as Ronan would have her believe. The man had taken food gratefully from her hand and had allowed Florie to place cool cloths and herbs on his wounds. He had watched as she turned pages, slowly sounding out Latin words as she pointed to the symbols.

But she could understand Ronan's nervousness, given that the Viking watched his every move like a lion waiting to pounce. His hatred was not veiled as it burned in those sea-colored eyes. Britta suspected that like Ronan, the Viking was a fearsome warrior, and both men sensed a worthy opponent.

Ronan caught the Viking looking at her. "I can make it easy for him," he whispered. "A knife to his throat as he sleeps and he would not feel pain."

She drew back. As a warrior, Ronan was surely capable of such violence, but he must see it was morally wrong to kill an unarmed man.

She controlled her voice, lowering it for emphasis. "You have given me three choices—to send him back, to kill him, or to send an emissary. His foot is still weak, and it needs more care than they will be able to provide in a makeshift camp, so he cannot return to them yet. As far as killing him, you know I cannot condone the murder of an injured man who cannot defend himself. So I will choose the last option—sending an emissary to the Vikings." She paused, forcing herself to say the next words. "And I will be that emissary."

Ari watched as Ronan's words grew heated. Although he gestured wildly in the air, it was clear he would not lay a hand on Britta. The two seemed to reach a tentative agreement, and the powerful man strode out the door.

She resumed her position, sitting back in the gold-studded chair by his pallet and picking up her holy book. She chose a page and began to read, but he interrupted her, croaking out a word for the first time in days.

"Ari." He pointed to his chest and repeated it, louder. "Ari."

She hesitated, her huge blue eyes searching his.

He nodded and said it again, motioning to himself. "Ari."

She leaned forward—if Ronan were here, Ari knew he would reprove her for a lack of caution, and Ari wouldn't blame him. She was altogether too trusting.

"Britta," she said, resting a pale hand on her embroidered ivory dress.

He repeated the word, enjoying the way it sounded with his heavy accent. "Bree-ta."

Her gaze returned to her book, and she seemed lost in her own thoughts. Finally, she pointed to a word next to a hand-drawn picture of a room filled with golden goblets and their holy cross symbol. "Mon-a-ster-i-um," she said, drawing out each sound.

It was a long word, but perhaps he needed to show her he was grateful for her daily teaching, even though the word she spoke was a reminder of the divide between her people and his. His ancestors had attacked such monasteries to gain the wealth needed to secure their power. Even now, his bronze heirloom bottle was hidden on the floor beneath his pallet, one side of it bearing a slight indentation from the misplaced blow of the mace. He would not leave this place without it.

With effort, his rough voice sounded out, "Mun-e-sterrr-i-um."

The smile that spread over Britta's face replaced all the anxiety that had clouded it when she exchanged words with Ronan. Ari wished he could think of other ways to make her smile.

Leaving Ari in Florie's capable, but still somewhat-resistant hands, Britta hurried to her room to change out of her ivory dress. She wanted to wear something that would indicate her position as princess.

Although her father's kingdom was small, it was well respected. It was quite an arduous journey over the hills for Father to discuss matters with the high king, and he only went twice a year. She hated that this was one of those times. She never knew how long such travels might take—once, he had stayed for a full month.

She hoped her actions would please her father, but deep inside, she was fairly certain that he would have agreed with Ronan and disposed of the Viking invader, instead of allowing the injured man to rest on a pallet in his room.

Shaking such doubts from her mind, she donned a tea-colored silk dress with pink roses scattered over the skirt. She placed a narrow, golden crown on her head.

For good measure, she pulled up her skirts and strapped a belt around her waist. Attached to the belt was a long sheath she tied in place on her thigh. From a drawer next to her bed, she retrieved her antler-handled dagger and carefully slid it into the sheath. She hoped the Vikings would not attack her when they realized she carried no sword, but if she were captured, at least she would have a secret weapon.

Yet her best weapon was Ronan, who had refused to let her approach the encampment alone. It was a foolish thing for him to come along, because if they were both killed, the castle would fall. True, he would place one of the guards in charge, but no guard was as vigilant and deadly as Ronan.

As she descended the stairs, she watched to make sure the chunky dagger handle did not protrude beneath her skirts. Realization struck her—how would she communicate with the heathen warriors? Hand gestures could prove deadly if they were misunderstood.

Perhaps Ari could teach her what to say, something that would make her peaceful intent clear.

She turned, hoping she could trust the Northman to share a word that would protect the castle, instead of one that called for an attack.

Chapter Four

Florie met her in the stairwell, her pink face anxious. "M'lady, I was just coming to fetch you. He's gaining strength in his foot, 'tis certain. He's trying to hide it from us."

Britta could not be distracted. Even now, Ronan was probably putting on his mail shirt and gathering his weapons. She patted Florie's hand. "We will watch him closely. For now, he will go nowhere—our guard Clancy stands just outside the door, and he is wider than the Viking. Do not fret."

Florie tucked stray wisps of hair beneath her kerchief and straightened her apron. "As you say, m'lady. I've dressed his foot, so I'll be going down to prepare our meal." She paused, her gaze trailing from Britta's crown to her nicer clothing. "Have you dressed early for the evening meal?"

"Ronan and I will be traveling today." Britta did not elaborate. Much as she longed to tell her nursemaid about her dangerous mission so she could savor some motherly sympathy, she would not allow herself to do it. Florie had already risked her own life, attacking the invader in the dark with a mace. What would she do if she realized the princess herself planned to stride into a Viking war camp? Britta could just envision Florie, her stout form clad in a man's mail shirt, spear in hand, accompanying her charge. She hid a smile. No, her loyal Florie must not know her plan.

As she entered the room, Ari turned his gaze from the window to her. His curious yet appreciative glance swept over her royal clothing and crown. Knowing she had no time to waste, she rifled through her stack of books on the floor, searching for one she had read many times.

When she found the volume she wanted, she searched out a particular picture in it then held it up for Ari to see. His cool eyes moved across the colorful page. It portrayed two armies facing off, but their weapons were no longer drawn. Two men met in the middle, helmets in hand. One carried a stick with a white cloth tied to it. They were obviously seeking a truce.

She pointed to the page where the two men stood. "Peace," she said, hoping he understood.

He gave her a blank stare. Did the Vikings have no concept of peace? It would certainly fit with the stories she'd been told as a child. The Northmen were villains who slipped onto Irish shores in dragon-head ships, killing to take what they wanted, stealing natives to make them slaves. There was nothing fair about the Viking attacks, no chance to be armed against a force that was nearly invisible until the last minute.

But she *must* have something to say to the Viking men in the camp. True, she could bring along one of Ari's things, like his sword, or the bottle he'd tried to hide under his pallet, but then the Vikings might assume he had already died at their hand. If so, surely their wrath would be swift.

With renewed fervor, she tapped at the men in the picture. Then she placed the book on her lap and rammed her fists together to indicate fighting. Finally, she abruptly pulled her hands apart, holding them upright to show that the warring sides were at peace.

"Peace," she repeated, praying for a word, just one word, that could save her family home.

Recognition sparked in Ari's face, and his lips slid into a half smile. He spoke carefully: "Greethe."

She repeated the word several times. When Ari nodded in approval, she placed her book on the floor then stood and hurried from the room.

As the door slammed behind Britta, Ari flexed his foot, pondering. She had been carefully dressed as royalty, and she had asked him how to say *grið*, the Norse word for peace. Although his thoughts were sluggish from something in the tea, he sat bolt upright as he began to understand.

She was going to see his men. She was going to ask for peace. That was the only explanation for her behavior.

How would Sigfrid react to Britta's approach? Thankfully, Ari's second-in-command never acted rashly, but when he determined someone was a threat, he would not hesitate to crush them.

Ari could not let his crew fall upon the helpless, trusting woman who had kept watch over him for days. He felt beneath his pallet, hoping they had not taken the knife he had hidden there, but it was gone. His eyes widened as he realized his heirloom bottle was also missing. The tea must have made him sleep through their pilfering. But why would they take something of no value to them?

He allowed his fear for Britta to flow through him. It washed away thoughts of the bottle and subdued the throbbing, heavy pain in his foot. Determined, he pulled his leg to the side of the pallet, allowing his foot to touch the floor for the first time since his injury. Although he could hardly bend his ankle, he tried to rotate his stiff foot before grabbing the back of the chair and pulling himself to a standing position.

The foot gave way, and he let out a light groan, which he quickly stifled. If he had to crawl to Britta's side, he would. Sigfrid would see him and stay his attack plans until he gave the word.

Someone shifted outside the door. Doubtless, they had left a guard behind. Where was his sword? Glancing around, he realized that not only had they taken his weapons, they had also taken his boots.

The still-swollen foot needed support. Unwilling to bend to the level of the low pallet, he struggled to take his tunic off then ripped into the bottom of the linen with his teeth. He managed to tear off a strip of cloth and wrap it around his foot. Each move was agonizing, but he could not give up. Wrestling his way back into his tunic, he scowled at the sight of his half-exposed stomach. It still bore a deep bruise from the impact of the mace on the bottle. Sigfrid would fear the worst had happened to him. But there was no time to search for another tunic.

His only advantage over the guard was the ability to surprise. He haltingly shuffled to the door, senses alert. The man outside sniffled then sneezed. Ari could only hope he was weakened with an illness.

An image of Britta, her pale cheeks flushing as she met his eyes, sprang to mind. If his men killed her, he would never forgive himself.

Gathering his strength, he pulled up the latch on the heavy wooden door, thankful it locked from inside. In one fluid move, he yanked the door back, thrusting his body forward to assault the unwitting guard.

Too late he realized that there were only two long steps between the landing and the first steep stair. When he collided with the large Irish guard's frame, he knocked them both into the darkened stone stairwell. Their bodies plummeted onto the jutting steps, tumbling over one another.

Fresh pain gave him a light head, and when they reached the bottom step, Ari's world went black.

Chapter Five

When Britta met Ronan in the great hall, she was not surprised to see that he was wearing his long mail shirt. His sword was sheathed, and he carried his mace over one shoulder. Trying to look at him as the Vikings would, she imagined he would seem like a regular demon, with his blazing eyes and red wool clothing.

She rested her hand on her friend's arm. "We must first pray."

Ronan nodded, taking the lead. "May the shield of God protect us from these pagans. May the angels of God give us protection. And may Christ be over all. Amen."

She felt safer walking toward the unknown with this God-fearing demon Irishman at her side. Their steps echoed as they entered the stone courtyard outside the entryway. The morning was brisk, and the cold air made her wish she had donned her woolen cape. But she wanted to appear unarmed to the Northmen.

Ronan led the way through the plush green grass, around the small streams she knew so well. She tried to forget her mission, noting how the clouds cast shadows and patterns on their hills. But after they climbed the final rise, she gasped. The field that edged the rocky gray coastline was dotted with drab-colored tents—at least twenty of them.

Farther off, where the grass gave way to the shoreline, they had dug a semicircular earthen rampart, blocking their long, dragon-prowed ships from easy attack. At least ten fully armed men guarded the dirt blockade.

As they drew closer, smells of cooked fish assailed them. The Northmen themselves struck her as incredibly hairy, with beards and fur vests and long, wild hair. Each one seemed to have several weapons on his belt.

These were barbarians indeed, handily shaping the land to their own purposes and sleeping outside in the elements. They were rough and rugged as the stags on Crow Mountain.

Ronan grasped her arm. "You do not have to be the one, Britta."

She shook her head. "Indeed I do. You cannot enter their camp alone. They will see you as a threat because you *are* a threat. You cannot hide the passion shining in your eyes—you would like to see them all dead."

He looked to the camp and nodded. "You are correct. But you must admit it is wise to be distrustful of these heathen. You have read the stories, Britta, and you have heard our monks' fearful prayer: 'From the fury of the Northmen, deliver us, O Lord.' These Northmen have ravaged our shores for so many years, I am certain they intend to plunder our castle." He paused, his russet eyes searching hers. "Your blond invalid is no innocent. He came to vanquish us—make no mistake. I see the passion in *his* eyes."

Britta could not deny it was true. Occasionally when he wasn't watching her, she noticed how a strange sadness would darken Ari's countenance. It was as if he were pining for someone. Was it a woman from his homeland? Perhaps a wife?

She shook off her doubts, pointing to a leather-clad, grizzle-bearded man who had silently moved toward them. When they glanced his way, he leaned on a tall spear, affecting carelessness. "It is too late to argue over this. They have already seen us."

With feigned boldness, she strode toward the man, holding her crowned head high. She could feel Ronan's solid bulk moving directly behind her.

About three feet from the scar-faced warrior, she stopped short and gathered herself to her full height, which apparently didn't amount to much. The Northmen towered over her as they began to form a semicircle around their leader. Their hands hung by their sides, but they had easy access to the sharpened swords and axes on their belts.

She closed her eyes, asking God to help her. Then she focused on the leader's one clear eye, since the other was merely a sightless, tight-lidded slit. "Greethe," she said slowly.

The man's lips twitched, and his gaze sharpened. She repeated the word.

Ever watchful, Ronan stood in silence slightly to her left. If any Northman moved her way, she would need to drop so Ronan's mace could hit him square in the head. He would follow that strike with a sword thrust to the gut.

The Northman scratched at his rough beard. "Greethe?" he asked.

She nodded. Hoping it was not a mistake, she slowly withdrew Ari's bronze bottle from a silken pouch she had tied to her belt. Taking a step closer to the obviously unwashed man, she held the bottle out to him, cupped in her palms. "Greethe."

The man snatched the bottle from her before Ronan could step between them. He spat out a string of clipped words to his men.

She caught one of the words and repeated it. "Ari." She put on a cheerful smile, trying to indicate that the Viking was healthy and alive. But how could she show them he lay abed, without leading them to believe he had died?

A stick lying in the dirt caught her eye, and she saw her opportunity. She slowly bent to pick it up. Silence fell upon the skittish Northmen. Ronan glided a step forward so he was at her side.

She took the stick and carved into the damp soil. It was slow going, but she was finally able to depict a rectangular castle with a jutting mountain behind it. Then she drew the sea and cliffs on the other side and scratches to indicate the camp. Finally, she drew a deliberate, deep line between the castle and the campsite. Her voice was firm and steady as she said, "Greethe." She tapped her crown to bring attention to her authority.

For a long moment, the bearded man did not respond. He gripped the bronze bottle tightly as he examined her dirt drawing. When he looked up, she slowed her erratic breathing so she could meet his gaze. Instead, the man fixed his eye on Ronan. Some wordless understanding passed between the men, and Ronan did not react when the Northman extended the bottle toward her.

"Ari," he said, his voice charged with concern.

She nodded, wrapping the cold bottle in her hands. Comfort flooded her. God had spared her life, and she would be able to return the vessel to its rightful owner. She let her voice soften as she said, "Ari. Greethe."

Ronan's hand squeezed her shoulder as he brusquely steered her away from the circle of Vikings. A truce had obviously been reached. The Northmen would not attack while Ari was within the castle walls.

But from the wild look in the Viking warriors' eyes, Britta knew the truce would end the moment Ari rejoined his crew.

She must find a way to delay him until her father returned home with his soldiers.

Chapter Six

Shifting on the rough board he rested on, Ari tried to recall what had happened after he attacked his guard.

Memories flitted around like swirling seabirds. He caught snatches of images: the Irish guard nursing a bloody lip, the sheath of the man's sword banging into his leg, and the pain that finally tore into his foot like a wild berserker charging his enemy. When the heavy guard's full weight had landed on Ari's wounded foot, the agony had knocked him senseless.

He could slightly remember two men moving him to a side room on the ground floor. They had placed him, none too carefully, onto a low board resting on two wooden blocks. A rough wool blanket was tossed over him, and they left, locking the door behind them.

Now it was night, given the darkness and the dim moonlight trickling through the high window. As he cautiously bent to touch his twisted foot, a metallic sound captured his attention. Someone was fumbling at the latch. He lowered back to the board, pretending to be asleep as he watched through narrowed eyes. A dark figure noiselessly stepped into the room, hastening to his bedside. The person leaned in close, as if listening for movement.

It was impossible to discern if the shape was male or female. But if it were Britta or Florie, wouldn't she speak up? The stillness grew heavy and ominous. He tried to slow his breathing, but his heart thudded like a bucking stallion. He could feel the intruder's breath on his face.

He could bear it no longer. He shoved his hand out and wrapped it around the person's throat—a thick throat, surely a man's—when the sharp tang of a knife blade pinched the skin on his own neck.

He tightened his grip. "No knife," he said, using Irish words.

Pressure from the knife lessened; then as he squeezed harder, the weapon dropped onto the blanket. Immediately, he shoved himself upward, slamming his forehead into the intruder's jaw and knocking the man backward.

As the man groaned, Ari flung himself from the bed, directly onto the prone form. He pinned him to the ground.

"Halt." The man's rough command was easily recognized—it was Ronan. The

Irishman had tried to kill him.

Lantern light shone into the room and Britta appeared in the doorway, unable to see them. She stood there, her white gown peeping from beneath a long, embroidered wrap.

Casting her light about until it fell upon the men, her voice rose in concern. "Ari! Ronan? What has happened? I heard noises. Did someone enter the castle?"

Ari rolled off the Irishman, glaring at the man as he grabbed the knife. He pointed the knife tip at Ronan. "This man tried to slay me."

"No." Her eyes flashed and color flushed her cheeks as she turned to Ronan. "Surely you did not?"

Ronan grunted. "Your father would have wanted it—in fact, I am sure he would have commanded this Viking's death the moment he stole into our castle. He has brought nothing but trouble to us. You have examined our valiant guard Clancy's arm after his tumble down the stairs, and you know his fracture will take many days to heal. We are left with only two guards and myself to defend these walls, should the Northmen invade. We will fall, Princess."

Unwilling to believe Ari had deliberately injured the guard, Britta boldly extended her open hand for Ronan's knife. Ari glanced at Ronan, then at her. Acknowledging her authority with a slight drop of his chin, he carefully placed the weapon in her hand.

She helped Ronan to his feet and handed him his knife. "Leave us for a moment. You can see he means me no harm."

Ronan's dark glare fell on Ari as he rubbed his reddened neck. "It is not wise. I cannot leave you alone with this unpredictable rogue."

"It is an order. I have the final say in my father's absence." Her feet were planted and determination charged her words.

Ronan strode to the door. His voice was thick with emotion. "I will stand outside, but the door will stay cracked. If you so much as breathe my name, he is a dead man. Be cautious, Britta."

Ari sensed the tenderness Ronan used when he spoke her name. The man cared for her—perhaps even loved her.

As the door began to close, Britta moved to Ari's side. It was not hard to imagine how the Irishman had fallen for her. Her touch was soft, yet firm, as she cupped his elbow and helped him to his feet. As he stretched to his full height, he realized that although she had such an imposing presence, she was far shorter than he. Despite her curves, she was compact. In fact, he could pick her up with one hand and throw her over his shoulder....

Where were these thoughts coming from? He was thinking like a lovestruck fool, like a man starved for affection.

Maybe he was.

As he looked down into her earnest blue eyes, he fought his base urge to lower his chin and cover her full, half-parted lips with his own.

She seemed to sense his intent, but instead of drawing back, she stood still, as if transfixed. He restrained himself and waited for her to speak.

She cleared her throat and spoke slowly. "I saw your men today." She withdrew his bottle from under her wrap and handed it to him. "I also wanted to return this to you."

He fingered its familiar bronze shape, always cool to the touch. It felt a bit gritty with patina and could use a good polish. He looked at the daring princess, acknowledging what she had said.

"My men?"

She nodded, covering one eye with her hand. "Your one-eyed man agreed on a truce, at least for now."

"Sigfrid," he said, incredulous. He had unwittingly thrown himself down a flight of stairs to protect Britta from approaching this very warrior. Yet without his aid, she had secured a truce with the battle-hardened man.

She looked shyly at the floor.

Who was this woman who carried such magical charm?

Britta braced her feet, trying to restrain herself from taking a step toward the tall Viking.

It was as if her senses were only attuned to his presence. No other smell mattered, save his leathery scent. No other sight mattered, save her upward view of his neat blond beard and ocean-colored eyes. No other sound mattered, save the husky tones of his words.

Standing so close, her senses conspired against her, pulling her toward him like invisible cords. She had read love poems in her books, but nothing had prepared her for the sheer physical force the emotion carried.

Even so, her head told her that love was more than an emotion. It was a commitment, such as Florie had with her husband, James, who had been sick in bed with the coughing, consumptive disease for almost two years now. He was useless at maintaining their small stone house, and they had to hire a boy to keep up with farm chores.

As Ari began to lower himself onto the board bed, she extended a hand to help. Her guards had given her little say in their decision to move Ari into this room. Once they saw Clancy's broken arm, they determined the volatile pagan could not remain in the king's chamber. Besides, he had already rolled downstairs, which made it easier for them.

As he settled back, she voiced the question weighing on her. "Why did you try to escape? Did we not treat you kindly?"

Ari's forehead wrinkled. "Yes, kindness. It was not escape—I went to aid you. With my men."

Britta caught her breath. He'd intended to accompany her, even though it was a fool's errand—he couldn't have walked all the way to the Viking camp.

"You worried about my safety?"

In answer, Ari took her hand in his own. Unable to look away, she stared at his strong arm, covered in blond hairs and a sinuous dragon tattoo. She allowed herself to savor the feel of his large, rough palm, gripping her own small hand.

"Yes." His eyes searched hers.

Unable to speak, she startled at the sound of shuffling shoes and deep voices in the great hall. Ari quickly released her hand. She stole to the door, peering out the crack.

Men moved around the great hall. Sensing Ronan's presence outside the doorway, she boldly edged forward, watching torchlight illuminate their features. Catching sight of a familiar face, she gave a short cry and pushed forward into the hall.

"Father!"

Chapter Seven

Britta threw herself into her father's outstretched arms. She clung to him, even though the small metal links of his chain mail shirt pressed into her exposed neckline. She pulled back to get a good look at him. His hair, streaked with white and gray, was trimmed and thick. He had not lost weight on his journey. His gray eyes twinkled. Things must have gone well with the high king—but hopefully not so well he had betrothed her to one of the princes.

"I see you have missed me, Daughter?"

She hugged him again, unwilling to be separated from him yet. "Indeed. The castle was empty without you."

Behind her, she heard Ronan slide the bolt across Ari's wide-planked door before stepping from the shadows. A heavy weight seemed to drop into her stomach as she waited for him to mention their Viking prisoner.

"Welcome, m'lord. Indeed, we are glad to see your safe return. I understand it is deep into the night, but we must discuss several things."

Father's face grew serious. "Of course." He motioned to his weary men. "Disperse to your own homes tonight. Tomorrow evening we will gather here for a feast."

Britta followed her father and Ronan upstairs, relieved she would have the chance to explain her actions to Father. But outside Father's chamber door, Ronan shooed her away.

Anger sparked through her, and she felt her eyes widen. "I am not some servant you can whisk away, Ronan. I am the king's daughter."

Father turned and gave her a thoughtful look. "Indeed you are. But whatever Ronan has to say, I am certain it is as one warrior to another. You can speak with me in the morning, but now you must get your rest."

Much as she longed to dig in her heels and explain what had occurred in his absence, Britta had learned long ago not to cross her father when he took that tone. He would not listen to a word she said and, in fact, would be more likely to go against her wishes.

Plodding into her room, she draped her midnight-blue embroidered wrap over a chair and tumbled into her bed. Pulling the heavy bed curtains shut, she yanked the blankets up around her. She wished her fire had not burned down to coals.

Sometimes the wind seemed to prod through every chink in the castle walls, pushing the chill right into her bones.

Despite her exhaustion from her meeting with the Vikings, sleep would not claim her. After trying unsuccessfully to get comfortable, Britta finally drew the curtains, lit her candle, and picked up a book near her bed.

As she read the tale of a mythical hero who fought sea robbers, she found herself picturing Ari. She remembered the long, intimidating ships docked near the Viking camp. It was easy to imagine the tall Northman, his blond beard shining in the sunlight, sleeves pushed up to show his tattoo, as he sailed to conquer new lands.

But this was her land. And she did not want it conquered.

Despite her growing attraction to Ari, if she allowed herself to look at the situation dispassionately, she knew he had not changed his intentions since he stole into the great hall. Ronan knew this, too.

Would Ronan recommend execution to her father? And was there any reason for her to stand against it, since not only was her life at stake, but the lives of everyone in her father's kingdom?

The castle forces had returned; Ari was sure of it.

His foot was stiff from the cold, so he could not creep to the door to observe, but the clamor of deep voices told him all he needed to know.

Britta seemed oblivious to his true intentions. Hadn't he come to kill everyone, to bring revenge for his brother's untimely death? He could never forget the turbulent emotions of that battle-torn day in Ireland so many years ago. He could never wipe away his mother's lifelong loss and his father's deep grief over the death of his firstborn.

He had come to make things right, not to become entangled with an Irish princess he could not give his heart to. When he healed—if they allowed him to leave—he and his men could attack, and this loathsome castle would be destroyed. How many years had he longed to tear it apart, stone by stone? To torch its wooden support timbers and watch it burn?

His room had no fire, so his thin clothing was altogether inadequate. He drew his blanket tighter. The stiff board beneath him made it impossible to become comfortable, and he was sure that had been the guards' intent. Until now, they had been meticulous with his care. After his bungled attempt to protect the princess, which must have resulted in an injury to one of their men, they would be wary and give him no sympathy.

Except for Britta, who seemed tethered to him somehow. She was not put off by his size, his people, or his violence.

A new voice seemed to penetrate his heart—a truthful voice that seemed older than time itself. The voice said only one word, but he heard it very clearly: *hope*.

From her window seat, Britta watched the muted pinks and yellows of sunrise seeping across the deep blue inlet. Seeing God's hand as He painted the world made her feel refreshed and composed. Perhaps Father and Ronan had decided on a reasonable course of action for Ari.

But her tranquility was undone as Florie entered her room, her words tumbling out. "I've already laid the morning meal for your father and Ronan. They will have many actions to carry out before the feast. I thought to myself, p'raps you might want to catch them first."

Understanding what Florie had left unspoken—that judgment would fall on Ari today—Britta sprang into motion, throwing off her nightclothes and pulling a red brocade dress from her wardrobe. Red was not her favorite color, but she had no time to stop and think. She must catch Father before he spoke to Ari.

Florie aided her, tightening the laces in the back. "You haven't been eating enough, 'tis sure, m'lady. But we'll have fresh meat tonight and one of those apple pastries you love so much."

The last thing she cared about was food, but she turned, taking Florie's round face in her hands. She planted a kiss on each cheek. "Thank you for looking after me, Florie. I know you are stretched thin with your James abed."

Florie shook her head. "There's naught I can do for him that I haven't already done. Looking after you and your family gives me a purpose, and James wants me over here, not clucking over him like a mother hen."

Britta squeezed her nursemaid's hand, hoping to derive a last measure of strength before she approached her father downstairs. As she pulled on her slippers and walked out of the room, Florie called after her. "May God fill you with hope, m'lady."

Hope. An invisible comfort that seemed oceans away. The Viking tide that had washed onto their shore carried with it only one promise: dread. And her father wouldn't tolerate it.

Ronan and Father were so deep in conversation, they paid no heed to Britta as she descended into the great hall. Only when she sat next to her father and tapped his arm did he look at her.

"My dearest." He brushed her cheek with a kiss then took a small bite of his potato pie.

Ronan's gaze fell heavily upon her, full of conflicted emotions.

Her heart sank. She took up her fork, absently tapping the shell of her soft-boiled egg.

Father spoke into the awkward silence. "Ronan has told me of the Vikings, and of this *Ari* who has enjoyed our hospitality although he arrived with evil intent. What have you to say to this, Daughter?"

Ronan spoke before she could reply. "I explained how we decided Ari was not a danger to us." His deep brown eyes held hers, imploring her to play along.

So Ronan had taken the blame for her own lapse in judgment. Probably for Clancy's resulting injury, as well. Her heart swelled with gratefulness.

She shared what Ari had told her. "Ari did not try to harm Clancy. He wanted to accompany me when I spoke to his men."

"To trap you, I shouldn't wonder," Father mused.

"No, he feared his man would try to harm me. I think he feels protective of me."

Her father shifted so he could look at her directly. "So he *says*, Britta. But a man will say anything to escape his prison, comfortable as it might be. No. I will speak to him myself and discern his motives."

She felt like spitting out the bite of chewy egg she had taken. Was Father right? Had Ari lied to her? He seemed so earnest, but she had only run across one liar in her life, and that was a mouthy chimney sweep her father had released from service before he had even finished his job.

After the men finished eating, she stood with them and filed into Ari's small room. If nothing else, she would be nearby when her father passed sentence on the Viking.

Chapter Eight

Ari was thankful for the fresh clothing Florie had brought him, even though the green tunic was a bit small and stretched along his shoulders. After her early morning ministrations with warm cloths and fresh linen strips for his foot, he felt strong enough to risk standing on it again. Despite the bruising, he could tell it had healed somewhat.

When the door opened, he sank quickly to the board. He did not want to let anyone know the speed of his recovery.

An older man stepped into the room, his gray eyes solemn. He wore a rich purple velvet tunic embroidered with a family crest. A heavy gold cross pendant hung from his neck. This was their leader, Ari was certain.

Ronan stood alongside the powerful older man, and Britta hung back, her gaze flickering from Ari's foot to his face.

The man spoke. "I am King Kacey O'Shea, ruler of this land, and Britta's father. You have come to our shore with plans for an attack. How do you answer?"

Ari understood most of the man's thickly accented words, like *ruler*, *father*, and *attack*, but when he paused expectantly, Ari realized he had missed some question. He looked helplessly at Britta.

To the obvious discomfort of both men, she walked confidently to Ari's side. She leaned toward him and spoke slowly. "Why did you come to Ireland?"

A lie would be easy and might spare his life. But there was no honor in a liar.

"Avenge my brother's death. . .killed on a raid of your castle."

Britta's eyes clouded, but she nodded that she understood.

"Blood for blood," he added.

As she explained to the men, her hands fluttered nervously. Dark hair slipped around her cheeks, but it did not hide the tears glistening in her eyes. She, too, feared the decision of her father.

Perhaps this was his chance to escape. Could he overpower both the king and Ronan before bolting for the door? He hesitated. The older man looked perplexed. He spoke rapidly to Ronan, and both seemed to agree. He turned and spoke to his daughter, but this time Ari understood every word.

"Vikings have not come to our shores before. It was not this castle. He is mistaken."

Britta knew Ari must have recognized the truth in her father's words, because he fell silent. When he finally spoke to her, the dangerous spark that had burned in his eyes was all but quenched.

"I feared this. The mountain. . .not the same as when I was young."

Her heart clenched. So Ari had been in Ireland alongside his brother when he was killed. She fought the urge to hug his shoulders, which were straining at the seams of his undersized tunic. Instead, she placed her hand briefly on his arm.

Immediately, Father shot her a sharp look. "Britta—"

He was interrupted by a guard's sudden appearance in the room. The breathless man's words were clipped.

"A rider came. King Tynan's lands have already fallen. The Normans have invaded."

Normans! Britta had heard of these clever, greedy men. Skilled in both rhetoric and military tactics, they were practically unstoppable in their conquests. In fact, the Normans were descended from the Northmen but had married the French and changed loyalties. They served no one but themselves.

King Tynan's realm was to their east. It was impossible to believe that it had fallen, with the king's extensive forces. There would be no hope for her father's smaller kingdom. The Normans would rule over her family and reduce them to peasants. Soon all of Ciar's Kingdom would belong to the invaders.

Ari continued to sit in his own stunned silence while Ronan and Father spoke with the messenger. She could not bear to hear the fear in their voices. The feast tonight would not be a time of celebration, but of preparation for war.

Suddenly, Ari's determined, booming voice echoed from the stone walls in the small room.

"I must speak with my people."

Father stared at him, obviously shocked by the impertinence of his demand.

Ronan did not hold his tongue. "Pray tell us, why?"

Ari turned to Britta, his pensive eyes searching her face. But he returned his gaze to her father, palms outstretched as if beseeching him for mercy. He began to string more Irish words together than he ever had before, which made her wonder if he had understood more of their private conversations than she'd suspected.

"I have wronged you. . .acted dishonorably. I rallied my crew for revenge, then led them to the wrong castle. My hatred blinded me."

Britta glanced at the men. Ronan looked dubious, but Father seemed convinced by what Ari had said.

He continued. "I must ask you to let me return to my men and tell them of my foolish mistake."

"But you cannot walk!" Ronan spat out.

Before she knew what was happening, Ari rose to his feet beside her. His jaw was clenched in concentration, and when he swayed a little, she grabbed his forearm to support him. He took two steps toward the men, and Ronan's hand dropped to his sword.

"With a sturdy stick, I could walk." His belligerent gaze challenged Ronan.

Britta could not restrain herself. She looked at her father. "Can't you see? It's the best solution. This way we do not have to take his life, thus incurring the wrath of his formidable crew. He can return to his men and sail before we have to battle the Normans."

While it tore at her heart to think of an abrupt departure for Ari, she knew it was the only way he could be safe. The longer he stayed with them, the more suspicious Father and Ronan would grow of his motives. If he left now, he had a better chance of surviving this misguided venture into Ireland.

Ari shook his head, placing his hand over hers. "You do not understand. I will order my men to sail, but I will stay. There is no one better to face the Normans than a Viking. I know how they fight. I am weak, but I can help you." He bent at the waist in a half bow before addressing her father. "It is an honor to clear my name by fighting for you, King O'Shea."

Chapter Nine

The king took his daughter's arm, walking her from Ari's room. Ronan trailed behind them, shooting the Viking a displeased glance. Ari caught a glimpse of two guards moving into position outside his door. They were taking no chances, now that they knew he could walk again. He recognized the burly guard he'd taken with him down the stairs, and the man gave him a murderous glare before the door latched.

After a short time, Florie brought him a meal, along with the surprising news that he was to attend the feast tonight. Did this mean the king would allow him to fight alongside his warriors? Perhaps he wanted to introduce them?

Or perhaps he planned to announce his death sentence.

He wished he could see out the high window to take his mind elsewhere, or that he had a book to look at. He missed those early days of Britta's unswerving attention, when she read to him for hours. Now he wasn't sure how she felt about him. She had suggested it was time for him to sail with his crew, so perhaps she wanted to be done with him.

He couldn't blame her.

He slurped down the hearty pea soup the nursemaid had brought then tore into a piece of dry bread to sop up the remainder. Were his men eating well? Had they been able to hunt? At the very least, they would have fish from the inlet and dried meat from their ships' supplies.

There was a soft rap at the door, and the guard opened it. Britta entered, carrying a pale green silken tunic and trousers, along with his leather boots. He hastily wiped pea soup from his mouth and stood.

She smiled shyly. "These clothes are for the feast. We had to borrow them from Clancy, since he is the only one your size, and the trousers may still be short. He was none too happy about it. Since there is no one with feet as large as yours, you must wear your own boots, though the servants could not clean all the dirt off."

He felt an actual blush creeping up his cheeks. Did she find his large feet repulsive? Taking the clothing and boots, he remained mute, unsure how to ask the question driving him mad. Would he live or die? Surely she knew.

She spoke up. "I know you are anxious. Please know that my father is a fair king.

He does not make decisions carelessly."

"I am sure Ronan has said much against me." He couldn't keep the spite from his tone. He knew Ronan's concern for this castle went deeper than loyalty to the king. The looks the Irishman gave Britta only confirmed that he cared for her deeply.

Her eyebrows crinkled. "You assume much."

"I assume only that he is not blind to the beauty living under the same roof and that he might want her for himself." He gave her a pointed look.

Now it was Britta's turn to blush.

"God will work things together for good." Britta managed to blurt the verse out before leaving Ari's room, unable to tamp down the fire in her cheeks. The Viking had no understanding of her God, so why had she felt compelled to say it?

She prayed Father would accept Ari's offer to serve with his soldiers, but it was impossible to know what his decision would be. This morning, she had told him that she believed Ari's intent was good, yet she did not say anything beyond that. If she pleaded for the Viking's life, it might make the king suspicious of her motives and give him further cause to eliminate Ari, or at least to expel him from their shores.

Instead, she put on her walking boots, told Florie she was going outside, and passed through the back door into the garden. Fruit trees had begun to blossom, and the heavy scent of their white petals filled the air. Honeybees from their hive box swarmed the holly bushes, humming past her ears. A bold squirrel chirruped at her from its perch on the rock wall.

How restorative spring was! And how fine to walk the pleasant land she would one day call her own.

Unless. . .

Unless Father demanded Ari's execution tonight at the feast. It was not hard to imagine Ronan, standing with his sword at the long table, prepared to fulfill such a command. No one would intervene. She imagined Ari's strong jaw dropping to his chest as his head slumped over, his powerful arms going limp as the blade cut into him.

She sank into the soft moss. Of course she would never allow that to happen, even if it meant throwing away any inheritance her father would leave her. The Viking wanted to learn—she saw it in his eyes as she read the Latin books to him. He was an adventurer at heart, like she was, although her adventures thus far had only been in her mind.

All these years, she had felt the draw of the unknown, even as she dreaded meeting it. Perhaps God was using this Viking to push her from her cozy nest. Perhaps she would need to free Ari then steal off with him as he sailed to his homeland.

She smiled at the image. Britta O'Shea, book-loving castle dweller, willingly joining a crew of Vikings. How absurd. She shook her head.

Florie stepped into the herb garden, cutting shears and basket at the ready. Snipping off a few sprigs of rosemary, she spoke aloud. "You're lost in thought, Princess. Anything you want to talk about?"

The woman was always sensitive to her moods.

"I don't know what God wants me to do with my life, Florie."

"What do you want to do with it?"

Britta laughed. "What does it matter what I want? God seems to want great sacrifice. Think of how brave Moses had to be, or the prophets. Think of our own Patrick, away from his home. Perhaps I must leave my home to find my future."

Florie gave her a thoughtful look. "Sometimes the greatest sacrifice is the one that takes you unawares. I had my own dreams of leaving this land, of returning to my home in England. But James became ill, and I don't regret staying here all these years—for him, and for *you*." She patted Britta's cheek then tucked several leaves of basil into her basket before leaving the garden.

Father greeted her with a kiss as she came into the great hall in the late afternoon. She hoped this was a sign that he had listened to her request to have mercy on Ari.

"You are the most beautiful princess in Ireland, my Britta. Fresh as a white rose."

She spun in the pale blue velvet dress he had brought her, enjoying the swirl of its flared skirt. Buttons ran in a straight line down the bodice, skirt, and wide sleeves, and dark blue satin trimmed the hem. She fingered the pearl crown on her head, hoping the twists of hair Florie had secured beneath it would not come loose and give her a bedraggled appearance.

Ronan positioned himself next to Father, his familiar red tunic draped with gold fabric. He could easily be mistaken for a king himself, even without a crown. He raised his dark eyebrows at Britta, and she detected only one well-hidden emotion in the depths of his eyes: sadness.

Had he and Father decided to execute Ari? Or was he upset because she cared for the welfare of a barbarian?

Her father's men were situated around the table, eating cheese and bread until the main course was brought out. The pleasantly heavy smells of herbed pork and stuffed pheasant filled the hall, stirring her hunger. She looked up at the dark oil portraits hung over the hearth, boasting generations of O'Sheas. Would her portrait and her children's portraits hang there someday? Or would the castle fall to the Normans first?

A hush fell over the room as the guards opened the door and Ari made his way toward the table. He clung to a wooden staff, yet his steps were more sure than she had expected. Even struggling to stand, his presence dominated the room. The pale green of the tunic seemed to cast a glow on his fair hair and beard, making him look almost angelic.

She wanted to stand and shout, "How could you ever take this man's life?" But she held her tongue, reminding herself this beautiful foreigner had tried to attack their castle. She would wait for her father's judgment.

After prayer, Father began to speak before the heaping dishes were passed. "You men know by now that this Viking, Ari, has offered to join our forces against the Normans. He regrets his hasty and misguided attempt to capture our castle, and he plans to tell his own crew to set sail without him. We have spent much time and prayer seeking fairness in this matter—for our people and for the Viking."

Britta looked into her father's gray eyes, praying for the right decision. If he chose to sentence Ari to death, she would be forced to act. Her heart would not allow her otherwise. She would have to steal into Ari's room, release him, and leave her treasonous shame behind and sail with him.

If he would let her.

Chapter Ten

Ari could not tear his eyes from Britta's anxious gaze. The appetizing smell of food only reminded him that this might be his last meal.

King O'Shea's voice echoed in the hall. "We have decided that we need Ari to help us fight the Normans. He can tell us of their weapons and train us to defeat them. We cannot let our kingdom fall, as King Tynan's did. We must stop the Normans here."

The soldiers looked to Ronan for his agreement, and the man slowly nodded. "It is the best way."

Britta clamped a fist to her mouth, eyes wide, as if repressing a cry. Ari fought the urge to rush around the table to her side.

"I will speak to my men this day," Ari said. "I am indebted to you and your people."

"Thank you, Father—and Ronan," Britta breathed.

Ari watched as the mighty Irishman rested a tender gaze on the princess. He did not speak a word, but it was clear Ronan had only spared his life for Britta's sake.

Florie had firmly instructed Ari to strengthen his weak foot by walking, so he changed clothes after the feast and hobbled out into the fading sunlight. A lone guard sat by the door, engrossed in eating a small pie.

Ari was thankful his bruises had begun to fade, and perhaps this brief activity would strengthen his foot still more, so he would not appear quite so shocking when he saw his men. He wondered if Sigfrid watched the castle, even now. Or perhaps he had stayed at the camp, honoring Britta's truce.

Lost in thought, Ari stumbled over a stray limb and his foot gave out. A gasp sounded from a tree above as his knees thudded to the ground.

He looked up into the drift of white blossoms that covered a gnarled apple tree. He could barely make out one black leather shoe that protruded from under a yellow skirt.

"I'm coming." Britta's voice sounded from her perch on a higher limb. She skillfully wove between the branches, keeping her skirts tucked as she descended. She carefully deposited a heavy book on the ground before dropping to her feet.

The guard grunted and looked up, but when Britta shook her head, he went back to his pie.

She braced her feet and grasped Ari's hands in an attempt to pull him up. Knowing she couldn't possibly bear his weight with her small frame, he used his good foot to thrust himself upward. As he returned to a standing position, she noted his labored breathing and gave him a half smile.

"I am afraid I was of little use to you." She handed him the walking stick.

"You tried to aid me. I do not deserve your kindness."

She led the way toward a wooden bench that was surrounded by silvery mounds of lavender. Silence settled as they lowered onto it, but it was not uncomfortable. He inhaled the honeyed Irish scents of spring, which mingled with the fresh fragrance of Britta's thick black hair.

"My book!" She jumped up, racing to retrieve it from its grassy bed.

He laughed. "Why drag such a heavy book into a tree?"

She was surprisingly serious as she answered, her voice charged with emotion. "This book is one of my favorites. It tells the story of Patrick, a man who was taken from Britain and made an Irish slave, yet he later returned to Ireland to share the truth about God."

"And you. . .admire this man?"

She looked over the gardens, unable to meet his eyes. "Like him, I have always wanted to tell others about God."

A quiet nudge moved him to say, "Perhaps you could tell me. Our gods have done nothing for me."

Tentatively, she shared the story of Jesus Christ with him. As she did, the voice he'd heard in the darkest recesses of his soul seemed to grow stronger, almost humming in anticipation. This God she spoke of had sacrificed His own Son for humans, so they could join forces with Him on earth then live with Him forever in His kingdom.

Her eyes shone as she spoke of how she could cry to Him in the depths of the night, knowing He would hear.

"When my mother died, all I had was Florie and my books. My father was often too engrossed in his royal duties to spend time with me. I began to read the scriptures then, and somehow my eyes were opened."

A sudden longing possessed him—he wanted to read. He wanted to know for himself what treasures her holy book held.

His hand fell to the bench, unwittingly covering hers. Instead of moving his hand like he should, he wrapped his fingers around hers, savoring the velvety feel of her skin.

Fighting the urge to bring her hand to his lips, he met her dark blue eyes.

"Teach me to read, Britta."

She smiled, and he had to focus on the apple tree to resist the pull of her innocent, upturned face. "I will. But only if you teach me your language."

Britta watched from the castle gate as Ronan and Ari rode on horseback toward the Viking encampment in early-evening light. Ronan had demanded to ride alongside the Viking, to be certain he did not try to break his promise and escape with his crew.

She watched Ari's movements carefully. His bad foot hung a bit too limply from the stirrup on their gray stallion, but he did not slump, so his stomach bruising must be healing.

Looking at the dirt road leading toward King Tynan's kingdom, she shuddered, imagining fully armed Normans charging toward the castle. They would probably wear steel helmets and chain mail. Perhaps they would laugh when they saw the size of her father's castle. How simple to take such a meager outpost!

Florie came alongside her, taking off her kerchief and smoothing her skirts. She was going home, goodies from the feast tucked into a basket at her side. Another townswoman would set out their food late in the evening, since there were many things left over from the grandiose banquet.

"Watching your Viking, are you?" Florie winked.

"What? I don't understand your meaning."

"Don't think I didn't see the two of you in the garden earlier, talking thick as thieves. Why, I even heard your father asking Ronan about your interest."

Britta snorted. Florie had likely been listening outside her father's chamber last night while the men talked. Her nursemaid believed it was her duty to stay abreast of all the affairs of the castle, on the pretense the princess needed to stay aware of such things.

Ronan. The man had listened to her, protected her, even stood up to her father on her behalf, for as long as she could recall. And now she returned his unspoken affection with open interest in a complete stranger's life.

Florie patted her hand. "'Tis naught you can do, m'lady. The heart will answer when it is called. No flood, no earthquake, no falling stars can stop it. I see how you look at him, how you cling to his every word. Ronan loves you, 'tis sure, but you've given him no promises."

It was true. "Thank you. Tell James I will visit him tomorrow to borrow his new book."

Florie huffed. "He paid out the nose for that trifle, I tell you. But the man loves nothing more than reading. Takes him away from his pains, he says."

How well did she understand that. In fact, she'd taught James to read so he could have some reprieve from his suffering. They had fallen into the habit of trading books so they could discuss their merits and inconsistencies. James had a simplistic way of looking at the world—he would often miss nuances in the writing—but he had a way of perceiving overarching themes that took Britta's breath away.

Would she ever have such intense discussions with Ari? Although he seemed the type who was a born warrior and leader, he also had a natural candor and seemed to delight in learning.

Florie hugged her briefly and set off toward her home, skirts kicking up dust.

Britta stared at the field that led to the encampment. If only she could have joined the men, but neither of them would have allowed it.

Ronan knew that if Ari turned on him, one word from the Viking leader would mean his death. She had to believe that Ronan saw some measure of trustworthiness in Ari, perhaps because of his willingness to stay behind and fight for them.

Regardless, she began to pray.

Chapter Eleven

As the Viking camp finally came into view, Ari exhaled. His friends—his people—watched as they approached. He took in the familiar earthy smells of camp. How he longed to join his men on their return voyage, to see his parents again. But he brought no news of a vengeful victory for his brother's death. Instead, he must now fight to protect the very people he had hated for so long.

Sigfrid strode over, his eye appraising Ari's injured foot, his foreign clothing, and the Irishman astride the large white mare.

He spoke rapidly in Norse. "What has occurred? Should we kill this man?"

Ari shook his head, motioning for the men to help him down. He groaned when his injured foot touched the ground, and his crew was visibly dismayed as he pulled the walking staff from his saddle so he could stand.

Sigfrid repeated, "What has occurred?"

Ari spoke loudly, so all could hear. "Many things, but the most important is this: I led you to the wrong castle. This family has done nothing to my brother. They are innocent of his blood."

Unbridled chatter broke out among the men, and Sigfrid commanded silence. At his shout, Ronan's dark gaze turned sharp and his hand dropped to his sword.

Sigfrid shot Ronan a glare then motioned to Ari's foot. His lips tightened and his jaw flexed. "But they have injured you."

"No. This was my own doing. It is too much to explain. You must believe that they have carefully nursed my wounds."

Sigfrid glanced at Ronan, looking doubtful. He suspected the Irishman had forced him to say this.

"You saw their princess," Ari added. "She is incapable of harming someone."

At this, Sigfrid finally relaxed. Britta had made an impression. He slapped Ari's shoulder, excited. "We shall sail tomorrow, then. The longships are ready, and it will not take long to pack up camp."

The men whooped for joy, but Ari held up his hand. "*You* may surely sail tomorrow. But I have promised to aid this kingdom as the Normans will soon descend upon it. I must do this for my family honor, which was marred when I brought us here."

Sigfrid leaned in uncomfortably close, gripping Ari's cheek in his dirty hand, his heavy breath on his face. Ari squirmed under the relentless gaze. He should have known he could not fool his old friend and battle partner.

"You want the girl!" Sigfrid finally declared, giving him a crooked smile. "This is not only about honor. I knew your heart was searching when we set sail, and now you've found the treasure you really sought."

The men had fallen silent, and Ronan shifted uncomfortably in his saddle, poised to gallop away if the men turned on him.

Ari decided to put his mind at ease. He spoke to the Irishman in his own language. "They understand."

Some of the fire went out of Ronan's eyes, but his expression remained wary.

Ari spoke to his men. "You will sail tomorrow. I will find another way back after I battle the Normans. There will be no plunder for you here."

The men murmured in agreement. They began to thump him on the back, saying their good-byes.

As the crew dispersed, Ari pulled Sigfrid into a hug and whispered into his ear, "Tell my parents of what has happened. Someday, I will find a way home."

The grizzled man nodded, but his eye glistened. He surely knew Ari's promise was in vain. This was likely their final farewell.

Burying his sadness, Ari turned toward Ronan. "It is settled. Now we return to the castle."

As the horses trotted off, he took one last glance at the men who had followed him so loyally. The Irish soldiers would never respect him as these men had—in fact, they probably despised him for breaking their man's arm. They would doubtless relegate him to the rear flank, given his foot injuries.

Yet it was no one's fault but his own. His bitterness and grief had culminated in this disgrace.

He would make amends the only way he knew how. He would lay down his hatred of the Irish, even as he laid down his life.

Behind them, the sun had nearly sunk into the horizon. The horses plodded on, anxious for fresh hay. When they were a good distance away from the camp, Ronan finally spoke.

"Why are you really joining us?"

Ari remained silent, letting his thoughts slide into order. Truly, he was motivated by the desire to restore his family honor. He had no wish to stoke the fires of fear and hatred the Irish rightly felt toward the Northmen, due to raids that had occurred centuries ago.

Yet Sigfrid had discerned a deeper need that had led him to these distant shores.

The need for answers to his unasked questions. Why had Egil died so young? What was the point of living if he didn't strive for the gods' favor? What hope was there for him if he doubted the existence of Valhalla? At home in Norway, he had suspected the Christian churches held answers, but he did not want to openly defy his parents' beliefs to attend.

Now he was in Ireland, at the wrong castle, and a princess had begun to tell him of the same Christian God he sought.

Ronan did not prod him, but he finally answered. "I must atone for my foolhardiness."

"There is another reason," Ronan said firmly. He gave him a stormy gaze that said he was unwilling to accept half-truths.

"It is true, I find Princess Britta very endearing. But I understand there is no hope for us. Her father would never let her marry a Northman."

"So you have thought of marriage." Although Ronan's tone was careless, Ari sensed calculation.

"I have," he admitted, as much to himself as to Ronan. "But I understand she is betrothed to you."

Ronan's expression soured. "There is no such betrothal."

The Irishman could have lied outright to protect his interest in Britta. Instead, he had told Ari the truth.

Ari took a long look at the glowering man riding by his side. He seemed to be in pain. Was his love for Britta so great?

The castle came into view, putting an end to his musing. Now was the time to prepare for battle, not to discuss the princess. Ronan seemed to understand the shift of focus and urged his horse into a trot.

Britta walked out to greet them, carrying Ari's sheathed sword. Her smile of relief was quickly replaced with a serious look. After he dismounted, she handed Peacebreaker to him. "Father says you must begin training immediately. The men are gathered in the courtyard. The Normans have been sighted, only a couple days' journey from us."

Chapter Twelve

Training began straightaway, even in the gathering darkness. Britta insisted on aiding the townswomen by keeping torches lit and giving the men water. Ronan had demanded that the handful of men who had chain mail wear it when sparring, so even in the cool of the evening, they overheated easily. Britta made sure the water bucket stayed full so they could occasionally wipe down with wet cloths, a luxury they would not have in battle.

After serving the men, she retreated up to her stone balcony, where she could get a better view of the clashing swords, shields, maces, and daggers. Some of the men wore bull-hide vests that would scarce protect them from the well-armed Normans. Some had no protection at all.

She felt grieved by the poorly dressed state of her father's soldiers, but most Irish kingdoms were the same. If only they were wealthier, able to afford well-crafted swords like Ari's. She had caught Ronan coveting that shiny blade, touching it to see how sharp it was.

Ari's family must be wealthy. Perhaps his father was a chieftain or king? She cringed, knowing the Viking royals probably rose to power with the aid of plunder they took from Irish monasteries.

The courtyard training was halted by a deep shout from Ari. He stood, one hand in the air, as if to silence everyone. Was he unable to spar with his injured foot?

Even as Ronan strode toward him, Ari began to guide the scattered Irish soldiers into a formation. He barked a word here or there to indicate what they were to do—some were to move forward with shields while others protected the sides with swords and maces. The men with daggers were sent away, only to return bearing spears.

From what Father and Ronan had told her, the Irish soldiers rarely used a structured formation in battle. They placed a high value on surprising their enemies, rather than meeting them head-on. Most of her father's soldiers were simply landowners and slaves; they understood more of farming than of fighting. Thus far, the only invaders they had faced were loose marauding groups from other kingdoms, bent on stealing cattle.

To be safe, her father had already ordered the women, children, and elderly to take the cattle and livestock into the caves of Crow Mountain. Although it would be slow travel at night, they would be out of harm's way by morning.

Father had recommended she accompany the group to the mountain, but at Ronan's insistence, he had allowed Britta to make the final decision. She wanted to be close to Father, no matter what happened, so she planned to stay with James and Florie in their cottage during the attack. It was doubtful any Norman would trail to the outskirts of the village, much less care about raiding a small farmhouse.

Her attention was pulled back to the sparring men below. Ronan and Ari stood off in a mock battle, but their intense, savage looks made her catch her breath. Ari held his gleaming sword and shield, and Ronan held his beloved mace and smaller shield. As the weapons clashed in a slow, deliberate fashion, it became obvious that although Ari still favored his injured foot, her father's toughest warrior would be bested by the Viking.

At the last moment, however, Ronan dealt a feigned, final blow that knocked Ari's sword to the ground. Both men nodded briefly out of respect then began to practice with the next man in line.

Would they be able to prepare her father's men in time? Would they know how to defeat the Normans?

As Ari effortlessly knocked an unprepared, helmeted man to the ground with his shield, she began to doubt it.

Ari had hoped the second day of sparring would be easier than the first, but it had proved more difficult. The men were tired from fighting yesterday and from doing farm chores in the morning. They hadn't had enough sleep to build up their energy.

But war never came at a convenient time. And these Irishmen had to understand how to counter the Norman attack.

If only he had one of his father's berserkers with him. Just one of those wild warriors could stave off many men and strike fear into the rest.

Sigfrid and the men would be under full sail by now. Longship voyages were always indescribably fulfilling experiences. He could almost feel the rush of sea air against his skin—that briny, fresh smell that made him feel so alive. How he loved pulling the oars those final lengths as they glided into the fjords of home. The deep blue sky and the formidable mountains always seemed to rein them in with invisible hands.

As Britta brought a loaf of bread to the table, he wished he could share his thoughts with her. Maybe she would someday sail with him and enjoy the delights of the sea, but if he could not stop the Normans, his death would be sure.

He did have one question to ask her before he fought, however. He withdrew his bronze bottle from his tunic and set it on the table.

"Around the neck of this bottle, there are letters. I wondered if you could tell me what they say?"

She traced each letter of the inscription with her finger. Some were worn, and he wondered if she could make them out. But it did not take long for a smile to break across her face.

"Spero." She carefully returned the bottle to his open palm. "It is a Latin word, probably carved by monks." Sadness briefly replaced her joy. "You have stolen this from the Irish monks?"

"Not I. But yes, my family did, generations ago." He could not restrain his curiosity. "What does it mean?"

She took a deep breath, a shiver running up her arms. "Perhaps it is a sign—a whisper from God. The word means *hope*."

He started. It was the very word he had heard so clearly in his spirit. Did it mean there was hope for him with Britta? Hope the Irish would triumph?

Or did it mean he had hope of salvation by the Christian God?

"There is always hope," she murmured, catching his gaze. "I have spent too much time fearing the worst. But God will watch over His own, even if it means carrying us home to heaven."

"I will not let that happen to you." He took her hand, toying with her amber ring. Perhaps someday he could give her a ring of his own.

Ronan stood abruptly, motioning the men back to the courtyard. As Ari rose to join them, he handed the bottle back to Britta. "Keep this safe for me. I will retrieve it after the battle."

Tears sprang into her eyes, but she cradled the bottle in her hands. "I am honored to do so."

He continued. "And to keep the bottle safe, you must promise me you will stay hidden, no matter what happens."

"I promise." Her voice wavered, and he had to fight the urge to pull her into his arms.

This was no time to go soft because of a woman. He strapped on his sword. He would channel the heat and fire of his emotions into sheer rage against the invading Normans. He would put thoughts of Britta, with her soft hands and heart, out of his mind for now.

Chapter Thirteen

Father joined Britta on the balcony to watch the warriors. She tried to read the thoughts behind his serious gray gaze but could not.

When the grunts and shouts lulled, he spoke. "I understand your desire to stay with Florie and James. But I have not been able to sleep, knowing the risks of that dangerous choice. It is too late for you to follow the others to the mountain, but you must allow me to set a guard outside their house."

She did not want to go against her father, but at the same time, she knew every warrior was needed for the battle to come. Although her father's men seemed to have improved in technique, their number was still abysmal. It would not require many Normans to overtake them, especially if they were on horseback.

Father gave her no time to respectfully decline. Instead, he patted her cheek, as if she were still a young child, and peered into her face.

"Britta, I must ask you. Have you any interest in Ronan?"

"Not as a husband." The speed and certainty of her response surprised her.

"Yet you know him so well, and you have been friends these many years." He shifted in his seat, adjusting the golden belt wrapped around his linen tunic. He looked at the heavy purple clouds that hovered above them. "I knew how he felt toward you, of course. But I implored him to approach you only as a friend and mentor. In fact, I do believe I threatened to banish him from the kingdom should he be bold with his feelings toward you."

So that was why Ronan had never declared his love! No wonder he had never discussed his heart with her. There had been too much at stake.

Father continued. "But now you are of marriageable age, and I must acknowledge there are many who seek to wed my beautiful daughter. I thought perhaps you had developed feelings for Ronan of your own accord, without his prodding."

As if summoned by their conversation, Ronan charged through the doorway. Removing his helmet, he ran a hand through his sweaty hair, making the front of it stand up straight. He unsheathed his sword.

Father jumped to his feet. "What is the meaning—"

"No time to talk," Ronan breathed. "I am taking Britta."

She stepped back, gripping the ledge of the balcony so she wouldn't topple to the ground below. "What are you about, Ronan?"

He dropped into a curt bow, his dark eyes apologetic. "I must rush you to Florie's home. Norman troops have been spotted on horseback, just outside our western wood." He turned to her father. "King O'Shea, Ari will guard you until I return. The men are preparing their weapons and armor, and Clancy is gathering our horses."

Ari stepped onto the balcony behind Ronan. His blue eyes were cold, like the frozen waterfalls she marveled at in winter. His jaw clenched, and his cheekbones formed angular lines. For a fleeting moment, she saw the deadly Viking who had fearlessly invaded their castle, and he was a terrifying sight—a Norwegian giant with no aim but to conquer his foe.

Ari pressed a hand on Father's back, leading him into the castle. Impulsively, Britta strode over to hug her father. He gave her a sad smile, kissed her forehead, and said, "Promise you will stay safe. You are my only heritage, my most valued treasure."

She nodded, and Ronan loosely wrapped his fingers around her upper arm. His sword remained in his other hand, ready to carve a path, should the need arise. She met his searching gaze. Did he hope for a declaration of love in these final moments of uncertainty?

"Come," he said gently, pulling her from the balcony. "You cannot be seen here. And leave the crown behind."

She had forgotten she was wearing her small jeweled crown today. Florie had instructed her to do so, to cheer the men as they fought for her and for their kingdom. She removed it, shoving it into a bookshelf as they left the room. She turned, remembering Ari's bottle on the balcony, but it was too late to retrieve it.

As they passed through the kitchen, she snatched Florie's long linen shawl and draped it around her silk dress, hoping to further conceal her royalty.

Ronan nodded at the wisdom of her action and then pointed to her long, flowing hair. She quickly knotted it as the commoners did. As they entered the back garden, she took a handful of dirt and smeared it on her face and hands.

"You are stronger than you think," Ronan observed.

The simple words made tears spring into her eyes. It was what she had always loved about Ronan—he believed in her, and he always spoke the truth.

"Will Father fight?" She could barely ask. If only Ari were whisking him into hiding, just as Ronan was hiding her.

"He must fight. This is no time for hiding in the shadows. Your father is a skilled warrior, and his presence will inspire the men to greater sacrifice." Ronan slowed, taking in her face, which seemed to be frozen in terror. Although he gripped her hand, it still felt chilled.

He rubbed her hand with his battle-toughened fingers. "You are going to live,

Britta. James and Florie will protect you. Your father will also live—you can be sure I will let no harm come to him."

She felt like bursting into tears, knowing Ronan would definitely lay down his life for her father's, but she nodded briefly and scrambled over the nearby stone wall. She would not detain this warrior any longer than necessary.

"Thank you," she said, knowing he caught every undercurrent of anxiety and sadness in her words.

"You are my princess," he replied.

After crossing several fields and pastures, they arrived at James and Florie's humble farmhouse. Britta tried not to think of the numerous cow piles she hadn't been able to avoid, but she knew her cloth shoes were utterly ruined.

Ronan gave five sharp raps on Florie's short wooden door, and the woman hastened to open it. Britta could make out nothing inside the hut, and she realized curtains had been pulled over the windows, plunging it into a deliberate darkness.

James spoke up from his bed. "We been waitin' on you, Princess. And prayin'."

She stepped over the stone threshold, turning to catch one last glimpse of Ronan. He nodded at her, a strange shaft of sunlight piercing the heavy clouds and lighting his dark hair. With his sword in hand and a fierce look on his face, he looked ready to single-handedly take on the Norman armies.

"Bolt the door behind me. If anyone comes and does not knock five times, do not open the door. Florie, do you have a weapon?"

Her nursemaid nodded. "Aye, we have a spear and James's sword. I will give Britta my dagger."

"It will do." Ronan looked directly at Britta's face. "Stay hidden. And if you are found out, keep the dagger close. We do not know how the Normans treat their conquests. . . ."

As his voice trailed off, she grasped his unspoken thought. Perhaps it would be better to kill herself than to be taken by the invaders.

"I understand," she whispered.

Florie hugged her. "Now, off with you, m'lord. We have everything in hand."

Ronan gave a short bow and left for the castle without another word.

As Florie bolted the door, Britta walked to James's bedside. She could hardly make out his face, but he took her hand in his. "Now you must be strong, m'lady. You must hide in the kitchen cupboard. It's dark and tight, and Florie will pack sacks of wheat and dried meats around you, so it might not smell the best. But I swear to you, they won't live to find you."

The certainty in his tone verified his words. Her sickly friend would doubtless stagger from his bed to protect her. And she shuddered to think of what her beloved nursemaid would do before she let anyone approach her princess.

"Thank you," she repeated, the inadequacy of the words squeezing at her heart like hot blacksmith's tongs. Would they live to see tomorrow? Would she ever be able to thank her loyal friends for their willingness to sacrifice their lives?

Would God let the O'Shea kingdom stand?

Chapter Fourteen

After helping the king into his battle attire, Ari paced outside the room. Ronan was taking a long time returning. Did it mean he had been waylaid? Surely he had kept to the back paths.

Ronan had told him not to assemble the troops until his arrival, but what if that did not happen? Ari had to do something—they couldn't be caught unawares. He approached the king's door and knocked.

"Enter."

Ari bowed his head as he stepped through the shorter chamber door, an unintended reminder of his lowly position here. He should be leading the troops, giving orders, yet he had to place himself under the king and Ronan.

"I believe it is time to move into position," he said.

The king turned toward his window, watching his men as they milled around the courtyard, full of restless energy. "I agree."

It did not take long to muster the men. Ari cringed again when his gaze traveled over the unimpressive force. Without Ronan's strength and experience, he and the king would likely be the most skilled warriors.

But the king had not practiced with them, presumably to save his energy. Ari suspected he was weary from his recent extended trek across the countryside. King O'Shea was not a young man anymore. Some older men, like Sigfrid, were strong warriors, but they had to train their bodies every day for the fight.

Perhaps this was Ari's chance to step up and lead the Irishmen. But he feared he would lead them to defeat instead of victory, given his lingering injury.

Britta's forlorn parting look filled his memory. She would be crushed if her father died and the castle fell to the Normans. Even worse, she might be abused at the hands of the bold invaders.

Fresh vigor filled his veins, a protective rage he had not felt since the day his brother returned to their longship, bloody and gasping for life. He would never let them touch her. She was so trusting, so compassionate. Perhaps her faith in the one God would be sufficient, but Ari would do anything to aid her God in keeping her safe.

Clomping hooves pounded the dirt and one of their spotters raced up the road, his stallion frothing at the mouth. The sentry attempted to speak several times, but words would not come forth. Finally, he gave a hoarse shout.

"Prepare! They are nearly upon us!"

Ari led the men as they surged forward, limping only a little. He refused to ride a horse, to show the men he would not seek to escape if the battle did not go in their favor.

Using rocks, ditches, and the trees lining the road, he pointed select men to their hiding places. They would try to use the terrain to their advantage.

The chains groaned and shook as the castle gate was drawn up behind them. The horsemen pulled up the rear line near the gate, both to keep the animals alive as long as possible and to give them a powerful advantage, should the initial attack come to naught.

The king produced a bright yellow sash for Ari to drape over his chain mail. "The men must be able to locate you quickly," he explained. Ari knew Ronan's red tunic was the one the men were accustomed to. He tried not to ponder what sort of person could have stopped the Irish warrior in his race to join the troops.

"Will you speak to your men now?" Ari asked.

King O'Shea shook his head. "You must rally them. You will be their commander in this battle. I must needs saddle my horse and take up my position by the castle door."

Ari nodded, accepting the task that had fallen to him in Ronan's absence. He climbed onto a nearby rock, ignoring a slight twinge in his bruised foot. At least he was able to keep his balance without his stick now. His words filled the air, silencing the men.

"Look here. I am not one of you, but I wholeheartedly fight for you. Call it fate, call it God, call it what you will, but I am here and I will not retreat. Hear me now: I will *never* retreat. We will win this battle and grind those half-breed Normans into the dirt. Not a one of them will live to tell others of their hideous defeat. Fight for your king, fight for your land, and fight for your honor!"

The men beat their shields in a slow rhythm, shouting their enthusiasm. As the Norman horses topped the first hill, the chants of the Irishmen roared in a wild cacophony.

Before the first arrow flew, Ronan shoved his way through the ranks, sword and shield at the ready. He took his place next to Ari. His voice rumbled out, full of determination and a deeper sentiment.

"For Britta."

Ari nodded, drawing his shield close. "For Britta."

Moments faded into hours as Britta lay on her side in the pitch-dark cupboard. Sounds were muffled by the food sacks that had been closely pressed around her.

Florie had not shirked in making sure the Normans would never suspect that someone could fit into the space she now occupied. If she ever emerged, she would smell like garlic cloves, and it might take days to comb the spilled grains out of her hair.

Was it day or night? Florie would not open the door to speak to her, for fear the Normans would burst inside that very moment. Before Britta had clambered into her hiding space, both Florie and James had given her a final hug and sworn again to protect her at all costs.

As a distraction from her tight, stuffy quarters, she let her mind roam where it wanted. She touched her mother's ring. Had Mother ever faced an invasion of this size? If so, did she run and hide, or sit proudly on her throne? Britta hated that she didn't know the answer to these questions. All Father had ever spoken of was her mother's beauty, but surely there had been more depth to her character?

And Ronan. The man was a wall of support to her, a friend from her childhood who had never failed to treat her with respect. A beautiful Irishman, truth be told, with his flashing eyes and dark hair. A man among men. He felt strongly for her, she knew. But was it the kind of love she wanted from a husband?

She couldn't stop herself as her thoughts jumped to Ari. What pulled her to the towering Northman who had come to plunder their castle? Was it his honesty, his willingness to admit he had been wrong? Or was it that love of learning new languages and words, a love she shared?

A tingle ran through her, forcing her to acknowledge that on some level, her attraction was purely instinctual. Every time the man touched her arm or hand, her mind danced into some star-strewn realm where it seemed nothing could ever hurt her again.

Yet she knew such visions were unrealistic. Hadn't she seen James struggle to make ends meet for his farm after he was struck with the coughing disease? Hadn't she watched Florie cry for days when she feared James had taken a turn for the worse?

One thing she knew: real love was not easy. It was not floating on a cloud of happiness. Life and death, survival and failure, happiness and grief were woven together with the unbreakable cords of marriage.

She had to choose carefully which man she tied herself to.

Chapter Fifteen

Things were not going well.

The Irish archers in the woods had initially caught the Normans by surprise, but it did not take long for the invaders to rally and gallop into their ranks, forcing them to scatter. Although the Irish warriors had managed to unhorse many Normans with their spears, they were at a disadvantage in hand-to-hand combat because the Normans were well outfitted with chain mail and helmets.

For each Norman Ari cut down with his sword, two Irishmen fell to the rocky ground they fought on. To make things worse, the heavy clouds finally burst into rain, making their leather shoes lose their grip on the uneven terrain.

As a helmeted Norman thrust his spear at him, Ari parried the blow with his shield. The deerskin-covered wood cracked, and he groaned. If his shield broke, he was doomed.

Ronan made his way to Ari's side, dodging the Norman's thrusts and driving the mace into the man's neck, dropping him to the ground. He turned and threw a bleak smile Ari's way, but not before a Norman stalked up behind him and thrust a sword into his shoulder. Ronan's mace dropped, and he sank to the ground, blood spilling freely from his wound.

Ari howled like a wolf and charged the Norman, bringing him down with little effort. Even as he took up Ronan's mace and attacked more Normans, from the corners of his eyes he saw how many Irishmen lay scattered around him.

They were overwhelmed. There was no hope. And now Ronan might die, because he had tried to protect him.

Suddenly, another howl met his ears, and he recognized it immediately.

Sigfrid.

His friend had come!

His hopes renewed, he charged afresh, bringing down two Normans with one blow. Viking warriors crested the hill. His entire crew had returned!

The leather-clad Vikings swarmed the Normans like an angry hive of bees. Sigfrid stood back-to-back with Ari and they cleaved their way through their enemies, dropping bodies in their wake. Driven by the bloodlust of war, Ari nearly forgot his foot was injured.

Thanks to his warriors, the Irish victory came swiftly. When the battle was over, Ari was shocked at the good-sized group of Irishmen left standing. King O'Shea himself was only bleeding slightly from a leg wound.

He scanned the bodies for Ronan, but to no avail. The king pointed to the edge of the wood, where someone had positioned the fallen warrior out of the way. Ronan writhed in pain, his left arm hanging useless as the blood continued to spill from his shoulder.

Ari moved as quickly as his foot would allow, dropping to his knees at Ronan's side. Sigfrid joined him, tearing off his tunic and pressing it to the wound.

"Don't stand there gaping," Ari shouted to the nearby soldiers. "His groans are a good sign! Fetch us a cot!"

When the men returned, they were able to roll Ronan onto the cot, although he cried in pain when his wounded torso was handled. Inside the castle, the men positioned him on the floor in the small chamber where Ari had been held.

Ari watched as his best healer, Valgerd, removed Ronan's mail shirt then stuffed the wound with cloth to stanch the flow.

"We need herbs," Valgerd said. "If they have yarrow, that might slow the bleeding. There are other things I could use, should they have them."

Positioning Sigfrid by Ronan's side, Ari led the healer to the herb beds.

His man pinched off a handful of leaves. Finally, he said, "This is good, but do they keep dried herbs?"

One woman would know where all the herbs were and would be able to aid his man. Her faithful care had good results, as he could attest from the way his nearly healed foot had performed in battle. Florie. And Florie watched over Britta. He had to retrieve them both.

Racing toward the stables, Ari said, "Do your best. I will bring you a woman who can help."

He dug his heels into the horse's flanks, finally acknowledging a possibility he could no longer ignore. What if the Normans had sent forces into the village and fields before they had attacked the castle? Would he even reach Britta in time?

Britta yawned. Her legs cramped beneath her. She tried to straighten them, knowing they would merely bash into the corner of the cupboard again. The only way to ignore her confined situation was to give in to sleep.

Just as she dozed off, thuds reverberated in the wood beneath her. What was it? She strained to listen for voices but heard nothing more than muffled movement.

She pressed closer to the cupboard wall. She prayed the Normans would not harm Florie or James, that they would not search the small farmhouse and discover her. The dagger lay beneath her. She would need to snatch it if they dragged her out.

She shuddered. Would she be forced to kill herself before the Normans could harm her? And how would she do it? Stab herself in the heart? Surely she would lose strength the moment the knife entered, so maybe it wouldn't work.

The cupboard door swung open, and a hand fumbled toward her. She was blinded by the light that poured in, but she managed to still her breath, even though she could not silence the pounding of her heart.

The hand shoved several bags aside then grasped at the bag on her head and yanked it down. She tried to shift out of reach, but the hand touched her face and a familiar voice poured through her soul like a healing balm.

"M'lady! Have you heard a thing I was sayin'? 'Tis the Viking come to retrieve you."

"Oh! Thanks be to God!" She crawled from her hiding place, much to the apparent amusement of the Norse giant, who quirked a half smile at her. His trousers were filthy, and his hair fell wildly about his shoulders.

James sat on his bed, beaming. "They've held the castle, Princess! The Normans won't try for it again, I'll wager."

Ari helped her to her feet, but worry creased his brow. "We paid a heavy price for our victory. In truth, I have mostly come for Florie. Her skills are needed. Ronan has suffered injury."

Britta gasped for air, unable to fill her lungs.

"Ronan?" she croaked. Her head felt like she was underwater.

Smoothly, Ari slid his arm around the curve of her waist, steering her toward a chair. "You must sit. This has been a shock." He turned to Florie. "You take the horse. There is no time to waste. I will walk the princess back when she is ready."

Florie nodded, taking a moment to kiss James before she hurried out the door.

Britta rubbed her head and looked at Ari through foggy eyes. She took another deep breath. Was this really happening, or had she fallen asleep? Perhaps she was still in the cupboard.

Ari knelt at her side, bringing her hand to his lips. The moment she felt the soft pressure of his kiss, the room sharpened. She knew what she had to do.

"We must go," she said.

James protested from his cozy corner, but Ari examined her face. "You are certain you can walk? Your legs must be weak after your long confinement."

"I *will* walk. Ronan cannot die without knowing of my gratitude, my. . ." She could not articulate the words, and the tears she'd been holding back flooded her eyes. She vainly swiped at them with her sleeve.

Ari hesitantly used his large thumb to wipe tears from her cheek, his serious gaze meeting hers. "First you must drink something to restore your strength. Then we will go."

Chapter Sixteen

Even after a cup of tea, Britta's legs still felt like wobbling jelly. She stretched several times up to her tiptoes, jumped around a bit, and then finally tucked her arm in Ari's to be sure she wouldn't collapse along the way.

James reluctantly let her go, but not before he gave Ari a stern lecture on what was expected in terms of gentlemanly behavior when walking alone with a woman.

Once they were halfway through the low grass of a hay field, a heavy sigh finally escaped her lips.

Ari did not probe, but he quirked an eyebrow, willing to listen.

She tried to give voice to her thoughts. "I am stricken that Ronan is hurt. But I am in awe that God has spared our castle." She turned to him. "I am thankful you fought for us."

"Were it left to me, all would have been lost." Irritation filled his voice. "We were outnumbered and underarmed, as we feared we might be." He squeezed her arm tighter, as if trying to protect her from the horrors he had seen. "Your Ronan saved my life."

She fell silent. He was not "her" Ronan. But she sensed there was more to the story. "Speak on."

He paused to sweep his unmanageable hair back into its leather tie. Without thinking, she reached up to help him, gathering handfuls of his blond locks. He stilled as her finger brushed his beard.

His voice was low and husky when he replied. "My men came to our aid. Sigfrid—the one you spoke to—said they had sailed but a short distance and something told him to return. If not for them, nothing could have stopped the slaughter."

"God must have spoken to his heart," she mused. Grass tugged at her skirts, beckoning her to sit and rest her weary feet. Releasing Ari's arm, she plopped down in the field none too daintily. "I need to stop," she said.

The sound of hooves pounding near the forest's edge caught her attention. Ari had already spotted the horse and rider. He bent and snatched her up, tossing her easily over his shoulder. He ran toward a rock formation perched atop an ocean inlet at the edge of the field. Placing her carefully in a damp crevice, he drew his sword and turned.

The horseman had not veered from their trail, and even worse, he wore Norman armor. He was shouting, but she could not make out what he said.

Yet the moment he stretched a finger toward her, repeating the same word with increasing vehemence, she knew what he had come for.

He wanted to capture her.

As Ari inexplicably scrounged for something on the ground, she shrank back into the shadows of the rocks. Had the remaining Normans already taken her father? How else would he know to search for a princess?

As the dark horse closed upon them, Ari rammed a long stick into the ground. To avoid it, the Norman flew past her rocky shelter. The horse jerked to a halt, plunging its rider over the edge of the overhang.

She wished she couldn't hear the man's groans as he wallowed on the rocks below. Ari turned to her, clasping her hand and pulling her back to her feet.

"I must finish this." His voice rose above the bloodcurdling sounds.

She nodded mutely.

Ari found an area where he could safely descend. The Norman continued to scream. In fact, the screams grew louder. What was Ari doing to him? Did the Vikings torture people?

Suddenly, Ari topped the overhang, dragging the Norman behind him. With each bounce, the man hurled insults in his language. When they reached Britta, Ari deposited the writhing invader at her feet.

"I thought this straggler could return to his people and share his tale of the Viking force that guards this castle." He sneered down into the man's cringing face, shaking his fist for good measure.

"Clever thinking. Thank you." She looked hopefully at the wide-eyed horse. The terrors of this day had taken their toll. "Perhaps we could ride the horse? You could bind the Norman here, and we could send one of our men out to retrieve him later. We aren't far from the castle now—it's just through that wood."

Ari nodded, removing the belt from his tunic and lashing the man to the trunk of a scraggly tree that had managed to withstand the ocean's blasts. For good measure, he tore a piece of the Norman's tunic and stuffed it into his mouth, stifling his continued protests.

Task complete, he took the horse's face in his hands. The beast started, but when Ari whispered into its face, it seemed to calm.

Ari extended a rock-solid arm to boost her onto the large animal. Instead of taking it, she turned to face him, taking in his dirty clothing, once-again loosened hair, and concerned eyes. His cheeks were reddened in the salty air and his lips had fallen open, revealing surprisingly white teeth.

Propriety vanished as she tipped up into his arms, meeting his lips. She had never kissed a man, but it required no training. Their kiss was as natural as the waves pounding behind them, as the robins singing in the trees.

He pulled back, his soft beard pressing into her cheek as he kissed it. Then he cupped her face in his hands, regret etching his features.

"James has instructed me what I am to do when walking alone with a woman, and this was not mentioned."

She laughed, and his eyes crinkled in response. He extended his arm again.

"We must not linger."

Of course. They had to return to Ronan—what if he were lying on his deathbed? How had he slipped her mind, even for a moment? What had possessed her to practically attack Ari?

The overwrought black horse munched grass nearby. Ari walked up to it, again talking in his low voice as he took the reins. But when it gave a sudden rear kick, he sighed.

"We will have to walk. It is not safe for you to ride him. Perhaps after a good watering and brushing, he might tame down."

She nodded, trying to keep up with Ari as he led the anxious horse to the stables. Even with his slight limp, she had to jog alongside, taking three steps to match just one of his.

When she was near him, the soft linen of his tunic brushed her hand in a gentle rhythm. He glanced down at her often, his gaze soft and unguarded. The truth began to stir and waken in her spirit. Her heart had already chosen who it wanted, and he was not the one her father would approve of.

Ari felt like a fool, his damp leather shoes causing him to stumble along the dirt road. But Britta seemed oblivious to his clumsiness, holding on to his arm as if she floated on a cloud.

What would happen if Ronan woke from his stupor? Would he regret that he had nearly sacrificed his life for a rogue Viking? And what if Ronan did not wake? Britta would never forgive him for costing her faithful friend's life.

Had Ronan ever been more than a friend to Britta? It seemed he had not, but the desire had been there, at least on his part. It was understandable. She was a woman who was easy to love. She delighted in small things, like books and flowers. She was loyal to her family and friends. She was even willing to crush her royal body into a small cupboard for hours, never demanding a softer hiding place.

Although she was not a trained warrior, she was as resourceful as any Viking woman, and that was saying a great deal.

He couldn't hide his smile, slowing his stride when he realized she was having difficulty matching his pace. She was so small, so vulnerable. . . . He could not bear to think what the Norman warrior might have done to her. He had heard tales of how they broke their conquests' arms and legs then threw their limp bodies over cliffs.

Violence for violence's sake. He had known some older Vikings who lived like this, who had embraced the killing. But his father had given up raiding when his brother died. And now, Ari realized he had no stomach for raiding, either. It was senseless.

As they neared the castle, Sigfrid came to greet them. His eye wandered over the fractious horse, the disheveled princess, and finally met Ari's weary gaze. He mercifully refrained from asking questions, motioning for a servant boy to stable the horse.

Sigfrid led them into the great hall, where Ari's men had gathered around the table. "You should eat. We've cooked up some of the meat that their healing woman told us to use."

Britta tugged Ari's sleeve. "But Ronan? Ask him how he fares. And my father?"

Ari knew she would not rest until she had a report. All thoughts of the Norman attacker flew as he put her questions to Sigfrid then translated his friend's reply. "With the aid of our Valgerd and Florie, Ronan will live. They watch his arm carefully, to be sure it will not need to be removed."

Britta let out a small cry. She understood that an armless warrior would not be able to lead, although he could still fight.

Hoping to soften her distress, he continued. "Your father's leg injury has been wrapped and it will heal. The cut was not deep."

Relief washed over her features. She glanced at his men, who lunged for their food like bears preparing for hibernation. "You should eat with them. I cannot imagine how weary you are from the battle. I must go to Ronan first."

"Of course you must," he said.

But in his deepest, darkest thoughts, some corner of his heart wished that Ronan would have died from that blow.

Chapter Seventeen

Ronan watched Britta's every move as she flitted about, adjusting his blankets and bringing him fresh tea. The Viking healer had steeped the smelly concoction, and although Ronan looked as if he might gag, he forced himself to swallow it.

"I suppose if they wanted to kill me, this would be an easy way to do it," he said darkly.

She drew up a stool, covering his cold hand with her own. "They mean us no harm, I am sure of it. Why else would they have returned to fight alongside our men?"

"Yes. . .I will admit Ari is a remarkable warrior. I suppose your father will place him in charge of his forces now."

The jealousy in his tone was palpable. "Ronan!" she scolded. "Do not think that way. Of course you will still be Father's commander."

"Not if I lose my arm." He would not meet her eyes.

She twined her fingers into his. "You will not. With the herbal ministrations of two skilled healers, your shoulder is healing quickly! Why, Florie only had to lightly stitch it."

He attempted to tighten his fingers around hers but could not. "I cannot strengthen my grip."

She, too, had noticed this but prayed it would be a temporary issue. "We must put our trust in God. He has spared your life."

He gave her a half smile. "Indeed, but perhaps this makes things more difficult for you."

"You are indeed surly and ungrateful tonight! I don't care if you are ailing, Ronan, you must not speak ill of God."

His dark beard had grown thicker and his hair was unruly on the feather pillow she had brought him. In such a state, he appeared strangely powerless, but she knew it was an illusion. Her father's best man would still rise and fight, should he have to. She checked a motherly urge to smooth his hair from his forehead.

He dropped his other hand over hers, taking her by surprise. His warm eyes glimmered in the lamplight, revealing an unfettered ardor. "Britta. Perhaps you know. . .surely you have realized that I have loved you for many years now?"

How should she respond? Her hand grew warm under his. Speaking the truth would not be easy, but she owed that to him.

"Ronan, it is true I care for you, most wholeheartedly. You are as much a part of me as our castle itself." She bowed her head. "But I cannot return that kind of love. I love you as a brother, Ronan. As a friend."

She waited a moment then untucked her chin and let her eyes meet his. He looked as if she had just kicked him, but his words were charged with tenderness and wonder.

"You love the Viking."

She nodded.

"And he loves you."

She responded quickly. "I am unsure."

He pulled her in with his eyes, and his grip tightened in urgency. "I must speak with him."

"Oh, no, I don't—"

"I will speak with him, now." Ronan's voice was firm. "Who can say if I will survive this wound?"

He was teasing her now, but she didn't like to think of Ronan's death. Embarrassing tears filled her eyes.

He placed his strong right hand on her cheek. "How I have longed to wipe your tears away, to kiss the pink of your cheeks. So many times I held back from embracing you, because your father's wishes weighed heavily on me. But it does not fall to me to do such things; I see that now. God has placed me in your life as a protector and friend, but not as a husband."

She burst into tears, and Ronan sat up and kissed her forehead.

"Now go, sweet child. Send the Viking to me."

Unable to speak or to decline his command, she left the room.

Sigfrid and his men were in fine form, sharing stories of their victory over the candlelit long table. One man claimed he killed two men with one arrow. One said Odin had smiled upon them from the raven-shaped mountain nearby. Ari leaned back in his chair, closing his eyes. The rush of urgency that had driven him in battle had dissipated, leaving him exhausted.

Sigfrid gave him a nudge. "My friend, we must sail tomorrow. You know we are well into planting season and our families will be worried."

Ari nodded. "Yes, my mother will imagine the worst." She could not withstand the death of her only remaining son.

"Perhaps you have a special good-bye planned for your Irish maiden." Sigfrid smiled.

He had no plan, but he knew he should. He could not walk away from Britta without explaining what she meant to him, although he hardly understood it himself. And this was the worst time to leave—when her attentions were focused on Ronan, and when the castle might still be vulnerable to a retributive attack.

In very fact, his desire to sail seemed to have been replaced with a pressing need to spend more time with Britta. They could walk in the gardens—he could imagine tucking sprigs of lavender into her sun-warmed hair. He could hold her small hand in his own. And perhaps he could kiss those generous lips once again. . . .

"Ari?"

Britta's voice broke into his thoughts. Her eyes were wide with anxiety. Had something happened to Ronan?

"Ronan wishes to speak with you," she continued. So the Irishman wasn't dead, but fresh apprehension stirred in Ari's heart. Perhaps Britta had told Ronan of the kiss, and he wished to issue a challenge on her behalf.

His sword lay in its sheath by the door, but his shorter seax was tucked into a leather sheath on his belt. He had retrieved it before the battle and didn't intend to give it up again.

His men's laughter died down as he approached the door to the side room. Pushing it open gently, he could see that Ronan had been transferred to a hay-stuffed cot—not to the board they had forced him to sleep on. It was fitting, of course, that they take better care of their own.

Ronan looked haggard, his face bloodless. Ari's mother would say the man needed barely cooked meat to restore the blood he had lost. He would suggest that to Florie.

The Irishman motioned him to sit close by. Ari lowered himself to a creaky stool that could barely support his weight.

"First, I want to give you thanks for joining us. You were admirable and honorable in battle."

Ari shook his head. "I am not the one to be praised. You were ready to offer your life for mine, and I am a foreigner. Why?"

Ronan's serious gaze softened in the waning lamplight. "There is no sacrifice greater than the death of Jesus Christ for my sins. It seems a small thing for me to give my life for one man, when He gave His life for all."

Ari pondered this. One sacrifice, lasting through the ages. One sacrifice that inspired others to give more of themselves, in contrast with the endless pagan sacrifices that were meant to make lives easier.

"I wish to know your Christ," Ari said.

Ronan smiled. "It is a simple thing, but following Jesus Christ will change your life. We will pray together."

Ronan prayed first, and then Ari followed the nudge of the quiet voice he had heard so often in his soul. He told the Christ of his bitterness over his brother's death and asked Him to forgive his blackened heart. He prayed he would be able to follow His leading, even in his native land. He thanked Jesus Christ for dying so he could live eternally.

When he tentatively said, "Amen," Ronan dropped his hand on Ari's shoulder. "Now we are truly brothers."

Ari choked back sudden tears as he realized God had brought him to this land for a reason. It had nothing to do with revenge and everything to do with the restoration of his soul. In the place of his lost brother, God had given him an eternal family.

Ronan gave him a rueful look. "There is something else we must discuss—Britta's future. I have no claim on her, as you know. And she has no desire to marry me." He held out a hand to silence any protests from Ari. "'Tis true. I asked her outright, and we both know she would not lie."

Ari shifted in his seat, wishing he could encourage the man who had done so much for him. Yet he could barely quell his excitement over Britta's confession.

He leaned forward, hoping to adjust the crooked legs of the stool beneath him. But a loud rip sounded as the leather seat tore in two, depositing him solidly on the cold floor. His face froze in shock and embarrassment.

Ronan's deep chuckle filled the room. "You are indeed clumsy, Viking oaf. But no matter. If you're not too injured, may I suggest you speak with the king tomorrow and ask for his daughter's hand in marriage? It is the proper course of action, and I believe you know that."

Ari sat, rubbing his seat and thighs. Visions of a future with the princess flashed into his head. Would they sail to his home? Or stay in her castle?

Did it matter?

"Thank you for your wisdom, brother, and for sacrificing the woman you have loved. I can never repay you." He pulled himself up to a standing position, rubbing his hip.

"You can repay me by choosing sturdier chairs, Viking," Ronan said. His good-natured laughter followed Ari out the door.

Chapter Eighteen

Sigfrid was alone in the great hall when Ari emerged. He jerked his thumb toward Valgerd, who lay on a makeshift cot that had been shoved into the kitchen doorway.

"He wants to be nearby, should the warrior have pains in the night," Sigfrid explained. "I will return to our camp soon." He paused, shooting Ari a knowing look. "The Irishman has given you something to think about?"

Ari nodded. "I must decide my course. Before we even sailed, you sensed that revenge was not the only thing that drove me to this land. I could not give it words, but restlessness jabbed like a dagger point into my soul. Yet now I feel a peace I could not lay hold of in our land."

"The princess?" Sigfrid guessed.

"It is true she has comforted me, but my peace comes from elsewhere. I have believed in the Christian God, Sigfrid. This is not the news my parents wanted to hear."

Sigfrid narrowed his gaze and muttered, "Perhaps you are wrong."

"What did you say?"

"Do you know your parents so little?" His old friend clasped his arm. "From the time your brother died, your parents have searched for meaning, for answers. Our gods offer them nothing. Just before you sailed, your father told me they were visiting the Christian church. They did not want you to know, for fear you would accuse them of foolishness in their old age."

His head swam. His parents? Visiting a church? He could not hide his awe. "This God is surely great, if He reaches into hearts in our land also."

Sigfrid did not agree, but he did not contradict him. "You will stay behind when we sail tomorrow?"

Ari hesitated.

Sigfrid filled in the words. "I have loved only once in my long life. You know my wife died too young. But I see in your eyes the same feeling I had for her, the same desire to protect her from the evils we have seen in the face of battle. This princess will be your first concern now—even above your parents. I will tell them of your decision to stay with her and to follow the Christian God."

He clasped Sigfrid in a hug, tears filling his eyes. "May we meet again."

"Surely we shall." Sigfrid unlatched a small pouch on his belt and handed it to him. "Here is something from home to remember us by."

Ari loosened the leather straps, and a piece of ivory walrus tusk rolled into his hand.

"Many thanks, my friend. I will treasure this as I do my bronze bottle."

Sigfrid smiled. "But soon you will have a wife to treasure more."

Britta sat curled on her bed, bare feet tucked up under her sleeping gown. Half-open books lay strewn about her like an abandoned fairy circle. She could not read more than one page tonight, it seemed. Her mind kept returning to her impossible situation.

Ari would sail tomorrow with his men. She would have to say good-bye.

Unless she stowed away with him. . .but no princess in her right mind would join a crew of Vikings just to be near one man who hadn't even declared his love for her yet. Besides, he was a pagan and not her husband. He would probably sell her into slavery or something equally barbaric.

She would stay home. Perhaps she would marry Ronan after all. She would be safe.

Yet in the Bible stories, God seemed to put a higher value on obedience and trust than on safety.

She prayed aloud. "Oh, heavenly Father, I do not know what You would have me do! I am so confused about Ari—the man is not a Christian, yet he pulls at my heart. You know my obligations here, that I cannot leave my father and our castle. Please point the way in the direction I must go. Close any doors I should not walk through."

Someone had stoked her fire, and her room was uncommonly cozy. She did not even pull the curtains on her bed but snuggled beneath the covers into her down mattress. Cricket chirps and night-bird warbles soothed her senses. Her thoughts ceased their tumbling and her limbs released the tension of the long day. She drifted into much-needed sleep.

A deep, guttural scream woke Britta. Disoriented, it took her a moment to ascertain that she was still on her bed. Though a tiny flame still flickered in the hearth, the room was cloaked in darkness.

She held her breath, waiting to see where the cry had come from. It only took a moment for a terrifying sound to rend the air: her father, calling for help.

Jumping from her bed, she grabbed a candle and shoved it into the low flame of the hearth to light it. Holding it close to her chest to protect the stuttering wick, she crept from her door and stood in the hallway. Two men raced toward her father's room—she couldn't be sure in the dark, but she thought one was Ronan.

Entering the king's chamber, Britta tried to make sense of what she saw. A dark pool of blood spread under a man in a leather vest who lay facedown on the stone floor. The red-blond hair told her it was not her father who had been killed.

For the man was surely dead. A sword protruded from his back. Even as Ronan and a guard felt for his pulse, it was obvious he had not survived the blow.

She looked at the sword closely. The beautiful sheen on the blade and the elongated, ornately carved hilt forced her to a horrifying realization.

It was Ari's sword.

As her father came to her side, she stepped into the comfort of his open arms. "What happened? Were you hurt?"

He squeezed her more tightly, as if he could protect her from the gruesome sight in front of them. "I was preparing for bed, and Clancy stopped in to give a report. He was going home for the night, and Garth was going to take his post and patrol this floor. I had asked them to stay tonight, in case any intruders were around."

Father didn't clarify, but she strongly suspected he counted the Viking warriors as intruders. Now it seemed his hesitation to trust them had not been unfounded.

He continued. "After Clancy put out the lamps, another knock sounded. He went to open the door, expecting Garth. I could not see who stood there, because my fire was low. But as Clancy turned to tell me something, he must have been stabbed in the back. He fell just as he is there. When he groaned, I shouted and lit a lamp. The scoundrel fled, leaving the sword."

She could not hold back her tears. Clancy had a wife and small children. Was it possible Ari would have committed such a ruthless murder?

Her father glanced again at the incriminating sword. His voice was both reflective and foreboding. "My deepest fear about the Viking has been realized. We never convinced him that we did not kill his brother. Yet I foolishly assumed his eagerness to fight on our behalf was proof of his loyalty. Instead, it was merely a means of winning our trust and infiltrating our castle."

She wanted to protest. But her father was so widely traveled, and he had met warriors of every stripe—both friend and foe. Although she wanted to, she could not deny that his conclusions were consistent with Ari's actions.

Father's words hit her heart like flaming arrows. "Indeed, I doubt his men ever sailed. They simply waited to swoop in as our saviors, all the while plotting our demise."

She clung to his arm, all the goodness slipping out of her sheltered world. Was it true? That sunlit kiss, those caring words? The invincible way she had felt with her hand tucked into Ari's?

She tried to catch Ronan's eye, but he was busy wrapping Clancy's large body in a blanket. The sword had been removed from the man's back, but she could not bring herself to look at it again.

A guard strode in and whispered in the king's ear. Her father nodded.

"The castle has been searched, and he is not here." He spoke loudly so the others could hear. "I doubt they will attack in the night, when they are spent from the battle. Tonight we will throw their sleeping Viking healer in a cell and set a guard on the castle. At first light, as soon as my troops can prepare, we will storm the Viking camp and take no prisoners."

Ronan simply nodded, shock etching his face. He would have to deliver Clancy's body to his wife tonight. She remembered Clancy's wife—a petite brunette with wide-set doe eyes. Innocent. Oblivious.

Just as she herself had been, until Ari's sword had ripped a hole in her heart.

Chapter Nineteen

Pale sunlight roused Britta from a mere hour's sleep, and she stumbled downstairs. She did not see Valgerd's cot, a sure indication he had been secured in a basement cell.

She peered into the scullery and found Florie pouring hot water into ceramic mugs. The nursemaid came to her side and hugged her gently. She motioned to the table, handing Britta a full mug of the fragrant liquid. "Please drink some, m'lady. This brew of lemon balm, lavender, and chamomile might ease your worries some."

Britta knew nothing could ease her worries, but she sat and sipped at it anyway, in hopes it would excuse her from eating. She could not eat until she knew the truth about Ari.

Father joined her at the table, wearing his tunic that would soon be covered with a mail shirt. Although she should not question her father's wisdom in kingdom matters, she had to ask one question. "Will you kill him, Father? After all he has done for us?"

He gave her a grim smile. "You have been strong, my daughter—like your mother. I regret you had to see what happened last night. But perhaps it was for the best. He had convinced us all of his goodwill—even Ronan, and that is no easy task."

Perhaps Father was right, and vengeance had driven Ari to contrive such an elaborate deception. Yet if his goal was to destroy their kingdom, surely he would not have hindered the Norman rider from capturing her yesterday?

She leaned forward, anxious to resolve the issue in her mind. "Father, where are we holding the Norman rider? Was he badly injured from his fall?"

Her father's soft gray eyes widened. "What Norman rider?"

She gasped. As soon as she had entered the castle yesterday, she had been consumed with Ronan's recovery. She had forgotten the Norman lashed to the tree, and perhaps Ari had, too.

"A Norman rider tried to charge and kill me yesterday. Ari—"

Ronan walked out of the small room, circles under his eyes. His limbs moved stiffly.

Meeting her concerned gaze, he said, "Do continue, Britta. What did you say about Ari?"

She sank deeper into her chair, sensing the disappointment in his tone. Hadn't he warned her about Ari from the start? And she had refused his advances for those of a murderous barbarian.

Guilt ridden at her own gullibility, she tried to redirect the conversation. "I am sorry you had such a sad task last night. I pray Clancy's widow finds comfort. Perhaps you should rest today, until your wound is fully healed."

Ronan shook his head, returning to the topic at hand. "You had something to share about Ari."

Before she could respond, an armed guard burst into the great hall, his sword tip pointed into the back of the very man they spoke of.

"Walked up to the castle gate, bold as bold. Asked to see you, King O'Shea."

Ari could not understand why the guard had such an arrogant tone. Hadn't he fought alongside him just yesterday? He turned to see if the man was in jest, but the sword tip pinched through his tunic into his skin, assuring him the man was in earnest.

"One more word from you, and I'll stab you in the back, just as you did our man."

Stabbed in the back? Who had been stabbed? Desperate for answers, he locked eyes with Britta. She looked tired and confused. Ronan's gaze was serious, his hand resting on his sword hilt.

King O'Shea stepped closer. "You have nothing to say, Viking?"

"Why should I say something? What has happened?"

The king's lips tightened. "Your feigned ignorance will no longer sway me." He nodded at the guard. "Take him to the cell. He can join his friend."

Friend? Who was he referring to?

The guard shoved him none too carefully to the basement door, then down the musty stone stairs. A torch on the wall hissed as it burned down, its light nearly extinguished. Valgerd's familiar voice greeted him.

"Welcome, m'lord."

They had taken the Viking healer hostage? But the man had saved Ronan's life.

Everything was upside down, the complete opposite of what it should be. The Irishmen should be praising Ari and his men, not throwing them behind iron bars.

When the door locked behind him, Ari clung to his only hope—the God he had so recently believed in. He fell on his knees and begged Him for mercy.

As soon as Ari was taken away, Father retired to his chamber to pray. Britta knew he had to act quickly or risk losing his advantage over the Vikings.

Ronan rubbed at his beard, meeting her eyes. "I am unsure."

She felt the same way, but she needed to make sense of the facts. "Ronan, we cannot explain his sword. None of our men would have killed Clancy simply to lay blame on a Viking. What Father said rings true—Ari won our trust so he could get close, and then he attempted to kill our king. We were blind and foolish."

"Yet you had come to love him," Ronan said simply.

"Yes, but perhaps my feelings led me astray—although I cannot understand why he didn't leave me to that Norman, if he wanted our castle."

"What Norman?"

"I could not elaborate earlier, but there was a straggler Norman horseman who charged us in the field. Ari thwarted him, and the man fell over a small precipice. We left him tied to a tree but forgot to retrieve him last night in my haste to come to your aid." She frowned. "I suppose the Norman's attack was fortuitous for Ari, because he protected me, making me trust him more."

"No one has checked to see if he is still there today?"

"I suppose not. After Clancy's murder—"

Ronan jumped to his feet. "Tell your father he cannot attack until I return. Then you must go and speak to Ari."

"But I—"

Ronan strode forward, cutting off her protests by gently taking her chin in his hand and forcing her to meet his brilliant gaze.

"You will never rest if we slaughter innocent men. Yes, *innocent*. Something was not right about that sword, Britta. I have looked cold-blooded murderers in the eye, and Ari is not one of them. You know I would never put you in harm's way. I am asking you to speak to the man and find out what he has to say in his own defense."

She did not want to ask Ari for his explanation of last night—hadn't she played the fool for the man too many times already? But the fervor in Ronan's voice forced her to capitulate.

"I will do so." She determined to be wise as a serpent when she questioned the beguiling Northman. "Just be careful with your wound, whatever you do. It needs time to heal completely."

He kissed her cheek. "Of course." His dark eyes probed hers. "And you must be careful with your heart. Real love is not so easily tossed aside."

Chapter Twenty

Ari sat on the cold stone bench, wishing Valgerd could recount what the Irish guards had said when they took him away. But his friend understood little of their language and was just as perplexed as he was.

His guard had mentioned that one of their men was stabbed in the back. It seemed they had concluded it was his doing, but why?

Unless...

He sat bolt upright. He had left his sword behind when he walked Sigfrid back to camp. He had only planned to stay a short time, to speak with the men before they sailed. Yet he was so bone weary at the end of a battle day, he had drifted to sleep by the warm fire. When the sun rose, he'd woken on the dewy grass, a wool blanket draped over him. He had come straight back to the castle.

There was only one conclusion: in the meantime, someone had used his sword to murder an Irishman.

He rubbed his hand across his forehead, abhorring the filthy state he was in. He had not washed himself since the battle, so his clothing and his body were still splattered with blood and dirt.

Would he be executed in such a state? He could not let his thoughts wander that direction, yet he knew it was unlikely the king would spare his life a second time.

Valgerd had fallen silent, his light brows knit in fury. Suddenly, he grunted and leaned forward on his bench. "We never should have trusted the Irish—slippery demons. We offered up our lives for theirs in battle, and what thanks did we receive? Gold? Jewels? No. They threw us in prison. And what evil have they planned for our crew, Ari?"

Ari's empty stomach clenched. It was a valid fear. If the Irish had been so bold as to capture him, knowing he was the Viking leader, what would they do to his men? Although his crew kept weapons on their belts nearly all the time, they were relaxed and not expecting any trouble. Would Sigfrid see the Irish approaching in time to prepare for another battle?

In desperation, he loosened his belt and wrapped it around the iron bar. Perhaps he could pull the door down. He yanked it backward with all his might, but it only gave a slight creak and remained fast.

Light cut into the dark dungeon, and a rust-colored skirt dusted the steps above. When Britta's pale face came into view, he wrapped the belt around one hand, shoving it behind his back.

"Britta, I am sorry for your man's death. I know nothing about it."

She held up a slim, small hand. Her slightly imperious gaze indicated that she had come in her capacity as princess, not out of love for him.

"Ronan is not convinced that you killed Clancy." Her tone remained aloof and impersonal. "But I am not certain what to believe. Your sword was in his back."

So it was Clancy who died. He shook his head in disbelief. First he had accidentally broken the poor man's arm, and now he could only assume his sword—his Peacebreaker—had taken the Irish warrior's life. Even more distressing, the man had been stabbed in the back, an action beneath contempt.

"I would never—"

"But someone did. And it makes sense it would have been you."

"How does that make sense? Why would I want to kill Clancy?"

"You thought he was my *father*." Her voice wavered, exposing the depth of her emotion. "You wanted the king dead so you could take our castle for your Vikings. It was your plan all along."

Did she truly believe these lies? If so, the past weeks had meant nothing to her. Yet those weeks had changed his life.

He recalled the sweetness of her lips as they had met his, the womanly feel of her waist under his palm, and how her heavy hair brushed against his hand. When he was injured, she had been so patient as she read to him, pointing out the Latin words so he could sound them out. Had it all been a ruse, a plan to win his trust before concocting an excuse to kill him?

Helplessly, he met her eyes, and he recognized an anguish that belied her harsh words. At some point, she had trusted him—perhaps even loved him?—enough to allow him to hurt her. Of course she was angered that someone had attempted to kill her father. He would try a different approach.

He pressed his face to the cold bars. "No Viking would ever leave his most treasured sword in a dead body. Ask anyone. Ask Ronan! If I wanted to slay your father—which I would never do—I would have been sure to stab the right man. And I would *not* have stabbed him in the back. I would have made him look into my eyes, even as he died. I would have been prepared to die an honorable death if captured. You know that what I am saying is true."

She stepped closer, her face pensive.

He spoke again before she could respond. "I am a Christian now, Britta. I would not kill a man in that way—like a coward."

A small gasp escaped her lips. "You are a Christian? But you never told me."

"You had already retired when I left Ronan's room." He grimaced, recalling how impatient he had been to speak with the king about marriage today. What a fool he had been, to believe a Viking would ever be accepted in this land!

As her gaze wavered between him and Valgerd, Ari spoke again. "Execute me if you deem it right, but do not attack my men. Allow them to sail home as planned."

"It is too late." Her face blanched. "My father already prepares for battle, and his men have gathered. When Ronan returns, they will attack the camp."

He gritted his teeth. Perhaps he would not be able to escape death in Ireland, but he must escape to fight with his men one last time.

"Lean in," he whispered.

She shot him a questioning look.

"Lean in toward this bar. I will not harm you, but I must go to my men and warn them. Do you believe what I have told you? That I am innocent?"

The confusion on her face melted into a slow certainty. "You have convinced me, despite my misgivings. Ronan was right to send me to speak to you. Now I realize you would never stab a man in the back, nor plot evil against my father."

She glanced at Valgerd, who stood by mutely, waiting to see what would happen. When her eyes slid back to Ari, her gaze was so intense, so searching, he had to say the words burning like hot coals inside him.

"I love you, Britta. You make my heart glad. I cannot leave this land without you."

All her hesitation seemed to give way, and she leaned into the bar, her cold nose nearly touching his. Holding her steady gaze, he took his belt in both hands and wrapped it loosely around her neck.

"Guard!" he shouted into the darkness. "Release me or I will strangle your princess!"

Heavy steps pounded down the stairs in response to his threat. He held his ground, hoping this deception would enable his release. He tightened the belt slightly to make it more convincing, and Britta let out a sharp cry. Immediately, he loosened it, but she winked, letting him know that she, too, could play her part.

Ronan strode into the dungeon, torch aloft. He had tucked his mace into his belt. His dark gaze was hard to interpret.

"Drop the belt, Ari. I know what has happened, and I have told the king."

What did this mean? Ari kept the leather strap taut. "I will not. You must explain."

Ronan walked up to the cell, inserting a key in the lock, which forced Ari to drop the belt before the door swung open.

Britta did not hesitate but rushed into the small space to stand by Ari. Ronan did not restrain her. That could only mean one thing.

The Irish warrior believed him. Relief and thankfulness flooded Ari. He boldly slipped an arm around Britta, and she sank into his side. But urgency to save his men propelled him to speak again.

"What did you tell the king? Will your men attack? I must know."

Ronan's smile unknotted the fears that had held him hostage. "I told the king to stay his attack on your Vikings. You did not murder Clancy. It was the Norman."

"The Norman!" His eyes dropped under Ronan's steady gaze. Of course. He had been so enthralled by Britta's kiss, then so distracted by her single-minded concern for Ronan, he had forgotten to send someone for the wounded Norman. He had eaten and slept and forgotten his captive strapped to a tree. It was shameful.

Ronan continued. "The man somehow loosened his binds and escaped, but he still craved a Norman victory. He crept into the castle through the gardens and took up your sword—"

"Peacebreaker." Ari strengthened his grip on Britta's waist, wishing he could distract her from the recitation of his failures. "I realized I had left it behind when I reached our camp, but I fell asleep before I could return for it."

As if sensing Ari's discomfort, Ronan hastened to tell the rest of the story. "The man did not take long to locate the king's chamber, and he decided to steal in and murder him. When Clancy opened the door, the Norman assumed the man was our king and took the opportunity to stab him when he turned. But when he heard the king's shout and realized others were coming, he tore down the back staircase."

Ari groaned. "He knew the sword would point to a Viking attack."

"Of course. Even though his plan to kill the king failed, it could still be effective if we rose up against your Vikings. Then the Normans could return and take the castle in the midst of the chaos."

Choking back his own guilt, Ari spoke. "And now a man lies dead because of my grievous mistakes. How many others could have died because of them?"

Britta did not respond with anger toward him, but toward the murderous Norman. "Where has this conniving Norman run off to, Ronan?"

Ronan put an arm on hers. "Steady. He was caught in the next town, raiding eggs from a henhouse. The farmer sent word to the castle that he had a Norman prisoner. Once I knew the man was alive, it was easy to ascertain the true events of last night."

Valgerd rapped at the bars, impatient with their discussion. He used one of the few Irish words he knew. "Freedom!"

"You will have it." Ronan calmly unlocked the other cell door. He motioned to Valgerd. "Now go, and report to your men that all is well with your leader."

Valgerd waited as Ari translated, adding his own instructions. "Tell them I am safe, and that they must sail while the wind is good." He allowed his gaze to drop to Britta's luminous, undoubting face. "And tell them I will not be sailing with them."

Chapter Twenty-One

Clinging to Ari's hand, Britta followed Ronan up the stairs into the great hall. Father and his men sat at the table. The warriors had removed their chain mail and spoke easily as Florie set food before them.

"See if that won't hearten the lot of you," Florie said. When she saw Britta, she winked. "It's been altogether tense without you around, m'lady. I take it Ronan has explained things to you?"

Britta nodded. Father summoned her closer, and she released Ari's hand to draw near to his side. His eyes were filled with regret.

"I have wronged you, Britta—and our kingdom. I made bad assumptions and nearly launched into a war with innocent men. We would have been no better than the Normans who attacked us without cause. Will you ever be able to forgive me?"

"Of course I forgive you, Father. But there is someone else we have both wronged." She looked at Ari.

The king stood and faced the Viking. Ari hunched down a bit, as if he wished to disappear from the eyes of the Irish warriors who had so quickly turned against him.

"Ari Thorvardsson," Father began.

Britta nudged his elbow. "It is Thor*vald*sson, Father."

"Yes. Well, it is best I learn to say your name properly, Ari Thorvaldsson. You have given much for my kingdom, and I have yet to repay you. I understand today is the day you set sail. Before you do, I would like to offer you your choice of treasure from my coffers. I will lead you to them myself."

Ari straightened. His appearance grew more imposing, even with his unkempt hair and clothing. Britta wondered again if his family was in a high position in his country, because his bearing did seem regal.

"There is only one thing I ask," Ari said.

Florie beamed at Britta from across the room, her cheeks rounded in a wide smile. Ronan was focused on the Viking, his lips in a resigned line.

Britta started, realizing what Ari might request. Her hands went numb, and she sat down abruptly to forestall a swoon. If he asked to marry her, her father might still refuse. Yet if he requested some other treasure, her heart might break forever.

"I would ask to be your bondservant for a half year," Ari finished.

Father's carefully positioned smile faded. "But why?"

A hush fell over the room as Ari explained. "Because, King O'Shea, I love your daughter. Yet our days together have ended in turbulence. This is no way to start a marriage. Instead, if I stay and serve you, I can prove my loyalty." He bowed his head in respect. "I also wish to aid Clancy's widow and family, to make amends for my careless behavior."

Blood rushed back into her hands. She rose to her feet and faced the king. "Oh, Father, please allow it! He is an honest man. I never should have doubted him. And now he has become a Christian man as well."

Her father's eyebrows shot up. "Is this true?"

Ronan stepped forward to answer. "Yes, I know it is." He paused, thoughtful. "And if we let him stay, he will become more grounded in the faith, because Britta could read the Bible to him. Perhaps he could share more about Christianity with his people, who have already begun to convert."

She gave Ronan a thankful look then clasped her father's hand as if she were a small child begging for a gift. "Please."

Father looked from her to Ronan to Ari. His men looked on, awaiting his decision. Florie wrung her hands on her apron.

Finally, he spoke. "I offered you a reward, and although you did not ask for any of my goods, I see you have a greater treasure in mind. As my daughter said, you are an honorable man. I grant your request. You have safe haven in my kingdom as long as you choose to stay. But do not stay as a bondservant. I ask you to stay as our friend."

Britta's tears mingled with laughter as she moved to stand by Ari.

He took her hand in his then responded to her father. "I will stay of my own accord, but I promise I will be here a half year." He leaned down to her ear, his low, determined voice setting her heart racing. "I promise," he repeated.

"It is settled," Father said. "Now please, go and bid your men farewell so they may sail in peace. When you return, we must determine where you will live. There is room in the castle, of course, but it might not be circumspect, given your feelings for my daughter."

Florie burst out, "He's welcome to stay with us, m'lord. Clancy's widow and bairns live near our abode, and if he wishes to work for his supper, my James could use an extra hand on the farm."

Ari smiled. "I would welcome the work."

Britta squeezed his hand, unable to contain her joy. Ari was willing to leave his family and friends behind, to learn more about her God, her people, and *her*.

How had her love so easily faded to distrust? Ronan was right—real love was not so easily tossed aside. Trust was based on a person's character, who you knew them to be. Ronan had guessed that Ari was incapable of such a cowardly murder.

Yet she had let fear drive her suspicions, overlooking the honorable way Ari had always behaved.

As Father and his men dug into their meal, Ari led Britta outside and through the castle gate. The fallen soldiers had been removed, so only bloodstains and torn turf remained to show what a vicious battle it had been. The crisp air and snow-white clouds gave her the feeling that God was trying to sweep the land of its sadness.

Ari stopped abruptly, angling her to face him. He located her wrists under her voluminous sleeves. Circling them in his fingers, he gently traced her arms up to her elbows. The sweetness of his touch contrasted with the strength of those hands— hands that had wielded swords and steered ships.

"Remember what you promised," he said. "You will teach me to read if I teach you my language. I want you to understand every word I say, Britta."

It would never become tiring, to hear her name on his lips. She looked into the limitless blue of his eyes, so like the ocean. His blond lashes caught the sunlight.

"And I want you to understand this," she said, wiping a smudge of battle dirt from his face. "You have showed me your valor and your honor many times, never once asking for my thanks. But I thank you, Ari Thorvaldsson. And I hope to kiss you again. . .once you have had a chance to wash yourself."

Laughing, she lightly pushed him forward, so he could say good-bye to his men. Would he be happy here, in her land?

Only time would tell.

Chapter Twenty-Two

Summer, One Year Later

D angling her bare feet in the creek, Britta knew her hemline would be drenched, but she did not care.

She munched an apple, puckering her mouth at its tartness. Florie would tell her that eating too many early apples would upset her stomach and ruin her meal, but she felt like fully indulging today.

After all, there was much to celebrate.

The Normans had agreed not to invade their kingdom again, once their prisoner had been sent home, bearing gruesome tales of Viking warriors protecting the area. Her father had banded with other Irish kings and it seemed that much of Ciar's Kingdom would be saved.

Ari had stayed longer than he'd promised—a full year had passed since he had arrived on their shores. James had taken him under his wing as if he were his own son. With plenty of assistance, Ari had learned to read Latin fluently. Now he and James challenged each other to memorize scripture.

She leaned back into the moss, resting her head in her hands as she watched the thin clouds drift by. A smile broke across her face as she considered the tangible proof of Ari's love for her.

Only this morning, Ari had finished building his own home—a longhouse in Viking style. He had asked for her preferences each step of the way, from the wood they chose for the door to the perfect spots for windows. Tucked into the hillside with its turf-covered roof and wooden beams, it looked cozy and inviting, nothing like the cold castle she had grown up in.

It looked like a home, and she prayed it could be hers.

He had not asked her yet. He was determined to build his house before the leaves dropped from the trees, and she had never seen a man so single-minded. What Ari determined to do, he most certainly accomplished.

Over the past few months, she had reveled in his touches, for Ari did not withhold affection from her. Yet there were times when the clench of his fingers, the darkening of his eyes told her they were on dangerous ground. At those times, he would inevitably remember some chore he needed to do for James, and he would leave her abruptly. She knew he was trying to protect them both, and she loved him all the more for it.

Ronan still lived nearby, advising her father. But he no longer looked at her in the same way. It seemed that as his friendship with Ari had strengthened, theirs had deteriorated, yet all was as it should be. Ronan, loyal as he was to her family, would not have been the man for her. She prayed every night that God would bring him a woman to soothe his wounded heart.

"Deep in thought, I see." Ari's voice sounded behind her, and she sat up abruptly, her half-eaten apple rolling into the creek.

"Now look what you've done! That was my last apple."

He opened his palm, exposing two more of the tiny green apples. "I know how you crave these sour beauties, although I cannot understand why."

She took them and tucked them into her favorite leather pouch. The pouch was useful when she went on walks, allowing her to gather unusual rocks, colorful feathers, or other things that caught her eye.

She noted Ari's bronze bottle dangling from a cord on his belt. "Why did you bring your bottle? Are you so very thirsty? This creek is full of fish."

He unlatched the bottle, and she noticed its gleam. He must have polished it recently. When he handed it to her, she touched the dent the mace had left.

"How different our lives could have been," she said, tears springing to her eyes. "What if Florie's aim had been true?"

"But it was not, for God willed otherwise." He shot her a curious look, as if waiting for her to notice something.

She turned the bottle over in her hands, examining it. "It looks beautiful, so shiny." Something rattled inside. "What is this?"

He took the lid from the top. "You won't know unless you look."

She peered into the darkness then tilted it toward the sunlight. A pale object clattered about then slid from the bottle's neck into her hand.

"Oh!" She managed to catch it before it fell to the ground. Looking at it closely, she realized it was an ornately carved piece of ivory. The ivory itself was slightly marbled, but the beauty was in the designs. She could make out a longship and a castle, as well as Crow Mountain. And in the middle were a couple—a warrior and a maiden—and the word *Spero* wreathed around their heads.

"Hope," she breathed.

"I carved this for you," he said simply.

"I know," she said.

He cleared his throat. "There is always hope. This bottle bears that word upon its rim, but the poor Irish monk who owned it probably died in one of our raids."

She nodded, unable to speak.

"Yet here we stand—a Viking warrior and an Irish princess—both hoping in the same God the monk believed in. Perhaps he is smiling on us from heaven."

She swallowed, touching the polished ivory. "How much thought you have put into this!"

"I have thought of little else. I wanted to give you a gift that was a piece of myself—my home—and that is what this walrus ivory is. I do not paint, but I thought you would like a carving of us."

"Thank you," she said, looking closer at the grooved pictures. "But what are these figures here behind me? They look as if they are tearing at my skirt! Are they wild dogs?"

He burst into laughter. "No, those are your children, clinging to your skirts."

"My children?"

"Our children." His smile faded into a look of earnestness that tore at her already surrendered heart. He touched her cheekbone, letting his fingers trail down to her chin. "I love you, Britta. You must know I built the house for you—for us. Your father knows of my plans, and he has given me his blessing. Will you be my wife?"

Throwing herself into his strong arms, she nodded. "Yes, yes! Please be my husband!"

He whirled her around, even as she clutched the ivory in one hand, the bottle in the other. When he set her down, she nearly toppled into the creek in her dizziness, but he pulled her close and pressed a tender kiss on her lips. She could not wait to kiss him more, anytime she wished.

"We will marry tomorrow," he said decisively.

She did not think twice. "Of course we will."

Her father came to her as Florie buttoned her wedding gown, which was nearly the same color as the ivory tusk. It was her mother's dress, and it fit perfectly.

He sighed. "You will stay nearby, in the longhouse? I would not like to have you far from me."

"Of course we will stay close. And now Ronan can live in the castle, where he can learn your ways and prepare to rule someday."

Father frowned. "Why would he want to rule?"

She turned, and a peach rose that Florie had twined in her hair fell to the floor. The nursemaid huffed amiably and searched for another one to replace it.

"Why, because Ronan will inherit the kingdom, of course. If he moved in, it would make things so much easier."

"Ronan is not to inherit my kingdom, Britta. *You* are. You are my child, my own blood, so you must take over for me. Unless you do not wish to do so?"

She grasped his hands, her knuckles turning white. All these years, she had been certain the castle and the kingdom would go to Ronan because her father had no male heir. But he had always planned to give it to her. She could stay in the land she loved, help the people she loved, for the rest of her life.

"But what of Ari? He will be my husband."

"It is your decision. If you want him to rule alongside you, so he shall. If you want to be queen, you may rule by yourself."

She did not need to ponder. "If I am queen, he must be king and command equal respect, even without the O'Shea name."

"It will be as you say, my dearest. Now I will go and let Florie arrange your hair, and doubtless weep a little, too."

She hugged him. "Thank you, Father, for understanding my heart."

"It is a queen's heart." He kissed her forehead before he strode out.

As Father had anticipated, Florie immediately burst into tears. When her sobs slowed, she said, "My little book-loving girl to be queen! Imagine!"

Britta glanced out the window, catching sight of Ari in his white tunic threaded with gold. She smiled. God had answered her prayers in a way she had never imagined—bringing peace and hope to her kingdom on the distant tide.

Heather Day Gilbert, a Grace Award winner and bestselling author, writes novels that capture life in all its messy, bittersweet, hope-filled glory. Born and raised in the West Virginia mountains, generational storytelling runs in her blood. Heather is a graduate of Bob Jones University and is married to her college sweetheart. Having recently returned to her roots, she and her husband are raising their three children in the same home in which Heather grew up.

A Song in the Night

By Amanda Dykes

Dedication

In cherished memory of Grandma Jean, a MacNaughton who knew how to fly.

*And to Grandma Diana, whose love shines strong and true,
and who shared with me the heritage of my own family's
bottle messages buried in the California desert.
As those notes said:
All is well. God is good.*

Chapter One

Argyllshire, Scotland
1715

Are ye ready, miss?"

Meg's stomach twisted at Mother Aila's question. She gave what she hoped was a smile and swallowed back a wave of fear. If she could but stay here in the elderly woman's croft, with the comforting spice of soil and peat fire warm about her. . . But that wasn't what a bride did on her wedding day.

The single candle in the room sputtered into smoke. Ah, blessed diversion.

"Shall I fetch another candle?" Meg made to rise, her pale blue dress with its delicate silver filigree swishing as she did. But Mother Aila placed her hands on Meg's shoulders with a strength befitting her eighty years of hard work. Meg sat again in the timeworn chair.

"Don't move," the older woman commanded. "Ye haven't answered my question. And we've work to finish here." She wove a ribbon of the clan tartan—pale enough to be properly modest—into the coils of Meg's braid. The eldest woman in the village, it fell to her to conduct the rite of preparing any bride before the ceremonies began—even, as in Meg's case, the laird's daughter. She reached for the table to retrieve the simple crown of clover blossoms and trailing ribbons, placing the adornment upon Meg's head.

"Fit for a queen," she said. "Now tell me. Are ye ready?"

Two answers rivaled on Meg's tongue. Was she ready? To secure the clan's land once and for all and put a stop to the feuding with the Clan Campbell? To see her father's burdens eased because of this union? Yes. But ready to tie her tartan in an unchangeable ceremony knot to the blue and green she'd lived her life fearing, until now? To marry the nephew of the Campbell laird, whom she'd seen only from a distance in her twenty-two years—so old was the strife between the clans? She shivered.

"I am ready." Perhaps speaking the words would convince her heart.

Mother Aila began to kneel, and Meg could see it pained her. "Please, let me—"

Up came a wiry finger, halting Meg and pointing back to her seat. Meg obeyed, sensing an air of reverence over what was happening. The woman lowered herself slowly to her knees and placed her hands around Meg's arms, the lines of her face suddenly solemn. "Be strong, lass. Hold fast the clan words."

Words Meg knew as well as her own name: *I hope in God.* 'Twas easier to say than to do, today. The destiny of an entire clan, resting on her shoulders.

"Now, off with your boots." Her smile was kind, and Meg rallied herself. She might not be able to fight alongside the war chiefs, or lead the people alongside her father, or make all the troubles of the people disappear, but this one thing. . .she could do. Put one foot in front of another and keep on till it was done. Meg tugged off her boots, the heavily draping skirt falling back over her bare feet. 'Twas the clan's way—for the bride to tread their land with nary a stocking between her and it upon her wedding day. A promise that come what may, she would be true to them, even in her new role as wife.

A knock sounded upon the door, and through the curtains stood the silhouettes of a gathering crowd.

"'Tis time," Meg breathed. She stood, slipping into the delicately knit gray *earasaid* Mother Aila held out for her. She let the shawl's billowy hood fall free down her back, and with one last squeeze of the hand from Mother Aila, she stepped from the rustic white walls and into the dirt pathway teeming with people. The road split the rolling green hills, wending like a river to carry her to a new life.

A cheer arose about Meg as two boys hoisted an evergreen bough above her. The joy of the people beat like the bodhrán drum that drove their song, until it thrummed right into her heart. How privileged she was to be one of this clan. To act on their behalf.

Two wee girls with the same russet curls tumbled through the crowd and nearly toppled Meg. "For you, miss," the taller of the two said, and held up a bouquet of white heather wrapped about the stems with a piece of long grass, crisscrossed and knotted.

"Wherever did you find this?" Meg hadn't thought it possible to find heather this early, and in this white hue, so near Loch Fyne.

"'Tis a secret," the smaller girl said, her grin contagious. "The man said a lady such as ye must have white heather on her day of union. And. . .and. . ." She scrunched up her nose, reaching for a memory.

Her sister piped up. "And the green grass of the hills of yer home to adorn ye."

Meg fingered the soft blossoms. "The man"—her groom, Ian Campbell? Perhaps he was not as severe as he was rumored to be.

"Well," Meg said. "Bonny lasses such as ye must have something, too," She removed her crown of clover blossoms. Curious looks crossed their faces as she untied two scarlet ribbons from the crown, tying one about each of their wrists with a tidy bow. "There, now," she said. "No one tells you how heavy those weddin' crowns can be. You'll help me ever so by taking away these ribbons." She winked at them and prayed today would make a brighter future for them. One void of the ongoing clan wars with the Campbells.

The sisters clasped hands with one another and dashed back into the crowd.

Villagers rallied about her, leading her in procession up the hill toward the castle to meet the piper. From the corner of her eye, she caught a snatch of joyful motion: a band of *Ceàrdannan*—summer walkers, who roamed from river to river chasing the pearl fishing. They ran from the road and their carts now to catch up and join in. Meg's spirits lifted at the notion of these Tinkers, perfect strangers, ushering her with such joy to the ceremony.

Such a flurry it was, with the young girls from the village twirling scraps of long, colored cloth, and the rolling beat of the bodhrán driving them on, and her heart right along with it—such a flurry indeed, it wasn't until she was nearly to the piper himself that she sensed it.

Something amiss. A heaviness in the air.

It was on the piper's face, too. He stood on the crest of the hill, watching her approach with a hollow, almost mournful look beneath a solemn smile. The curves around his mouth strong but gentle. She hadn't known which of the pipers it would be—for Father had summoned three more for the festivities, in additional to their own Duncan Blair. But it was Duncan's familiar form standing stalwart there. She felt a wash of peace at that knowledge, so like a brother was he. Still, there was a deep anguish in his eyes she had never seen before.

All was still of a sudden. The drumbeat hushed, and the voices of the people ceased their song. It was to be a moment of peace before her last journey alone, that small stretch between her and the piper. But the silence felt like glass, ready to shatter.

Mother Aila gave her a gentle nudge from behind. "Now's your time, lass. I canna go farther, but listen for the sound of the wedding bells, for we'll set them a-rollin' over the hills. Away with ye, and be wed!"

Such a foreign notion. The bell was rung only for the laird's family, but she'd not had cause for it to ring for her since the day she was born.

She breathed in the salt air of the sea lake. Something odd tinged it. Smoke, such as should hover after autumn harvests and into the winter. Not on a spring day like this. But perhaps she imagined it.

She took her first step forward and just as she did, a gust tumbled down the hill. Her skirts whipped about her ankles, and she stumbled back against the blow.

Duncan started toward her. But she caught her balance, shook her head to stop him. She would make this journey alone. Then the path would lead her to the castle, just her and him and the bolstering anthem of the pipes.

This one thing, I can do.

She gathered her skirts so her unshod feet could step wild and free through the tall grasses. And slowly, as she reached the top, the drumbeat started again behind her. Steady, strong. A herald for the pipes.

Duncan's eyes met hers. Something inside of her gave way at the sight of his soul-deep pain, whatever it was. She wished she could lift a hand, smooth away this nameless despair—for he was family. Not MacNaughton, but through ties forged in battle and celebration alike, he was loyal. True.

She rested her hand on his offered arm, wishing away the brief tremble that came over her. He turned with her toward Castle Cumberave, and side by side, they stood facing the long stretch of green ahead of them.

He lifted his mouthpiece, and just as he made to blow, the far-off sound of pipes came.

Not his. And not the nuptial music.

It was a battle song. Meg searched the landscape, trying to place its source. Her eyes landed on the gray cobbles of Cumberave. Her home. All appeared still beneath its corner turrets. No movement came from the tree-covered mountain behind it, nor the loch before it. But the music grew louder. There, from the low walls of the courtyard, a spiral of smoke began to snake its way into the blue sky.

Meg's feet sprang forward, a force she'd never known propelling her toward the castle. For within those walls stood all she had in the world. Mother. Father. Her twin brother, Graeme.

Someone took hold of her arm with such urgency she whipped back in pain. But she would not stop. An arm wrapped about her waist, pulling her close to the rough wool of a jacket. A familiar voice broke through the pounding in her head.

"Meg." She fought against it. Sounds of attack grew louder. *Mother. Father. Graeme.* If she could but climb the last rise—

"*Meg.*" Duncan. He would help her. He must— "Ye must go, lass." His voice was low, fervent. "As far as ye can get. 'Tis the Campbells."

And as sure as he spoke, the Campbell battle cry seemed to shake the earth. "*Cruachan!*" Moments later, a flag bearing the boar head of their crest unrolled from the tower window.

Her legs were crippled beneath her, and Duncan draped her arm about his neck and guided her stumbling feet away from the scene. The villagers had scattered—some running toward the castle, others retreating for the woodlands.

Only the traveling folk remained near their wagons. All their voices knotted together as they surrounded Meg, creating a wall between her and the castle, until she reached the nearest cart. Duncan helped her up to sit among rough sacks of burlap.

He released her, turning to go. He stopped only long enough to speak to an older man, glancing back at Meg with protection in his eyes. "Meet us at the Tinker's Heart," she heard this new, gruff voice say to Duncan. "When all's safe, we'll bring her there."

Duncan nodded, turned toward Meg. She saw him take her hands again but could hardly feel a thing. "Go, lass. I'll see to them." He pointed at the castle. "Ye'll be with yer family once more."

"Duncan." Meg clasped his hand.

His eyes searched hers.

"Haste ye back, Duncan."

He did not speak—only gave the briefest bow and charged over the hill. Within moments, the air filled with his music. A song to instill courage in the hearts of the brave. She knew he made himself an easy target in doing so, but she also knew he believed this was the reason he was alive. For such a moment as this.

The Tinkers carried Meg to safety several miles away, deep within the shade of the forest. 'Twas a good many hours before all was quiet and the patriarch of these travelers, a man they called Thistle Jimmy, escorted Meg back to Tinker's Heart. In truth, the rustic landmark was their own site, this outline of rocks in the shape of a large heart in the ground. Yet for as long as Meg could remember, they'd shared it with the MacNaughtons on days like today—for the final knot-tying ceremony of the tartans after the bride and groom had been wed. But gone were the wedding banners that had flapped in the wind here scarce hours before. Burned to ashes. A mockery of the peace this day was to begin.

Meg knelt, brushing away the debris. "Hold fast the clan words," she whispered and grasped for them. *I hope in God.*

But covered in ashes like Job himself, she found no hope. For Duncan did not come. Not a single soul came. In the dark of the night, the only sound was a hollow ringing. A death bell, tolling slow and solemn into the night for three different souls: *Mother. Father. Graeme.*

Meg knew not how long she waited there. But the moon was high and bright when she finally stood, pulled gently to her feet by the man who'd brought her. Behind him came a young woman with large, kind eyes, who draped a heavy woolen blanket around her, and Meg realized she'd been shivering. Her numb, bare feet stumbled over the ashes and up into the wagon. It lurched into motion and took them again into the cover of the woods.

Chapter Two

Two Years Later

Meg caught a snatch of motion from the corner of her eye—a small object falling. It splashed into the creek, causing droplets to spring past the white apron Meg was washing and into her face. Her heart leaped and she whirled, ankle-deep in the water, to face the woods behind her and see who the culprit was.

"Very funny," she said, forcing calm into her voice, though her senses stood on edge. It was a joke, no doubt. One of the summer walkers trying to startle her. But it was ill timed, to be sure. Two years it had been since she'd been back here to Argyllshire. Two years since the day that had turned a wedding march to a dirge in a matter of moments. And returning here now had every nerve on end, for what once was home was now Campbell territory. She must take care here, lest she be recognized by them.

"Meg," someone whispered. A tree rustled behind her, and her eyes darted across the tree line. *'Tis only a trick.* All the same, the jokes of the Ceàrdannan, family that they were to her now, spooked her betimes.

Meg brushed her skirts, as if doing so could brush away the fear, and hung the apron on a reaching tree branch. "Who's there?" She infused calm into her voice. A white-winged snow bunting released a trill, and Meg breathed easier. "Ye're a fool, Meg MacNaughton," she spoke aloud. "A silly fool. Jumpin' at the sight of a wee bird." She cocked her head at the bird above her. "Carry on," she said. "'Tis a right winnin' tune!"

She knelt again to dunk the apron one last time, humming a few notes of her own, and skimmed her fingers through the water as it carried away the grime of the summer's travels through the highlands. 'Twas peaceful here. She could almost forget the shadows that mangled her life's story.

One glimpse at her reflection in the currents showed her those shadows were written on her face, in the dark circles beneath her eyes and the wan countenance that changed her so. All the better, if she were to traverse this territory unrecognized with the Tinkers.

"Meg!" The lilting voice of her friend Kate came, and Meg smiled at the hurried footsteps. From the moment Kate had wrapped the blanket about Meg's shoulders that night long ago, they'd been fast friends. "Come! They're waiting!"

Kate splashed straight into the stream, yellow hair flying loose behind her, and snatched the apron away. Linking her arm through Meg's, she tugged with a wiry strength. Meg would be alarmed at such urgency from anyone else, but this was Kate's way. Everything an adventure that could not wait.

She was breathless. "What a crowd this time, Meg. I swear it—your fame grows every day. Ye'll soon be wantin' to take leave of a rowdy bunch like us and take your stories to the courts of kings!"

Meg plucked her wet apron right back, shaking herself loose of Kate's hold with a smile. "Nonsense. They come for a glimpse of the famed beauty of bonny Kate, that's what."

Kate placed her hands on her hips and drew back with a smirk. "See for yerself." She pulled Meg into a run. Past the cluster of canvased bow tents and their domed roofs, rising from the ground like low boulders. Past the men gathered about the fire with hammers and anvils, smithing tin as was their way in the afternoons after a morning of pearl fishing. Snatches of conversation wafted her way—the gruff voice of Thistle Jimmy, their leader, saying something about the pearl fishing going nigh unto dry, hereabouts.

Thistle Jimmy was a man who defied time. At times he seemed as old as the land itself, but most of the time, he had the energy of a young man. A whole lifetime on the road had made him weathered but strong, and it was with hard-earned wisdom that he led their small band of travelers with such care. Like a shepherd toward his flock.

At last, they burst through a wall of willows, and Meg lurched to a stop. Humble farm folk filled the green meadow, eyes large against hard-worked, hungry faces. Their tattered clothing created a tapestry of muted reds, browns, and greens.

"They're here for you," Kate whispered in her ear.

"They canna be," Meg said. What had she to offer? Would that she could pass around bannocks or fresh water—anything to quench the thirst behind their gazes. "And even if they are, I cannot appear. This close to home. I mean—this close to Cumberave. If there be Campbells in the crowd. . ."

"*Nae.* Thistle Jimmy checked first thing after we made camp. Castle Cumberave is abandoned," Kate spoke softly. Meg felt ill. For all that—the wedding, the attack, the death of her family—the Campbells had abandoned her family's castle? She hardly knew whether to weep in relief or explode in anger. 'Twould still be their territory, and a place she had no speakable right to.

"The Campbells are mostly away at Campbelton, for their laird is there before going to London. Something about a show of support for the king."

Meg felt behind her and found support by steadying her hand against a tree. The crowd of faces reflected so much of the pain she knew all too well. They, too, had lost much that day. And she had been nowhere in sight to help them. A wrong she would never be able to right.

"They heard a story weaver was amongst us. They need hope, Meg." All traces of jesting gone from Kate's voice, Meg knew she spoke truth. Mother Aila's words echoed in her mind. *"Hold fast the clan words. . . ."*

Meg stepped back. She wasn't enough. She would disappoint them, surely.

A rustle sounded, and the gathering of people turned, a pathway parting between them. From their midst, a wee girl of no more than six approached, large waifish eyes fixed on Meg. "If ye please, miss," she said, "is it true what they say? Ye'll tell a tale for a shilling?"

At the edge of the gathering, the tall form of a man moved slowly, his face hidden behind the hood of a rustic brown cloak. Meg shivered and fought the urge to run. Instead, she knelt to take the girl's hand. And with each feature she registered, the crowd around seemed to blur until all she saw was this creature—waves of auburn hair dingy but combed with care and tied back with a piece of twine. The sight of the longing in her eyes pulled Meg's heart until it hurt. Such solemnity did not belong on the face of one so small.

The girl clasped her hands in front of her and as she did, a dull ribbon bracelet dangled from her wrist. Two thin red ribbons intertwined, tied in a crooked bow. Meg narrowed her eyes, unable to look away from it.

The girl caught her staring. "'Twere a fine lady who give them us," she said.

Us. A thread of memory flew at Meg: two sunlit faces full as they thrust a bundle of white heather into her own nervous hands on her wedding day. Her stomach sank with the weight of realization.

This one, a steady voice within told Meg. This was the one she was to speak for, today. Her spirit quickened, and she said a quick prayer for wisdom to spin a story to speak to hope to this girl's heart.

"Nary a shilling needed, lass." She would be loath not to have anything to contribute to the coin jar come nightfall, but neither could she take money from the girl. "Just your name."

"Jemma, miss." She bit her lip, which trembled as if she'd just given Meg all she had in the world.

"Well, then"—she sat upon a low rock and guided Jemma beside her, vaguely aware of the lookers-on and their listening hush—"look around you, wee Jemma." The girl sat with wide blue eyes and leaned in. "If you could choose one thing in this bonny glen to tuck into the pocket of your heart, and to carry with you all the days of your life, what would it be?"

Delight nestled into the peasant girl's expression as she looked from the blue July sky to the wild roses spilling around the edge of her rock.

"Anything?" Her young voice was light on the breeze.

"Anything. Be it the very wind"—Jemma's brow wrinkled—"or the delicious oatcakes I smell from the camp." Meg winked. The girl smiled as if she held a secret too precious to tell. She cast a glance at a woman standing just behind her, who returned an encouraging nod despite the sheen in her eyes.

A boy elbowed his way through the perimeter. His face was flushed with mischief beneath hair of the same red as Jemma's, and Meg could sense his shenanigans before he said a word. Several rows behind him, the cloaked man watched on. A shiver traversed Meg's spine, and she turned her attention back to the boy.

"My sister'll be wanting that shawl of yours." The boy pointed at Meg's threadbare earasaid. "To use as a blankie, like a bairn!"

His laughter hit its mark, and Jemma slumped in her place.

Meg leaned forward and whispered, "Never ye mind him, lass." She gave a gentle touch to her shoulder. "Brothers grow up, and that teasing will turn into something rich and good as time goes on." Meg knew this all too well. The truth of it sharpened the void her brother, Graeme, had left when he perished. Her very heart had lost its shape that day. "I hope ye'll treasure each other long, indeed. Now, what will ye pick for the story, then?"

Jemma looked timidly around until her gaze rested on a pair of butterflies.

She pointed. "The *dealan-dè*," she said.

"That one?" Meg pointed at the one taking flight.

"No," the girl said. "Both, together." Such resoluteness in her voice, more than her small frame seemed able to hold.

Meg studied the white-winged creatures, both at rest now upon a sprig of yellow broom. Then she studied the girl and inclined her heart toward heaven. *Give me Your sight, Lord. Help me to understand this young heart you created.*

The silence of the crowd pressed in upon the prayer, and she fought to forget them and what they might think. A quick glance around told her the dark-cloaked man was gone now, at least. She thought of the two girls, the smiles they shared when they'd delivered her heather.

Meg's breath caught, the way it did when understanding began to unfurl and a story took form. And so it began. "You know, of course," she said, "about the two butterflies of the Great Glen of Inveraray." Jemma shook her head back and forth quickly. "No? Well, then. Let me tell you. They were inseparable. They went everywhere together! Nary a day went by that they didn't have the grandest adventures in all the land."

A fleeting smile crossed Jemma's dimpled face. Meg's voice rose and fell with the tale of a grand journey, of the brave way the butterflies spurred one another on until they reached the famed field of daffodils. "And now to the bravest part of all," Meg said, her words swimming in the rapt silence of the crowd. So many of them battle scarred. "The day came that a giant of a wind carried one of the butterflies away." Her voice dropped, thick with familiar grief and gentle with the handling of the girl's heart. "The one left behind flitted and flew, searching everywhere for her friend. And when she could not find her, she flitted and flew once more, searching for how she was to continue on alone."

Meg paused. She had no easy answers to give the girl. *Give me wisdom, Lord. . . .* Jemma leaned in.

"Well. The butterfly gave up flying altogether one day. She could not figure it out, and so she rested upon a log until a cricket came along, singing a song and asking what troubled the lovely creature. She told him, and do you know what that cricket said?"

Jemma shook her head.

"Seems to me your wings were made to fly. Your heart was made to beat. The air about you was made to carry you. You will not be the same as before, and ye need not be. . .but ye can fly, and fly ye must," she said. "Ye fly, sure and true, for that is what you were made to do. Ye never need forget your friend, but neither must the life ye shared disappear."

It took everything in Meg to end the tale with a smile. *Help me believe that, Lord,* she prayed. For to her, a quiet log in the forest looked much more appealing than all the flying in the world.

"Thank ye, miss," Jemma said in a near whisper. "'Tis a brave butterfly." And with that, she dashed away and wrapped her arms about her mother's legs. The older woman met Meg's gaze with a quick curtsy, eyes shining.

"Well done," Kate said, clasping Meg's trembling hand and helping her up. Together they walked back through the trees, toward their camp. The peace that had wrapped her during the telling was gone, as was the scattering crowd. "And just as I said, no one recognized ye. Come,"—she dashed ahead—"the others will be achin' to hear all about it." She picked up her faded green-striped skirts and ran ahead, leaving Meg alone.

With the crowd's retreating footsteps to her left, the clink and murmur of the camp to her right, and the whisper of the creek ahead of her, Meg suddenly felt a hollow vulnerability at her back. The same unease she'd sensed earlier.

She turned, and at the same moment a shadow moved from behind the trees. He stepped from shadows—the man in the cloak.

Panic seized her, and a single thought overtook her consciousness: *flee.* But as she turned to run with all her might, a hand caught her wrist from behind.

"Meg MacNaughton," his low voice said. "Stay."

Chapter Three

Meg's pulse raced. At her back, sounds from the encampment, the metallic ring of meal preparations, stood like the assurance of an army. *Help is near,* the noises seemed to say. She let that knowledge embolden her.

"Let me go." She pulled in a breath. "I'll scream." She kicked, her foot colliding against the man's shin. Pain exploded in her toes, but she pursed her lips, holding back a cry.

"*Ach,*" the man uttered, shifting his weight to his other foot but maintaining his hold. He held her at a distance as she kicked again, harder this time, and with her heel. She hit only air and threw herself off balance. His hands flew to her shoulders, steadying her. "I mean ye no harm, lass."

His assurance bounced right from her. Something about being back in Argyll, a stone's throw from the place she'd lost all trust—she wasn't about to take the man at his word. Not when he'd been lurking in the shadows so. Meg shrugged free and stumbled backward. The man stayed still, letting the distance breathe between them.

"Please. Just listen." There was strength in his voice, its edges rounded by something gentle.

But she would not be fooled by another false offering of peace. "I will not," she said. The man could work for the Campbells—or worse, be one of them. She plucked a branch from the ground and held it back over her shoulder like a shinty stick, ready to strike. "Who are you?"

He held up his hands and took a step back.

A sick feeling hit her, remembering Jimmy's warning as they arrived here yesterday. "*Be on your guard, for the Campbells may yet be seeking ye.*" Had the man come to retrieve her?

"You'll not take me," she said. And neither would she run. It was a hard lesson, two years in coming. Fleeing was the worst of her failings. "Ye've done enough harm to my family."

The man froze, his stiff posture exuding guilt. So he *was* a Campbell, then.

"Mark me," she gritted her teeth. "I will never step foot outside this clearing with a Campbell."

He lifted his hands and removed his hood. Meg's stick clattered to the earth. It could not be...

"Please," he repeated. His eyes pleaded, warm gray as the loamy earth. "Meg." He let her name linger, seemed to sense she was already pulled asunder by shock. Indeed, he was as much a part of her home as her own brother, so faithfully had he marched with her family. "'Tis only I,"—he seemed to struggle over the next words—"your piper."

A whirl of emotion cinched the breath straight out of her. "Duncan. . .Blair?" She could not keep the corners of her mouth from pulling into a smile. He, the only link in years to her life when it was whole.

He stepped closer, brow furrowed. "Are ye well?" he said, voice curving the question downward as he beheld her earnestly.

"Am I well?" The words felt distant as she repeated them. A simple enough question. But no simple answer could she find. In the distance a pot banged—a signal that the meal was nigh ready. "I'm meant to be helpin' with the food," she said reluctantly and turned to hide the flush of heat in her face. "Perhaps you'd join us?"

"Can ye not wait a small while? I've aught to tell ye," he said. "News of home."

Please don't. The words were on Meg's tongue. She could not bear to hear again of the empty Cumberave.

"Home is everywhere but here," she said. But when she lifted her gaze to his, there was a longing there—something near desperate to be spoken.

"Please, Meg. I did not mean to startle ye. Not now, nor earlier. . ."

Earlier.

"It was you in the woods?" Gooseflesh pricked her arms. It could have been anybody.

"'Twas a. . .*right winnin' tune* the bird sang, just as ye said," he offered. Such a look of sheepish hope crossed his face, and in it she a glimpsed the subtle spunk she'd encountered in him when he'd first come to her family eight years before.

And was not this the man who had saved her? Given her a chance at life, such as it was? He stood before her, asking something within her grasp to give, small as it was.

"Will ye eat with us tonight?" She spread an arm toward the camp. "I will hear whatever ye have to tell."

The relief in his posture was fleeting, for a look of solemn concern soon took its place. "Thank you."

"'Tis nothing," Meg said. Though she began to suspect it was much, much more.

Duncan watched Meg slip through the trees, the last of the evening sunlight playing across the shadows. She looked slight enough to blow away on the wind, but he knew better. There was a strength in her like iron, and it had only grown in these years since the battle. To the point that there was a chill about her he hardly recognized, and she wore it like a cloak.

"Coming?" she asked, holding a branch back for him to follow. He grasped the branch and stepped through the grove and into the camp. Low, rounded bow tents like canvas half barrels on their sides peppered the clearing, supper fires beside them. Jolly voices seasoned the air along with the salted scents of herring and tatties. A humble supper from land and sea.

Instincts trained to the very second, he spotted the most direct route through, scanned the periphery for any signs of trouble. All seemed safe. He pressed on.

"What're ye doing?" Meg's amused question halted him, and he turned to find her behind him. "Do ye think we're headed into battle?" She stood with her arms crossed and a look of friendly amusement on her face. "By all means, *good sir.*" Laughter was barely concealed in her voice. "Lead the way. Since you know just where we're going." She emphasized the word *just* with a sarcastic lilt. "And since these fearsome foes are clearly such a threat." She motioned wide to the small clusters of jovial summer walkers, who sat with tin plates and laughter to commune together. One of them pulled out a fiddle and began to play. A sparkle lit Meg's face, and she leaned in as if to impart a great secret. "Such formidable weapons they wield."

Embarrassment burned in the back of his throat. He swallowed it away, only to be chased by jaw-tightening anger. "Very sorry, *my lady*, for doing what I once vowed to do for your family." The words were out before he could stop them, and the moment they were, he wished he could snatch them back. Everything he knew of Meg MacNaughton told him she meant no harm, even down to the warmth of her voice as she'd jested. It was what had caught his attention eight years ago, when he'd first come to serve the family at twenty years of age. A warmth that had burst uninvited into his life, when all he'd known was coldness.

She'd been racing two of the young scullery maids up the back stairs at Cumberave, wearing a simple brown dress, her laughter bouncing about the cold stone walls like sparks. He'd been going down to find his quarters below, and she'd been running up, carrying a bucket. They'd nearly collided. She'd turned that bonny face up toward his, brown eyes dancing.

"Ye'd best give watch where ye're goin'," she'd said.

"Yes," he'd replied. "If there be banshees such as yerself flyin' through these halls. I'll keep watch for ye."

And he had. For a week after, he'd watched at every turn for the mirthful maiden who occupied his thoughts. It wasn't until the feast days later, when he was first summoned to play for the family, that he found her. And his gladness both swelled and shattered.

For there she sat between the laird and lady, clad in silken finery that puzzled him. *Was she a lady's maid, then?* Dark hair falling over her shoulders in curls, fair face sprinkled lightly with a dash of rose and freckles across her high cheeks—a feature whose effect somehow gave the impression that the same sun that had touched her face now warmed the room from within her.

"Margaret," the laird addressed her. "It is you we celebrate this night. Sixteen years is a noteworthy age. Will you choose our dinner ballad this evening?" He opened a palm toward Duncan. "A fine piper whose reputation precedes him. He'll know many a tune, I'm sure."

Duncan bowed, evading the young Margaret's gaze when he straightened. She was family to the laird, then.

But he felt her gaze on him, and when at last he lifted his eyes to hers, her face was solemn as stone. Perhaps she did not recognize him. Fool that he was, had he imagined she'd been watching for him all the week long, too?

"Aye, Father. I think a cautionary tune. Perhaps 'Keep Watch, Ye Lads and Lasses'?" She paused after the first two words of the name, a lightning-quick smile lifting the corners of her mouth. *"Ye'd best give watch,"* she'd said to him that first day. So she did recognize him, after all.

That dreaded heat overtook his face. He tried to mask it by quickly filling his lungs and lifting his pipes. When their eyes met just before he was to play, she tilted her head to the side ever so slightly, suppressing a smile. He could not look away.

And he'd been watching for her ever since, though he knew now that any future with her in it was foolish and impossible. For more reasons than one.

He'd played the tune, making eye contact with her only when, had anyone been singing, the song would have said "keep watch." And the delight he'd seen in her eyes was one that held him fast over the years, try as he might to forget how she captivated him.

She slipped past him now, leading on through the camp without a word. So changed. They joined a small encampment at the far edge of the clearing.

A flood of stilted introductions followed as a plate of steaming stew was ladled from a bubbling pot. The folk gathered: a lively older man, the young woman—Kate MacGregor, he learned—who'd been at Meg's side all afternoon; Mrs. MacGregor, Kate's mother, and it showed, for the yellow hair and blue eyes they shared; and two younger families, a handful of boys and girls circling their parents in a pre-supper blur.

They'd stood with wary faces when he and Meg approached. Meg assured them it was all right, that he was "an old. . .friend." The pause between those last words was painfully long. Even as they dined in seeming ease, he did not miss the watchful glances cast his way from all directions.

At length, Mrs. MacGregor began to gather the tin plates. She took theirs and lingered in front of Meg and Duncan. "Go on," she said, "have a dance, then." She nodded to where Thistle Jimmy was tuning a fiddle, wincing as he plucked a discordant string. He uttered something about a storm-a-blowin' in and meddling with his fiddle, though nary a breeze rustled. Then he shrugged and resumed twisting the knobs until at last, he struck up a lively reel.

"Well?" Kate's mother looked between the two of them in a way that made Duncan want to release a bitter laugh. If she had matchmaking notions between him and Meg, she'd learn soon enough that such a thought was wretchedly absurd.

Meg sat close enough to him on their shared boulder, he could feel her tense.

"Yes, do!" Kate scurried over, touching her friend on the shoulder. "'Tis high time you danced again, Meg. What better time than with an old friend?" Meg hesitated, looking toward Duncan with a fragile question on her face.

And though it struck a hollowness into his chest to do it, he shook his head. "I don't dance," he said. True though it was, he hadn't meant it to sound so abrupt.

All three sets of eyes were on him as if he'd just declared night was day and day was night. "'Course you do," Kate said. "Everyone does."

Meg's words were more knowing, tinged with a soft mix of sorrow and curiosity. "You used to, Duncan. All those sword dances and reels. What's happened?"

The near-constant ache in his leg burned, as if it knew it were being spoken of. He shook his head. She didn't need to know. It would only add to her burden. "'Twas long ago," he said and left it at that. Her face fell. Kate pulled Meg up from the rock and looped her arm through Meg's.

"Come, Meg," she said. "I'm in need of a spritely friend to whirl with, and there's none better than you."

Meg whispered something to her friend, glancing back toward Duncan. Kate studied him then whispered something back—and not very quietly. He didn't mean to overhear, but she was as discreet as a bear. "Have pity, at least. Poor man looks like he's been wandering lost for two years." She paused. "Same as you."

Meg stood alone and still as the others swept off into the dance. The late-summer sun stretched the dancers' shadows into a churning pool about Meg, and she turned to face him.

"Duncan," she said simply. "I was hasty before, in the woods. And cruel. You came to bring me news, and whatever it is—I will hear it." She swallowed. "And thank ye for it."

He nodded. "Come, then," he said, and he prayed grace upon his words as she sat again beside him. This would not be easy, and he wanted to take care with the shock it would surely bring. Best to ease into it from a sideways approach.

"Meg," he said. He searched for words. He was never very good about easing into things. "Come with me to London."

He winced at his own directness.

She drew back, bewilderment on her face. "Duncan Blair, why would we go to such a place? So far away—"

"Ye must come, Meg. To make things right—for me to make things right—"

"Nay," she said, shaking her head. "I've never so much as left the highlands, Duncan. The Tinkers—they're the closest thing I have to family, now. I cannot leave them." She sighed. "If not for them,"—she gestured to the dancing folk—"I may never have stepped foot back in Argyllshire. They follow this route every few years when the pearl fishing brings them, for 'tis their livelihood. I'll move with them wherever the rivers call them."

"Then move in the general direction of London," Duncan said with a desperate laugh. Time was so short. "I'll be your guide. The journey is not easy, but. . ."

The song came to a close, Duncan's voice too loud over the sudden silence. The others gathered around Thistle Jimmy in low conversation, who stooped to draw in the sand with a stick as he explained their route for the next day. So, they were leaving the encampment already. Duncan's time was shorter than he'd thought.

Meg spoke, gentle finality in her tone. "I. . .will visit the graves of my family while I'm here. To say good-bye. 'Tis one good thing that can come from facing this place again. And you, Duncan. I am glad to see you. That you are well after—everything. You did much to save us that day." She took a deep breath. "Anyway," Meg said. "Did ye not say ye had news of home? What has London to do with all this?"

He wanted to burst out and tell her but did not want to startle her yet again by speaking too bluntly. It would be a shock to her, no doubt.

Jimmy's voice rose with excitement as he spoke to his gathering. "With the pearl fishin' running low hereabouts, we'll go west tomorrow," he said.

Duncan leaned in closer to Meg. "Go south."

She whispered back, "Ye're mad, Duncan."

Jimmy carried on with his plan for the group. "Across the land, to the sea, and on to Skye and the other isles after."

"Go to London," Duncan countered again, but for Meg's ears only. 'Twas a bit too loud, for Jimmy shot him a puzzled look before moving on with his plan. "Ye needn't go with *me*, Meg, if that's what's stoppin' ye. I needn't be your guide." Though he'd give anything to, to make what he'd done right. "But just—"

"Ye're daft," Meg said, shaking her head in refusal and fixing her eyes on Jimmy.

Jimmy continued, "We'll outfit with boats at Craignish. . . ."

Duncan set his jaw. This would sound insane, but there was no going back now. If Meg would not listen. . . He stood and stepped toward Jimmy. "If I might, sir." Jimmy nodded. "If it's pearl fishin' ye're after, you might think of the river Esk." If he couldn't get Meg to London, perhaps Thistle Jimmy could get her as far as the borderlands. It was on the way and nearly into England itself.

Jimmy's eyes narrowed, and a vague look of recognition dawned. "Lowland territory? Too far south for us," he said. "Not our normal grounds. We stick to the highlands and islands for our trade."

Duncan's mind raced, grasping at arguments and assembling as fast as he could. If he could but get Meg even partway to London... "You're right. 'Tis a fair journey, and not an easy one. But many a walker has said just that, and the plentiful pearl fishin' is proof." All eyes were on him now. "I came from there just a month past. 'Tis fair beggin' for someone to come and pluck the mussels from the waters."

Meg leaned in, anger in her low tone. "What're you doin', Duncan?"

"Take a barge or a ship from Campbelton," he continued aloud and felt stiff ire take over Meg beside him at the mention of the place. "It'll even carry your carts and horses. Cross the Irish Sea and go south to camp at Gretna Green. You could spend the whole summer there on the river, maybe more. I'll guide ye, if you like."

The others began a low chatter among themselves, this new possibility bandied about with alternating doubt and hope.

"Duncan." Meg took hold of his shoulder and turned him to face her. "I'll thank you to leave us be. You come here with such a plan, turning everything upside down, and look at the trouble you've caused." Meg gestured at the others, but the smiles beginning to dawn on their faces did not support her. She dropped her hand and led him to the edge of their tent cluster. Light was fading to nearly nothing, and so was his hope. "Please, Duncan. 'Tis getting dark. Perhaps 'tis best if ye head home."

She was pulling on his arm now, leading him away for a send-off.

He thought of Meg as she had been: warmth to his cold life. He looked at her now, barely a thread of that girl hiding behind her sorrowful eyes, and hated what he was about to do. She'd despise him, too, once she knew all. He pulled in a breath and stopped in his tracks, causing her to stop as well.

Face-to-face with Duncan, her shoulders rose and fell quickly with her breath. "Ye promised news and have only brought trouble. Perhaps ye meant well, but... Please. Just go."

"Meg," he said at last. "'Tis Graeme. He is in London."

Meg blinked. Shook her head. "What cruel trick is this?"

He closed the small gap between them, putting his hands on her arms. "No trick, Meg. He is there."

'Twas as if he'd struck her with a blow that turned her to stone. "You mean his grave is there," she said. "Was he buried there? I know he loved his time at Eton, but surely..."

She was stiff but let his hands remain on her shoulders. And there—just in the very depths of her eyes—he saw it. A flicker of hope—distant and elusive as a will-o'-the-wisp light upon the loch. If she could dare to believe... But then she shook herself as if to shrug off a snare, his hands right along with it. And just like that, the light was gone.

"I heard the bell ring for his death. For my parents—and for him." She paused, as if trying to convince herself. "I remember it, for I counted the bells, and one was with his number of years. I would never have left if he'd lived."

"Listen, lass." His voice was low now. The press of ten sets of eyes from behind, all fixed on the pair of them, seemed to weigh each moment down into a slow crawl. "Graeme is in London." She watched him, hanging on his words. "Alive as the day."

Chapter Four

Daybreak never looked so like the night. The sun should be shining, but blue-gray mist cloaked land and loch like a curtain. Fog such as this swallowed people alive, or so Tinker lore said. Stole away years from them in the blink of an eye then released them back into the world, left to find their place where time had marched on without them.

Standing here at Tinker's Heart, Meg began to think it wasn't just lore. For just a dash down the valley and over the covered hill, the very one she'd climbed on her wedding day, Castle Cumberave awaited, same as the day she'd disappeared.

She clutched the rustic brown knit cowl about her neck and shoulders, shivering beneath the billowy sleeves of her ivory blouse. A peasant's dress over it, in the same muted blue as the mist, a length of brown twine crisscrossing back and forth in front of her bodice. It felt like a tether about her lungs just now.

"Ye dinna have to go back there," Thistle Jimmy said beside her. He slipped his weathered hand around hers.

"I do," she said. "And I thank ye for coming with me. I need to see for myself whose graves those are."

At the campfire last evening after Duncan's revelation, Jimmy had insisted he'd seen three graves, all new since two years ago, in Cumberave's *kirkyard*. Duncan insisted Graeme was not buried here. The men both drew up until, fearing they'd come to blows, Meg had stepped in the middle. *"I'll see for myself,"* she'd said.

Duncan had protested. It was best left alone, he said, and it was too dangerous—Campbell territory that it was. Jimmy sided with Duncan, and suddenly the two were allies, insisting that Meg trust them.

As if trust were something to be given freely. Or at all. Her thoughts were so thick by then, she didn't even protest when Kate intervened and led Meg away to their tent for the night.

But come dawn, when Meg had slipped out of the tent to make her way to the kirk of Cumberave, there was Thistle Jimmy, knobby and strong as the tree he leaned against. "You're going," he said gruffly. Perhaps she imagined it, but there seemed to be a prickly sort of respect at the edge of his voice. "Thought as much. Well, then. On with it." And he'd led the way deep into the thick fog, until they stood here on the brink of the place.

They followed closely the tree line now, for—though the Campbells were rumored to be away and, according to Duncan, Cumberave was empty as the tomb on the third day—they all knew there was still danger, her being here.

Croft after abandoned croft they passed, and Meg could not help but wonder what life they might hold now, had things been different. The trees grew thicker until the heavy presence of a rock wall loomed dark to their left. She ran her hand along the dewy stones until at last they reached an opening to the kirkyard. Her toe caught on a tree root, and she tumbled over the hallowed ground, catching her balance and freezing. For there—dark silhouettes against the fog now lit by the rising sun—were three wooden crosses. Not the elaborate stone typical of a laird's family. Jimmy hung back, crossing his hands in front of him and bowing his head—a show of respect for what this moment would mean. Confirmation of what she'd already mourned and would mourn once again. . .or a complete upheaval of all she knew to be true. Her heart beat wildly as she drew near enough to read them:

ROBERT MACNAUGHTON

ILISA MACNAUGHTON

And the third one, smudged with mud. She wiped the dark earth away to reveal the deep engraved letters beneath:

MARGARET MACNAUGHTON.

She stumbled back a step, pressing herself against the rock wall. This could not be. She saw a dash of motion and someone beside her. She reached for Jimmy's hand, thankful for his swift presence.

"The villagers wanted to protect you," he said. Only the voice was decidedly not Jimmy's gruff one but of low and steady timbre. *Duncan.* Meg turned to look at him. He studied the lifting fog ahead as he spoke. "They risked their own lives, stealing in to give your parents a proper burial in the land that was rightfully theirs."

"And—and that one?" Meg removed her hand from his, pointing at the cross marking her own name. Jimmy drew closer to them.

"Ian Campbell swore he would take you, alive or dead. Some of the villagers saw you go with the summer walkers and knew you lived. . .but they buried any hope Campbell had of you there in that grave. Said it was the only way to set you free. 'Twas you they rang the bell for that night."

Twenty-two hollow clangs of that bell, rolling over the hills and reaching her ears in the darkness that night. Never suspecting it was her own death they marked.

Meg released a breath. "So this grave. . .is empty."

The hesitation was enough to tell her otherwise.

She swallowed. "Tell me."

"Many were lost that day, Meg. Graeme was wounded. I took him to London. I knew he had friends, safety there—and when I came back, it was already done." He hung his head. She waited. "'Tis Mother Aila's resting place," he said.

The air went out of Meg. She stepped forward, stooping before the headstone just as Mother Aila had kneeled before her that day. She traced the top edge of the marker slowly.

"I know 'tis the family kirkyard," Duncan began, regret in his voice.

Meg shook her head. "'Tis right she has a place here," she said. "Family is more than blood." All the wisdom and generosity the woman had poured into their lives. "I only wish she had her own stone. She deserves better."

Duncan clamped one of his wrists with the other hand, bowing his head in a show of respect.

She stood, retreating to the gate. "There's more you should know," Duncan said. "Though Ian has proclaimed a high reward for anyone who will return to him his 'wayward bride'"—the words dripped with bitterness—"they have come to accept that she is gone." He faced Meg now. "Even Graeme believed it."

"What? And you let him?" She pushed the gate open, threading numbly through mulching leaves toward the castle. Spiced air followed her tread, and so did Duncan, with an oddly uneven gait to his step. She stopped with the castle in view and faced him, awaiting an answer. Jimmy trailed warily behind.

Pain swam in Duncan's eyes. "I returned to try and bring news, let ye know he was safe. But the travelin' folk had gone, and you with them. From the villagers, I learned ye were safe, and I've watched for ye ever since. I wrote to Graeme, but the letter was never delivered."

Jimmy was beside them now, appraising Duncan with a wary look. "And he's in London, you say."

"Yes," Duncan said. "But if we're to catch him before he leaves, we must hurry."

"Where is he going? How did ye come to know?" Meg's voice sounded too tight. Keen panic made her mind race. "Will he be back? I could write him, tell him I live. I'll ask him to come back."

Duncan was shaking his head. "I had a letter from him a month past. Writing him now will take too long. And there are highwaymen on the stretches of road who steal the mail. . . too many ways for it to go missing and not enough time."

"What do you mean, 'not enough time'?"

A stroke of silence. "He's bound for America, Meg."

America. The word hit her with the force of a boulder. Duncan continued. "He's to stay long enough to see the governor of Edinburgh through an important political event in two weeks' time. And then he's to sail for the Carolinas to take on a position of leadership. They're in need of good leaders who will not leave the people unprotected in times of attacks. Leaders who can represent the Scots people well, who know their tongue."

Was this what Graeme had been spared for? Survived such plunder, only to forge his way across the world and fight again? Her spirit sagged with the grief of losing him all over again. Opening her eyes once more to the warmth of the sun, she decided. "I will go."

Relief broke across Duncan's face, lifting the corners of the mouth that always seemed chiseled into solemnity. She couldn't help smiling in return. He glanced over his shoulder, where Jimmy waved an arm at him.

"We're goin', too," Jimmy said. "At least as far as the river Esk and Gretna Green. Hope ye ken what you're signing on for, guidin' a wild pack like us."

Duncan strode over and clapped Jimmy on the back. "Never did I see better travelin' companions," he said. "I'll get my things and meet ye back at the camp." Duncan dashed into the woods in the direction of his croft, a short jaunt from the castle. He ducked his tall, dark-haired form beneath a low-hanging branch and tossed a boyish dimpled grin back at Meg, one her heart caught with an odd jump.

"*Craicte*," Jimmy uttered, looking on. Meg laughed. Yes, Duncan was a bit crazy. "But I believe you are right to go, lass."

Meg spoke past the thickness in her throat. "D'ye think so? If I don't get to Graeme in time, or if something happens on the way. . ."

"But if you *don't* miss him. If nothing happens on the way. There will always be reasons not to do something. The question is—is this what you were made to do?"

His words stirred in her the memory of Mother Aila's voice. She'd said something similar, and look what had happened. But could this be a second chance? To put one foot in front of another, all the way to London this time, until she brought peace, at last, to what was left of the clan?

"If the answer is yes,"—Jimmy's worn boots shuffled through the bracken until he faced her—"if this is what you were made to do, lass, then do it. Come what may." He rested a hand on her shoulder. "Ye're stronger than you think."

Jimmy was kind to say so. But even as Meg resisted it, her own battle cry came back to her. *This one thing, I can do.* A deep breath and she slipped her hand inside her dress pocket, where her last remaining scrap of tartan lay.

Help me to hope, Lord. Help me to trust. Help me to—did she dare ask something that seemed so impossible? But God was in the habit of redeeming death, and a grave marker in the woods told her she had nothing to lose. *Help me to find my brother.*

A sudden *crack* sounded. Meg's eyes flew open. *Crack*—it sounded again, an ax head upon a tree, or something just as forceful.

"Come," Jimmy said and wove through a thicket of willows. Meg followed, feet carrying her over ground she knew so well she could have navigated these trees blindfolded. Men's voices sounded now. Still Jimmy moved ahead, Meg letting her ear guide her into his quiet footsteps as she kept watch over her shoulder behind them. And when she looked ahead at last, her hand flew to her mouth to stop the wordless groan. For there, looming above them, a lone fortress yawned with want of life. Castle Cumberave.

The urge to run burned in her muscles. To hide away from the betrayal this place held, looking down on her from those stone-framed windows like great, empty eyes.

But the voices drew nearer, the cracking sound louder.

And the urge to run from the castle grew stronger. Each force closed in on her. She was stuck. Caught fast in Campbell territory, a price on her very head.

Chapter Five

Here's another," a gruff voice said. "Mark it."

"Too young," said a more robust voice. "They'll be wantin' thicker trunks for Inveraray."

Meg pressed her back against the cold stone wall of her former home. The overgrowth of the shrubs was a boon. She cast a furtive glance at the kitchen door to their left.

The men spoke of Inveraray Castle—the seat of the Campbells. Suddenly she felt the price on her head as if it were a physical weight.

The voice continued. "Such saplings wouldn't stop a Jacobite from tumblin' over his own feet, let alone stave off an attack." A dry laugh. "Such as it might be, and long live the king."

Jimmy and Meg exchanged a look. Though the Tinkers—and Meg's family, for that matter—did not much enter the politics around them, word was spreading of a second Jacobite rising against the monarch of the newly united Great Britain. With a king newly crowned on the throne—an outsider from Germany, of all things—tensions were thicker than ever before, clans divided across the highlands.

Jimmy grabbed her wrist and pulled her into the kitchen doorway, where a splintered door hung barely open on its hinges. He backed in, Meg following, fighting against the urge to get as far from this place as she could. Her sleeve caught a plank, the hinges groaning their protest. She froze.

"What was that?" the older man said, all trace of humor gone.

"Watch yerself," the other said. "'Twill be one of the MacNaughtons, come back to avenge them all." His voice grew theatrical.

Meg peeked outside at their kilt-clad forms, axes in hand—just in time to see the older man's fist land a solid *thwack* against the younger's arm. She pulled back, flattening herself against the cold wall behind her. Jimmy did the same. Footsteps thudded nearer and louder.

She could not look away as a weathered wooden ax handle butted against the door. A loud groan of the hinges pierced the air—high and low, high and low as the door swung back and forth in response.

"'Tis a right shame," the man said. "We could be livin' here. Relations of himself the laird, watchin' over the loch from its head. 'Stead of seein' it fall to pieces like this. If his hotheaded nephew would learn a thing or two—"

"Stop yer gripin'," the gravelly voice said. "We'll be late to Campbelton if we're not back with the boat soon. Come."

Meg felt ready to empty her stomach. But she took a deep breath. Mentally traced the plans of these men: south along the loch to Inveraray near their own castle, then farther still to the Irish Sea peninsula, where Campbelton perched on the edge of the loch as it turned into ocean.

"Don't worry, lass," Jimmy whispered as the men's footsteps receded into the forest. "We'll take the high road. They'll be on the water. We'll not cross their path."

She nodded, easing herself away from the wall at last. She stood in the center of the room at the end of the thin shaft of light let in by the door and turned slowly around. Odd silhouettes within greeted her like lonely fossils. The stool she'd stood on as a girl was toppled in a corner, where once their cook's arms had wrapped about Meg to guide her in stirring the soup. Meg had loved it down here. Always the comforting warmth of steam and spices. A stack of cobwebbed bowls, spoon still resting in the top one, seemed to greet the bride they'd been preparing a feast for when interrupted so suddenly and finally.

What had once been her home was now one gaping tomb. She could not bear it.

She pushed her way out into the morning daylight, the only trace of mist a few stray tendrils at her feet. Her feet carried her away from thoughts she could not revisit.

"Wait, lass," Jimmy said, gaining on her.

She paused, catching her breath. She hadn't meant to bolt. "I'm sorry, Jimmy." He waved it off. Yet still she felt too close to the castle. "Should we help Duncan pack?" Any excuse to keep going. Jimmy gestured for her to lead on. Past the empty stables they went, down a hillside, up into Duncan's thicket.

But he was not there. And neither was his stone blackhouse. A hearth and chimney stood in the middle of the clearing, looking incomplete without a home around it. The earth was raked carefully, and a pot sat beside the open hearth.

Jimmy stepped around the chimney and surveyed something intently. "A wonder he'd ever be willin' to leave, with riches like these about him." He motioned for Meg to come look.

On the ground was a thin, uncovered bed of straw, the length of a man. A plank of wood next to it rested upon two rocks, where stood a single tin cup and a chipped plate that matched the bowls she'd seen back at the kitchen. A pile of rocks stood beyond the makeshift bed, a low wall of the same stone incomplete beside it. Someone was rebuilding.

Had Duncan lived here, all this time? 'Twas no rougher than the bow tents she'd grown accustomed to, but the sight of the ruins heaped heaviness upon her heart. It looked so exposed, so solitary. And he, who could be playing his pipes in the finest castles. It did not make sense.

All other small belongings appeared to have been carried away already, so she took hold of the tin cup with a thought of returning it.

Back at the camp, walkers were tying the last of their things to the two horse carts they shared. Duncan stood on the edge of one, lashing a canvas down with a worn rope and looking quite at home among these wanderers. A rough-woven sack was strapped to his back, odd lumps shaping it. A wooden pipe—a drone, Meg recalled him telling her long ago, protruded from the top, slung over his shoulder like a musket.

Mrs. MacGregor pushed her gray sleeves up and asked him about the journey. He pointed toward the road they'd be taking. As he hopped down to lift a sack from one of the men, they laughed, and Duncan clapped his shoulder.

She felt so small. Undeserving of all that lay before her. The Tinkers changing their route for her. Duncan searching her out to bring news of her brother. Much more was at stake here than herself, and she must do better to remember that.

He glanced up from his work beside the cart just then, catching her gaze. She held it fast, studying him. He straightened to his full height and held hers just as steadily, until it dropped to her hand at her side. To the cup.

Meg closed the gap between them, holding the cup up by its handle. Her finger tapped a crooked dent on the side. "Yours, I think."

"Aye," he said, not making eye contact. "Thank you." He reached to accept it. But she did not let it go, even as his fingers wrapped about it and touched hers.

"Duncan," she began. "Have ye made camp there in the woods?"

A fleeting pause. "Ye might say that."

"For how long?"

He gently pulled the cup from her hand, tucking it into the cart, and pulled the rope so swiftly the threads of it released a light *zip* into the air.

"I promised I'd watch for ye." His only reply before he strode away.

The cooling air stung Meg's eyes as his meaning struck her. She ran to catch up. Nearly an entire day since they'd crossed paths, and she only now thought of what all this must have meant for him. To see her brother to safety so far away as London. To watch over the MacNaughton land when all others had forsaken it.

She caught up to him, keeping stride as best she could with his long steps. Just as her legs worked double the pace of his to keep up, her thoughts tumbled, grasping for words good enough.

"Thank you," she said at last, breathless from nearly running to keep up.

He looked upon her, an instant of shared understanding passing between them. "'Tis nothing," he said.

"Nae," Meg said. "'Tis everything."

"*Bag gasag an tur!*" Jimmy shouted. The walkers clambered to their places in the caravan, and Duncan slowed his pace, looking to Meg for help.

"What did he say? I fear I don't know much of the Gypsy language."

Meg laughed. "Don't let Thistle Jimmy hear ye call them that. Call them Tinkers. Pearl fishers. Summer walkers. Travelin' folk. Ceàrdannan. But *do not* call them Gypsies. Quite another people, so he'll tell ye."

"Understood," Duncan said. "So then. In the tongue of the summer walkers." He smiled, and it warmed her. "What did he say?" Meg had traveled with them long enough to learn much of the Beurla Reagaird—their secret language.

The wagons clattered into motion. But Duncan stood still, awaiting Meg's answer.

"Put a match to the fire," she said. Jimmy's way of beginning every journey. And this time Meg knew more than ever—there was no going back.

Chapter Six

A river of deep green trees spilled down the hillside into Campbelton. The travelers, energized by the sight of it after a wearying two days' journey, rushed to the hill's curving edge as soon as the burgh came into sight.

Duncan smiled at their chatter and exclamations over the smallish port below. By their wide-eyed looks, it might as well have been Glasgow itself. Over the miles, he'd begun to see how these humble people of the road wore the dust of their travels like the robes of kings. How simple peasant garments cloaked their bodies, but souls afire with story and song and hard, hard work lived within. No wonder Meg felt such a fierce loyalty to them.

He issued a warning about the boggy wetland beyond the short stone wall they stood along but knew it wasn't needed. More than anyone else, they doubtless understood the danger of the spotty terrain, the hidden depths masquerading as shallow pools.

Duncan set down his bag as the others rested. Three men huddled at the end of the wall, looking at a hand-drawn canvas map and making plans. Mrs. MacGregor unbundled a parcel of thick oatcakes, passing them to each person, including Duncan. Meg followed, dispensing handfuls of the *blaeberries* she and Kate had gathered along the way. She barely looked at him as her palm opened into his, but he dipped his head in thanks all the same.

A satisfied hush settled as they ate and lingered. It was simple but heartening fare, and they'd all greet the town the merrier for it. And the more alert.

With that thought, Duncan's gaze sought out Meg again. She stood next to Kate, the sun of the afternoon crowning her dark hair. Kate pointed wildly—first to the fishermen's white shanties dotting the waterfront below, then to the criss-crossing streets, and finally to the bustle of market in the center of it all.

And then there was Meg. Smiling amiably at her friend, but Duncan did not miss the way her hands pressed to her stomach. Nor the way her gaze kept stealing to the swaying masts in the harbor, like foes she did not trust.

Kate dashed off to speak with her mother, and Meg was left alone. Searching the horizon with such a longing look, as if her brother would come riding over the hills at any moment and spare her what she was about to do. She pulled something from a plain brown satchel. A small square of something—a scrap?—and fingered it as if it were her greatest treasure. He shielded his eyes against the sun and caught a faded snatch of plaid.

A gust off the loch curled up the hill and plucked the treasure right from Meg's hands. It spun in the air, her face registering distress. Had she anything left of her family besides that piece of tartan? The very thought had him bounding toward it.

"Duncan, wait!" Meg's voice was urgent but somehow distant.

He sped around the stone wall. At last the item fell, and he closed his hand around it just before it hit the ground.

Soggy, wet ground, he realized too late. Mud was thick around his ankles, bouncing oddly beneath his feet as he tried to catch his balance. A thin web of peat was all that kept him from the hidden pool below.

"Brilliant," he muttered. At that instant, the web snapped. Sludge engulfed him up to his waist, cold and thick. He grasped onto the bank, but the muddy mass of roots came away in his hand. He reeled backward, splashing into the muck. The stench was nearly suffocating. He lunged for the bank again, grasped harder, pulled himself halfway up. He could make it—if he grabbed the ground with both hands. But Meg's scrap was held fast in his left hand, and he would not let it go. His hand alone kept it from being soiled irreparably.

A branch thrust into view, nearly colliding with his stomach. Two bare feet stood on the grassy bank. His eyes traveled up from the muddy blue hem of a dress to the fair face looking down.

"Take hold," Meg said, a mass of her curls falling over her shoulder.

He was about to protest—for if she got pulled in, too. . .

"Quick!" Meg shouted. Behind her, Kate and Jimmy and one of the younger men of the party came running, grasping fast to the long end of the branch.

"*A h-aon*," Meg began to count in Gaelic. "*A dhà*." Tension spread across the branch; a slight cracking sounded. "*A trì!*" On the third count, he fought with all his might against the mud, and the company on the other end of the branch heaved back. He emerged, dripping with brown muck like a swamp creature from the tales of old.

"Just thought ye'd clean up a bit for the townsfolk, did ye?" Jimmy clapped him on the back, releasing a full-bodied laugh.

Duncan leveled him with a glare but let it morph into a low laugh. "Thank ye kindly," he said. "One and all." Meg looked half-bewildered and half-amused, the way she scrunched her eyebrows together and stifled a smile. The rest seemed on the verge of laughter, turning redder in the face by the moment. Probably holding back to spare him embarrassment. Well, 'twas too late for that. He breathed deep, shaking his head. "I told ye to beware the bog."

Every pent-up laugh burst forth with abandon, the tide of it carrying them back to the wagons. Duncan ducked away to scrub off in the creek then ran to catch up just before they reached the outskirts of town.

Meg trailed the group. When she looked back and saw him, she stopped, letting the caravan move ahead. And for the first time since he'd seen her three days ago, there was her smile. Real and true and full. The same one she'd given him the day they'd first met. It lit her whole countenance.

"You're back," she said with gladness in her voice.

"And human again." He shifted his weight, and his boot released a loud squishing sound. "Nearly." He matched her smile then held out his hand to return what the wind had stolen. It was indeed a square of soft wool tartan, no bigger than the palm of her hand. Interwoven squares of red and green, with threads of light blue outlining bits of the plaid.

She took it gingerly, smile fading. "Thank you, Duncan." She studied him. "Truly. You can't know how much this means to me."

"Your family tartan," he said. The very colors he'd worn with pride all those years.

"Aye, and the only piece of it I have left. All I have, really, of any of them. Mother Aila tied it into my hair on my wedding day, and"—she closed her palm around it—"well, you know the rest."

"Come on, lollygaggers!" Kate motioned afar down the road.

Duncan's boots continued their loud narrative, the unevenness of his limp maddeningly loud. After a few strides, Meg spoke again. "I am sorry," she said.

"Ye've naught to be sorry for. I'm the one who plunged into the bog like a fool. And I know it could have gone much worse."

Meg laughed softly. "No, I mean—I *am* sorry for all that, but. . ." She cast a glance down at his feet then pursed her lips as if unsure how to proceed. "When you found me in the forest the other day." She paused, expression hopeful.

Duncan narrowed his eyes, not following.

"When I. . .kicked you." She bit her lip, eyebrows raised, an expression of guilt. And remorse, probably. "I never meant to truly harm you."

His uneven gait punctuated the silence between them—a rhythmic *stomp-pause-squish, stomp-pause-squish* that sounded off kilter. His limp. She thought she'd done this to him? How easily he could free her of that burden. But. . .he held back a smile.

"Ach, yes," he said. "I do recall a scrappy rapscallion attacking me. I'll never walk the same now."

Meg looked askance at him. "Scrappy rapscallion, is it? And who gave me a fright to last a lifetime? Letting me think you were a Campbell, ready to carry me away."

That silenced him. The look of fire-lit terror in her eyes in that moment was burned into his memory. As much as he wished to, he could not undo that. But he could at least ease her worry. "Dinna concern yourself over this." He patted his leg. "Aye, you gave me a muckle kick." Enough to leave an impressive bruise. She hung her head. "But this particular friend"—he kicked his wounded leg out—"has been with me for much, much longer."

She tipped her head to the side, listening.

He did not wish to trouble her, for he knew she'd find a way to carry fault for this, too. He exhaled. "The day of the wedding," he said. "We all lost something. He tipped his head toward his leg, remembering the deep and long-healing gash. "My loss was far less than all others."

Again, Meg seemed to search for careful words. "Is that why you don't play the pipes anymore?"

Duncan kicked a pebble in the road, noting the arched stone entryway to the town ahead. The proverbial hornets' nest was just minutes away.

"You don't have to answer that," Meg said, filling the silence.

"No. 'Tis a fine thing that ye'd ask. The answer is a simple one." He shrugged the bag carrying his pipes higher on his shoulder. "The day I came to Cumberave was the day I became piper to the MacNaughtons. When everything happened. . . I swore I would not play until I'd done all I could to reunite the family I owe every-thing to."

Meg stopped in the middle of the road. "D'ye mean to tell me, Duncan Blair, that ye've not played a single note since then?"

"Who would I play for?" He was still walking, but he stopped at last and turned to see her worrying her scrap around and around one finger, an intent study on her face. "Best to hide that," he said, nodding toward the tartan. "We're nearly there." She nodded, hesitating only briefly before slipping it into her satchel. The others had already passed under the stone arch, their wagons clattering down the cobbled streets.

"It would nae have a warm welcome here. Not from some."

A serious look crossed her face. "Duncan," she said and paused as if turning something in her mind just as she had the fabric in her fingers. "Do ye think Graeme will take me with him? To America, I mean."

He stopped in his tracks, a tension girding him. "Is that what ye'll be wanting?"

She hesitated only a moment before nodding. "'Tis what seems right," she said. "To be together."

"If I know Graeme, he'll not step foot aboard any ship until he's secured a place for ye if that is what ye want."

She dropped her gaze. "It is," she said at last. "Thank you, Duncan."

The arch stood before them, and Duncan could not shake the feeling that it was a portal to another life. Once they passed through, there would be no going back.

The last piece of Argyllshire soil Meg MacNaughton would tread.

The thought sank heavy in him. But his feelings were not what mattered. Her life was. Meg set her satchel down and removed from it her earasaid, draping it over her head like a hood. 'Twas good she did so. The faster they could get through Campbelton, the better.

Chapter Seven

Meg knew she should be thankful for the bustle of the town, overwhelming as it was. The streets flooded with the smell of salt air, the warmth of fresh bread wafting from a bakery, the jumble of people milling about the market. Spritely fiddle music played from somewhere nearby. 'Twas easier to blend into such a scene, but easier, too, to lose Jimmy and the rest. Meg hurried to keep close.

They congregated at the center of the market near a towering stone cross. Meg studied the intricate etchings swirled into it and wondered at the hands that had placed it here, probably hundreds of years ago. What would they think of the wavering faith in her heart?

Jimmy began assigning duties. They were to procure supplies for the next leg of the journey and meet on the dock in a half hour's time. Kate and Mrs. MacGregor for the salt pork. The others for fish and oats. Jimmy for the potatoes.

Meg hadn't been named in any of the jobs. "What can I do to help?" she asked.

Jimmy closed the gap between them. "You and Duncan head straight for the ship."

"I can help, though."

Jimmy leaned in. "I know ye can, lass. But 'tis best ye move on through."

Duncan closed in on them. "He's right."

Meg looked to the waterfront. It was horrid to be such a burden. "At least let me get the potatoes," she said. She pointed at a booth where an older man and woman were bundling lumpy cloth parcels. "We'll pass them, anyway."

Jimmy searched her eyes. "Ye're a brave lass," he said.

Meg smiled. "Indeed. The bards shall sing for ages to come of the girl who purchased potatoes."

Jimmy gave a hearty laugh. "Go on with ye, then." He turned, started up the street toward the church.

"Where is he off to?" Duncan asked.

"The kirk." They watched as Jimmy pulled a bottle from his jacket. Aged bronze, the vessel's sheen was long dulled, but strength of life filled it from within. Much like the man himself. "Every town we stop in, he goes into a church, finds the Holy Scriptures, and copies down whatever he can. Just a line or two, but he says it's a way to carry the Word with him when he has no other way. He keeps them on a scroll in that bottle."

"A Bible in a bottle," Duncan said.

"Yes. Well, parts of a Bible, anyway. He says there's no tellin' how far God's Word will travel, no matter what vessel it's in, 'be it a bottle or a book or a braw brave brain,'" Meg recited Jimmy's oft-repeated chant.

They watched the man disappear within the red door of the stone building.

"I respect a man who will search out the truth," Duncan said. And then he turned to her. "And I respect a woman who dares to vanquish fearsome potatoes, too," he said with a wink.

At the booth, Meg thanked the couple, offered a few of her meager supply of coins, and walked a little surer for having done even a small task to help the others. Even if Duncan refused to let her carry the sack of them.

They had not walked ten steps when a shout stopped them.

"Blair!" A jovial voice, from behind. Meg's heart pounded in her ears, and she searched for the source.

A man with deep red hair bounded down the lane, dodging shoppers. "Duncan Blair!"

Duncan muttered something under his breath and, in one fast motion, set himself between Meg and the man. "Quick," he whispered in her ear, gesturing with a nod to the open door of a milliner's shop beside them. "'Tis one of Ian Campbell's nephews."

Meg ducked inside the white building, just far enough to be out of sight. Wishing her heart would quiet down. *He is just a relation,* she told herself. *Not all Campbells are Ian Campbell.* Perhaps this nephew was of the laird's—Ian's uncle's—camp, who reportedly were more interested in wars between countries than wars between clans.

She slowed her breath so that she could hear.

Rows of fabric rolls lined the wall like books in a bookshop, and Meg took hold of one of the lengths as if to examine it. But her every nerve was trained on the scene unfolding outside, just beyond her view.

"Come to make good at last, have ye?" the man said, out of breath.

Meg ran her finger across the fabric of the bolt in front of her. Make good. . . ? Duncan did not seem one to be beholden to anyone.

"Angus," Duncan said. "Off to rid the sea of its fish?"

"Not I." He laughed. "Not unless you mean the Irish Sea," he said. "Or the river Thames."

"Are ye headed all the way to London, then?" Duncan asked, his tone one of ease. As if they didn't also happen to be planning the same trip. Meg caught a reflection in the wavy glass of the open door. The man patted a fishing basket.

"Aye," he said. "Most of us are. The Campbell wants to show support for King George. Says a Campbell contingent must represent us well at this concert he's planning."

A touch on Meg's shoulder made her jump.

"Didn't mean to startle ye," a woman clad in deep burgundy said beside her. "Will ye be wanting a length of the black watch?" She gestured at the fabric Meg fingered.

"The black watch?"

"Aye, the Campbell tartan," she said.

Meg pulled her hand away from the blue-and-green-plaid fabric as if it had burned her. "I. . ." She was being ridiculous. They were threads. Threads with their own name, apparently. But they could not harm her.

Outside, Angus laughed and talked on. Duncan glanced her way, their eyes meeting fleetingly.

"Ah, a gift for your beau?" the shopkeeper leaned in with a warm smile and asked conspiratorially.

"No, he is. . ." What? Her oldest friend? Her guide to a land she'd rather not see? She shook her head, leaving the sentence behind. "I wonder,"—she faced the woman, noting the gentle lines creasing her smile and eyes—"do ye know aught of a concert in London?"

"Oh, aye," the woman said. "The floating symphony. The king has had an entire series of pieces written just for the occasion by a fine composer. Can't recall the name. Begins with an *H*. Hanford, maybe? Hanover. No, that's where the king hails from. Han. . .Handel. Yes, that's it! The musicians will board a boat, of all things, and play as they float down the river."

"An outdoor performance," Meg said. A fine thing indeed, for most people never dreamed of hearing a single orchestral piece in their lifetime, let alone an entire grouping. Such joys were reserved for royalty and the like.

Outside the window, Angus was gesturing wildly, consumed with a tale of some kind. "Will you be goin'?" Meg asked.

"Me!" The woman laughed. "No, not the likes of me. But many a Campbell will be, for 'tis a great act on the part of the king. Governors and courtiers and all the fine, fine people will be along, and they hope 'twill soften the hearts of the land toward the king."

In the shadows of her mind, Meg latched onto something. These words this woman spoke. . .and Duncan's words of her brother. *"He'll stay to see the governor through an important political event."* The two strands of words wrapped about each other inextricably.

So. She was headed to London. Without a day to lose. To see her brother at a floating symphony, it would seem, and the very people who'd driven them apart would be surrounding them.

"Are ye all right, miss?" The woman said. "Here." She bustled across the shop, pulled a kettle from the stove in the corner, and poured steaming amber liquid into a teacup. "Have a *strupak*," she said. "'Twill warm life back into those white cheeks of yours." Meg took the earthenware cup pressed into her hands and sipped. The chip on the clay-colored rim made the whole gesture somehow even more comforting.

"Thank you kindly," she said. She reached into her satchel to dig for a penny. She had barely a farthing to her name after the potatoes, but such kindness. . . She took hold of a coin and pulled it out.

"Oh, no, no, no," the woman said, bending to retrieve something that fluttered down from the satchel. "No coin needed for that. If we Campbells can't pour a simple cuppa for our visitors, then I dinnae know what we are about," she said, her merry face brightening.

Meg swallowed too fast, the liquid nearly scalding her throat. *We Campbells. . .*

She froze. For the woman stood, every trace of her smile gone. She held her palm out toward Meg, displaying what she'd plucked from the ground. Her own faded tartan scrap.

"Oh, lass. . ." Just two words. Yet the compassion and sorrow and knowing in them seemed to reach straight into Meg's heart, cradle it like a mother with her bairn.

"Please," Meg said. "I know I shouldn't be here. I—"

"*Wheesht*, child." She pressed the scrap into Meg's palm, easing the cup away. "You've nothing to fear here. Not from the likes of me. Do wait here until young Angus skiddles away." She shot a worried glance out the window. Duncan had shifted toward the street, drawing Angus's vision away from the shop. "Tuck yer plaid away, for some here dinnae look so kindly upon the Clan MacNaughton." She leaned forward and whispered with a smile, "But not all of us."

Relief untied a thousand knots that had held Meg's muscles captive. "Thank you," she breathed.

"Meg." Duncan's voice came from just outside the shop. He bowed toward the woman then spoke to Meg. "We'd best away. The ship'll be leavin'."

"Ach, you're on a journey, then!" The woman said. "Take these." She scurried behind the counter, pulling out a bundle wrapped in muslin. It looked to have been packed as her personal supply for the day's work. "The best scones in Alba," she said. She leaned in and dropped her voice. "And if I don't miss my guess, ye're a lass of the highlands just as I was. That makes us sisters enough. Just take care in this town, and may your journey be swift and smooth."

Meg thanked her heartily, clinging to the woman's blessing even as a distant roll of thunder tried to chase it away once they were out in the street again. Duncan guided her quickly to the docks. She pulled her hood forward, keeping her head down as much as possible. Only when they passed a large boat did she look up. "Is this it?" she asked.

"Nae," Duncan said. He looked almost longingly at the boat. While large, it was yet smaller than most of the other vessels looming on the waterfront. "This is a schooner," he said. "'Twould serve us well if it were ours. She's a limber one, the schooner is. Small and fast. But that bark"—he pointed just ahead toward a three-masted vessel—"is the boat we'll find passage on."

Meg took in the behemoth of a ship. Its weathered wood tired, its masts worn and sluggish. Another distant roll of thunder sounded, and Meg breathed it in, letting it bolster her.

"Well," she said. "Looks as though she's earned her salt. Shall we?" And with that, they boarded the ship that was to take her away from this country she'd called home all her life.

But she would not think of that. Not as the rest of their party scrambled aboard. Nor as the sailors pulled in ropes, hoisted sails, and shouted to one another as the gray sky began to release its drizzle. And not as she lowered her hood for one last, unobstructed view of the rising green hills and this long sea loch pointing to its end at Cumberave somewhere in the distance.

The small schooner's sails raised, too. A shout rose up in a familiar voice from its deck. "Good journey to ye, Duncan!" The man Angus waved his cap from its deck, and too late, Meg pulled her hood back up. His smile froze on his face then vanished altogether as he angled his head to the side, staring hard at her. The look sent a spear of nausea through her: recognition.

Keep calm. Meg dipped a small curtsy. Perhaps she was wrong. Perhaps he did not recognize or remember the wayward bride.

But the way he stood unmoving until the bark began to move and the port grew smaller in the distance. . .

Thunder clapped so close it shook her from her trance. She seated herself on a wooden crate out of the way of the flurry of activity on deck. Hours passed, snatches of the sailors' narrative helping her to follow their course. They were out of the sea loch and into the open Irish Sea, heading into the channel between Ireland and Scotland. The wind blew hard. Phrases bandied about, anchoring her spirit: *Off course. Too close to Ireland. Behind schedule.*

She couldn't sit any longer. She looked about the deck. Wasn't there something she could do? Swab the deck, or something? The others in her party were sitting about in a circle on the deck in the twilight as Kate entertained them with some account. Jimmy, whose back was turned to her, must have felt her stare. He turned and rose, crossing the deck in his steady, sure way.

"What ails ye, lass?" Jimmy strode in front of her, polishing his bottle with his plain brown jacket as he did.

"'Tis nothing," Meg said. And wished she could believe it. She fell into step with him, walking the deck. "Did ye find a new pearl?" A pearl fisher all his days, he often said the real treasures were the words of life scratched out upon his scroll, copied from the scriptures. The true pearls.

"Aye," he said. "Listen to this." He lifted the bottle's cap and reached a finger in, removing a worn scroll. Handing her the bottle, he unrolled the paper and read, "I call to remembrance my song in the night: I commune with mine own heart: and my spirit made diligent search." His eyes moving over the paper as he read it again silently to himself. "What a thing."

He was a man of few words, Thistle Jimmy, and Meg tried to piece together what he might be thinking.

The thunder grew nearer as the ship carried them into a gray sky roiling with storm clouds. "Night will come, Meg MacNaughton. Ye know that more than any-one." He crossed his arms, lifting his chin in a gesture toward the clouds. "I'm thinkin' on that song the scripture speaks of. How the dark doesn't have to snatch it away."

There was so much Meg would not "call to remembrance." But the steady cadence of Jimmy's voice nudged her to brave the waters of the past. His words knocked at her heart, asking for her to open the door even a crack.

"Here," he said, rolling the scroll and tucking it into the bottle she held. He put the cap back on it.

"Shall I hold it for ye, Jimmy? For the voyage?" She ran her thumb across the etchings on the bottle. SPERO, it said around its mouth, each letter encompassed in wending Celtic swirls. Jimmy liked to tell the story of the trade he'd made with a scholar in Edinburgh to find out the word's meaning. He'd played his fiddle and regaled the man's handful of university students with tales of the river. And in return, the professor had interpreted the bottle's intricate markings. Monastic carv-ings from the likes of Ireland, hundreds of years before. *Hope*, it said in Latin. A fragile thing Meg hardly dared think of.

"Aye," Jimmy said to her. "Hold on to it for me. For good. I've carved those words in this old brain. Time for them to find new life."

The metal warmed in her hands. "Jimmy, ye canna mean it."

"Take it, lass. 'Tis a brave thing you're doing. Take these words, and that bottle they're in, and let them give ye strength when ye most need it."

"But—"

He placed a hand on her shoulder. "Ye ken what I have to say. There's no tellin' how far God's Word will travel, no matter what vessel it's in." A tap on the bottle, a moment of silence as he looked upon it and recalled—what? The day he pulled the empty bottle from a crevice in a stone wall in Ireland as a young man? It had been encapsulated with care in the ruins of an old castle, doubtless the great treasure of an important family from another time. She'd heard the tale more than once.

"Time for these words to travel in new hands," he said. "The bottle is a fine thing, but it was never my treasure. It was the words that mattered to me. That bottle's just a messenger. And it does its job well."

"Thank you, Jimmy." She felt as if some great responsibility had just been entrusted to her—this bottle with a legacy far beyond her. But with it came a fluttering of hope, a settling of strength. For she carried the words that had survived the fires and waters of the past, landing in her own arms now to spur her on. Meg hugged it to her heart, protecting it from the rain as it fell harder. As if the bottle hadn't weathered countless storms in its hundreds of years already.

And it looked as if it was about to weather another.

The sky, dark as it gave way to night, unleashed its torrents. The whitecaps of the sea snapped like hungry fangs. Shouts arose around them on deck, Jimmy pulling her close to a mast. Strong footsteps pounded from behind, and Duncan appeared.

His dark hair hung wet about his handsome face, a smoldering wildness behind his eyes. "We've a problem," he said.

"The storm," Meg began. "What can I do?"

"Nae. I wish that was the problem." He pointed behind them, and Meg could barely make out the form of a silhouette. A smaller ship, headed their way. The schooner.

"Angus," he said, and then he quickly gave Jimmy the details of the man's relation to Ian Campbell. "If he knew of Meg. . .with his loyalty to Ian Campbell, the reward money. . ." He left the rest unsaid.

Meg drew her arms tighter about herself.

"He did see me," she said. "'Twas my own fault. I took my hood down too soon."

"Nothing about this is your fault, Meg. You did not ask for this." Duncan's words eased the knot in her stomach a little. "All the same, I do not believe it is safe for you here."

She shook her head, looking around. Sea in every direction. Dark night and a storm tossing them about. "When we get to land tomorrow, we could take cover," she suggested.

Duncan shook his head, droplets of water on his dark eyelashes gathering, coursing down his rugged face. "That boat will overtake this one before then. It shouldn't even be out here, for it sails close to the coastline."

Meg looked about, fear tumbling into her, desperate for some other explanation. "Perhaps they're in distress. Coming for help in the storm. Lost their way."

"The sailors aboard are as able and knowing as ours. We must take action," Duncan said. He locked eyes with her. "They're coming for you, Meg."

Chapter Eight

We must divert."

Meg burned with protest at Duncan's words. But without warning, he turned, making straight for the front of the ship.

"Duncan!" Meg shouted, flinching against the bucketing rain. He could not—or would not—hear her.

A mighty wave slammed the ship. She scrambled for something to hold. Her back collided with a mast. Pain splintered through her. She steadied herself, clutching the rough surface of a rope wrapped up the mast, and strained to see through the frigid sea spray.

At the helm stood the captain and Duncan. A few clipped words exchanged, a handshake, and Duncan bounded back across the slick deck.

"We'll take a *currach*," he said, motioning toward one of the smaller boats tied to the side of the ship. Two of the sailors rushed to prepare it. "The wind has blown us close to the Irish coast. We'll camp there for the night."

Meg shook her head, desperation creeping into her very bones. "No," she said.

"Pray God they do not see us," he said, casting a glance back at the schooner. "The lanterns from this ship should lead them on, and we'll slip away."

"Slip away." Meg drew herself up. "In a wee currach—in this storm. Are ye mad? And we've no time to spare if we're to be to Gretna Green in time for the coach to London."

"D'ye not remember your wedding day, Meg?" Kate's voice interjected. Meg clamped her mouth shut. They'd witnessed it, each one here—Duncan, Jimmy, Kate. "What d'ye think they'll do if they find you?"

Meg dropped her gaze. "If they keep me from Graeme—if it is too late by the time we get to London. . ." Her voice was raw. She could not finish the sentence.

Duncan turned her gently toward him. "They saw us in Campbelton. They know 'tis you. Diverting is our only chance, Meg."

Meg fought to breathe. "We cannot."

"We must."

"But Graeme—"

Duncan brought his hands up, gentle but sure, until they cradled her face.

"Please," he said. "Do not let him lose you again, before he's found you." His thumbs moved to brush the storm's wetness from her cheeks, and at last she met his eyes.

She could feel it tangibly—a rending within her. England just around the bend and a road unfolding to her brother. Ireland in the other direction, pulling her to a haven she could not see or be sure of. And a ship behind, gaining on them.

The storm within matched the storm without until she thought her heart would collapse. She surveyed every hopeless direction. *Lord, help me see what to do. Make a way, please. . . .*

"I'll not leave ye, Meg," Duncan said.

"Nor I," Jimmy's rough voice piped up above the torrents.

"You won't be rid of me, either," Kate said.

Jimmy spoke again. "We'll away to Ireland. Cross the sea in the morning if we can. The schooner will have passed by. And we'll meet up with the others of our group again at Gretna Green."

It all sounded so final. Yet in the midst of it, a whisper of faith stole through her, hushing the cries of protest. The sea did not part. The sun did not break through the night sky. But the strength that came in the sound of those three voices was enough to bolster her courage long enough to breathe deep. . .and speak the words that could either keep her from Graeme forever—or might just give them a fighting chance.

"To Ireland," she said.

The moment the words were out, the deck erupted with movement, leaving nary a moment to consider the gravity of what this meant. She was passing ropes, gathering oars, heeding directions to board the currach. A quick embrace from Mrs. MacGregor and the others, and at last they were being lowered over the side of the ship. The bottom of their small vessel hit the ocean with a slap and a splash. The ropes retracted, slithering up and over the top of the ship.

Within minutes, the ship was sailing away toward England, storm beginning to wane at last.

The foursome sat in the small currach on the glittering waves of black waters, the night swallowing them into solitude. Meg clutched the handle of an oar across her lap, fingers wrapped so tight they ached.

The waters were choppy, but the storm left an eerie quiet in its wake. The only sound a single oar dipping into the water. Duncan, taking them on toward Ireland.

Meg breathed deep, lifted her own oar, and leaned in to row.

Chapter Nine

A great wall of black, jagged silhouettes rose against the navy sky in the distance. "Ballyfír Monastery," Thistle Jimmy said. His voice was solemn. "What's left of it, anyway. Ashore, then, and we'll shelter there."

"*Shelter* is a generous word." Kate's attempt at a joke floundered in the solemnity of the moment as they drew nearer the ruins. "Oh, come now," she said, voice rising with a forced buoyancy. "Not a soul will find us here."

"Indeed," Meg said. "Not a soul would dare."

True to her misgivings, navigating their way to shore was no easy task. It took all of them paddling and leaning and praying and counteracting the crash of the waves against the sabre-like rocks. The boards groaned with cracking sounds that twisted fear into Meg.

"Hold fast, lassies!" Jimmy shouted just as the boat was hit by a wave from the left, then another from the right. Another came at them from a pillar rock, away from the shore as if to warn them away.

But at last, the scrape of gravel beneath them slowed their boat, and Duncan leaped out and pushed them onto shore. Jimmy jumped to the rocky beach. Kate clambered over the side, following Jimmy to scout out the land. Just Meg and Duncan remained at the shoreline, an entire ocean welling up behind them. Waves lifted the tail end of the boat, propelling Meg toward him. But the lingering argument from the ship stood as a wall between them.

He offered a hand to her but looked as though he'd enjoy a doctor's leeching more. And just for that, she thrust her hand straight through the invisible wall between them and took hold. She hopped down, and as soon as her feet touched the ground, she withdrew her hand. She knew she should thank him. 'Twas the proper thing to do, regardless of how she felt.

"Thank you," she said. He gave a solitary nod of acknowledgment.

She caught a glimpse of Jimmy and Kate closer to the mass of land. Cliffs rose before them like legs of giants. Meg shivered at an image that suddenly came to mind—then laughed promptly at herself.

"All that cold water getting to you at last," Duncan said dryly as he wound the rope of the boat around hand and elbow in a quick, adept motion.

"No." To which he only raised skeptical brows. "Well, perhaps," she said. "I was just thinking. Graeme used to tell me a story of an Irish giant who so reviled a certain Scottish giant that he built a stone path across the sea to confront his enemy." She eyed the cliff top where a single, circular tower perched. From the corner of her eye she saw Duncan follow suit, looking up.

"And you think this is where he lives, then?" Duncan's voice was lined with a feigned gravity. He tugged the boat higher on the rocky beach. Meg moved behind to help push.

"Aye." She matched his tone, shoving the boat with Duncan's next pull. They paused. "That tower there." She pointed. "'Tis no tower at all." She rested her hands on her hips, catching her breath. "'Tis his boot. Ready to come down upon Scottish foes"—this last word punctuated by the angry scrape of gravel beneath their next push—"who do not know when to listen to a lass aboard a ship in the middle of a storm."

"Ah," Duncan said. "So he's a merciful giant, then. One who'll put a man out of his misery." He gave a final heave, pulling the boat away from Meg and tying it off to a boulder. His words sailed through the air like a victory banner. Meg didn't know whether to laugh or retort and had just decided not to dignify his quip with a reply when he cast a quick glance over his shoulder, letting his eyes rest on her. A flicker of depth warmed her in his gaze, but just as fast, he gave a wink—and the spell was broken. She fought a smile until he looked away. The scoundrel.

With his back to her as he tromped ahead toward the cliff, she did not need to hide the smile that climbed its way from the past and onto her face. It was nearly like old times. And it was welcome relief from what had transpired today.

She ran to catch up, despite the weight of her soggy skirts. The climb up the angled path along the cliff side would take every ounce of concentration, for it was mangled with overgrowth, slick with rain, and dark but for the cloud-filtered light of the moon. Duncan motioned her to go ahead, and while the gesture was kind, it made the climb all the more nerve wracking. That he could see her every misstep. That when the ground came to life in a slick hiss beneath her feet and she slipped toward the edge of the path with nerves firing panic, his footsteps behind her battled the same ground to steady her. A hand upon her arm, nothing more. Ever so brief, but she knew without it, she may well have tumbled straight down into the waves.

At the top, they joined Jimmy and Kate, who stared in hushed awe at the stark silhouettes of the ruins. While not a shadow stirred from the fallen rocks and remnant walls, Meg's skin pricked with the richness surrounding this place. She knew life in seaside monasteries had been filled with peril for monks. Especially along this coast, where Vikings had raided the strongholds. Yet such strength remained in these stones. Each one seemed to proclaim the courage of those who came before—and even more, the strength of the One they followed. The whole place was cloaked in a sense of resolute hope.

The ruined structure and its nameless stories drew her. She could not help breaking from the line formation that she and the others stood in, and taking a step toward it. And another, and another, and—

Kate grabbed her wrist, halting her. "Look," she whispered. Her friend's finger pointed, following the outline of the ruins. "Listen."

Meg froze, straining to see and hear. And as she narrowed her eyes, she saw it: movement. Ever so slight, like the whole structure shivered. And with that shiver came a rustle, a whisper through the darkness.

Meg's imagination sparked a thousand different directions, sending her mind to chasms and dark corners better avoided. Part of her wanted to flee, and part anchored her here, thirsty for answers.

"Birds," Jimmy's low voice said at last. A single word, but it lassoed the wiles of her imaginings and focused them in until indeed—she could see it. Little cobbled bumps atop the ruins, each one a bird. "'Tis a good sign. Come." They followed him to the tower, the single-roofed building. "They would not roost there if predators were about," he said. "We'll keep here for the night and cross the North Channel tomorrow."

Jimmy took a step, and as he did, a slick sound of mud sliding beneath his footfall gave way to a heavy thud as he hit the ground. Meg, Kate, and Duncan clambered to help him up.

"Can't a man blunder in peace?" he grumbled, shaking their hands away. He stood and struck a match, igniting a lantern he'd brought from the boat.

Kate took it from him, the firelight showing the stubborn set of her mouth. She, whose hardheadedness matched even the indefatigable Jimmy's. She knelt, examining his injured foot. "Sprained, at least," she said of his ankle. "The only blunder ye'll be making, Thistle Jimmy, is to put weight on that foot." Kate planted her free hand on her hip. "Ye'll let us help you, or ye'll roost out here with the birds. Shouldna be a problem. There aren't any predators about, as ye said."

"I've half a mind to. The company would be more peaceful." But under the wrath of Kate's raised brows, he nodded, letting Duncan come alongside him. The second Duncan put a hand under Jimmy's elbow, though, Jimmy jerked it away. "I can still walk," he said.

The two men led the way inside the tower on the cliff's edge, Duncan a few steps behind Jimmy all the way. Dripping water echoed down a spiraling staircase, and Meg forced her imagination not to conjure up images of what might await them at the top. Four pairs of footsteps echoed as they climbed. Finally they reached the opening to a single round room with nothing to boast but an open window to the sea.

The breeze was sharp but calming and had kept the room free of creatures over time. The next moments blurred together as exhaustion set in. Meg and Kate were to sleep in here, it was decided, and Jimmy and Duncan would bed down on the landing outside the door opening.

Meg skimmed the surface of sleep for what seemed like hours, but despite her fatigue, she could not enter that sweet promised land. She could hear Jimmy's snoring, and she could see Kate's steadily sleeping form, but perhaps Duncan was as awake as she.

"Duncan," Meg whispered.

No response. Just the waves below. She breathed deep of the salt air, closing her eyes and leaning her head back against the wall between them. Was he doing the same? A warmth seemed to come from the other side. If he was asleep, there was no harm in saying what she'd meant to say, even if he did not hear.

"Do you remember the nights on the loch," she said, "when you would play your pipes on the hill at sunset?" It was done for the villagers, the sheepherders, the residents of Cumberave. A recognition of a day completed and the miracle of another on the way. It was an archaic tradition, but Father insisted that in times of darkness, such a reminder was lifeblood to them all. That each day held purpose yet, that each day was a gift worth celebrating.

Duncan didn't reply, but she thought she heard the steady breathing of deep rest. She did not wish to wake him. After a length of silence, she continued, quieter this time, for the tale of it somehow settled her own heart. "We would gather by the window, the four of us, and listen. Father would close his eyes, and it was as though all the battles and hungry stomachs and dwindling accounts of his tenants—the weight of it all vanished and for a moment in time, he had peace to renew his strength. Mother used to say if we listened hard enough, no matter how heavy the darkness, God would always give us a song in the night." The very words in Jimmy's scripture, she realized.

The memory of her family made her ache with longing. But oh, the gift of it. After pushing away such thoughts for years, to let one slip into her heart was like someone lighting a small candle. She held it with grateful tenderness. 'Twas like coming inside after playing in the highland snow as a child. Hands so cold that the warmth of the fire stung fiercely. . .but soon, the stinging gave way to thaw, to movement, and she could unfurl her fingers again.

She closed her eyes. The unfurling ache sent a tear down her cheek, brought Duncan's song afresh to her mind. Time passed, she knew not how much, until she heard a quiet stirring in the corridor. She did not wish to wake the men, nor Kate, but she felt such a pull on her heart that something deep and true was happening within her. She made her way past Kate in the middle of the circular floor, who slept with arms splayed in exhausted abandon. Resting her own arms on the window, the song coiled inside of her.

One by one, the haunting notes of Duncan's tune made their way up through the cracks in her heart, past the burn in her throat, and into the spray of the midnight waves. The words, too, came. Slow but sure, like old friends.

"All glory to our Lord and God. . .for love so deep, so high, so broad. . ."

The moon was high as her song dropped among those waves, telling of a love that defeated darkness. Off in the sea, far beyond her view, their pursuers sailed on.

And below, off to the right on the rocks rising from the shore, stood the figure of a man. Watching. Turning from the sea, facing her.

She should have jumped straight out of her skin after the events of the night, but instead a settled peace wrapped around her. She could not see his face, but she knew his stance. The man who awaited her with such a broken expression atop the hill on her wedding day. The man who had stood watch, just so, a thousand times for her and her family. *Duncan.*

And try as she might, though her song froze between them, she could not look away.

It took all of his strength to rip his stare from the window. Duncan tromped over wet, black rocks, trying not to think of the way Meg's face looked up there in the moonlight. He must find sleep again if he was to have strength for the morrow. He'd slumbered fitfully, upright against the wall in the corridor earlier. It was the sound of Meg's voice whispering his name that awoke him—but surely he must have dreamed it. He hadn't responded. But then her voice curled around the open doorway, recounting her tale about the evening song on the loch.

He had not known she'd cared that much. Or even stopped to listen. It tied into knots all the strings inside of him holding the idea of Meg where he knew it should be: far from him. So when she'd gone silent from her tale, he'd snuck down the stairs. Away from her.

Yet there she was at the window, tossing his own song out into a salt wind that delivered her notes straight to him. Clear, sure, true. Just like Meg. When she saw him, he forced himself to look away. At the rocks, the waves, the tower, the jagged ruins beyond—anything but her.

But even as he trod silently back up the stairs and a thick wall of ancient rock stood between them, that fair face filled his dreams until he woke again to the first light of day. 'Twas high time she got to her brother. And away from him.

Chapter Ten

Arms afire, Meg pulled her oars through the river waters for what felt like the ten thousandth time. It was with a wash of mingled weariness and relief that the wee village of Gretna Green came into view. After a day of rowing across the channel, skirting the Isle of Man, muddling through the firth and up the river, they were ready for a good night's rest.

Jimmy had rowed along with Duncan as best he could for the first half of the day, gritting his teeth and pushing through what was clearly increasing pain, despite Meg and Kate's protests. At last, they'd managed to get him to elevate his ankle and let the ladies take turns rowing from the stern. If Meg's arms burned—and she only rowing a portion of the time—what must Duncan be feeling? She caught his eye as their oars slipped into the water in sync.

They pulled the currach to land and walked in twilight into the wee town. The last Scottish ground they would tread, direct upon the border of England. Two simple, white-stoned buildings faced each other. A blacksmith's shop to the right, and to the left, the small inn. In the distance where the road wended up a low rise, the glow of a campfire beckoned them. 'Twould be the Tinkers' camp, and a welcome sight it was. Mrs. MacGregor would be waiting for them with warm food and blankets, as was her way. But first, Meg must find out what she dreaded to know: whether they'd missed the London coach. And the inn, she hoped, would have the answer.

"You go on ahead," she offered to the others, noting how Jimmy looked toward the camp. "I'll be only a moment here."

"Nay," Jimmy said. "We leave none behind."

Meg smiled her gratitude. The black door was flanked by posts covered in fragrant red roses. The flickering noise of bush crickets welcomed her. Just as she raised her hand to knock, the door flew open with such force it seemed to fracture the whole evening. Meg's hand tightened around the pillar as she gaped at the ruffle-clad shadow blocking the glow from within. A gown so wide it extended beyond the doorway, making the woman's silhouette look otherworldly.

"Well!" The voice was mature and amused in its polished British tongue. "If it isn't a merry band of rogues!" She sounded utterly delighted. Meg's eyes adjusted to the mix of fading evening light without and glowing lantern light within. The woman rubbed gloved hands together like a child on Christmas. She stepped onto the stoop, shifting to face Meg. Silvery ropes of hair crowned her. She looked slightly upward at Meg, but what she lacked in height she made up for in dominating presence. "Are you here for a room, poppet? Oh, I do hope they'll put you next to mine, you poor drowned mouse. Lovely drowned mouse, mind you. I've smelling salts to help liven you back up. Come in, all of you! We shall dine on fine Scottish fare. There is nothing like it!"

"I. . ." How was a lass to respond to being called a drowned rodent? And it had been said in such a way that somehow warmed Meg's heart. "Thank ye, milady. But ye see, we only just—"

The woman interrupted, chattering on without a breath. From the corner of her eye, Meg saw Kate dash away toward the boat and return, satchel in hand and eager look upon her face. Thistle Jimmy watched the older woman and straightened, tugging at his ragged shirt and transfixed with a sort of awed respect.

"I was just going out for an evening carriage ride," the woman said, "but now *you're* arrived, just follow me and we'll see what we can do." She spoke as if she'd been waiting all evening for the lot of them. "Come, come! All of you, now."

"If ye please, Mrs. . . ," Meg said, taking a step back.

"Eugenia Bettredge. What sorts of cheeses do you like best? We'll see if we can talk some out of the kitchen. Mr. Bettredge preferrd the cheddar in his day, and I always toast his memory with a bit of it. You'll join me of course."

"Your kindness is more a gift than I can say," Meg said, "and I do believe my friends would be glad of refreshment." She looked their way. Jimmy gave a solemn bow of affirmation. "But first, is the goodman of the house about?" She craned her neck, looking for the innkeeper. "I'm needin' to inquire about the coach to London."

"That rattletrap?" Mrs. Bettredge gestured for them to follow her. "It passed through today at the noon hour." Meg went cold. So it was as they'd feared. This would put them a week behind. "Chin up, my dear! Never say you meant to take that contraption. Oh, love, you're lucky you missed it. Unless you enjoy being swallowed whole by piles of splinters masquerading as carriages."

She ushered them in, Kate, Meg, Duncan, and Jimmy, who paused at the threshold, bowed, and said resolutely, "Your servant, my lady."

His words released a peal of exclamations from Mrs. Bettredge about "an authentic highland gentleman!"

They entered a dark-wooded parlor and sat as trays of boiled eggs, slices of bread, thick pats of butter, canisters of jam, and steaming pots of tea were brought up.

"And my favorite." Mrs. Bettredge leaned in, lifting the lid of a platter. "The food of kings!"

Kate and Meg exchanged a glance. "Rumbledethumps?"

"Ah! You see? Pure joy, even to utter it. *Rumbledethumpsss*," she said with a flourish. Meg had never thought of the potato, onion, and cheese dish as royal by any stretch, but the savory smell was a welcome gift.

They fairly inhaled the feast as Mrs. Bettredge talked on about her exploits traveling the lowlands. Once they'd eaten every last crumb, she ended her tales and looked at Meg.

"Now. I know it isn't as exciting as traveling in that forsaken coach, but I've been mulling over something."

How she'd had a chance to "mull" when she'd hardly paused for a breath, Meg could not imagine. She was a wonder. Or a whirlwind. Perhaps both.

"I've a carriage and a driver, and I'm stuck by my lone self all the day long. Do tell me you'll come with me to London-Town." She twirled a hand in the air. "If you were of a mind to go there anyway. . ."

Meg hopped to her feet, nearly dropping her teacup as she went. "You would do that?"

"My dear. You would be rescuing me from unspeakable boredom."

Meg looked to Duncan. He nodded. Her glance skirted to Kate, who mouthed an enthusiastic *yes!* But when she looked to Thistle Jimmy, he rose slowly, steady eyes first on Meg, then on Mrs. Bettredge.

"My lady," he said. "I'm to rejoin the rest of our group here for the summer. 'Tis no small honor ye offer, but I've pearl fishin' to do, ye see."

"Why, if it's pearls you're after, take these," she fidgeted with a strand of pearls from her own neck and coiled them in her palm, holding it out to him. "Do come with us."

Thistle Jimmy stretched a good bit taller, as if a platform of quiet pride had risen from the ground beneath his feet. "Very kind of ye to say so, but these old fingers only know one way to get pearls. And wi' respect, that's to earn them. Pry them out of the shells myself."

The woman beheld him with a sort of wonder upon her face then clamped her fingers shut around her pearls. "Of course," she said. "I could learn a thing or two from you, sir." They made quite the picture, this woman in all her finery, standing in awe of this humble man of the river before her.

He bowed once more and turned to Meg. "But ye go, lass. 'Tis the good Lord's provision, sending such a generous soul to carry ye the rest of the way. Besides. . ." He leaned in closer to Meg. "I fear this old leg would slow ye down." He winked, patting his bad leg.

"Never, Jimmy," Meg said. "But if ye do want to stay, and ye're sure 'tis all right. . ."

"It is." He furrowed his brow. "Ye go, lass. Get to that brother of yours."

Joy washed through her. Deep and tinged with pain at the thought of leaving Jimmy, yet somehow that pain bolstered her courage.

"Well, Mrs. Bettredge," she said. "I think ye've got yourself a band of grateful travelers."

"Wonderful! We'll leave first thing in the morning. Eleven o'clock agreeable?" Mrs. Bettredge said.

Meg and Duncan exchanged a look to share delight over her concept of an early morning. But it was a look wrapped in astonishment, too, at this turn of events.

"Eleven o'clock it is, Mrs. Bettredge." Meg curtsied. "And we'll do our best to not be too dull."

"I'll hold you to that," the woman said.

Meg awoke before the sun the next morning. She slipped out of the tent she shared with Kate and Mrs. MacGregor, Jimmy's bottle in hand. Across the low-rolling lands she went, away from the village and river, to where the grasses reached high enough to tickle the palm of her open hand. Closing her eyes to drink in the pure air of the field, she twisted the cap of the bottle until she felt its notch click into the needed opening. She lifted the lid, tucking it into a fold in the earasaid she wore crisscrossed over the top of her dress.

Just as she pulled the scroll from the bottle, a figure approached in the distance. Duncan. Her heart jumped at the sight of him. Instantaneously, a single word shot through her mind: *Home.*

All the things of home she'd never dreamed of having again strode toward her in the form of Duncan Blair. Belonging. Knowing. Being known. Memories shared, schemes concocted, comfort, loyalty. . .and something more. Something she dared not put a name to.

"I see I'm not the only one who could not wait until the early hour of eleven in the morning," Duncan said. His smile, slightly crooked, warmed her.

"Aye." Meg laughed.

Dawn crested the distant horizon with a reverent stillness. Meg hugged the bottle to herself.

"'Twas a braw thing Jimmy did, giving that to ye," Duncan said.

"More than we know, I think," Meg said, unrolling the rolled record of scriptures. "I wonder sometimes what each of these words meant to him when he wrote them. Jimmy is a good man, but his life has been far from easy. This one." She held the curling edges open to show his straight-etched letters, and Duncan read them aloud as if considering as he went:

"'If I take the wings of the morning, and dwell in the uttermost parts of the sea; even there shall thy hand lead me.'"

"He's a man who holds his deepest stories closely," Meg said. "But I would dare to say he knows the truth of God's faithfulness in 'the uttermost parts' very well indeed."

"And you, Meg?" Duncan's eyes in their deep gray were searching.

"I begin to learn that truth, I think." She paused. "I hope." So many of the "uttermost parts"—places she'd felt alone and afraid—were of her own doing.

Across the field, a single bird rose from the grasses and flitted away.

"I know what that's like," Meg said, watching the bird as she returned the scroll and lid to the bottle.

"To fly?"

"No. To run away. 'Tis all I've done." She paused, eyes on the clouds skidding across the sky in the same breeze that now rustled the grasses. "Do you ever wonder what would have happened that day, if. . ." She swallowed. Never before had she attempted to put this into words. It had just been a dark and leaden weight, hidden always in her own heart to carry.

She sighed, trying again. "If the wedding had happened."

Duncan hung his head, expression grim. He pulled a handful of grass, twisting it into a rope. Listening.

"I would be married," she said. It seemed as foreign a thought now as it had that day.

"To a scoundrel." Duncan's jaw worked.

Now it was Meg's turn to hang her head. "Yes," she said. "But my family would be alive. Together. You would not be. . ." Her gaze shifted to his injured leg. He saw, and she scrambled for more thoughtful words, cheeks burning. "You would never have been harmed. And you would be playing your pipes across the highlands for all to hear, not bearing them like a mourning garment."

He winced. Instantly she regretted her words. She hadn't meant them to be harsh. Only a lament for what he had lost, for she recalled the force of life and purpose in Duncan when he played.

"And. . ." She closed her eyes and exhaled. "I would not have spent the past two years running like a coward."

When she opened her eyes, Duncan was beholding her with an expression so faceted and knowing, she could not speak.

"Meg," he said. He let her name linger there. It was cradled in his voice with such tender strength, she knew not whether to bury her face in her hands at how exposed she felt, or to dwell here in the fragile safety of the moment. Rise up and meet that strength, somehow. "Is that what you think?"

"No. 'Tis what I know."

Duncan opened his mouth, a concerned expression on his face—but said nothing. For in the distance, a pounding sounded. A wild stallion ran toward the very place the starling had arisen from. Its chestnut coat and flaxen main shone with a halo of early sunlight.

And in its wake, a massive veil of black-winged specks shot into the air. A dark cloud rising like a phoenix, taking ominous, changing shape low in the sky. Birds—thousands of them—headed straight for Meg and Duncan.

Feathered applause swooped over them. So close Meg closed her eyes and ducked—but opened them again in time to see flashes of iridescent purple-green coming from their feathers. Pointed beaks, wings, and tails made them look like urgent stars darting across the sky. Starlings, they were, in a performance that captured Meg's breath. The very second one of them changed direction, the rest condensed in near collision, changing direction at the last possible moment to follow the new course. Again and again they did this. Thinning, turning, flocking in an awe-striking dance.

Startled into flight by something unfathomably larger than each one—yet as they flew, they formed a cloud greater still, webbing across the sky and hills as they swooped, spun, dipped, and soared together as one. One mammoth, marvelous creature. Enchanting. Terrifying.

Duncan's hand around hers squeezed. "Never let it be said, Meg MacNaughton. . ." He paused. "That when something sets a body to flight, there is not purpose in it."

His eyes were on her, suddenly, the birds disappearing beyond the village and river, on toward England. "There are those who will stand in awe at what the Lord intends. At the courage that rises." He stepped closer, facing her. "There is a difference between fleeing"—his free hand lifted, brushing a hair away from her face, the backs of his fingers grazing her cheek—"and flying."

Hot tears stung Meg's eyes. She blinked them away. Clasped her hands behind her back—willed them to cease trembling. Duncan's words felt too large.

A quickening in her heart harkened her to prayer. To grasp hold of this transformation he spoke of. *Give me courage, Lord. Turn my fleeing into something good.*

She thought of what lay ahead. The Lake District. The Peak District, famous for highwaymen. And on and on until her thoughts reached the thing that loomed largest on the horizon: the city of London, bigger and grander than she could imagine herself a part of.

Help me to fly.

Chapter Eleven

After spending the late morning bidding the Tinkers a long farewell, they'd embarked at last. The next three days on the road in Mrs. Bettredge's carriage rolled rhythmically one into another. They passed through the crumbling remnants of Hadrian's Wall built centuries before. Duncan couldn't help but relish the irony. It had been built to keep wild and barbarous highlanders such as himself out of the more civil realm of England. And here he was, riding in a fine carriage toward the land's very heart in London.

Meg sat across from him stitching something upon her tartan scrap. It wasn't long before Mrs. Bettredge discovered Meg's gift of story weaving, and every landmark they passed became fodder for a fairy tale. Tales of scraggly tree stumps and shepherdesses and all manner of things.

As they passed a ruined estate in Leeds, Mrs. Bettredge broke a rare silence. "Tell me of the ruggedly handsome man we left behind," she said. "He's full of tales of high adventure, I shouldn't wonder."

"What, Jimmy?" Kate smiled preposterously. "Ruggedly handsome? Have ye set your cap at him, Mrs. Bettredge?" she asked with joyous scandal in her voice.

"My cap is too old to be set for anyone, young lady." The woman snapped her fan out, winking at Kate. A youthful spark shone in her smile-creased eyes. "Pray, Miss MacNaughton. Tell me instead, what possession of madness caused such a grand estate to be built upon such a forsaken hill?" She gestured out the window at the ruins.

Meg paused a moment, and a tale spilled forth about a lone shepherd, who had nothing to his name but his staff. His master wouldn't pay him in coin, instead offering him anything upon the hillside that he could carry. So he carried one stone after another until he'd built an estate on the hillside next to the sheepfold, living like a pauper king as he tended his woolly friends the rest of his days.

"Clever man!" Kate clapped.

Meg smiled. "'Twould not be the first time a man has made a home for himself on the land he faithfully worked." She looked Duncan's way knowingly. "Even when he deserved much better."

Duncan shifted on his seat. He was hoping she'd forgotten his encampment in the woods. There was much that would be difficult to explain. But still she waited, a question on her face.

Kate pointed to something out of the far window, asking Mrs. Bettredge about it. The two broke off into chatter, leaving none but Duncan to bear the weight of Meg's unspoken question.

At length, he answered. "Nor would it be the first time a man stayed to watch for someone he'd promised to watch for."

Surprise lit her face. She opened her mouth as if to respond but closed it again. Duncan restrained a laugh, enjoying the turn of roles a bit too much.

"I. . ." Meg reached into her satchel, pulling out a canteen. She shook it. "We're out of water," she said. "And I daresay you all must be hungry. Is it time yet to stop?"

"A fine idea," Mrs. Bettredge said, and she thumped her cane atop the ceiling. The carriage stopped, and Duncan helped the ladies down.

They picked their way over to a mound of rocks for a picnic lunch. But just as they'd settled, a mighty gust blasted debris into their faces.

"Ach, ye monstrous bluster!" Kate clutched her skirts, hollering into the wind as if challenging it to a duel.

"Come," Meg said, tugging on her friend's arm. "There's shelter there!" She helped Mrs. Bettredge to her feet, placing herself as a buffer between the wind and the lady and holding her hand as she led the way to a chasm in the deep bedrock.

The walls of sheer rock were topped in trees and draped in moss and trailing greenery, creating an open-roofed tunnel of sorts. And immediate respite from the wind.

"Did you fear I would be blasted to smithereens?" Mrs. Bettredge patted Meg's hand. "I'm not that frail yet, child."

Meg laughed. "On the contrary," she said. "I was clingin' to *you* for dear life!"

Duncan caught her eye and her cheeks tinged a pleasant pink when he did. 'Twas good of her, caring for Mrs. Bettredge so.

He journeyed farther into the chasm, a chill traversing his spine. The deep-earth path forked into a maze, and the walls soared higher in both directions.

Meg released Mrs. Bettredge's hand, looking to the top of the gorge they now stood in. "'Twould seem we've found the entrance to the center of the earth," she said, running her hand against the wall of cleaved rock.

"Lud's Church," the coachman, Thomas, said behind them. "Not a church, mind you, though there are those who have worshipped here in hiding, in times past." He hefted down a hamper of food on a table-like rock. "Watch for arrows of old. They say 'tis where Robin Hood once sheltered, too."

"Indeed!" Mrs. Bettredge brushed her hands together. "And is that water I hear? I declare I'm as parched as the Sahara. And if it's good enough for a rogue like

Robin of Loxley, well then. I've always wanted to be a rogue. Come." She linked arms with Kate and met them at the fork. "You two go that way, we'll go this, and see if we can't find a stream."

Mrs. Bettredge and Kate were already poking their way through the muddy ground of the right fork of the canyon.

Meg looked down their own canyon, and Duncan could feel the way curiosity pulled her on. Shafts of light filtered through the canopy of trees ahead.

Duncan reached out his hand. "Shall we walk?"

The corners of her mouth turned down in a deeply dimpled, restrained smile. "Nae. I'll race ye. Like old times." She darted away, skirts flying behind. And he followed. Down the stretch of ever-rising walls, like children running through corridors of a castle. Only here, in this earthen keep, he was laird and she was lady, and the world was theirs if just for a moment.

They turned a bend, and Meg stopped suddenly at the foot of a mossy, gradual stairway. Laughter shone in her eyes. "'Tis like the day we met," she said. "D'ye remember?" Flyaway strands of her dark hair fell into her face.

He furrowed his brow. This should be fun. "The day we met, ye say?" He paused, cast his eyes to the side as if thinking. Slowly he shook his head. Meg planted her hands on her hips. "Nae, I don't seem to recall—"

She swatted his arm. "Ye don't recall nearly knocking me to my feet on the stairs."

"Oh, that. Yes, I remember very well a certain scullery maid. Very bonny indeed, she was."

Meg's smile froze. She searched him and seemed to see the earnest threads beneath his jest.

"And right clever I was to think so," his voice grew serious. "For as the years drew on I saw she was bonny through and through. In her kindness. . ." He swallowed. He should not be speaking so. "Her spirit. . ." Meg's hands dropped to her side. "Her soul." He stepped closer to Meg. She turned her head ever so slightly, shifting her gaze away from him and to the wall beside them. He'd overstepped. He should stop. But pushing him like the mighty wind itself was the knowledge that he had only days left with Meg. . .and then she'd be gone.

"That lass," he said. "Aye, she was bonny." He said. "But she was more than that, as I soon learned. She was true, and good, and showed me a light outside of the darkness I'd come from."

Meg lifted wide eyes to his. "What darkness, Duncan?" The melody of her voice was soft, curving up and then traveling down in the burr of their people. A question spoken in a tone not hungry for knowledge, but eager to share a burden. An invitation.

For a second, he thought to tell her all. The people who had disowned him, the weight of their schemes. The details he'd never disclosed, for worry of burdening the MacNaughtons.

But the way her eyes swam with a thirst for understanding, a tender care he'd known nowhere else. . .

He opened his mouth to speak. To drag the truth by its chains from deepest part of him, raise it to the surface. The leaden words piled up on his tongue, ready to spill—when a sudden noise stopped them.

Kate emerged from around the next turn, breathless. A somber look on her face.

"Kate?" Meg said. "What is it?"

"'Tis nothing, I'm sure," Kate said. "But we just met up with a fisherman. He asked if we were with the others."

"The others?" A foreboding swept through him as he stepped forward.

Kate nodded. "A band of Scotsmen. Headed to London for the symphony."

Duncan looked to Meg, whose face was ashen. "It may not be Campbells," he said, hoping it might bring some measure of comfort.

"True." Meg lifted her chin a mite. "Well. We can but go onward. Shall we?"

Duncan nodded, and the threesome began the walk back to Mrs. Bettredge at a clipped pace. The merriment was gone. They would stop ahead for the night, as planned. But lodgings off the main road would be in order.

One look at Meg and he knew it must be so. He would not take any chances with her. Not when her freedom, her reunion with Graeme was finally within reach.

Chapter Twelve

A ch, me bones," Kate moaned dramatically. The coach clattered down a road so rutted, none had spoken a word for miles over the noise of it. "I'll be shaken all the way to kingdom come!"

Meg's own head pounded, too. When Duncan had said "off the beaten path," he had meant it. After making inquiries in the last village, they'd learned of a country inn that was seldom frequented because of the condition of the road leading to it.

Meg laughed and slipped her arm through her friend's. "Let's hope you won't be shaken *quite* that far. Unless 'kingdom come' is the name of the inn." She pointed through the window, where in the high twilight, smoke curled from a red brick chimney poking up above a clump of trees.

The road smoothed into a well-groomed drive. The wheels ticked across a bridge over a creek, and as they rounded the bend, a stunned silence swallowed them all. The inn was lovely, to be sure—window boxes spilling their blue bouquets down over the bricks, three stories of windows glowing soft yellow light from the boxlike structure. But the entire clearing was filled to the brim with coaches and wagons. Their carriage halted a ways from the open double doors, from whence strains of fiddles sang.

Duncan eased forward, eyes narrowing as he scanned the scene keenly. Meg sensed the change in him—the peace that had finally found him miles after they'd left Lud's Church, eclipsed now by sharp tension. "Quiet country inn, indeed," he said.

Their seats bounced with the driver's dismount. As he opened the door, fresh evening air whooshed in. "My apologies, madam." The coachman bowed toward Mrs. Bettredge. "I cannot draw nearer the entrance as there is no room, but I'll dodge in and have a word—"

"You'll do no such thing," Mrs. Bettredge said. "We've feet enough, haven't we? We'll walk."

The man offered his hand to help each of the ladies down. How he kept such a straight face in the wake of Mrs. Bettredge's endless upturning of all that was proper, Meg did not know. She was thoroughly enjoying the woman's surprising antics.

"Before you know it, Mrs. Bettredge, you'll be dancing a highland reel barefoot with the likes of us," Meg jested.

The woman's solid form stopped, and she turned in slow delight. "Now that," she said, "is a superb idea. I am a rogue now, after all." With a wink, she led the way.

Warmth unfurled from the door, the very energy of the assembly sending a thrill into the atmosphere. The others went in, but Meg turned, all too aware of Duncan's presence behind her.

She lingered on the step, the smell of sweet alyssum spicing the air. "Duncan?"

He gave another wary look around.

"Is everything all right?" Meg stepped down to the ground, tilting her head.

He shook his head, reaching his thumb and finger across his forehead as if to scrub the worry away. "Aye," he said. "'Tis fine. Not the hermitage we were wanting, but. . .it will be fine."

Meg released a soft laugh. "Hermitage, is it? Now if anyone knows a thing or two about living like a hermit, Duncan Blair, I suspect it might be you."

He smiled, but the reference to his shanty in the woods seemed to drive the shadow deeper within him. "Shall we?" He offered his arm.

As she rested her fingers upon the sturdy cloth of his jacket, the single instant tore right down the middle. It felt at once the most natural thing in all the world—and the most terrifying. For the last time she'd taken his offered arm, their world had shattered.

"Tomorrow, Duncan." She smiled through the threatening panic, refusing to let it overcome the hope she'd begun to trust. "Tomorrow we'll be in London at last. Tonight"—she gave his arm a gentle squeeze—"we celebrate."

The innkeeper handed over a single key on a hoop large enough to fit over Kate's wrist. Their last room, and Duncan said he'd bunk beneath the stars.

Meg would have protested, but she thought back to every place he'd slept along the journey. His open-air ruins back home. Sleeping outside at the monastery. Had he always craved such freedom?

He carried Mrs. Bettredge's trunk up the stairs, and Meg's cheeks burned when Kate mentioned her state of dress within his hearing as they climbed. "We'll have to shine you up for the symphony. These dresses of ours are fine enough for a country dance, but they may turn us away as ragamuffins in London!"

But a quick glance over her shoulder told her he was busy easing the trunk around the hall corner and did not appear to have heard. Silly of her, anyway, to let her state of dress bother her. Her garments were plain but still held up, and that was all that mattered. Perhaps it would be dark enough at the symphony that no one would take note.

Once they'd freshened up, Meg, Kate, and Mrs. Bettredge descended once more and followed the music into the assembly room. A dance for the villagers, the inn-keeper had explained, to cheer their spirits. Most were farmers and could not leave the land long enough to travel to London and hear the floating symphony. 'Twas unheard of, a public symphony, and something they were breaking their hearts to miss. So they'd rallied their spirits and put together their own celebration this night. Guests, the innkeeper said, were most welcome indeed.

High wooden beams lifted the roof far above them. Three round iron chande-liers, each bearing a ring of candles, lit the room. A thrill stole through Meg. She would be so glad to watch, to take in the joy of the night. She would not dance herself, for she did not know the fine dances of the English folk. And Duncan, she recalled from their fireside encounter, did not dance.

Mrs. Bettredge bustled through the crowd, balancing three crystal cups of water. "Mrs. Bettredge!" Meg rushed toward her. "Here, let me help."

"Thank you, my dear," she said, letting Meg take two of the cups. "One for your own parched mouth, and one for that of the unceasing Kate."

Meg nearly spewed the sip she'd taken. "Unceasing Kate," she repeated. "It does have a ring to it."

"Yes, and she's disappeared, I see."

Meg turned, scanning the room for Kate's long golden braid. She was not to be found in the throng of dancers, nor anywhere among the onlookers.

A flutter of applause drew her attention—and there was her friend. Clapping as she jumped for joy, nodding adamantly at something the conductor of the fiddle orchestra was saying.

She threaded her way back toward Meg, cheeks rosy.

"Well, Mrs. Bettredge,"—she plucked the extra glass from Meg's hand, gulp-ing the water down in four unladylike sips and setting the glass firmly on the table behind them—"you are to have your reel."

"Ach!" The woman put on what was presumably her very best Scots accent. "Ye be certain, lassie?"

Kate doubled over laughing and pulled both of her companions to the floor. "Aye! We be not the only Scots here tonight," she replied in kind with an exagger-ated accent. "'Twould appear many have made the journey for the symphony, and many have stopped over at ye olde Quiet Country Inn." Kate leaned in and whis-pered to Meg, "Take heart. I see no Campbells."

A massive shifting of formation took the dance floor, groups gathering in four circles. Men and women dashing to the dance floor in couples. A pang shot through her at the sight of all the couples. . .and through the steady stream of them, there across the room, she saw him. Duncan. Studying her carefully. When their eyes met, one corner of his mouth pulled into a smile, and he nodded toward the dance floor as if to usher her in, away from these sudden nerves.

If he would cross the room, offer her his hand, the dance would be so much more. But she knew he would not, and she would never ask that of him. But with the smile he gave, and the surge of joy she felt at it, she stepped onto the dance floor.

Duncan watched as the fiddle orchestra struck bows to strings twice in quick succession, signaling the merrymakers to bow and curtsy. Deep pride welled in Duncan. Whatever may be said about the Scots, they worked with all they had in them and celebrated just as furiously afterward. The tradition of dance was a stronghold, an unflinching resolve to rejoice and commune even when the perils of such a life weighed heavy upon them. Deadly exhaustion, dwindling hope of crops, mounting odds in warfare—their foes were as real and dark as the night. But come evening, they pushed through the resignation that threatened to isolate them each, joined hands, and set their feet to flying together.

Tonight the people did just that. On the eve of a symphony held to break through tensions and forge trust. During a time when this new Great Britain of theirs faced enemies from without and within. These country folk and sojourners gripped one another's arms as if on a battlefront. . . and began to march in dance.

The music was lively, the souls even more so. To an outsider, it might look like an utter tangle at first, but every step of a reel was planned, every weaving movement as intricate as if the dancers pulled strings behind them, tying an elaborate Celtic knot as they went.

Kate hollered instructions to Mrs. Bettredge around the poor fellow in between them. "To the right! Now left! Now clap and—yes! There you are. Less like a rabbit, if ye please. More like a gazelle, Mrs. Bettredge."

"Cow's bell?!" Mrs. Bettredge tipped from side to side with great confidence.

"*Gazelle!* Yes, there! Now to the center, and take your partner's hand. . . ."

"Aha! Here I go! Did you see that? Rather like a gazelle!" Her face flushed with alternating concentration and delight as she swished herself side to side. Her feet did not know the intricate steps, but she caught the movements of the circle dance fast and was soon hollering her own whoops and trills along with the others.

And then there was Meg. Her bowed lips parted in a smile so warm it made him ache. Oh, how she laughed. Tossed her head back, dark hair flying like freedom itself. Eyes alight as she danced with abandon, like a bird in full and stunning flight. She looked his way, searching—her smile brighter when she found him.

Duncan swallowed. Longing filled him for the fine light of Meg's spirit. If all went well in the coming days, that spirit would fly far across the ocean with her brother. The very thought snapped something within him. *Father above, keep her. Keep her fast and well, even if ye keep her not for me.*

She set to the center of her circle, hands clasped behind her back as she awaited her first partner. A wide-set man with a curling gray mustache bobbed in. They each raised a hand to meet as they stepped in time and turned together. She turned, faced her second partner to repeat it, and Duncan held himself back from bursting in to meet her himself, bad leg and all. The circle broke into an intricate weaving pattern, the dancers joining hands to travel under the arch the next group over made for them. Another weaving to and fro to intermingle the groups, and they faced fresh partners.

Meg was nowhere in sight. Duncan shoved away from the wall, moving along it as he craned to spot her. When he saw the deep red of her sash, he breathed again. He began to count off the dancers. Trying to find whom her next partner would be. Not that it mattered, but—

Duncan's stomach knotted. The man who would clasp Meg's hand in a matter of moments—Duncan could not see his face. But he could see the unmistakable blue, green, and black plaid of his kilt.

The black watch.

Chapter Thirteen

Meg dipped to the right with the reelers. Then to the left, barely noticing the stifling heat of the room. If she could stop time and soak in every corner of this moment, she would. Each strain of the dance seemed to feed her heart with something more to be grateful for. Her sides ached from laughing over Kate's and Mrs. Bettredge's volleying dialogue. Each time she joined hands or linked arms with one of the kilted officers, she was reminded that only a matter of hours, if the Lord saw fit, remained until she'd see her brother's face once more.

And then there was the matter of the silver candelabra in the corner. For each time the dance brought her closest to it, she had an unhindered view of Duncan Blair. And each time she looked his way, his eyes were fixed on her. The corners of his mouth turned down in a stifled smile when she made a wrong turn once. His eyebrows lifted, mouth in a full, open smile when her dancing partner whooped and hollered for his entire turn with her in the center. 'Twas as if, through his antics and rhythmic clapping, Duncan had joined the dance, though he did not budge from his place against the wall.

When her circle broke into the grand chain and then threaded through the tunnel of arches created by the next circle, it took her a moment before she could glance back at Duncan's place.

It was empty.

She searched the crowd, smile fading as she passed from face to face, with no sign of him. Her feet carried her through the steps, her gaze anywhere but on the dance. 'Twas her turn in the center of the circle—but even as she assumed her place there, she could barely concentrate.

Her new partner's hand met hers as they began to turn, and still she could not focus. She pressed her eyelids closed just long enough to talk sense into herself. This would not do. She needed to give her partner the common courtesy of attention. The same moment she thought this, her slippered foot collided with his.

"Will ye not watch for yer piper, then?"

Meg's eyes flew open.

Duncan. But it could not be. He did not dance. Because of her. She moved her thumb across his, time slowing, the warmth of it quite real.

Those gray eyes, gray like the storm they'd weathered together and gray like the morning just before dawn, held her. Seeing her, knowing her fears and follies and somehow looking at her that way still, like a man who had found what he'd searched for all his life and would not let it go.

They turned together in the circle, not speaking a word. His steps were uneven, but somehow all the stronger for it.

And just as they were to part ways as the dance steps required, his hand closed around hers entirely. He leaned in, and her breath stilled. "Follow me," he said.

A chill wrapped her at the gravity in his voice. As he led her out of the circle, weaving around the puzzled onlookers, his pace quickened, and so did her pulse. Something was wrong.

"Duncan."

He did not stop. He cast a glance over his shoulder, but not at her. Whatever he saw, it made his grip on her hand tighten. Faster they moved, out of the assembly room, through the entryway. The night was dark, the carriages oddly unsettling as they dashed through the maze they created. "Duncan!"

But he did not stop, not until they'd reached the clearing's edge.

"What're ye about?" She broke her hand away from his, breathless.

"Shh." He skimmed the scene. She whirled and did the same. The woods at their back, the inn glowing its golden light from the windows, the strains of the reel finishing and applause drifting their way. . .along with the crunch of slowing footsteps.

"Blair!" a whisper hissed. "Duncan Blair, show yourself!"

Duncan leaned close to Meg. "Stay here," he said. He hesitated only long enough to lift a hand to her face and sweep his thumb across her cheek with a strength that trembled with restraint. "Whatever ye hear," he said, "I am true to you, Meg Mac-Naughton. I swear it."

And he was gone. She listened hard, trying to hear above the wild thumping of her heart. The men began to talk in clipped words—and she recognized the voice. 'Twas the man Angus, from Campbelton. The one who'd sent Duncan on his way, the one with the rough sort of kindness. But his voice now was laden with anger. If he meant any harm to Duncan. . .

She gave thanks for the slow-moving cover of the clouds and lifted a rock from the ground, clutched it. It wasn't much. But it was something, should the man have any ill intentions.

With every muscle in her body held tight to keep quiet, she closed in on the pair. Pressed herself against an empty carriage.

"Return her, Duncan."

Duncan's voice grew lower. "I'll thank ye to leave her be. Even if she was the 'wayward bride'"—the words dripped with disdain, as if they were shackles about Meg—"she's no object to be carried away at your whims."

Heat crept up Meg's neck.

"Not my whims. The Campbell—he is in no good humor about his nephew's antics. He will restore the alliance, make right by the MacNaughtons."

Meg felt sick. She did not know which was worse—Ian's price on her head, or his uncle's plan to see them wed after all.

Duncan scoffed. "Too late for that, don't you think?"

"I'm no fool, Duncan. But you are. To let a lass drive you to such madness. It'll bode no good for ye with the clan. Ye've lost yer brain to yer *Neach-Gaoil.*"

Meg's heart lodged in her throat. His. . .*beloved?* Her thoughts raced, barely registering that something was terribly awry with the other things spoken. Her heart swelled, and her stomach sank. Why would Duncan's clan—these Blairs she'd never met—object to Duncan's actions?

Silence cut like a sword through the night.

At last, Duncan spoke. "I've borne the wrath of my clan for eight years now." The very length of time since he'd arrived at Cumberave. "Ye can tell the Campbell I'll be stayin' my course."

The words slogged through Meg's mind. These words that did not go with one another, lining up and scaling a wall inside. *The Campbell. . .Duncan's clan. . .*

It could not be.

The clouds overhead began to break apart, a slip of moonlight stealing through. She leaned around the corner and saw deep pain, and even deeper resolve, carved on Duncan's face.

But those words, they kept right on with their attack, smashing around her head until a tremor swept down her spine, her arms, her fingers. The rock dropped from Meg's hand, hitting the ground with a sickening crunch.

She winced. If this carriage at her back could somehow swallow her up. If she could vanish away and never be seen—

But then there was Duncan. And his. . .his. . .clansman. Both of them, staring right at her. And all she could do was stare right back, mouth clamped shut, breath coming shallow through her nose, eyes wide until they hurt.

Duncan ducked his head down and to the side toward Angus. "Leave us," he said. "Please."

Angus turned to go, stopped, and spoke two words, not even turning to face Duncan.

"*Ne Obliviscaris.*"

And like a millstone sinking all trace of hope, the motto of the Campbells cinched around her heart. *Forget not.*

As if she ever could.

Angus departed, leaving Meg and Duncan and an ocean of impossible.

She knew not how long it was before either of them spoke. She sensed it—that the moment either of them did, they would be irreparably broken. Shattered. Whatever this shifting truth was, she wanted to vanish into the woods with him, outrun the revelation that quaked her soul.

He took her hand in his. Covered it with his other hand like a pearl to be kept safe from the harsh currents of this world. Her mind told her this should not be—that if what they said was true, she should be pulling away, running from him and never looking back. That perhaps he'd been behind the attack all along, that he was even now setting a trap. But her heart. . . Its whisper was stronger, surer. *Stay,* it seemed to beg her. *This is Duncan. Your own Duncan.* The man who'd given up his own livelihood, the very thing that made his heart beat, to keep a vow to restore her to her family. *Hear him.*

Without a word, he led her to the bank of the creek, a thin line of trees between them and the carriage-filled clearing. The water whispered past them at their feet. She would not look away from the long grass that cloaked her bare ankles.

At last, he lifted her chin. Ever so slowly. Ever so gently. With all the courage she could gather, she met his gaze. The depths of it were fathomless, aching, this man who knew her very heart. He lowered his forehead to hers. Closed his eyes, brows furrowed against the fragility of the moment.

And then her lips were rising to meet his. Defying the dam that would be broken. Standing fast on it before words were spoken and it crumbled beneath them. 'Twas no joyful kiss—not like in the tales of queens and kings and light shining down upon their union. 'Twas a requiem for the love slipping through their fingers, the heartache swelling between them in this place of what could never be. There, she lingered in his arms. Holding off the inevitable for just. . .a little. . .longer.

At last, they pulled apart, the air cold upon her face.

"Please," she said at last through pain in her throat. "Help me understand."

He nodded, expression grim. Her dress billowed about her as they sat upon the grassy bank, and he began to chip away at the rocks in that dam holding back the truth. One by one, letting the tide of history trickle over them. He released one of her hands as he told how the Campbell laird had a sister. . .Duncan's own mother. Who married a Blair, and Duncan was born.

Meg traced his hand slowly—this hand that had held the tale for so long, with no one to share the burden. The tale went on—how the Campbell laird also had a brother. . .Ian Campbell's father. How the cousins—the young Ian and Duncan—had grown up, first as friends, but with a growing chasm of philosophies and ambitions cleaving deep between them. His voice was hollow. So heavy with the loss of something deep and true when he'd lost the friendship of that cousin.

Plans had stirred among the clan about their neighbors, the MacNaughtons. Their land. Their people. The plans had taken an unprovoked dark turn, and Duncan could not in good conscience stand by and do nothing—but neither could he stand in the path of an entire clan to stop them.

"I did the only thing I could think of," he said. "The Campbells are fiercely loyal, whatever their faults may be. I thought—I *hoped*—if one of their own lived among your family, they might not take violent measures. But that fierce loyalty backfired, for they then saw *me* as a traitor. And perhaps they were right," he said. "It wasn't until much later that Angus brought news that plans had changed. That all was well, for they'd arranged a peaceable union." He swallowed, hard. "Between my cousin. . .and my new laird's daughter. That I could come home now. Only"—he tossed a pebble into the stream—"I couldn't. My home was there now. With. . ." He left the sentence unfinished, an unspoken *you* landing with such force in her heart, it knocked the rest of that wall clear away, the truth flowing full and fast now.

Meg's stomach churned. That the man before her—the one to save her from the Campbells. . .was one himself. That he'd been wounded just as much as she by their actions. Lost all his family. Both his original family, and the one that had taken him in as their own. And she had been blind enough to miss the love of the man who'd given everything for her. But oh, how she knew it now. Her heart bursting with such strong, tender love.

"That day," she began. Remembering the look of desperation he wore as she'd walked up that hill toward him. To link arms with him, whom she viewed as a brother. How wrong she'd been. The shift had occurred so gradually, it had snuck into her heart until it was a living force that could not now be ignored.

But there he'd stood, braving the day to deliver her hand to his own cousin. How much heartache would it have saved them if she'd been awake enough to him to see him this way sooner? How much loss?

Hot tears trickled down her cheeks. In a slow enfolding, she was wrapped in his arms. She leaned into him, cold night air gentling around them.

"What now?" she said at last.

"Now. . ." Duncan looked at the sky, clearing of clouds and pinpricked in starlight. "'Tis the same as ever, Meg." The huskiness in his voice drew deeper the pain in her chest. "I'll take ye to your brother. And make right what I can."

Graeme. This did not change the fact that she had this one chance to be reunited with her brother.

They would find him. She would go with him to America. It would be good, and right.

And she would leave her heart behind. . .with a Campbell.

Chapter Fourteen

H ome at last," Mrs. Bettredge declared. Twelve days since Duncan had first startled Meg in the woods. An entire lifetime ago. If he had not found her, she'd be on the road with the Tinkers right now. Probably gathered 'round a fire on Skye, achingly unaware of her brother's heart beating a country away.

Yet here she was, just as Mrs. Bettredge said. *Home at last.* Meg pressed a hand to the warm glass of the carriage and searched for anything that resembled home. But gone were rolling hills and limitless skies. London's monstrous expanse seized her—a terrain sharpened with rooftops and steeples as far as she could see. She tried to concentrate, but its bigness sent her further inside herself—desperate for a pocket of familiarity. And there was the matter of the empty place across from her that would not leave her thoughts.

Duncan had volunteered—rather too eagerly and without so much as a glance in Meg's direction—to ride atop the driver's seat for the remainder of the journey. Kate protested and shot Meg a scolding glance when she did not join her campaign. But she didn't have the heart. Not when every mile crossed brought her closer to life without him—and closer to the reality that they might be too late even to find Graeme.

Meg breathed deep, drawing up her scattering courage. A low ceiling of mingled smells hung over the city. Mrs. Bettredge moved her fan about, pushing waves of alternating scents and stenches across the increasingly small space.

Meg drew her satchel close against her, feeling the hard form of the bottle through the fabric. SPERO. She ran her thumb over the engraving. *Hope.* She breathed the word until it became a heartbeat.

"Prepare yourselves, poppets. There are some who think my dwelling a bit *fantastique*, as the French would say."

"What, yours?" Kate piped up. "A rogue like you? Never." She winked.

"See for yourselves, if you will." Mrs. Bettredge gestured out the window. They were coming upon a low ribbon of gray, a great divide in the city. And across it, a bridge whose surface was packed with buildings. Surely Mrs. Bettredge couldn't mean she lived on a bridge. Could she?

"The river Thames," Meg said. "Isn't it?" In a matter of hours, this water could carry her at long last to her brother.

"Indeed, child. River to all. Livelihood to many. For me? Home." She opened the door and leaned out while the carriage rolled slowly onward. "Let us off before the bridge if you please, Thomas!"

The coach stopped. Outside, people milled about in their finery. Men strode with canes swinging and top hats reaching into the sky. Women seemed to glide, their silken skirts billowing great widths.

She spread her hands across her own faded blue skirt, its rough cloth suddenly seeming so very thin and rumpled. Duncan would appear any moment to open their door, and there she'd be, a rustic from the wild moors standing plain among such beauty.

"Don't worry, child," Mrs. Bettredge spoke into her ear. "You're lovelier in a frock than any of these women could be in the crowned jewels themselves."

Bless this woman. A moment of rare subtlety, and it gave Meg just the strength she needed to face—

The door opened. Her heart thudded. A hand reached in and—that same heart sank. 'Twas Thomas. Offering a friendly smile and a "Welcome to the London Bridge, miss."

Out in the street, she searched for the familiar Blair plaid. She turned in a full circle, the press of the crowd flowing in some chaotic system that they all seemed to know and understand. Behind her she caught snatches of Kate's voice conversing intently with Mrs. Bettredge. About what, she could not decipher.

"Make way, miss!" a hearty voice hollered, and Meg ducked to the side just in time to avoid being knocked into by a man rolling a barrel labeled SALT.

He wove through the crowd, on past the threshold where the street ceased being a street and became, almost imperceptibly, the famous London Bridge. It stretched across the Thames, laden with homes and shops that even extended over its edges, odd boxes of architecture dropping closer to the river that flowed beneath it. 'Twas a wonder the bridge hadn't fallen down under such weight. But what did she know of such things? It would probably last for ages to come.

Still, no sign of Duncan. Hollowness dug within her in the sweep of the crowd until she grew dizzy. She knew their plan: he would find out which barge Graeme was to be on this evening for the symphony, and they would meet at Whitehall in time for the boarding.

"Come, love!" Mrs. Bettredge called, and Meg followed, her senses beginning to numb and retreat. They walked partway down the bridge, minding the *clip-clop* of horses and the roll of carriages. Meg dodged low-hanging arches, nearly like tunnels, these passageways beneath the houses that straddled the bridge. In the middle, they came to one that reached four stories in golden hues. A veritable palace-house, complete with white domes atop its side towers, arched windows with countless panes winking in the afternoon sun.

"Yes," Mrs. Bettredge said dryly as they stood before it. Meg realized her mouth was agape. She clamped it shut, giving Mrs. Bettredge an apologetic look for such a display. "Say what one will about the late Mr. Bettredge. . .one can never say he learned the art of blending in. That makes two of us, I suppose. Our humble abode, Miss MacNaughton."

Inside, Meg took in the sky-blue ceiling doming the grand foyer, adorned with white framework. Mrs. Bettredge doled out instructions to the stream of servants who flowed in and out of the room before them. It wasn't until Meg was being led past the wide, graciously curving staircase that she sensed something else amiss.

It was quiet. Too quiet.

"Where is Kate?"

"I've sent her on an errand," Mrs. Bettredge said. "And never you mind asking what it is. You'll know soon enough," she said with a wink. She led the way into an opulent parlor for tea, talking until the clock in the corner had struck a full hour's passing. Meg tried to concentrate. But her eyes were on everything but her tea. A newspaper lay before her, proclaiming a new act of Parliament—*Transportation Act to Rid England of Large Criminal Population*. Criminals of all sorts would be shipped to the American colonies for years of labor. Perhaps she'd share a ship with them.

A white-capped maid entered and dipped a curtsy. "Ah, perfect," Mrs. Bettredge said. "Martha will show you to your room to prepare, Meg. Spare no luxury, for you'll be in the presence of kings come nightfall!"

Meg was led into a bedroom on the second story. A porcelain tub in an attached room steamed with crystal-clear water. Dried purple blossoms dimpled the surface as Meg ran her tired hands through it, the soothing scent of lavender swirling.

Meg washed as quickly as she could, fighting the temptation to close her weary eyes in the peace of the room. There was too much to do, yet. Upon a porcelain-tipped brass hook hung a pure white *sark*—*shift*, she corrected herself, for she was in England now. Clad in its light form, she entered the adjacent bedchamber and searched for her dress. She'd use the lavender water to clean what spots she could from it.

But the dress was nowhere to be seen. Not in the ornately carved wardrobe in the corner, nor on the russet-canopied bed. A knock sounded. Kate burst through the door, arms about a large package. She wore a dress of royal blue, edged in black ribbon, with black brocade across the bodice. She wobbled slightly, the dress looking at once becoming and entirely cumbersome upon her free-spirited frame.

"Kate!" Meg steadied her friend. "Where have ye—"

"I am your humble messenger, me lady," she set the package on the bed and twirled her arm in an exaggerated bow.

"Where did ye find such a beautiful dress?" Meg couldn't stop smiling, it was such a thing of finery. "Ye look grand, Kate. Positively grand!" Kate's eyes were as vivid as bluebells, her yellow hair twisted in a halo about her head. Meg gave a hapless look at her own shift then eyed the package. *Nay. Could that be for. . . ?*

She dared not wish, but such a hope was twirling up in her all the same. More so at the sight of Kate's mischievous smile.

"Mrs. Bettredge got it into her head to dress me up. I didn't s'pose there was a chance of making me anything like presentable, but she declares London needs to be shaken up, and a dose of the Highland Tinkers is the way to do it!" She released a happy sigh. "Now! If you will be so kind as to open yonder package." Kate's attempted London accent was endearing, if not convincing.

Meg untied the twine about the pure white box and lifted its lid. Nestled inside was a sea of mild green and ivory silk, a soft sheen glancing off it.

"Oh. . . ," Meg breathed, pulling the dress out and smoothing her hand across the buttery softness. "'Tis so fine."

Kate faced her toward the oval mirror that stood in the corner. Meg clutched the dress against herself and felt immediately an impostor.

"I cannot wear this," Meg said. But even as she spoke, she held it tighter, hand pressed against the cream-colored bodice where beneath crisscrossed golden cord, embroidered blossoms in hues of sunshine, raspberry, and blue sky intertwined betwixt vines. Like a walk in the heathered hills of Scotland, it was. Home, so very far from home.

"In with ye," Kate said, and she helped Meg into it, layer upon layer. Every detail had been considered, right down to the pockets that nestled against the petticoat and opened discreetly into the folds at her waist.

The cool weight of it against her skin brought such strange comfort. Like an embrace, it was. The sage green of the petticoat and skirt draped like still-form waterfalls over the panniers at her waist, giving the folds a gently curved edge to spill over.

Meg lifted a hand to push her unruly waves of dark hair back. As she did so, she marveled at the lightness of the long, delicate lace cuffs, draping from the sleeves' ends beneath her elbows.

"What'll you keep in the pockets?" Kate asked. "Ye could fit a whole island in the likes of them!" She leaned in as if to impart a scandalous secret. "They say some ladies keep all manner of delicacies in them. Biscuits. Sandwiches. Bonbons. Imagine! Ye'd best pack bonbons, whatever they be. Ye've not eaten a bite since this morning."

"I can't," Meg said. "These nerves." She forced a laugh. Retrieving her satchel, she pulled Jimmy's bottle out, running her hands across the letters, thinking of all that lay within. If her own courage should fail her, she would have this to remind her that there was more at stake than her own wavering bravery. SPERO—hope itself etched upon it and scrawled on the scroll within in Jimmy's hand. And the tartan, too. "This will keep my strength better than bonbons," she said with a wink. She removed the scrap she'd been stitching on throughout the trip, slipped her worn needle in and out a few last times, and tied off the thread.

"I hope in God," Kate read slowly. 'Twas the one thing that embarrassed her spunky friend, her difficulty with words, but 'twas a wonder she'd learned as much as she had in her years on the road.

"Aye," Meg said. "Our clan motto." She tucked the scrap safely back into the bottle, and the bottle into her pocket. "I'll call it to remembrance often tonight," she said, braving a smile. A comfort, that the future lay in the hands of a God bigger than all of this.

Kate stood back and beamed at Meg. "Ye're a picture, my friend. Ye can hardly tell the dress is a mite big. But with no time for a fittin', and ready-made pieces so rare. . ."

Meg shook her head. "'Tis more than I ever hoped for," she said. "Mrs. Bettredge shouldn't have done such a thing. So generous. . ."

"She didn't," Kate said, and, lifting a brush, she motioned for Meg to sit.

"But she said you were on an errand for her. . . ?"

"Aye," Kate said. Her fingers worked Meg's curls, twisting and weaving. "She did tell us where to go. But not for her."

"Then who. . . ?" Kate did not have a penny to her name. Neither did Meg, and the only other person who even knew they were here—but that was impossible.

"Oh, a very kind soul," Kate said. "He's not one to say much, but he was very particular that I tell ye what he said, and not a word different. Let me see. . . ." In the mirror, Meg saw her look up and to the side as if deep in thought. "Ah, yes. 'Tell Miss MacNaughton' "—she took on a theatrically serious face for the recitation—" 'that a lady such as she must have the white of heather on her day of union. And'. . ."

Meg turned to face Kate. These words she spoke—a memory rolled out of the past, across the miles, burrowing deep within her. Two young girls, giggling and reciting.

Kate halted. "Daft brain, don't fail me now," she groaned. "What were the words. . ."

"The green grass of the hills of her home to adorn her," Meg said in almost a whisper.

"Yes!" Kate cried in delight. "How did ye know?"

How could she forget? The words that, moments before the attack, had made her suppose Ian Campbell mightn't be as coldhearted as he was reputed to be. A wash of panic struck Meg. Was the dress from him?

Kate dug within the pocket of her skirt and pulled out a plain brown paper. She handed it to Meg. "See for yerself," she said.

The paper crinkled as Meg opened it. Letters straight and solid, dear and familiar spanned the scrap in a single line: *The white of heather on her day of reunion, and the green grass of the hills of her home to adorn her.*

Beneath that line stood a signature that made her heart beat so loud she feared the passersby on the bridge below would feel tremors from it: *Duncan.*

Meg stood, reading the words again. Hearing them in the voices of the young sisters on her wedding day as they'd thrust a grass-tied bouquet of heather her way. Somehow in all her naïveté and girlish hope back then, she'd thought such a thing had come from Ian Campbell?

"Oh, Kate. . ." How wrong Meg had been. And oh, how dearly she would pay. How dearly a lone piper had paid for so long. Her heart ached anew.

His words swam before her unspilled tears, and she wiped her eyes.

Kate led her to the window, which looked straight out over the water that carried her destiny. It was a rare moment of silence from her friend. But Meg had to know for certain how this all came about.

"Do you mean to tell me that this"—she smoothed the dress—"is. . .from Duncan?"

Kate's smile lifted her blue eyes. "None other. Well, he did have a wee bit of help choosing the actual dress. 'Green and white!' was all he could say." Kate laughed at the way she lowered her own voice. "Every time I asked what it should look like. 'Green and white!' Poor man looked like he was being led to the slaughter the moment we arrived outside the dress shop. He would not step foot inside—said it wouldn't be fitting. Some of the faces he made when I held up dresses through the window!" Kate tossed her head back, laughing. "I declare, the man must think ruffles and lace the deadliest combination on earth! But this one. . ."—Kate leaned in, whispering—"when I knocked on the window and showed him this one, his pacing halted, and he could not look away. I know he was seeing you, Meg."

Meg could scarce believe it. She fingered the skirt, green like the highland hills she might never see again. Pressed her hand against the stomacher of heather white, thinking of the piper's kind eyes. . .and the thought of never seeing them again grieved her deeper still. It would be unladylike of her to ask. But a horrible sinking feeling urged the words from her. "How did he afford such a thing?"

Kate looked away.

"Kate?"

Her friend began working Meg's hair once more. Meg caught her hands and looked Kate in the eye.

"Tell me," she said.

Kate pursed her lips then spoke at last. "I gave my word not to." She tilted her head resolutely.

There was only one possession Duncan had that could fetch such a price—and it was his very livelihood. Or should be.

"His bagpipes," Meg breathed. Such a wretched tangle this was. For every step that brought her closer to Graeme drove Duncan further from himself. And her further from him.

"Ye do not have to go, ye ken," Kate said quietly.

"I do." Meg wiped the sudden wetness from beneath her eyes. "The symphony is the only place I can intercept Graeme before he leaves. You've all given so much to make this happen."

"No, ye goose." Kate's brows wrinkled into sympathetic humor. "Ye need not leave him."

"I won't leave Graeme." Meg was pacing now, concentrating. Pushing images of Duncan out of her mind. Again. And again. "You know the plan. I'll board the barge,"—she ticked the list off on her fingers—"find him before the grand dinner makes it impossible with its crowds, and we'll sail for America first thing in the morning when it's all said and done, if he'll let me."

"Margaret MacNaughton." Kate placed her hands on Meg's arms and stood squarely in front of her. "Ye are the daftest maiden that ever was. Listen closely. Ye do not need to go to America. Ye do not need to leave Duncan Blair. Anyone can see that ye are each other's very hearts."

Memories strung together in her mind like pearls on a string. The stairway where they'd nearly collided, where he'd thought her a scullery maid, and she'd thought him the kindest face she'd ever seen. The moment he'd stood in her father's dining hall, playing "Keep Watch, Ye Lads and Lasses." The moment he looked her in the eye in the carriage and confessed he'd lived on the forest floor, if only for the chance to keep that promised watch for her. His vow to reunite her with Graeme. His careful touch in Lud's Church. The dance—when he'd sworn never to dance.

Moments begun as absolutely ordinary, held close for so long, they'd been transformed, layer by layer like sand in a mussel, until they shone. *Treasures.*

"'Tis my own fault, Kate. If I'd opened my eyes to see the man before me all that time. . . But it is past. I will go to America. He will finally be free to play his pipes in all the land once more, for he vowed not to until Graeme and I were together again. And God be thanked, I will have the brother I'd never dreamed of seeing again on this earth."

Kate opened her mouth, but Meg shook her head. "Please, Kate." She could manage no more words, her throat was so raw. "Keep care of him, if ye can."

Meg could tell that Kate was holding back a fiery lashing. She offered measured words instead. "He needs no care taken, Meg. Except what's given from you. But I'll look out for whatever I can." She turned to go, pausing with her hand on the doorknob. "Until ye come to your senses, that is."

Meg closed her eyes, closed out the world around her with the only prayer she knew in that moment: *This one thing, help me do.*

Chapter Fifteen

The night was large around Meg. And she was ever smaller among the growing throngs upon the riverbank. Meg stood sandwiched between Mrs. Bettredge and Kate, each of them searching for Duncan. It was so far from what she'd pictured. She'd imagined a park along a peaceful river, with children racing stick boats and picnickers awaiting the festivities. But here, at the starting point of what was to be the event of this monarch's reign, the wide Thames loomed beyond a wall of people.

Boats packed the river. From rowboats, to fishing boats, to merchant ships, to rafts piled high with roped-down barrels. Every vessel in all the kingdom, it seemed, had come out to meet their king. Never had they been in such close proximity to him, nor even dreamed of hearing a symphony in their lifetimes.

Meg spotted an open bench beneath a tree, and before she could stop herself, she picked up her fine skirts and stood atop its seat.

"Look!" A young woman in black-and-white servant's garb jumped up and down. "Are those the musicians?" Two other girls dressed identically to the first stood on tiptoe. Meg followed their gazes and, indeed, saw a barge, the white-wigged musicians boarding with late-evening sun glinting off their brassy instruments.

Meg wove through the masses and edged along the river's bank, her fine slippers sticking in the mud.

"Meg!" 'Twas Duncan's voice.

"Duncan?" She called out, searching.

"Meg!" His voice was closer, his hand reaching through the crowd. She could not reach him, feet stuck in the mud. She pulled one foot free of its shoe, stepped on the toe of her other to release her second foot, and leaped, giving her a clean landing on the grassy portion of the bank. She was shoeless. . .but she could reach his hand.

The moment their eyes met, Duncan froze. The same longing on his face that he'd worn on her wedding day. And she could not look away from him.

"Duncan, the dress. . ."

"Ach, Meg MacNaughton. . ." He stepped closer, keeping her hand within his. He leaned in close to her ear to be heard over the crowd. "Ye know, don't ye, what ye are?"

Meg tightened her grip.

But in his next breath, Duncan was halted by the brassy tones of a trumpet herald. The crowd stilled, all eyes on the row of boats and the small procession of royally clad men and women.

"On this seventeenth day of this seventh month of the year seventeen seventeen," the herald began.

"Quick," Duncan said, leading her through the crowd. "This is your chance!"

The herald continued, and Meg raced against his every word. Surely the end of his speech would signal the launch of the boats, the symphony. . .the future.

"The famed composer George Frideric Handel, by commission of His Majesty King George the First, shall unveil for the first time, the symphony composed for the people of this kingdom."

At the back of the queue to board the boats, Duncan offered his arm. And as if he'd done so a thousand times, he escorted her into the royal procession, looking every bit the highland contingent. Chin raised in sure strength. Together they stepped forward, and all at once it was her turn.

The herald paused significantly, and Meg could feel the crowd hanging on his words. "His Majesty presents to you. . .*Water Music*."

The musicians' barge floated past these royal vessels to lead the way, jolly notes ascending into melody. It was regal and joyous, this floating symphony. But suddenly, all Meg could hear was her own heartbeat.

They stood before an attendant clad in royal red. Duncan gave a bow. "Margaret MacNaughton," he said. "Sister to the new Lord Proprietor to the Carolinas, Graeme MacNaughton."

Meg stood a little taller at the sound of her brother's title. The man gestured to the boat on the right. Duncan stood beside her and—did she imagine it?—gave the slightest pull on her arm when he reached the place she must leave him. She halted. This was all wrong.

"Duncan, I—"

"Remember the starling." Brief words, but their strength filled her. "Ye were made to fly, Meg. Go."

He stepped back. There she stood, alone.

"If you please, my lady," the attendant spoke. "The barge will embark shortly." He gestured aboard, where ladies laughed and men in uniform strode about and somewhere among them her brother lived and breathed.

But just as her foot made contact with the ornately carved black boat before her, she looked to her left.

What she saw made her wish she had never turned her head. A single motion in a single instant and everything changed. There, on the deck of the boat to the left, stood Ian Campbell.

"*Fly.*" Meg heard Duncan's voice in her heart. The impossible choice would not wait: miss the chance to tell her brother that she lived, or let Ian Campbell rule their past. And worse, Duncan's future.

"Madame?" A man on board her brother's boat offered her a white-gloved hand to help her.

"I—" She looked at it, at him. She thrust her hand into her pocket before she could change her mind, gripping the warm bronze of the bottle. "I'm to journey on the other boat,"—she tipped her head slightly and managed a smile—"but I'm needin' to get this to a gentleman aboard yours. Graeme MacNaughton. Please tell him to wait when we dock, before he goes in for the dinner." She placed the bottle in his hand with a prayer that Graeme would see the tartan inside and wait for her when he disembarked. The attendant tipped his black three-cornered hat to her in agreement.

In a blur, Meg boarded the smaller boat just as it pushed off and away into the river, floating with its current. She edged a cluster of courtiers, feeling horribly out of place. If she could disappear somehow—if this dress could magically become the true grass and heather of home and she could run barefoot across the land with no care in the world. . .

But that land was not hers. There was only one thing to do.

Meg craned her neck to see to the center of the boat. There was Ian Campbell, conversing beside an older man in matching tartan. They bowed in tandem to a man seated on a red velvet bench, and Meg's stomach dropped. King George himself. She dodged behind the woman in front of her as the two Campbells turned, striding away from the king and joining another man on the far end of the barge. Meg followed.

Within earshot now, she heard the older Campbell speaking. "Indeed, Governor. My nephew will be invaluable to you in that regard. He is a strategist of the highest caliber. . . ."

The words twisted Meg's heart. And before she could think, she was striding straight toward the men, the deck smooth beneath her hidden, unshod feet. What she planned to do when she got there, she had no idea.

"That's all very well," the man they called "Governor" said. "For with regard to English and Scottish relations, we've much work ahead of us. Some of them still view us as savages, if you can believe such a thing."

"Savages," Meg spoke. Her voice was calm. Glass over the tempest within. "Indeed, I cannot imagine why." She looked at Ian, who turned uninterested eyes on her only for a moment. Not a flicker of recognition.

"Ah—yes," the governor said. "My apologies. I do not believe we've been introduced." He looked about for a companion, someone to do things properly. But Meg was far beyond caring about etiquette.

"Lady Margaret MacNaughton," she said, curtsying deeply. When she arose, all three sets of eyes were on her. Including Ian Campbell's, much more keenly now. "Formerly of Argyll." The older Campbell seemed to scrutinize her, though there was an almost fatherly concern on his face. A face she'd seen sketched before—the laird himself.

The governor spoke again. "George Hamilton, governor of Edinburgh Castle." His brogue was light beneath his refined accent but accentuated when he spoke of their country. He bowed. "And these are—"

"I'm acquainted with the Clan Campbell," she said. "Very closely." She looked the man in the eye who'd promised peace and turned around and robbed her of everything.

"I did not mean to eavesdrop." She addressed the governor again. "But it sounds as if you'll be availing yourself of Ian Campbell's services?"

"Indeed," the man said. "We've much at stake in Parliament just now and have need of a native liaison as the Scots law converses over these things, too."

"Yes," Meg said, a surge of recollection giving her fresh energy. "You refer to the"—what had it been in the newspaper?—"the Transportation Act, I believe?"

"You are acquainted with it," the governor spoke.

"Only just. I took special interest in the part about damage to property."

"Aye." The man seemed to come to life at that. "The English have adopted strict consequences for arson, robbery, and the like. I think if the Scots will follow suit—"

"Many would heartily agree." Meg raised her brows and leveled Ian Campbell with a look. "Such plunder as takes place in the highlands."

"And how do you plan to help in such matters?" Duncan's voice. Behind her.

Meg turned, nearly knocking into him. How had he come to be here? She could have embraced him then and there, were it not for the company at hand. And the fierce look he directed at his cousin.

The air between the four of them was full of unspoken things. The governor seemed too shrewd to carry on in such a way.

"I. . . ," Ian spoke. This man, whom she'd approached with such trepidation on their wedding day, seemed suddenly weak to her. Nerves shooting his glance back and forth between his uncle and the governor. And finally to Meg, with a cold smile. "I think it would behoove some to include 'breach of promise' in that lot. There are many who have run from their commitments, after all." The man dared insinuate Meg was at fault. She narrowed her eyes.

Duncan's arm pressed against Meg so that she felt the restraint he fairly trembled with.

Meg settled her hand within his elbow, as if he'd merely offered it to her as a courtesy. As if there weren't a universe of meaning in that one gesture.

"Excellent thought," she said. "So a man who had promised to wed a woman to join rival clans, for example. If he were to turn on that promise, and, say, plunder that clan instead. Ooh," she breathed as if in sympathy, shaking her head. "What a penalty he'd be in for, then. Damage to property *and* breach of promise."

By now the governor had taken a step back, folded his hands, and seemed to be following along with creased brow almost as a judge.

It was the laird who intervened, catching the invisible ammunition shooting back and forth between Meg and Ian. "Such a case would be a tragedy," he said.

Ian's mouth opened in protest, but a single hand held up by the laird halted whatever words were on Ian's tongue.

The laird faced Duncan and Meg. Sorrow in his eyes. And something deeper, more fragile. *Hope.*

"Such a case would find many at fault. Men in authority who should have planned differently," he said, regret in his voice.

Duncan dipped his head then looked at his uncle. "Men who acted rashly in the heat of their youth," he replied.

A silence laced them, during which Meg gripped Duncan's arm tighter. The laird looked between them, understanding softening his face. And Ian stood like an agitated twig, shifting his weight and looking in the direction of the governor, who had silently excused himself, no doubt long since aware that they were not speaking in hypothetical wonderings.

"In such a case," the laird said, "the man who had unspeakably harmed an entire clan would pay. His uncle would see to finding him a position where he would be watched closely, and not allowed free access to his own plots and schemes. He would be under the watch of a governor, or his uncle himself. And"—he looked at Meg—"he would not be allowed to *touch* the land he had plundered."

The castle. The cobwebbed kitchen. The whole place groaning with emptiness. It had not been a waste, then—it had been preserved? Protected from Ian.

The laird continued. "So that when the family returned, it would be awaiting them." The man's eyes, deep blue as the ocean and turned down at the outer corners in such a state of sadness, crinkled up ever so slightly.

"Margaret MacNaughton," he said. "I know it cannot undo what's been done. But please. Take the seat of Cumberave as your own once again. 'Tis yours. Rightfully, lawfully yours. Please know I had no knowledge of what my nephew planned. . .and he has not left my side since that day. The Clan Campbell may be known for many things, but betrayal is not acceptable. Be free of him. Be free of us." He looked to Duncan and then back at where her hand rested on his arm, Duncan's other hand now covering it. "If ye care to, that is." And with that, he turned, jerking his head at Ian, and the pair of them disappeared.

Meg's shoulders rose and fell in shallow breaths, the courage that she'd held to with every ounce of strength she had releasing her muscles so suddenly she thought she might collapse.

Duncan pulled her closer to himself. "Now, lass," he said. He lifted his finger to point, and Meg followed his gesture. "What do ye think of that?"

The boat was docking. Lines of ladies and gentlemen were disembarking the royal barges and wending their way up a path toward a grand house for dinner at Chelsea. The symphony played on buoyantly. And there, at the end of the dock, was a sight that unleashed a thousand silent, happy tears.

A man in red uniform, gripping the bronze bottle and tartan in one hand, shielding his eyes against the evening sun with the other, and intensely searching the barges.

Their eyes met. Everything else about them faded into a world of silence, and all she could see was her brother. Desperate happiness breaking across his face. He clambered through the onslaught of the crowd, bumping haplessly into people as he went, for he would not take his eyes off her. Meg did the same until at last, at last—

She collapsed into Graeme. Touching her own flesh and blood. Living impossible hope.

"Thank you," her prayer choked through sobs. "Thank you."

Chapter Sixteen

One Month Later

Golden wind of evening lifted tendrils of hair from Meg's shoulders. She stood at the shore of the water that stretched between her and her love. Waves rippled, settling around her ankles. A gentle washing of her feet. And she watched for the man who'd watched for her for so very, very long.

How different things were from what they might have been. Looking at the long, narrow sea loch now—why, this could have been the entire Atlantic. This could have been another day in a lifetime without Duncan.

But it wasn't. It was home—and her wedding day.

"Haste ye back, Duncan," she'd whispered to him when she'd left him in London. He was to stay there with Graeme while arrangements were made to delay her brother's voyage. Her heart had been full to overflowing. . .so different from the last time she'd begged him to hasten back.

She'd left London with Kate and Mrs. Bettredge—*"Fry London,"* the older woman had said when Meg protested her offer to transport them, arguing that she'd only just returned to London. *"There's love in the air. Get me to Scotland!"*

And so the threesome had retraced their path. They made two stops while in London, at Meg's request. First, a church. She brought the bottle, and she searched the scriptures for one last verse to inscribe. She etched the words upon her paper, wiping tears away as the scratch of the quill echoed in the soaring ceilings of the chapel: *mourning into dancing. . .put off my sackcloth. . .girded me with gladness. . .*

A testament to what God had done. A message of continued hope, to pass the gift she'd been given on to the next person the bottle might deliver such news to. She dripped white wax from a candle, sealing topper to lid. *Bless the next hearts to hold this,* she prayed.

And the second stop, a squat red-roofed building with white walls and dark trim, Curiosity Shop lettered above the door. Inside, Meg gaped at scattered pieces of armor, rusty weapons, and dusty books, vases, and carved artifacts. Such a place deserved a story of its own, she thought. But it was the bagpipes in the corner that interested her. She proposed a trade to the proprietor: a bronze bottle of great personal worth, and probably great historical and monetary worth, or so she hoped. In trade for the set of pipes sold to him by a Scotsman days before.

When the moment came to hand over the bottle, she'd tightened her grip, nearly changing her mind. It had meant so much to Jimmy, to her, to Graeme. Could she really trade it? Was she so heartless?

Kate, apparently sensing Meg's hesitancy, had leaned in and spoken through gritted teeth—*"Jimmy'll kill ye if ye don't do this thing."* And the guilt dissipated right then, for she was right. Dear Jimmy. He'd at least force her to eat mussel shells for a week straight. So she'd arranged for the pipes to be delivered posthaste to Duncan.

They'd left London and traveled north to Gretna Green to rejoin some of the Tinkers, who'd hopped in the carriage when they learned what happened and made the rest of the journey north by land with them.

So here they were, weeks later. Kate and Mrs. Bettredge stood at Meg's back, forming a line of witnesses along with Jimmy and Mrs. MacGregor, wee Jemma with her fire-bright hair and ribbon-woven bracelet, the girl's family, and a minister from Inveraray. All waiting in stillness for what was to come. Castle Cumberave peeked out from the green tree line behind them like a great sentinel.

And then the sound came. Pipes that had long lain dormant, keeping their song for this day. In the distance, a currach appeared. Her brother, rowing the groom who wore his full piper's plaid. The tune sounded so familiar. She gripped the skirt of her dress—the same heather green she'd worn to the symphony—and remembered. A lilting movement, sounding slightly strange and foreign on the bagpipes, for when she'd heard it, it had been on the strings during the floating symphony in London. "Air," they'd called this movement.

And as the boat drew nearer, "Air" gave way to something more lively. It spun into her soul and emerged with lively laughter: "Keep Watch, Ye Lads and Lasses."

"Oh, Duncan," she laughed into the wind. "Always, I shall."

Then they were upon them, nearing the shore, and the music took on a slower, more steady rhythm and melody. Meg's hand flew to her heart and clutched the clan brooch there. The song from the tower ruins—the song heard nightly, sitting beside her mother and father, listening to Duncan play the sun down to its rest each evening. How she wished they could be here tonight.

And with his approach, she remembered her mother's clear voice and sang along with the pipes under her breath:

"All glory to our Lord and God. . .for love so deep, so high, so broad. . ." The words became a prayer of thanks. For such a love as His. Such goodness in creating Duncan and letting her love him. For hope that did not disappoint. . .and for songs in the night.

The breath went clean away from her when he set down his pipes, stepped into the shallows, and sloshed toward her, gait sure even in its barely detectable unevenness.

She clutched her simple bouquet of heather tied in highland grass—and when he drew near, she tucked a sprig of it behind his sashed wool.

He drank her in as she did, sliding his hand down her long, free hair. "I never told ye, Meg."

"Told me what?" She took his hands as the minister stepped forward.

"What ye are. The night of the symphony. . ."

She pressed her eyes closed, remembering the heartbreak in his voice. *"Ach, Meg MacNaughton. . .ye know, don't ye, what ye are. . ."* And then had come the blow of the trumpet.

She looked into his gray eyes, waiting.

"If a man could pile castles upon seas"—he looked to his right at Cumberave, then to his left at Loch Fyne, and the Irish Sea in the unseen distance—"tempests and ruins upon rivers. Wild horses and forests and country dances and floating symphonies. Heap it all together and tell the world where the treasure in all of it lay. . ."

Meg's breath caught. Pictures flooded her mind of each place he listed, and in each one of them, there he was. Strong and true. Waiting for her to open her eyes and see him.

"'Tis you, Meg MacNaughton."

She shook her head, lacing her fingers into his. "'Tis you, Duncan Blair."

The exchange was so simple and pure, Meg often thought, looking back on the day, that the words were their true vows. For the minister, perhaps sensing the sacredness of what had already been spoken, added only a few more words of wisdom and truth to the ceremony. And what he did add was treasure, too. A prayer, for the hearts being joined this day. 'Twas a union wrapped in light as the sun slipped behind the hills.

Amanda Dykes is a drinker of tea, dweller of truth, and spinner of hope-filled tales. She spends most days chasing wonder and words with her family, who love a good blanket fort and a stack of read-alouds. Give her a rainy day, a candle to read by, and an obscure corner of history to dig in, and she'll be happy for hours. She's awed by the strong thread of God's grace and provision woven through every era and hopes her stories reflect that grace. A former English teacher with a BA in English education, she is the author of the critically acclaimed *Bespoke: A Tiny Christmas Tale*, and enjoys connecting with her readers at www.AmandaDykes.com.

The Forgotten Hope

by Maureen Lang

Chapter One

New York City
June 1798

Abigail Van de Klerk opened the door to the house she shared with her father on Pearl Street. At this hour, neither of them expected any servants to be up—although keeping Bromley from waiting up for them, no matter the hour, had been a recent accomplishment. She suspected the faithful butler's door was still open at the back of the house, and he would rest only now, hearing them return.

"Long day, eh?" Father said as they made their way toward the stairs. Neither he nor Abigail paused when passing the hall to the kitchen. Another dinner missed, but sleep was the greater need right now.

"Sleep well, Father," she said as they went up. She was as eager as he for rest, but at the top step, her father's voice detained her.

"Abigail, you mustn't let me depend on you as I did tonight. I say this for your good, not mine."

As she reached the door opposite his, she offered a half smile, all she could muster. "Ah, but Father, helping you is what I want to do."

He rubbed the back of his neck, shaking his head. "Still, tonight was particularly nasty. I warn you, darling, in the morning we will have an argument—after we've both regained our fortitude."

She took two steps closer to him and planted a kiss on his cheek. "Thank you for the warning. I'll dream up my defense tonight."

As she was about to enter her room, she saw him reach for something just inside his door. She knew a small table stood there, the traditional spot where Bromley left important letters or missives. He'd given up leaving notes by the front door, a place Father always rushed past whether coming in or going out.

"Go to bed, Father," she called. "No letter is more important than your rest."

He held it up to the light from the moon filtering in from the hall window. "But it's from that gentleman, the one working with my friend Charles in the West Indies. Perhaps the young man has agreed to join me here in New York, after all. Shall we see?"

With a sigh, knowing he wouldn't resist, Abigail made a slow approach as he neared the fireplace in his room to light a narrow spill of twisted paper, then the candle's wick. As he read the letter, she guessed it couldn't be good news, because instead of a smile of anticipation emerging on his tired but kindly face, he frowned.

"Now that is sad news, sad indeed."

"He isn't coming?"

Her father hesitated, finally nodding. "But he is."

"I thought that would be good news?"

"Only because Charles has died. I'm sorry to hear that. Very sorry indeed."

"I'm sorry too, Father. I know he was dear to you."

"But he died serving others, for which he should be proud. I'm proud for him."

"When is this gentleman coming? This protégé of his?"

"Dr. Tallery says he must see through some cases Charles left to him, but that he should arrive here in New York this summer."

"So there is a silver lining. Perhaps you will sleep, after all."

"And so shall you, I hope. Good night, dear. Don't forget our argument scheduled for breakfast."

She issued a tiny laugh that sounded more like a sleepy sigh then made her way to her own room.

Lizzie, Abigail's lady's maid, roused Abigail in the usual way. Abigail didn't hear a thing until after Lizzie drew back the curtains that let in enough light to instantly wake her. With a stretch and yawn, she mumbled a good morning to Lizzie's cheery greeting. She was tempted to roll onto her side and stay abed another half hour, or at least complain that three hours was hardly enough sleep, but she didn't waste energy on something so pointless.

Instead she allowed Lizzie to help her dress, knowing another day's work waited for both her father and herself. How in the world had Father done this for so many years? He'd been a physician since he turned twenty—some fifty years ago—and learned the art of medicine from his father the same way Abigail and her older brothers had learned it from him. She doubted any one of them had ever seen a consecutive week's worth of uninterrupted sleep.

Abigail made it only halfway down the stairs before the scent of cooked bacon and eggs obliterated her fatigue. Hunger took its place.

Her father, already seated and served, winked at her as she accepted a full plate from Bromley at the sideboard.

"Today is one of those days when Marta's excellent cooking skills will be wasted on us both," Father said instead of greeting her. "I asked Bromley to turn his back while I ignore all manners and eat like a barbarian. I invite you to do the same."

Looking at the especially large pile of scrambled eggs next to not one but four pieces of bacon—an amount of food she never would have accepted had she not skipped dinner last night—she sat down and proceeded to join her father. Neither bothered to spend a moment on conversation. Instead, she filled and refreshed herself in a way that refined society could never condone.

She'd made quite a dent on the heap of food when Father accepted a second cup of coffee then regarded her with the little grin he seemed always to wear. But this morning the look was accompanied by unmistakable concern.

"I assume you're feeling fit this morning, despite the lack of sleep?" he asked.

Deciding Bromley had been a bit too generous with the amount of food he'd given her, she set aside what little was left to wipe her napkin at the corners of her mouth. She had just enough room in her stomach for Marta's strongest coffee, something the cook always knew to prepare on such mornings as this.

"I am. And you? Ready to take another young doctor under your wing, this Dr. Tallery?"

He chuckled. "Dr. Tallery hardly needs my protection—or instruction. I expect Charles finished his training, if any was needed after Edinburgh. He'll be a great asset."

She savored her coffee, at last able to taste something now that her hunger was abated. But she knew her moment of enjoyment would soon come to an end. That concern in her father's eye had wiped away his grin.

"Now, Father," she began, hoping to forestall the argument she knew he had every intention of initiating. "We discussed long ago how it shouldn't matter that I'm a daughter instead of another son. In fact, my training is likely more thorough than John's or Matthew's, because I began shadowing you from the moment I could walk. Mother, God rest her soul, kept my brothers home far longer than you ever kept me."

"Only because I didn't have the time to argue with you. But I've been too indulgent of your whims and much too selfish. Goodness, you must be nineteen already, or close to it."

She was twenty, but she didn't bother giving him more fuel.

"You opened your own medicine room when you were twenty, Father. Both Matthew and John left home to practice on their own when they weren't much older. So if age is to be discussed at all, I hope it will only be in terms of my readiness to work independently, should I ever develop such a desire. Which of course I won't. Age is only important as it relates to experience."

"Age is another thing entirely as it relates to you. You're a young woman now. Instead of sending you off to the best school here in New York or Boston, or even in Europe, I've monopolized your time. I cannot even remember the last party you attended. Can you?" He sighed, but then his white brows lifted with a touch of horror. "My dear girl, can you even dance? But of course not. When have I given you time to learn? Ah, I've failed you."

"Oh, Father, don't be ridiculous! I wouldn't change one single solitary moment of my life working with you."

"Some work it's been, too." His frown deepened. "Amputating an arm and a leg last night was hardly a pretty thing for you to witness."

"But you saved his life! Who cares about pretty? You did it fast and sure, and that's all anyone can ever hope for with such an operation."

"Now we've changed the subject," he complained. "I asked you if you could dance. I suspect you cannot. And so let us begin the argument. Abigail, I've taken the liberty of contacting the Pipperday family to ask a favor regarding you and your future."

"Mindia's family? Why?"

"Because Mindia's mother and your mother were the best of friends, and because despite my claim on your time, you and Mindia have somehow managed to be friends. At least that is how it appears when you see each other at church on Sundays."

"Yes, she's my friend." *My only one*, but she didn't see fit to add that, either. Arguing with her father was always polite, quite in contrast with the traditional sense of the word. The procedure was also familiar—they would voice their concerns then work out common ground. The last time they'd argued had been over letting her serve at the hospital with him. When he told her even the impoverished patients being treated there instead of in the comforts of home didn't trust a woman to do the job, she'd convinced him the only way to change such an attitude was to prove herself. Going there on a regular basis, even as little more than a nurse, was the only way to solve the problem. That argument was still ongoing.

This discussion, however, had something new: he'd acted before consulting her, before the actual argument had even taken place.

"What have you asked of the Pipperdays?"

He paused, showing a caution that equaled her own. "I've asked them to take you in for the summer. A condensed course, if you will, in all Mindia's training as a lady. You're a quick learner, my dear, so that should be plenty of time to—"

"Put myself on the marriage market!" she finished, aghast.

"Well, I wasn't going to put it quite that way, but yes, that does express the actual goal."

"How could you?"

Those concerned, ever-so-friendly brows rose in surprise. Raising one's voice was rarely part of any of their arguments.

"Abigail." There was a gentle warning in his tone. "I'll not go to my grave having done you the greatest disservice, that of keeping you from a life of your own."

"I *have* a life of my own! I have far more freedom than a hundred Mindias and enjoy doing something important with it."

"But when I'm gone, who will keep you company? Who will share your breakfast table, your home—your heart? And who will give you children, the greatest joy of my life?"

She stood, rounding the table to reach her father's side. Taking his hands in hers, she kissed one, whispering, "I'll get to that in my own time, Father. I promise you the minute I feel lonely, I'll do as you say and learn to be a society lady. But right now I'm just too busy."

He stood, too, turning his hands to engulf hers. "I'm sorry, my dear. I am putting my foot down. Mindia will be here tomorrow morning, and Lizzie is already upstairs packing for you."

"But. . . But I have a number of visits in the neighborhood today *and* tomorrow. What about Mrs. Erdmann? Her baby is due any day now."

"If she wants you as her midwife badly enough"—he chuckled—"then she ought to have that baby within the next twenty-four hours. Because after that, my dear, you will be enrolled in the Mindia Pipperday private summertime course for one not-so-very-young lady. By the end of summer, with luck and God's blessing, you ought to already have a particular husband in mind."

Chapter Two

On a Sailing Ship Leaving the West Indies

Calvin Tallery watched the whitecaps of the Sea of Antilles dance between him and the coast of Saint Kitt's. The island's black, jagged rocks shouldn't beckon anyone to its shore, such an unfriendly guard to the verdant green hills and lush mountains barely visible in the mist. Even now the screech of a coot balanced on one of the crags seemed to say, "Be off! Be off with you!"

Soon the island before him would be a memory. Nothing held him here any-more, now that Charles, his mentor and teacher, his friend, had gone the way of so many before him. Cal would miss the man whose heart was far larger than his own had ever been. Other than him, Cal would miss little else from this place with its wars and riots, fires and floods, hurricanes and earthquakes.

Still, part of Cal would remain amid the hidden pristine harbors and coral reefs, cavorting with the turtles and dolphins and whales, and on land with the island's improbable population of monkeys. But he would not let himself care.

He turned from the sight before it disappeared, even though he knew it would be the last time he'd set eyes on the place.

"Goin' home, boy?"

Cal turned to see a sailor standing nearby. He wasn't looking at the vista; he seemed to have stopped whatever he'd been doing with the heavy coil of rope dangling from his shoulder to address Cal instead. The man was far older than most sailors, his tanned skin thick and leathery, white whiskers sprouting in uneven patches along a jawline that, despite his wiry form, now sagged.

"Yes." Cal had no wish to extend the conversation, so he left it at that.

"Good to have a home," the sailor said then shifted the rope and went on about his job.

Cal watched him, wondering at the odd exchange. The sailor's words had been few, but somehow they brought comfort. It *was* good to have a home.

He was leaving sooner than he'd expected, but it would still take nearly three weeks to get to New York, even on such a sleek frigate as this. He preferred not to take a larger British or French vessel. Although that might promise a more comfort-able passage, the two nations were picking at one another again. It wouldn't do to get caught in a battle or stalled by privateers from one side or the other.

New York City likely offered as many woes as the ones Cal was leaving behind in Saint Kitts, but at least it offered a deep sense of familiarity. His family was gone: his father and older brothers lost in the war, his mother having followed by sheer will and pneumonia that set in the first winter after the war. But he still had a variety of cousins left in New York, one of whom was caring for the home Cal had left behind when he'd gone to Edinburgh to study medicine.

America didn't pretend to be the kind of paradise Eden might once have been, the way all these islands did with their sparkling beaches and flowers and birds and sun. All of the sins and blemishes in America were as blatant as the freedom it offered. So long as a person arrived in freedom, America didn't promise anything more than what could be earned.

A peaceful home and the chance to heal others: that was all Cal wanted now.

It was hard for Abigail not to blame Mindia for this sudden, unwanted turn in life. After all, if Mindia hadn't been so chatty with Father last Sunday and invited them to her family's country estate on the Hudson, Father might never have pondered sending Abigail there.

It was, however, impossible to be angry with Mindia Pipperday. If Abigail had a thousand friends instead of only one, Mindia would still be her dearest. She was two years younger than Abigail, and kind and clever and pretty, too. It was no surprise she'd been proposed to four times since her parents had introduced her to New York's elite last year. Indecisiveness was one of Mindia's few flaws: She'd confessed to Abigail that whenever she was with a young man, she was sure it was he whom she should marry. Until a half hour later, when enjoying the company of another young man...

"I think it's positively magnificent that your father insisted you come, Abigail," said Mindia as they sipped lemon tea on Mindia's terrace.

"Magnificent, Mindia? A sunset is magnificent, a work of art, a symphony. What my father did by banishing me is—well, it's nearly unforgivable."

Mindia put on an exaggerated pout. "Thank you so very much for categorizing your visit here as banishment." Then her pout disappeared in favor of one of her familiarly dazzling smiles. "Darling girl, I'll tell you what is magnificent about your father's action. He cannot talk to anyone five minutes without admitting how much he depends on your help. With your patients in the neighborhood, in his medicine room, or even at the hospital. You are, by his own admission, an extension of what he hopes to accomplish on any given day. Do you not see what a sacrifice it is for him to give you up for an entire summer? Since when is love not simply magnificent?"

Abigail rolled her eyes. Another flaw of Mindia's was her penchant for embellishment. "Please let me hold on to my anger just a little bit longer. It's the way he's gone about it, sending me here without considering my objections. I'd have gotten round to socializing in my own good time."

Abigail had barely finished the last word before Mindia laughed in a most unladylike manner, loud and guffawish. She reached across the table and grabbed one of Abigail's hands. "Don't you realize *this* is the life your mother expected her daughter to have? Her mother, your grandmother, would have been appalled that you never received proper training. I heard my mother say so."

Had Mother lived, Abigail's life would have been far different; she knew that. She didn't want to call being motherless a benefit, since she no doubt would have loved her mother. Father said she'd been the most wonderful woman in New York, and he'd always been grateful she'd let him marry her—a humble doctor marrying the daughter of a wealthy shipping magnate. That didn't happen every day, he'd said.

But Mother, and her parents, too, were long since gone, having left Abigail, her brothers, and her father with enough money to live like the Pipperdays. Instead, all of them went Father's way: practicing medicine, living comfortably but simply.

Why was she the only one to be thrust into a way of life not of her choosing?

"It's just that I'm not comfortable with the kind of society my mother must have enjoyed. I've never been part of it."

After letting go of Abigail's hand, Mindia patted it. "In three weeks we return to New York, and our house will be teeming with guests for our Independence Day gala. That gives us—me, you, my lady's maid, and my dressmaker—three weeks in which to transform you from a first-rate physician to a first-rate lady. In fact, we might as well start right now, since we're approaching the task several years behind schedule."

She grabbed Abigail's hand again, running a thumb over her knuckles. Even Abigail had to admit they were rough and red, not smooth and white like Mindia's. But following her father's habit to wash them often demanded a price.

"Come with me."

Abigail had little choice but to obey, since Mindia still held her rough hand captive. Upstairs in Mindia's room, her friend introduced her to a new sort of medicine, even though many were of the botanical variety she and Father preferred. But these offered remedies she'd never considered: scented lotions for her skin, cool cucumbers for her eyes, flower fragrances for her pulse points, the right kind of oils for her hair. By bedtime, Abigail was afraid she would slip right out of the satiny bedsheets and land in a heap on the floor.

Chapter Three

For three exhausting weeks, Abigail succumbed to every beautification ritual tried or rumored from various schools and society clubs to which Mindia Pipperday belonged. Abigail suffered egg whites painted on her face at night, rather enjoyed the added herbs to her bathwater, but drew the limit at the extravagant wastefulness of milk baths. She giggled with Mindia over remedies they found in an ancient book from her mother's library on Egyptian beauty secrets. The use of crocodile or nightingale dung made them both erupt into fits of laughter that would likely have invited censure had Mindia's so-called school for ladies been real.

In spite of Mindia's happy company, Abigail missed her father. She found the pain of separation that much sharper whenever an opportunity to carry on the work she'd learned from him presented itself. A stable boy fell and broke his arm, something Abigail set before any other help could be summoned. Cook's assistant burned a finger, and Abigail used one of Mindia's beauty ointments in a far more practical manner, having noticed it smelled much like the salve she'd left behind in the city.

Unexpectedly, dancing turned out to be Abigail's favorite subject. Accompanied by Mrs. Pipperday at the pianoforte and one rather shy but skilled fiddler from the village, Mindia proved herself an admirable instructor. While the minuet was complicated but almost conquerable, Abigail found the contra dance outright fun. She was fairly exhausted by the end of each day but every morning woke so invigorated that she wondered if the fresh country air, regular meals, and unprecedented exercise weren't the best prescription for good health.

Seeing Mindia interact with her mother sharpened an ache Abigail had long tried to ignore, stirring thoughts of a mother she'd never known but somehow always missed. Yet it was hard to long for one kind of life if it meant giving up the other.

She used to think of the marriage market as frivolous and of little benefit to women. But Mindia and her mother talked of marriage as more than just the fruition of flirtation, more than the fulfillment of a little girl's wedding-day dreams. They were alliances for a stronger future, the fabric of this new American life where generations to come would be nurtured and taught and equipped to meet challenges everyone faced; and to raise up the next crop of children to carry on under a government far less authoritarian than any other before it.

"Mindia," said Abigail on a stroll along the river, "you and your mother have opened my eyes to so much. But you know, don't you, that for me to find a husband who would put up with me working with my father, carrying on after he's gone, is a nearly insurmountable task?"

"All you need is to be so irresistible that potential husbands will agree to your stipulations. It's what you'll demand of yourself that I see as the biggest challenge, not finding a man who will 'put up with you,' as you say."

Abigail sighed. "If all you've taught me these last weeks doesn't help me to succeed, then I'll just find a way to convince my father marriage isn't for me. The future of America will be fine in the hands of women like you."

Mindia laughed. "Be the coquette I taught you to be, and you'll have men lining up with proposals in hand. They'll happily accept your aspirations, just wait and see!"

After three weeks away, Abigail returned home—just a few days before her first Independence Day ball. Father was as glad to see Abigail as she was to see him, until, after dinner, a familiar, concerned light reappeared in his eyes.

"You know, don't you, darling," he began tentatively, "that it's best for you to continue staying with the Pipperdays? Even here, back in the city?"

She'd half expected this, since Mindia hinted her mother's understanding was that Abigail was to be their guest for the *entire* summer. But Abigail had hoped her father would be so happy to see her he'd have changed his mind.

"You haven't discovered you can do without me, have you?" she asked.

His gentle laugh warmed her heart; she'd pined for it these past weeks. "I do miss you, of course. But this is for your own good. How can you attend a ball unescorted? You know I cannot accompany you, at least not regularly. At the Pipperdays', you'll be one of the family, escorted as Mindia will be."

Abigail tilted her head to regard her father. He'd avoided looking in her eyes before speaking, but now, seeing her study him, he returned her gaze in earnest. In that moment, she believed what Mindia had said all those days ago, that her father was sacrificing more than she knew. *"Magnificent,"* she'd called it.

Well, maybe so.

"I'll find a husband, Father, if it'll please you. But only if he'll let me work at your side."

"Now, Abigail, no sense putting limits on your choices. You must follow your heart where it leads. Perhaps you'll find marriage will keep you busy enough without working all day."

"I am following my heart by only considering a marriage that will allow me to carry on at your side." She dabbed the corner of her mouth with her napkin. "Tomorrow night is my first test, a smaller soiree at the home of a Pipperday acquaintance, as practice for the larger Independence Day ball the night after. You will accompany me tomorrow night, won't you?" She didn't dare ask him to attend the Pipperday gala on the night when their medicine room fairly bustled with emergencies every Fourth of July.

He nodded. "Yes, darling. Tomorrow night, no matter what, I'll fill the role that I should have before now."

Just inside his old front door, Cal dropped the seabag he'd carried from the Battery Park docks. He placed his small medical satchel on top. He'd hadn't brought much with him from the tropics, leaving behind many of his books, most of his equipment, even some of the light-weave clothing so well suited to hot weather. The man who'd taken his place would have far more need of all that than Cal would; whatever Cal required he could replace easily enough here in New York.

He hadn't bothered to knock—this was, after all, his home. He was only a little surprised to find the front door unlocked. Back when he'd lived here, just after the war ended and the Brits had been cast out from their occupation of the city, he'd heard his mother say she was weary of hiding behind locked doors. Perhaps his cousin had carried on with his mother's sentiments.

Noise of his arrival did, however, summon a butler. Not the one Cal remembered, but the man could only be a servant based upon his manner of dress.

"I beg your pardon?" the man inquired, looking not exactly alarmed, but wary.

"I'm Calvin Tallery," he announced. "Owner of this home. Is my cousin here? Early Goodwin?"

"Mr. Goodwin is not at home, sir. He's on commission at the home of Mr. and Mrs. Pierpont."

Cal lifted a brow. "Is he now? So he's gained success with his art, then, since I've last been home?"

The butler's gaze shifted away, and he smoothed a lapel that needed no attention. "I shall let you be the judge of that, sir, according to Mr. Goodwin's account of himself. Now, is there any way I can be of assistance to you? My name is Hogarth, and I've been in Mr. Goodwin's—er, should I say, *your*—employ for two years now."

"I'd like a bath in my room, the clothes in this satchel laundered—all but the linen shirt and gray trousers, which I will wear after my bath. Also, have Mrs. Downing send up something for me to eat. She is still here, I hope?"

"Oh, yes sir. I'm sure she'll be pleased at your return."

Cal was three steps up when it occurred to him he might need to know another thing or two.

"Cousin Early—that is, Mr. Goodwin—which bedchamber is he using?"

"The master's suite, sir. He finds the light pleasing for his painting."

Just as well. Cal wouldn't have taken his parents' bedroom anyway. Still, it would be hard to return to the room he'd shared with his two brothers, knowing he'd never have their company again this side of heaven.

"You're positively the most beautiful girl in attendance tonight."

Her father's words couldn't be true, but he'd always had a way of convincing Abigail he was sincere. That was enough for a cloud to slip under her feet so she practically floated into the room, just behind Mindia and her parents.

By the fourth dance of the ball at the home of a Pipperday associate, Abigail forgot to worry about steps still new to her. Mindia was right; movement came naturally if she listened to the music. During the course of the evening, she discovered a part of her she never knew existed: one who knew to laugh at just the right times, who could send the blood rushing to an attentive gentleman's cheeks with the bat of her eye, who could feign feminine weakness to sit out a minuet in favor of light-hearted conversation or refreshment.

Before the midnight supper was served, Mindia pronounced to Father that Abigail wasn't only a success, she was a much finer pupil than Mindia herself had ever been. She cast Abigail an excitedly conspiratorial wink.

"You're the talk of the night! Everyone is impressed and intrigued. What a perfect prelude to our Independence Day gala tomorrow where we introduce you to all of our friends!"

Abigail was almost looking forward to it, if she didn't let herself ponder the possibility of failing to catch a husband—that was, after all, the whole idea. What a waste of time this summer would prove to be if she failed! Even if this party was more enjoyable than expected and dancing fun, she couldn't help but think how busy her father must be without her.

Mindia must have sensed her wandering attention, because she tapped Abigail's wrist with her fan. Then she leaned closer to whisper, "I can name three gentlemen who will likely ask for your hand before the end of this year."

Abigail followed Mindia's gaze. She saw three men in the vicinity, each of whom she'd danced with at least once. Reginald Marks, Ordell Lebsock, and Montague Barteau.

"Montague Barteau!" she fairly hissed. "He can't tear his gaze from a lady's form to speak to a woman eye-to-eye."

Mindia flipped open her fan to hide a giggle, no doubt hoping no one heard their whispers. "Not him, silly. There is Reginald, Ordell, and DeWitt Henshaw. He's a bit old, but that could work in your favor. He'll likely be so grateful for your hand he'd let you spend your days as you wish."

Abigail sighed. Marriage to any one of the three didn't make her heart so much as flutter. Wasn't there supposed to be some of that when it came to marriage? According to Mindia, a heart could flutter faster than any fan could cool her. Oh, to feel that way, at least once, as if her heart had wings. . .

Yet Mindia might be right about her choices. For being so indecisive, she was being surprisingly sensible on Abigail's behalf.

"What about you, Miss Fickle?" she asked Mindia. "Many young men here tonight would ask for your hand if you winked their way, including the three you seem to want to share with me."

Mindia gave a swift, feminine shrug—a movement that vanished quickly enough to avoid the attention of her mother, who stood nearby with Abigail's father. "I have plenty of time," she said. "My father hasn't set a deadline, after all. Besides, you have more stipulations than I do. Your marriage will be fairly unconventional. That means one thing: you must choose someone who will fall so madly, *hopelessly* in love with you that he won't hesitate to let you do as you please."

Now it was Abigail's turn to use her fan to hide a barely suppressed chortle. "That should be easy!"

Mindia narrowed her eyes. "I'm not jesting, Abigail. Don't doubt yourself. Finding a man who won't keep you too close to home is no laughing matter."

"And it's likely not a realistic matter, either," she said. "Where am I to find such a generous husband?"

Mindia closed her fan then grinned. "Not to worry, my dear. This is only the first of many parties for you. Wait until tomorrow night! We've only begun."

That evening, bathed, shaved, fed, and with his legs becoming more accustomed to New York's terra firma, Cal sat at the writing desk in the parlor. He composed a note to Dr. Daniel Van de Klerk, letting him know of his arrival and that he would be available to work with him as soon as possible. Cal had never been one to put off working.

Just as he was sealing the folded note, the door opened, and a familiar voice called from the foyer.

"Hogarth!"

The summons was followed by the sound of various items falling to the floor.

Cal stood, walking slowly to the archway that separated foyer from parlor. "Good evening, Early."

His cousin, rubbing a hand through his untethered, shoulder-length hair, stood behind the mess he'd just made—a toppled easel, dry pallet, a box of pig bladders inflated with various colors of oil paint, and a sprawling number of paintbrushes mimicking a game of pick-up sticks. He stilled abruptly then gazed at Cal with wonder before bursting into a smile and hopping over the heap to simultaneously grab Cal's hand and thud his shoulder.

"Welcome home, Cal! Your letter said not to expect you until August, but by thunder, here you are and July's barely begun. It's good to see you."

Cal couldn't help but smile, an exercise of facial muscles he hadn't used in quite some time. But Early always dispelled frowns from anybody standing inside his radius. Just then Hogarth appeared, gathering the abandoned goods as he spoke.

"I see you've reunited with your cousin, sir," he said. "I'm glad to see it's a happy occasion. We've held dinner, which can be served whenever you're ready."

Cal found himself already hungry again, even though he'd lunched so late, and Early patted his flat stomach and pronounced himself famished.

"We can talk about what you've been doing these past few years, cousin, all about your island adventures. And I'll tell you how things are here. Then—most importantly—we'll make plans for you to attend a few parties with me."

"I haven't suitable clothing," Cal protested. The last thing he wanted was to impose dancing on his barely regained footing. "Besides, I'll be working again as soon as possible."

"Yes, we're all working, aren't we?" Early said, draping a comfortable arm about Cal's shoulders. "But in between we'll surely have fun. Don't worry about what to wear. If we can't find what you need at the shops tomorrow, you can borrow what you need from me. It's the least I can do. Starting tomorrow night, I'll introduce you back into society."

"I came home to work, not to be caught up in all that."

"Ha! No wonder you've remained a bachelor so long. You're a year or two older than I am, and at twenty-five I'm considered quite the catch. Well," he added with a wink, "only by those foolish enough to think my artwork allows me to live here, but you won't spoil that secret, will you? Come on now. You can't live in New York and not socialize. It's against every law of polite society."

Cal felt another smile coming on, if only half of one. Attending a society ball was the last thing he wanted to do, but if he remembered his cousin's ways, Early wouldn't take no for an answer.

Chapter Four

On the night of the Pipperday Independence Day gala, the ballroom on the second floor of their spacious city home was alight with candelabra and chandeliers. Silks and satins shimmered, ivory fans swished, intricately coiled hair—some undoubtedly enhanced by wigs and hairpieces—glimmered with strategically placed combs winking with gems. The men, with their dark, close-fitting trousers, crisp cutaways, and white cravats were a subtle contrast to the bejeweled women.

A tinge of uncertainty surged inside Abigail as the room rapidly filled. On previous Independence Days, she'd worked with Father. Boys and gunpowder never failed to produce mayhem. She was sorely tempted to join him, and she might have if she didn't believe both her father and Mindia would have a fit.

So she swallowed her disappointment, determined to appear as carefree and lighthearted as Mindia. How could she not, considering she'd been practically adopted by the Pipperdays? She would stand in the welcome line as if one of the family.

All three of the men Mindia had picked out for Abigail from the night before arrived among the first guests. One offered the longest kiss to her hand, another the promise of as many dances as she would spare, the third a request to sit beside her at dinner. And so, eyelashes fluttering, smile quivering, fan engaged, Abigail played the role of society coquette just the way Mindia had taught her. If she could perform it successfully, if she could convince someone she'd be the perfect society wife, then she would, at last, be allowed to set it aside for the woman she wanted to be.

Cal followed Early up the wide staircase to the ballroom on the second floor of the Pipperday home. He'd never been here before, not even for a ball during the year he had in New York society prior to taking up his medical studies in Edinburgh. He hadn't gone to many such functions, despite his age and his family's place in society, which had been earned by his father's military rank and sacrifice, along with that of Cal's two older brothers. Back then society hadn't been very festive; it hadn't yet recovered from the war.

Tonight's celebration of the fledging nation's eventual victory wasn't enough to lift his spirits. Coming home to an empty house—empty, at least, of his own immediate family—had been harder than he'd expected.

The pain of losing his brothers should have scarred over by now, but somehow these years of struggle to heal his patients, who too often died, had kept the wound open. Losing his mother, then his mentor Charles to a fever had been the match in the powder keg that blew whatever remained of his heart to pieces.

"There she is," said Early once they reached the ballroom. Cal followed his cousin's gaze toward the host and hostess line in the grandly lit room. An older couple, perhaps only a bit younger than his parents would have been, welcomed their guests. At their side, however, was not one lovely young woman, but two. Early had said he wouldn't have missed tonight for anything, the reason being the young Pipperday girl. He hadn't mentioned she had a sister.

"Which one?" he asked, with an equally quiet voice. Probably the one in yellow. They were both pretty, both greeting their guests with youthful enthusiasm, but the one in yellow had something about her that would have caught his own eye if she wasn't already in Early's sights. Her dark blond hair was swept up fashionably, but she had a sense of maturity the one in pink lacked. She offered her hand gracefully to the gentleman being introduced to her, with a more level gaze and slower smile— even when the younger man being introduced held her hand too long.

"The one in pink. That's Mindia. I don't know the other girl. Mindia doesn't have a sister. Let's go find out, shall we?"

Surprised at the answer, Cal's breath unexpectedly caught. But then, in the time it took to cross the room he reminded himself he wasn't interested in laying bare his heart again, just to have someone taken from him. He was even less interested in the kind of girl Early had described Mindia Pipperday to be: happy, frivolous, talkative, and a lover of society galas like this. Such a person would bore Cal before the evening was out. Even on Saint Kitts, women were expected only to build up the ego of the men they supposedly loved. Well, Cal didn't need such a shallow relationship as that.

Someday, if he ever did risk getting married, it would be to a woman who involved herself in more than the simple parlor games too often enjoyed during an evening like this.

"Ah, Mr. Goodwin," said Mr. Pipperday to Early, "so good of you to join us tonight. I trust you remember my wife?"

The lady nodded somewhat regally in his direction; then her gaze traveled to Cal quizzically.

"This is my cousin," Early answered the unspoken question, "recently returned from the tropics, where he's been serving as surgeon and physician. Dr. Calvin Tallery."

Was it his imagination, or had a gasp come from one of the two girls at Mrs. Pipperday's side? But he wouldn't let his gaze go there, not until he was properly introduced. He may have been a novice at society parties when he left, but his Edinburgh education hadn't been strictly in medicine.

"Mr. Goodwin, Dr. Tallery, may I present to you my daughter, Mindia, and her very good friend Miss Abigail Van de Klerk."

Now it was Cal's turn to gasp, and he nearly did, though he caught it before any sound emitted. Van de Klerk! Surely she was related somehow to Dr. Daniel Van de Klerk. As Mindia Pipperday offered a slight curtsy, he kissed the back of her hand but finally let his gaze travel to the woman at her side.

"I hope you will both spare a dance for us tonight," Early said, lingering a moment or two longer than necessary in the receiving line.

"Of course we shall!" Mindia Pipperday responded, following with a little giggle that instantly grated on Cal's senses. Giggles and batting eyelashes! Part of the silliness he hadn't missed. "We must make a pledge immediately to ensure no set is played without us. I insist! You agree, do you not, Mr. Goodwin?"

"I do indeed!"

When it was Cal's turn to bow to Miss Van de Klerk's curtsy then accept her hand, he was dismayed to see her flutter her lashes in a mirror display of Miss Pipperday's.

"I believe you're acquainted with my father," she said to him in a demure, almost teasing tone that hardly matched the reasonable words. "Dr. Daniel Van de Klerk?"

Her father! By his absence in the receiving line, he guessed the man mustn't be present. Obviously he wasted no time at parties. When, exactly, had she the time to discuss her father's acquaintances if she spent her time at functions like this? Instead of asking, he said, "I know him only by letter, and most recently by an exchange of notes. I hope to meet him as soon as tomorrow."

"He will be most happy to meet you in person, I'm sure," she said, then another bat of the eyes.

"No more so than I," he murmured, grateful for the line of newcomers still behind them cutting short any further opportunity to talk. He and Early walked on.

"Well?" Early elbowed Cal once they'd joined the gathering crowd filling the ballroom. "Glad you came, then? You already know one of the two prettiest girls here!"

"I don't know her at all."

"You know her name, and that's the same thing." He let his gaze travel back to the two girls. "I heard she made quite an impression just last night. My friend Reginald couldn't stop talking about her today. If you set your cap for her, you'll have some competition. But then, it sounds like you can work your way into her good graces through her father, so you'll have an advantage there."

"Who said anything about setting my cap for her? I'll be working with her father, not socializing with him. I doubt anything from either of our personal lives will come up."

At least, that was how he planned for things to go. He'd let Charles become a surrogate father to him, and look how that had ended. No sir, he had no intention of getting close to anyone these days. Neither Van de Klerk nor his daughter.

No matter how pretty she was, she was still just a silly girl who likely hadn't a serious thought in her head.

"I'm going to ask Mother if we can be excused from the line," Mindia whispered to Abigail. "Look, the mayor is taking his place by the orchestra. He'll start the ball soon by reading the Declaration of Independence, and then the dancing begins. I refuse to miss a single moment!"

Abigail nodded, but her attention had left the incoming string of guests several minutes earlier anyway, between spotting something oddly charged in Mindia and, more so than that, meeting Dr. Tallery.

While Mindia turned to her mother, Abigail's gaze floated again to the handsome doctor. She tried recalling every bit of information her father had shared. He'd been trained in Edinburgh, hadn't he? Where he'd heard about Father's friend Charles Woodridge, working in the tropics. Dr. Tallery had gone straight from university to Dr. Woodridge and had been there ever since.

And now he was interested in working with Father. *Goodness, he's fine looking.*

She caught her breath when she thought he was looking her way. A flutter! A real, honest-to-goodness heart flutter!

Whether she was merely succumbing to Mindia's prediction or whether this reaction was truly unique and worthy of further consideration, she had no idea. But she did look forward to dancing with him.

While the mayor called for everyone's attention, Abigail brought up the other matter on her mind. "Is it my imagination, Mindia, or has someone entered this room tonight who ignited something in you not previously lit?"

Mindia sucked in a breath, looking at once both horrified and pleased. "So I can't hide it!" No sooner had she uttered the words than she turned her back to her mother, who couldn't possibly hear anyway from where she stood. "It's Early Goodwin. Isn't he the most delightful man you've ever seen?"

Abigail knew exactly where to find him, since he was still accompanied by the doctor. "I suppose he's charming," she said. "But you've said so about any number of others. Is he different?"

"Well, for one thing, Mother doesn't approve of him. Only because he's an artist! You'd think that would make him more intriguing, wouldn't you? Why, his artwork could make his name practically immortal!"

"But your mother doesn't think so?"

Mindia shook her head. "He wouldn't be here at all except I convinced Father to invite him. So I intend to make the most of my time with him. And you, my dear,"—she pointed her closed fan at Abigail—"ought to do the same with the handsome doctor. In fact, I aim to make such a thing happen." Winking, she added, "Just leave it to me."

And so Abigail followed Mindia, letting commence more eyelash batting along with sugary words to pink not only her own cheeks but also the nearby gentleman's as well. She laughed, fanned, fawned, and flirted, and danced without reservation the steps she'd only just learned. All the while she hoped for an audience with Dr. Tallery, for him to be struck by her performance as a society coquette, and for him to ask permission to dance, perhaps even a contra dance. There was always time to exchange a few pleasantries during those steps.

But though she never lacked a dance consort, not one of them was Dr. Calvin Tallery. He neither sought her company nor asked her to dance.

Just when she believed Mindia had thoroughly forgotten her promise of help, Mindia approached with not only the attentive Mr. Goodwin trailing her, but the young doctor as well. Abigail had just excused herself from a contra dance, intent upon finding a spot near an open window for a breath of fresh air. Mr. Goodwin had two glasses of punch in his hand. One he handed to Mindia and the other to Abigail, which she gratefully accepted.

"Miss Pipperday has just told us you've been spending the summer with her family," said Mr. Goodwin. "I'm surprised we haven't had the pleasure of your company before tonight."

Abigail exchanged a cautious glance with Mindia. "Other obligations have kept me busy until recently."

She couldn't help but notice one of Dr. Tallery's brows rose, but whether it was from curiosity or skepticism she couldn't tell.

"Miss Van de Klerk is my dearest friend!" Mindia proclaimed. "We share everything from a love of poetry to our great passion for reading. Isn't that right, Abigail?"

She knew better than to admit her favorite reading material was Dr. Mitchill's periodical, the *Medical Repository*, even if it might interest Dr. Tallery. That was just the sort of thing she'd been told to keep hidden. Still, she nodded and could honestly add, "We were alternately thrilled and scandalized over *Charlotte Temple* recently."

Mindia immediately giggled with the confession of having read such a novel, and Abigail couldn't help but laugh with her. Mindia's giddiness was so contagious even Mr. Goodwin joined in.

"We ought not laugh," said Mindia upon catching her breath, "since Mother approved of the novel because of the warnings it contains, but goodness! It spelt so very clearly how a young girl can be swept away by a dashing young man."

Then she cast a slow blink Mr. Goodwin's way, and he blushed a deep shade of scarlet.

"Isn't this evening the most fun?" Mindia went on, setting aside her empty punch glass on a nearby table to free both hands as she boldly looped her arm with Mr. Goodwin's. "Father has arranged for a troupe of actors to perform the last act of *Bunker Hill*, right outside in our garden. We can sit together on the veranda for the best viewing. Shall we?"

Mindia chatted all the way to the edge of the ballroom and down the hall, while Abigail dared only a furtive glance in Dr. Tallery's direction. He looked straight ahead, as if not even aware of her company. Everything Mindia taught her about engaging in playful conversation came to mind, something she hadn't had much trouble practicing all evening. Somehow the task wasn't as easy with someone as distant as Dr. Tallery. Nonetheless, she persevered. *Express extreme interest, as if any and every aspect of their life is fascinating.* Such were the instructions that came to mind as they followed the hall out to the upper verandah of the house.

Why was it so difficult to think of a suitable question? Personal, but not private. Interesting, but not complicated. Elegant, but not simple. If only she could ask him about his work! Or how certain treatments might differ in the islands compared to here in New York. "I trust your voyage from the tropics was pleasant?" she said at last.

He glanced her way for the first time, as if reminded she was there. "Uneventful."

"Ah! The most enjoyable kind of transportation, then," she said, adding her mimic of the little laugh Mindia promised was music to a potential beau's ear. Abigail wanted to follow with reference to her father's work but held back. How many times had Mindia said a man's ego simply wouldn't tolerate a woman speaking of anything serious? So she said, "Will you miss the islands, Dr. Tallery? I've never traveled from our own shores, of course,"—she added a shy tone to her words and batted her eyes over the rim of her fluttering fan—"but there are wonderful poems about the beauty of such places."

He did not speak, as if walking took every bit of his concentration. Finally, when they approached the double doors leading to their destination, he said, "The islands are filled with savagery, Miss Van de Klerk. From the constant threats between the British and French to the daily horrors of slavery practiced in the sugar fields. Besides those tensions, disease and death are rampant."

He looked at her as if daring her to try brightening his mood and showing not the least bit of regret over his morose recounting of a place she'd heard offered only goodness and beauty. Though his words should have shocked and dismayed her into silence, they did not. "I wonder," she whispered as they paused near the chairs

Mindia had led them to, "if your profession hasn't gotten the best of you. Perhaps, Dr. Tallery, you ought to try recalling something lovely in your memories of that place. For the good of those around you, of course, if not for your own."

If Mindia had heard her scolding the man, she would have been horrified. But Abigail lifted her chin, every bit as confident as him. After she took the seat Mindia indicated, they hadn't any more time to exchange conversation as the performance started below.

Cal barely watched the reenactment of battle being waged beneath the balcony. He didn't care to watch a rendition of something that took so many lives: his father's, his brothers'.

He gave up his seat as others filed in behind them, so he could stand in the shadows. He'd watched Miss Van de Klerk laugh, tease, and cajole her way through the night so far, proving herself as shallow as any other girl he remembered from his youth. It was easy to believe she was Mindia Pipperday's dearest friend. The two had profiles lovely enough to mint on a coin, but obviously possessed as little depth. How could a doctor Charles had held in such high esteem have raised a daughter so flighty that she was incapable of expressing a single well-composed thought?

For the rest of the evening, Abigail did her best to ignore thoughts of Dr. Tallery. Yet her gaze sought him anyway. She shouldn't be so sensitive to his obvious dislike, since it appeared he didn't enjoy anyone's company with the possible exception of the cousin with whom he'd arrived.

She consoled her wounded pride by convincing herself he acted as one who did not want to be present in a room filled with gaiety and dancing. Perhaps he didn't like festivities; more likely, he did not know how to dance. She ought to at least pity him there, since she was so recently proficient at it herself. But her speculations died when he asked Mindia's mother to accompany him for one of the more complicated minuets. It took less than a few, heart-dipping moments for him to prove himself first rate in the dance department. That confirmed the worst. He hadn't asked Abigail to dance because he simply hadn't wanted to.

Long after the ball ended, Abigail lay awake in her borrowed Pipperday bedchamber. Mindia's artist couldn't have pried himself from her company, a fact that emphasized Abigail's failure to catch Dr. Tallery's attention. He'd snubbed her with his harsh description of the islands, saying things no lady ought to hear. Even if his heart was otherwise engaged—something she hadn't considered earlier, since he'd arrived with Mr. Goodwin—surely he might have been interested in asking her about her father, at least?

Still, of all the men Mindia had introduced to her, he'd been the only one to inspire such a stirring reaction. Should she give up after only one attempt to get to know him? There was, after all, another way to insert herself into his company. All she had to do was go home.

If only Father would let her!

Chapter Five

Cal didn't rise as early as was his habit; instead, he was grateful for an afternoon appointment with Dr. Van de Klerk, which allowed him to enjoy a leisurely morning. But to Cal's surprise, Early was in the dining room when he entered for the breakfast he'd ordered served at ten rather than eight.

Cal hadn't expected to see Early at all that morning, especially after the late-night party. "Working early today?" Cal resurrected an old tease from their childhood to add, "Or should I say: Early's early today?"

His cousin lifted a brow. "Good to see your sense of humor hasn't completely disappeared. After last night, I was beginning to wonder."

"Why? It was a very nice party."

"I know *I* enjoyed it. I believe everyone did, with the possible exception of you—who deigned to dance only once, the obligatory minuet with your hostess. If I hadn't talked about Miss Pipperday all the way back here, I assume you'd have been as quiet then as you were during the rest of the evening. What's wrong with you, Cal? Have you completely turned off the spigot of fun in your life?"

He felt compelled to protest, knowing the accusation was laced with reproach. The words seemed to echo the criticism he'd heard in the reprimand from Miss Van de Klerk, as if she'd had some insight into why he'd spoken so dolefully about the islands. Surely neither she nor Early had so quickly discovered the truth: Cal was miserable and wasn't at all sure what to do about it—except to fill his days with so much work he would fall asleep exhausted. Such a routine would leave neither time nor energy to contemplate anything except the tasks before him.

He offered a grim smile. "I haven't gotten back into city living yet, cousin. Once I establish the rhythm of working again, I'll be a veritable merry-andrew."

Not surprisingly, Early snorted. "I'll believe that when I see it. You missed an opportunity last night, and I don't understand why."

"What opportunity?"

"Why must I spell it out? With the Van de Klerk girl! Didn't you find her beautiful?"

No reason to lie about that, not to an artist with an eye for such things. "Yes."

"And yet you barely spoke to her, never asked her to dance."

"How could I? There was a constant parade of admirers circling her all evening."

"Ha! No less than the pack around Miss Pipperday, but that didn't stop me."

Cal waved away the topic. "All of this game playing is silly. It's not for me."

"Listen, there is much competition in courtship. It's not a game—it's hard work. If you want someone of your own choosing, you'll have to allocate time and energy, the same as any other task."

Cal's tattered heart was hardly in condition to offer anything to anyone. Who would want a heart so bruised and battered? Without admitting the face of the Van de Klerk girl had somehow made it to the recesses of his mind just before he drifted off to sleep last night, Cal changed the subject.

"Speaking of working," he said, "is that why you're up and about? Are you going back to the Pierponts' for the portrait work?"

Early looked strangely stiff for a moment as Cal took a seat, having filled his plate with ham and eggs at the sideboard. "Yes, well, about that. I shouldn't have let you believe something that's not quite true."

"You're not working?" This was also no surprise, since Cal had left the house open for his cousin's use because he was notoriously quixotic about any type of employment. Artist's flamboyancy and all that, or so Cal believed.

"Oh, I'm working. Just not doing a portrait, as you assumed."

"What, then?"

Early set down the fork he'd been about to shovel into his mouth, redirected his gaze from Cal to the plate in front of him, and then under hooded eyes said, "I'm painting the Pierpont dogs."

"What?"

"The dogs. I'm painting their pets."

For the first time in a long time, Cal felt the stir of a belly laugh. But he refrained, seeing his cousin's obvious embarrassment.

"Well, what's wrong with that?" In spite of his best effort, the words tottered on mirth. "You're being paid, aren't you?"

Early nodded, but even though he raised his gaze and started eating again, he frowned. "I've learned a thing or two about being an artist."

"I should think so, after a half dozen years at it."

"For one thing, being an artist is harder than anyone might guess. I never expected talent isn't enough. Success is like chasing a path impossible to chart. . . ." He seemed to struggle for clarity. "Like trying to grasp a will-o'-the-wisp, an ignis fatuus." He leveled his gaze at Cal. "What I've discovered is that if I want to earn a living, afford my own home, protect a family from financial insecurity, but still work at what I like doing, I'll have to take jobs I'd never dreamed of when I first discovered I wanted to be an artist."

"Painting dogs, for example?"

He nodded.

Cal sighed. "If it's any comfort, I couldn't afford to live in this house if it hadn't been left to me, along with the shipping income that still arrives to support it. Yet I've worked round the clock since I graduated from Edinburgh. It hasn't resulted in a feeling of success." Particularly when it seemed he'd lost more patients than he'd saved.

Early took up his coffee cup. "Well, we're quite a pair. Failures together, then."

Cal raised his cup to meet Early's salute. "Cousins in blood, and failures in calling."

Abigail sat beside Mindia in the Pipperday dining room. As hungry as she'd felt when she woke that morning, Mrs. Pipperday had just chased her appetite away.

"Well? Don't you agree that the new doctor in town will enhance the parties this summer?"

Despite every doubt that the doctor was even remotely interested in her company, Abigail wanted to pipe up with an enthusiastic *I do! I do!* She refrained. The question—the prodding—had obviously been aimed at Mindia. That made the note hidden in Abigail's lap, written to her father asking him if she may come home, that much riskier to send.

Her friend slid a sideways glance at Abigail. "Dr. Tallery didn't seem very inclined to dance."

"Perhaps because he felt new to our community, having been gone from New York so long." Her mother followed her statement with a wink, clarifying her hopes for him on Mindia's behalf. "He's a fine dancer, polite and well mannered, obviously intelligent. Besides, everyone remembers the sacrifices of the Tallery family: Mr. Tallery, along with his older boys. There isn't a family in town who wouldn't welcome the doctor into their fold."

"Mother," Mindia said, a hint of exasperation in her tone, "I'm sure Dr. Tallery is all you say. But do you know he'll be working with Abigail's father? I daresay Abigail and Dr. Tallery will have far more time to get to know one another than I shall."

The heat of a blush stemmed from the back of Abigail's neck and spread fully into her face, curtailing any convincing denial of her own secret hopes. She averted her gaze when she glimpsed Mrs. Pipperday's disappointment, wondering if she ought to apologize. But for what? Dr. Tallery hadn't seemed interested in either Mindia or Abigail herself.

"Dr. Tallery is cousin to Early Goodwin, Mother," Mindia went on. "Shouldn't his family be counted in the sacrifice the Tallerys made? He lost his uncle and two cousins, after all, and his oldest brother fought even if he didn't give his life, thank God."

Mrs. Pipperday placed her coffee cup back on its saucer with a bit less care than was her norm. Instead of speaking, she pursed her lips and glanced at her husband as if hoping he might join the conversation.

"Mindia," she said once it was clear Mr. Pipperday would offer no reinforcement, "your father and I will not encourage any thoughts you might entertain regarding a young man who everyone knows has nothing to his name. He lives in this neighborhood only because of the generosity of Dr. Tallery."

Mindia raised her chin. "Dr. Tallery is perfect for Abigail. Not for me."

Abigail wanted to sink under the table. Instead, she crinkled the note she and Mindia had written together. She couldn't send it now, at least not until Mrs. Pipperday sorted through the unexpected twist to her plans for Mindia.

"I agree with what you said earlier, Mindia," Abigail said softly. "Dr. Tallery's lack of interest in dancing—though he obviously possesses the talent for it—must mean he won't be pursuing anyone at the moment."

"Sadly true," Mindia said.

A hint of softening reached Mrs. Pipperday's face. "Perhaps he will once he's been home longer." Then she sighed. "I apologize, girls, if I was a bit too eager to assign the new doctor to only one of you." She exchanged a fuller smile with her husband, who looked visibly relieved the conversation hadn't degraded any further. "I have great hope for you, too, Abigail, that you might make a suitable match. Let's leave the future to be what it will, shall we?"

The meal ended, and Abigail slipped the crumpled note under her sleeve as they left the dining room. Only an ungrateful houseguest would go behind her hostess's back to assert herself into the good doctor's company.

Besides, she and Mindia hadn't exaggerated when cautioning Mrs. Pipperday's hopes that the man might choose either one of them.

They made it no farther than the front hall before a Pipperday servant approached Abigail, announcing a note had arrived from her father. With delight, Abigail tore open the sealed page then read the missive with astonishment.

She looked at Mindia with widened eyes. "I'm to go home tonight and play hostess for my father's dinner—with Dr. Tallery."

Risking her mother's wrath, Mindia offered a high-spirited clap. But Mrs. Pipperday didn't even look peeved. She threw up her palms with a smile of surrender.

That afternoon, Cal walked to the address he knew belonged to Dr. Daniel Van de Klerk, having let Early use the family carriage to go the farther distance to the Pierponts'. The Van de Klerk home was plush for a physician, standing three stories high with matching sets of mullioned windows symmetrically placed on either side of an impressively carved wooden door. Near the curb, a sign had been erected, embellished with the profile of a hand with its forefinger pointing the way to a separate entrance covered by a white awning. Below the hand was inscribed: THE MEDICINE ROOM AND OFFICE OF DR. DANIEL VAN DE KLERK AND FAMILY.

And family? Cal recalled Charles mentioning that Dr. Van de Klerk had two sons who had followed in his footsteps, but he'd been under the impression they'd started their own practices elsewhere.

Cal contemplated going to the front door but decided using the office door best suited his purpose. He was, after all, here to apply as an associate to the patient circuit Van de Klerk had established. Front doors were for social visits, and this was anything but.

The side door had a small, mullioned window embedded beneath its rounded top, but it was clouded so he couldn't see inside. He twisted the handle and, as expected, it opened easily. Inside, each long wall was skirted with chairs, all empty except for what he guessed to be a mother and child. She held a boy on her lap, gently rocking despite his being too old for such a thing.

Since neither she nor the child greeted him, Cal ignored them as he took a seat on the opposite side of the room. Before long the boy's moan drew Cal's attention; the child was deathly pale, his lips stark purple in comparison to his cottony skin. He seemed barely conscious.

"Have you been waiting long?" he asked.

She looked startled by the question, her eyes slightly widened as she looked his way for the first time. "Dr. Van de Klerk is with another patient before he leaves for his afternoon visits. He said he'd see my boy before he goes."

"How long has he been like this?"

"A day and a half. He's a healthy boy! But last night he couldn't sleep, and this morning it's worse. I don't know how to help him."

"Has he a fever?"

She nodded. "I think so."

"Stomach pain?"

"He cries out if I even try touching his stomach."

"What of blockage? Is he able to void?"

"Oh, yes! Too much! It helps ease his pain for a little while, but. . ."

"Vomiting?"

She nodded.

Cal stood, approaching them. "My name is Dr. Tallery, and I'm here to meet with Dr. Van de Klerk. Do you mind if I have a look at the boy while we're waiting?"

She looked half-grateful and half-suspicious, but gratitude won. The boy was perhaps eleven or twelve, and she shifted him between her seat and the one next to them so that the child was more accessible. She pulled open his jacket and tugged at the cotton shirt beneath.

It took only a moment to see the skinny boy's swollen abdomen, just to the right below his belly button. Cal frowned. No one looked forward to a surgical procedure, certainly not any patient, but neither did any doctor he knew, himself included. He and Charles viewed surgery as a last resort. If patients didn't die from the shock of pain, they all too often didn't survive the aftermath. But sometimes, as he believed now, it was the only choice.

"Please wait a moment, madam," he said; then without delay he went to one of the closed doors and rapped on it soundly.

Instead of it opening, he heard a call from the room opposite, nearer the woman seated with her sick child.

"In a moment, please." It was a man's voice, unperturbed and far too calm to have recognized the urgency of Cal's pounding.

Cal approached, put a hand to the knob, but refrained from intruding. "There is a boy here who suffers a swollen appendix," he called. "I believe he needs immediate attention."

"A moment," came the excruciating reply.

Silence followed, and Cal fell victim to the nature of time. Each second ticked as a minute, each minute far too slow. His hand hovered above the knob, resettled upon it as if to go in anyway; then he decided against it to retrieve the bag he never traveled without. He returned to the boy, reaching inside for the small wooden ear trumpet that he placed upon the boy's bony chest to see if his heart was strong.

A moment later Cal withdrew a small bottle of laudanum. Treating pain wasn't always popular, and he had no way of knowing how Van de Klerk viewed such a thing. But Cal would be hard pressed not to do something to ease this boy's current condition, not to mention what was to come. Cal carried doses in careful quantity, mixed with sherry wine and saffron then blended with powdered cinnamon and clove to improve the awful taste. He extracted one of the smallest vials he carried for children and, without even asking the mother, administered the elixir. Thankfully, the boy swallowed without any trouble, and Cal only hoped he'd be able to keep it down long enough to take effect.

"How far is your home?" he asked. Perhaps surgery would be best done there, where he wouldn't have to be moved for recuperation. Cal preferred surgery any-where but in a hospital, where disease seemed to abound. "Did you carry him here?"

She nodded. "It took me a half hour, but I had to stop often to rest. He's getting so big!"

Cal took the boy up into his arms; he barely seemed to notice it was not his mother coddling him. "Lead the way, and hurry," Cal said, blasting himself for not having his carriage. Certainly that would be faster and more comfortable for the boy.

They'd just exited the house when he heard a call after them.

"Wait! Where are you going?"

"I'm Dr. Tallery," Cal called over his shoulder without even looking back. "And this boy needs surgery. Immediately."

Instead of following, instead of calling after them again, the man Cal assumed to be Dr. Van de Klerk disappeared. Cal didn't look back to see where he went, but he'd barely walked a half block behind the woman when he heard the wheels of a carriage clank against the cobbled street.

"Bring him up," said an older man dressed only in a white shirt, dark trousers, and open vest thrown on but not buttoned. "Madam, have you a clean room? A kitchen table large enough to accommodate your son? A bed all to his own in which to recover?"

Blast! Cal hadn't thought to ask any of that. If the woman lived in a hovel, even a germ-infested hospital would be preferable.

"Yes, my husband is away at sea, but we have a home near the Battery. It's not large, but it's clean, and our kitchen table is long enough." Though her words were calm, her eyes suddenly filled with tears. "Surgery is truly the only hope? Is that—really necessary?"

Dr. Van de Klerk, sitting where a driver would have sat in a carriage better designed for two than four, nodded grimly. "If it's his appendix, then yes, madam, I'm afraid it is. He'll die otherwise."

And, Cal thought grimly, *perhaps anyway.*

Chapter Six

Abigail dismissed Bromley from the dining room, knowing he would stand in wait until the house crumbled if he thought the slightest possibility existed of her calling for him. Instead of sending for a meal that had already been holding for well over an hour, she stood and extinguished the nearest candle on the table. There was still no sign of either her father or the enigmatic Dr. Tallery. Try though she had, she possessed no appetite to eat alone. Besides that, the new gown she'd brought from Mindia's dressmaker pinched just below its high bodice, and the ribbons in her hair were tied so tight she'd developed a headache.

She was used to waiting for her father if she wasn't at his side; often their obligations took them in two different directions, leaving one or the other to dine alone. But tonight was different. No one seemed to know when Father had left the medicine room, or even if Dr. Tallery had arrived to accompany him on his rounds as arranged. Bromley only knew, since the horse, Sissy, and the carriage were both gone, that Father must have set out without notifying anyone of his departure. That signaled an emergency of some kind, which wasn't unusual, but she'd still hoped he might be home for the promised dinner with Dr. Tallery. When he hadn't arrived she assumed Dr. Tallery must be in on whatever emergency had taken Father away.

Surely Father wouldn't expect her to leave in the morning, without having met Dr. Tallery in her role of hostess? She wandered from the dining room into the library, where a number of periodicals waited on her father's desk. They often went over them together, studying the papers written by colleagues eager to share their knowledge or expertise. Settling into the chair she usually occupied in front of the fireplace—which remained unlit in the warmth of the night—she decided to start reading without Father, but soon her eyelids grew heavy.

Abigail had no idea what woke her, and so, confused at first as to her whereabouts, she sat up and listened. The clock ticking on the mantel was barely visible in the dim light; the oil in the lamp was low, the light scant. Past eleven o'clock. Surely Father was home by now!

She stood, and the periodical fell to the floor. Scooping it up, she replaced it on her father's desk, and, adjusting the lace at her nearly bared shoulders and another ribbon in her hair, she went out to the hall to make her way upstairs. The lace suddenly scratched at her skin, and she wanted to be free of it.

But in the foyer she stopped. Her father was indeed home, and at his side was Dr. Tallery. Bromley greeted them while taking Dr. Tallery's hat and gloves. Father didn't seem to have either, confirming that he'd been called out unexpectedly with Dr. Tallery.

"Good evening," she greeted them, and both men turned to her with similar looks of surprise.

"It's late, darling," her father said, coming to her and bestowing a kiss on her forehead. "I didn't expect you to wait up. You're as bad as Bromley."

It was on the tip of her tongue to remind him of the many times she herself had kept Bromley waiting, but she refrained for what it would reveal to Dr. Tallery. Instead, she forced a smile to her reluctant lips and faced the young doctor.

"I see you've met my father."

He bowed. "Good evening, Miss Van de Klerk."

"We were about to ask Bromley if he might put together whatever's left of dinner," Father said. He might be exhausted from the day, as he always was at this time, but he hid it well. Not even his voice sounded tired. "Would you care to join us, if only to watch two hungry doctors outeat one another?"

"As a matter of fact," she said coolly, "I haven't had my own supper. I waited, you see, but then must have dozed in my chair. So yes, I will join you."

She knew she wasn't playing the best of coquettes, not at all the way Mindia had modeled, but between her own suddenly growling stomach and having been left out of whatever had kept them busy since that afternoon, she was short of temper.

Cal watched Miss Van de Klerk approach the seat to the left of her father at the head of the table. Seeing past the ribbons and frills, trying not to notice the creamy quality of her skin that the new fashion revealed, it was clear she was miffed. Last night, with the exception of her final words, her behavior might have been frivolous, but at least she'd been far warmer. Tonight she was brittle, just as he imagined any doctor's wife might be should a physician be unfortunate enough to have one. Miss Van de Klerk personified the neglected, ignored, forgotten women he'd been hesitant to envision when first warned of them in medical school.

The butler scrambled to show the way. After the dining room was alight, he hurried out ostensibly in search of the long-delayed meal.

Three and not two table settings awaited, attesting to Miss Van de Klerk's claim that she'd forgone her meal to wait for them.

"I assume an emergency kept you away," she said, her voice guarded. "Care to share any of the details?"

What an odd question, even from the daughter of a physician who might have heard far too much of his business.

"Now, Abigail," Dr. Van de Klerk said gently, "we won't talk of such things except to say we're both sorry to have kept you waiting all of this time. Aren't we, Dr. Tallery?"

"Indeed," he said, though even to himself he didn't sound very convincing. It hadn't occurred to him that he might have been expected to dine with Van de Klerk and his daughter; in fact, he'd asked Van de Klerk to take him home after the last visit of the night. The removal of the boy's appendix had taken several hours, so they visited only one patient after. The family had been grateful for the late-night call, awake and standing vigil over their soon-to-die loved one. But death's hour was as unpredictable as ever, and so they had left knowing the family was as prepared as they could be.

Cal hadn't wanted to come to dinner; in fact, he didn't know why he'd agreed. He certainly hadn't expected Miss Van de Klerk. He wondered if she always gave her father such a chilly welcome whenever he was late. Yet in the very next instant, as she shifted her gaze to Cal, a small transformation seemed to take place. With a sigh, almost one of acceptance or resignation, a smile slowly grew on her face, and if the candlelight didn't deceive him, he thought she even offered a leisurely bat to her eyelids. The gesture was oddly discomforting, and he wished he hadn't stayed. Her changeable mood was harder to accept than her previous chill.

"Father is right, of course," she said. "I'm sure you've both had enough worries of the day so we'll talk about something more enjoyable. You must take the time to see a new play about Joan of Arc at the Park Theater. I went with the Pipperdays and thoroughly enjoyed myself."

"Did you?" said Dr. Van de Klerk, with more surprise than such a trivial admission warranted. Didn't all ladies in the Pipperday and Van de Klerk circle go to the theater? "Tell us about it."

And so she went on, even beyond the time it took for the butler to return and serve the meal. She spoke of the costumes, the spirit of liberty infused in every breathing word, even of the lighting and quality of acting. Cal was covering a yawn with a sip of water when she looked at him directly.

"Dr. Tallery, perhaps you might tell us about Dr. Woodridge. He was a great friend of Father's, so I'm sure he must have been a pleasure to know."

"Yes, he was," Cal said, tempted to leave it at that. The barrier of caution he'd ignored since caving in to Dr. Van de Klerk's dinner invitation now waved like black flags in the recess of his mind. On the wind of those flags came clear warning: *Do not share your grief over losing Charles.* Sharing too often led to caring and that inevitably to loss.

Still, to leave his answer so brief was rude. So he added, "He spoke highly of you, Dr. Van de Klerk, so I didn't want to miss the opportunity to accept your invitation into the medical community here."

"After today, you certainly have that," the old doctor exclaimed. "Abigail, you should have—" But then he cut himself short with a wave of his hand. "Ah, but I won't trouble you with details. I'll be happy to introduce you to other colleagues, Dr. Tallery, starting at New York Hospital just up the street, and then to the health commissioner and various officials who will be important to know sooner or later. Have you a place to set up your own office? Or might I hope you could join me here?"

"I do have a home large enough to accommodate an office," he admitted. "But I'm currently sharing it with my cousin. Once he finds his own footing, I will make modifications for an office. I live about twenty minutes north, by foot, so the location might be beneficial to patients from that area, if there aren't any other doctors immediately around my home I'm not aware of."

Dr. Van de Klerk mentioned a name or two of those who might be close by. "There is another hospital up the river," he added. "Well, I suppose I shouldn't call it that. It's our almshouse, but the entire upper floor is dedicated to treating the sick. Fever victims, mostly. I imagine you've seen a number of fevers in the islands?"

"Yes, some," he said. He didn't add that he himself had wrestled with a slight case of yellow fever only last summer, and it was that same fever that had killed Charles only a couple of months ago.

Between Miss Van de Klerk and her father, the conversation was carefully directed toward social niceties: questions about life in Saint Kitts, acquaintances they might have in common through his family, his recollection of the Pipperday gala just the night before. The only remotely serious topic came unexpectedly from Miss Van de Klerk, who asked details about his recent ship voyage. Had he worried about the trouble from a new French general called Napoleon? But then she commented on the cut of "pretty blue French uniforms," and whatever depth Cal mistakenly detected disappeared with the silly observation.

It wasn't as hard as he'd expected to remain aloof, because this was just the sort of polite conversation he detested. Perhaps it was the normal course of things between people who barely knew one another, but he had no wish to waste such time. Eating alone was far more efficient.

By the end of the meal he couldn't have been more exhausted, even if he hadn't spent the afternoon cutting open a boy who screamed in agony before blessedly falling into a stupor.

The only good thing that had happened all day was that the boy had revived and, despite the lingering pain, was likely to recover if infection didn't set in.

Cal planned to take that satisfaction to bed and forget all about this tedious dinner.

Chapter Seven

One Month Later

Abigail hid a yawn behind her fan. As frivolous as she'd first thought them, fans did come in handy. Particularly during this wet summer's heat!

She'd been back with Mindia's family for a month and had been to more balls and dances than she cared to recall. Father hadn't actually ordered her back to the Pipperday home; she'd returned willingly the morning after the disappointing meal she'd shared with Father and Dr. Tallery. She'd have been a fool not to recognize he had absolutely no interest in her, and she wasn't about to parade herself before him. She vowed if she ever saw him again she would present herself in complete candidness; no more pretending to be the society maiden Mindia was trying so hard to make of her. It was arduous, this effort to stir a man's interest, but as soon as she was finished with the task, she could return to work. She had no doubt her father would be true to his word; once she found a beau, she could return to the work she was called to do.

Abigail had become so proficient at dancing she didn't shy from the most intricate minuet. She'd developed genuine fondness for many of Mindia's friends and acquaintances, and for Ordell Lebsock in particular. Of the three gentlemen Mindia had identified as potential mates for Abigail, if Abigail had to choose it would be Ordell. He was pleasant looking; had strong faith in God; and although he wasn't the best dancer, gave every spin his best effort. As a new pastor assisting the older leader of a prominent church, Ordell wasn't as financially blessed as DeWitt Henshaw, nor as handsome or graceful as Reginald Marks. But she sensed the manner in which Mr. Henshaw had accumulated his wealth had as much to do with enthusiastic frugality as with anything else, and she'd caught Mr. Marks in earnest conversation with several other girls and knew she hadn't been the only lady to catch his eye.

Of course, the name Lebsock lacked the elegance of Van de Klerk, and she also had to admit that the yawn to which she'd just succumbed hadn't been the first in his company. He did tend to talk quite a bit about morbid things like burial procedures and the best sort of songs for funerals. He had also gone so far as to recommend she ask her father, knowing he was a physician, if he might tell families to request a layer of straw be laid upon a coffin at the gravesite service before the first clods of dirt were thrown in. The straw, he whispered, softened the ugly, echoing sound of dirt meeting the loved one's final resting place.

She forgave him his tendency toward the morose in light of the fact he was just getting used to performing funerals. Some small part of her, perhaps equally morose, thought a doctor and a pastor would make a fine team, since even the most dedicated and modern doctors like her father and herself lost far too many patients. How reassuring, not to mention convenient, to have Ordell handy to administer the spiritual consolation so vitally needed after the few tools of medicine failed.

Just now, happening to see Mindia alone for once, Abigail excused herself from Ordell and made her way quickly to her friend. They walked to the punch bowl together, something they'd done often during the past weeks. It wasn't only an opportunity to fill in one another on the night's doings; the summer had been unbearably hot not to mention rainy, and other than their fans, punch offered the only respite.

"I see your young artist hasn't shown up tonight," Abigail said sympathetically. Whenever Mr. Goodwin's name came up, which was often when she was alone with Mindia, Abigail couldn't help but think of the man's cousin. Other than the Independence Day gala, Dr. Tallery hadn't attended a single social event this summer. She liked to think Mrs. Pipperday was the only one disappointed in the lack of opportunity to get to know the eligible doctor, but Abigail's pride still stung.

Mindia hardly looked disappointed. In fact, she was grinning over the rim of her punch glass. "He sent me a note! Will you come with me tomorrow afternoon to the park? He'd like to meet me there!"

Abigail, only a little shocked, glanced about to be certain no one overheard. "Are you sure it's wise? Since your mother hasn't changed her thinking of him?"

"Oh, fiddle on that. Father thinks Early is a fine young man, and I'm not afraid to remind Mother of such a fact. Besides, we'll only take a stroll—if it'll just stop raining long enough! Say you'll help, Abigail. You will, won't you?"

She squeezed Mindia's free hand. "Of course I will. You know that."

"And now for your future," Mindia said, though her excitement cooled as she looked over Abigail's shoulder at the waiting Reverend Lebsock. "Have you spoken to him about your plan to work after you're married?"

Abigail paused, waiting to feel an intimate reaction at the mention of marrying Ordell. A wave of delight, anticipation, something to inspire the kind of excitement she'd seen on Mindia's face over a rendezvous with Early Goodwin tomorrow. Nothing. Her heart and mind remained as calm as ever. Perhaps Abigail was too old for such a fanciful reaction. She was, after all, two years ahead of Mindia and had a far different upbringing. She'd seen the harsher side of life, the suffering and stink of a sick human body. Necessarily, she was more objective than emotional. It made perfect sense for her to marry Ordell; she could easily grow to love such a sweet and honorable man. Provided, of course, he allowed her to do the work she hoped to do.

"I suppose I ought to speak to him about it."

"You mean you haven't yet?" Mindia asked. "Not even a hint?"

Abigail shook her head.

"My dear girl, you've allowed him at least three dances at the last several balls, sat beside him as we dined at nearly every function, let him monopolize most of your time. It's high time you said something or he'll wonder why you didn't sooner."

Abigail sighed. There was still so much to learn.

Abigail fluttered her fan, smiling over its rim at Ordell. "Perhaps we might find some respite from the heat on the verandah?"

It was nearly a scandalous invitation, even though verandahs were hardly the place to find a real retreat. Countless couples sought the spot in search of privacy. But Abigail's suggestion surely interested him, because Ordell smiled with a look somewhere between astonishment and caution. Then he took her elbow and led the way.

"I've so enjoyed tonight," Abigail said as they found a place still within the spill of light. She had the feeling there were at least two other couples hidden in the shadows but didn't care to see anyone in particular. "In fact, I've enjoyed so many parties because of your company."

"Thank you," he said. "I can certainly say the same."

"We've been able to talk about things that are important to us, haven't we? I'm glad you think so highly of my father's work. He is, in my opinion, one of the greatest men alive."

"I'm sure you're right."

"Oh! I'm so relieved you agree. I haven't talked about how I've enjoyed working at his side, learning to help others."

"Yes, I've heard from more than one of my flock that you tended to their ills and even set broken bones." He reached for one of her hands and held it gently. "You're quite admired, which makes me admire you all the more."

"Now I'm doubly relieved," she said, and her heart did feel cheered at such a perfect start to the subject. "I've often thought how a pastor's work meshes with that of a physician's. Patients are often in great need of comfort after seeing a doctor. Do you see how the two professions might complement one another?"

"Do you wish for me to partner with your father and be available to his patients after I have a flock of my own?"

"No, not at all." She pulled her hand from his, rubbing at a temple where her pulse had decided to throb. "I haven't expressed myself well. You see, I wish to keep helping my father, to continue working at his side."

He tilted his head, looking at her curiously. "After marriage?"

"Well, yes. Marriage doesn't debilitate a woman, after all."

He stroked his chin. "How interesting that you wish to spend more time with your father than with any prospective husband. Do you think that's fitting?"

"To help others, could it be anything else?"

"You're close to your father—I guessed that from the moment you mentioned him. But when a woman leaves her family, she gains one of her own. You'll have plenty to do in establishing and then taking care of your own home."

"Yes, that's true. But why leave behind all of the work I've loved?"

"Won't it be enough, tending to your family, helping your husband?"

"That will be part of daily life, of course." She rubbed again at her temple.

"Only part?"

As promising as the discussion had begun, it seemed to have sailed quickly south. "Perhaps we might think about the topic a little more before we continue? Now that we've begun understanding how each of us feel?"

"Yes," he said, "that's the wisest idea of the night. I do care for you, Miss Van de Klerk. So very much. And if I've said anything to make you care less for me, I wish to have another chance. Will you do me that honor and let us really talk of this again, after some contemplation?"

Relief set in. So he wasn't lost to her, after all. "I'd like that very much. It's so important to understand each other."

"I want nothing more than that."

Chapter Eight

The following afternoon, the heavens banished any showers long enough to encourage Mindia's hopes of seeing Mr. Goodwin. Abigail drove the Pipperday pony cart, and they'd barely reached the bowling green before Mindia spotted Early. He made no attempt to hide the prearranged nature of their visit by waving and quickly helping Mindia to alight.

Abigail stayed with the cart as the couple walked off alone down the grassy path, wondering if she would ever be half of such a couple. Ordell would never meet so clandestinely. He must, after all, set an example for others.

She sighed, suddenly dissatisfied. Being with Mindia had taught her more than just frivolities. Working with Father left Abigail little time for pleasantries, and Mindia was the right tutor for enjoying life. Surely, though, there must be a balance? A little time for adventure, apart from work that was so much more important?

Ordell's words replayed in her head. Was he right about marriage, that she ought to be her husband's helper instead of her father's? Could she leave medicine to be Ordell's helper instead? After all, she would still be serving others.

But her father and men like him—yes, why deny it, she thought of Dr. Tallery among them—were vital to the city. When in the grip of sickness, people took comfort from someone who knew what to expect, a voice of knowledge and solace that alone might aid in healing. And if not, a doctor's experience brought serenity in the hour of need. Surely that compared to the kind of help she could be to Ordell.

They'd parted on good terms last night. She expected him to ponder what they'd talked about, just as she'd been doing. If Ordell truly wanted to marry her, he would accept her desire to practice medicine. Surely God had designed her to help heal others; she saw how different she was to those like Mindia who would likely faint at the sight of most of the things Abigail easily handled.

Whether it was the gathering of more clouds and the prospect of muddy paths or solely their discretion, Mindia and Mr. Goodwin returned to the carriage before Abigail had grown weary of waiting.

Mr. Goodwin, who had been so eager with eyes only for Mindia upon his appearance, now waved a greeting to Abigail. "How good it is to see you, Miss Van de Klerk! Perhaps I should ask you how my cousin is doing, since I rarely see him."

"I beg your pardon?"

One of his brows bent. "It's only that he spends night and day working at your father's side, what with all of the fevers they've been tending. I thought perhaps you'd seen him."

Summer fevers were hardly a rarity, but it did seem troublesome that someone outside the circle of medicine was aware of any particular ailment these days.

"No, I've been staying with Mindia and haven't seen my father for some time. I suppose now I know why."

"Well, don't say anything to my mother about fevers!" Mindia warned. "Else we'll be sent straight back up the Hudson to escape the closeness of the city."

As he aided Mindia back into the cart, Early kept hold of her hand even after she was seated. His face was far more serious than Abigail had seen it during the galas where he'd been so attentive to Mindia. "Perhaps you should go upriver. It might be best."

She laughed, patting his cheek. "And miss the fun of the city? I don't think so."

Nonetheless, he shook his head. "If your parents suggest going, promise me you won't argue. Please, Mindia?"

The urgency in his tone warned Abigail this young man whom Mindia obviously cared for—because he was so cheerful and amusing—was resolute. What did he know, even rarely seeing his cousin, that she did not now that she wasn't living with her father?

"Only if you go with us," she whispered, but Abigail had no trouble hearing her.

It was his turn to laugh. "Oh, that's likely! Your mother permitting me to be a houseguest? I don't think so."

Mindia's face took on new intensity; then her brows rose in outright joy. "I could speak to Father about having you paint my portrait!"

But Mr. Goodwin shook his head. "He'd be more likely to hire me to paint his favorite mare, if he has one."

"Well," she shrugged, all feminine, "either way is fine with me."

They said their farewells, but Abigail barely listened. A fever in the city. Perhaps this was God's way of telling her she ought to go home.

Cal roused with a start at the call from the driver sitting atop the hired hack he'd used to bring him home from New York Hospital. In spite of the sun peeking through the clouds, he was grateful to be within walking distance of his very own bed. Cal paid the man then went directly to his room. His cravat was already loose, but he didn't bother to remove his vest. He wouldn't do anyone any good if he didn't sleep, and at the moment he thought he could stay abed for the next twenty-four hours.

Briefly, he wondered how Dr. Van de Klerk kept up the way he did, between his patients and traveling his circuit. Cal had all he could do just to go back and forth to the hospital these days, where they had recruited him for the duration of the summer fever season. Van de Klerk was unquestionably a hero. . . .

But as Cal drifted off to much-needed sleep, he refused to care for the man. Or allow the lovely face of his daughter to invade his dreams again.

Abigail didn't bother seeking her father's permission to leave the Pipperdays'. Even if she wanted to ask, when she arrived at her family door late that afternoon, he was nowhere to be found. So when Bromley sent for the footman to retrieve her baggage from the Pipperday carriage that had delivered her, there were no objections. Trunks considerably heavier than they'd been upon being taken out two months ago were placed in her room, and Lizzie set about unpacking her things, new and old alike.

Abigail dined alone that night, which did not surprise her. She was, in fact, a little relieved to put off the initial meeting with Father until breakfast. He was notoriously chipper in the mornings, so that was the best time of day to speak to him of her plans anyway.

Abigail arrived in the dining room earlier than their normal eight o'clock breakfast, so she would have the advantage of greeting him as he arrived. But it was she who felt the brunt of surprise when he walked through the threshold a few minutes later. Her energetic, ruddy-faced father looked anything but, and he barely seemed to notice her until she stood to gain his attention.

"Well, Abigail! What a pleasant surprise."

Even his voice sounded strange. "Father? Are you keeping up with your rest? You've always told me to do so, especially when the demands are more frequent than usual."

He took a seat at the head of the table, at the same time touching her elbow as if that was all he could spare. Evidently a welcoming embrace was too much for him. "Thank you for asking. I am a bit tired this morning. I came in late, but then you probably already know that if you were here. Were you? Or did you arrive at this uncommonly early hour today?"

"I came last night. You must have been very quiet when you returned, because I didn't hear a thing."

"That's good," he said, taking a sip of coffee as if grateful for it.

"Father," she said carefully, "I've come back to stay. I think you'll approve, though. I've gotten to know a young man who is most agreeable to me."

"What's this, then?" Father asked. "You've taken a beau? A serious one?"

"I'm talking about a young reverend, Ordell Lebsock, serving right here in

New York. He's aware that I want to help tend the sick, and I couldn't help but think his way of ministering to others will be a natural partnership with the kind of work we do."

"Then we must have him here so I may meet him. For dinner. As soon as possible."

She patted his forearm, which rested beside his plate. "I do want him to meet you, but there's no particular hurry."

His eyes, rimmed in a deeper shade of pink than normal, gazed at her leisurely. "Are you not smitten enough to be eager for things to progress? As I recall from my own youth, patience and romance don't often meet."

Afraid he might send her back to Mindia's until satisfied this was the right beau for her, she offered an amused smile. "Mr. Lebsock is, after all, a reverend, Father. We cannot be rushing into anything, can we? In the meantime, I've moved back home."

He appeared more concerned than pleased. "And you want to work again, at my side, even now?"

"Yes, of course. I thought that was understood."

He paused, neither taking up his fork nor looking at her as he spoke. "I've been spending a bit more of my time on my rounds these days, in between regular visits to the hospital. My absence from the office has reduced the number of people visiting here."

"That's all right," she said. "I'm sure once word gets around that I'm here to help, they'll return." Although tempted, she asked nothing of how Dr. Tallery was doing at Father's side.

"I welcome your help, Abigail," Father said, a hint of the old twinkle in his eye. "With midwifery, setting broken bones, extracting teeth and such. But I must ask you one thing: do not think of tagging along on my rounds. Is that clear?"

"But why ever not? If it isn't busy here, I'm sure you can use my help."

"No, my dear, I must insist. You're to steer clear of the hospital, too. I mean it. Do you understand?"

She eyed him closely, convinced he wasn't telling all. Perhaps Dr. Tallery was enough help on his rounds. Nonetheless, she was certain there was something Father didn't want her to know, confirming every fear Early Goodwin had inspired.

Chapter Nine

By the third day home, Abigail was still treating fewer patients in her father's medicine room than she could remember. She told herself word simply hadn't gotten around that she was back, available when her father couldn't be. She refused to contemplate old insecurities about people not trusting their health to a woman.

But the city *did* seem quiet, something she hadn't noticed at Mindia's and in the circles she frequented. Perhaps it was only the foul weather keeping everyone indoors or under a shade tree when the sun shone mercilessly between storms. While she was glad there were fewer children with broken arms or legs to be mended and fewer adults in need of a tooth extraction, she couldn't help but notice crowds on the street in front of their home seemed thinner. Even babies didn't seem to want to enter the world these days.

Though she searched the newspapers, there were no reports of fevers. And she hadn't seen Dr. Tallery once.

Father was still away more often than home, making her suspect his patients demanded more of him than he ought to allow. Instead of waiting to speak to him that evening, she donned her bonnet and gloves and set out to walk up Broadway to the hospital. She wouldn't find her father in the city on his rounds, but she might find him there. It was silly for her not to be of some help with whatever kept him so busy.

The two-storied, H-shaped building was set back from the street. Father didn't send many of his patients here, preferring to offer whatever treatment he could in the comfort of a home. But some did go to the hospital, and Father often met with other doctors on its staff, as well. When she worked there herself, she was referred to as a nurse, though in practice she handled many tasks entrusted only to doctors.

As usual, a variety of carriages waited outside. Nearly every window of the building was open, no doubt in hopes of catching a breeze even if it was a hot wind. Inside, the halls were anything but quiet. She wasn't sure what she'd expected, given the peace she'd left behind at home, but it took several minutes to find someone on staff among the unfamiliar influx of visitors.

"Miss Pasario!" she called after the nurse she knew. She'd worked often with

Miss Pasario, who offered only a grim smile in greeting.

"Ah, Miss Van de Klerk, I'm glad you've finally returned to us. You can help, can't you?"

"Of course—but I wasn't called. I simply came looking for my father."

Miss Pasario's eyes—already large on her narrow, olive-skinned face—widened further. "How can you not know?"

"Know what?"

"Goodness, Miss Van de Klerk! The city is besieged by fever. Hasn't your father told you?"

She shook her head. "I'm sorry to admit it, but no."

Miss Pasario put a hand to Abigail's elbow. "He must want to spare you, because like it or not, this is a nasty outbreak." Then she leaned closer to whisper into Abigail's ear. "Some are calling it yellow fever, but don't repeat it in the company of Dr. Dawson. He doesn't want to start a panic."

Yellow fever! She'd been only fifteen when the great fever had caused the near collapse of Philadelphia, and every time the fever reared its ugly head since then, she hadn't been the only one to imagine the worst. Although the fever had never risen to the level of '93 here in New York, who could be certain that it wouldn't? No wonder the streets were empty! In spite of the lack of official notices in the newspapers, people were no doubt shutting themselves away in terror of catching the deadly disease.

Nonetheless, she knew what had to be done. She'd treated yellow fever victims in the past and had yet to succumb. She would do so again.

"Tell me where I'm needed most."

And then she went to work.

⌒↻

"Oh! Doctor!"

Cal ignored the horrified exclamation coming from the nurse two beds over who must have witnessed what just happened. He knew any hint of fear or revulsion in his reaction would spread throughout the hospital, and that was the last thing he needed. Despite the noxious odor of the black vomit now spattering his jacket, he bent over the exhausted patient and took up the rag sitting on the bedside table. Then he gently wiped away the stream of blood-speckled spittle from the patient's chin.

"It's all right, young man," he said calmly. "You'll not let this get the best of you, will you? Here, then, some sweetened wine to refresh your mouth." He pressed the glass to the man's lips, setting it aside after he managed to swallow. "And some quinine to fight the fever."

"Thank you, sir," the patient whispered. He couldn't be much older than Cal himself, but at the moment with his yellowed skin and haggard cheeks he looked twice as old. "I'm sorry, so sorry. . . ."

"No need for that," Cal assured him, helping the man to swallow the quinine.

Afterward, stopping only to clean himself as best he could at a basin, he decided removing his jacket was the only answer. He must order more broth and creamed rice for those patients who could tolerate such things. More tea, more wine, and definitely more quinine. None of it would cure them, but they would do far more good than some of the old-fashioned treatments he'd seen here since leaving Dr. Van de Klerk's practice.

They'd agreed that Cal was needed here, but Cal wondered if Dr. Van de Klerk had noticed his eagerness to sever ties. He likely hadn't guessed it was too easy to admire the man, his work, and his dedication to healing. The last thing Cal needed was to grow fond of another mentor, and even in the short month they'd worked together, that had happened. But mentors, like fathers, too easily died.

Several patients had been admitted this very day. Cal's visit to the health officials had produced no result. He would go to the hospital committee next, to see what they intended to do. Already he'd given explicit instructions to every nurse he encountered—not nearly enough for the growing number of patients—about cleaning soiled linens quickly, keeping the patients, the beds, the floors, the walls, everything under this roof as clean as possible. Fresh air helped to alleviate some of the worst odors from the illness, but he was convinced that in and of itself wasn't the cure, either.

He turned and scanned the room. With every new crop of patients in the few days he'd been here, it seemed they lost either a doctor or a nurse. Some to illness, others fleeing the city altogether.

Movement on the far end of the long room caught his eye. A new nurse? Although she wore the familiar white apron, she was missing the white cap that went along with it. Not that it mattered, but it was unusual for any of the staff not to wear the complete uniform.

Then he went on to the next patient, too busy to pay attention to anyone but the sick.

"Which orders are we to follow, then?" Abigail asked after being told this ward was adopting different treatments than the one just across the hall, which was under the direction of Dr. Dawson. She knew Dr. Dawson, not well, but he'd been a doctor for at least as long as her father. New York Hospital had invited her father to the permanent staff several times every year, but he'd always refused. Although he never said it aloud, she thought her father's resistance stemmed from reluctance to work with Dr. Dawson.

"Just don't get confused about which side of the floor you're on," whispered Miss

Pasario. "This side, it's tea, sweet wine, fresh air, and quinine. Over there, it's the old ten-and-ten."

Abigail knew well enough what that meant. Dr. Rush's cure, they called it, though some never gave it that much respect. Ten grains of calomel with ten grains of jalap, two poisons powdered together and administered so the body would work to void itself—ridding, it was hoped, the fever along with the poisons.

"Who is in charge on this side, then?" she asked.

Miss Pasario nodded in the direction of the opposite end of the long room. "Dr. Stanfield was quick to hand over authority to our newest staff member since he came straight from the tropics. He's dealt with yellow fever himself."

Abigail's heart tumbled around in her chest, but she held back her gasp. "Not Dr. Tallery?"

"Why, yes, how did you know?"

"I thought he came to New York to work with my father."

"Ah, yes, someone did mention that. Well, then, you already know him so I won't bother to introduce you. Not that he'd take much time for any social niceties. He's aloof, stiff as a plank, but he's a saint in his efforts to relieve suffering. I'm surprised your father could let him go, but then your father's a saint, too."

Nurse Pasario filled her in on the amount of quinine each patient was to be given, followed by what food to allow, and special emphasis on cleaning each and every bed as often as the supply of linens could withstand.

After that, Abigail was simply too busy to worry about letting Dr. Tallery know she was now working under his direction.

Chapter Ten

If Cal was thankful for anything, it was for the nature of a forgiving nose. Smells that made his stomach turn could be tolerated if exposed to them long enough, and there was no shortage of exposure in a ward besieged with a fever often known as "black vomit."

He sat alone in the dark corner of the main hall. He'd discovered the spot underneath a staircase last night when he'd decided to stay here rather than going home in the hope of saving time. Although a veritable army of hospital maids still remained that came to wash floors; take away soiled linens; and empty buckets, pans, chamber pots, and anything else that had been used in association with the indignities of disease, this little corner was seldom disturbed because it led nowhere.

He knew he wasn't the first to discover the spot; the chair he sat upon had been placed there intentionally, opposite another just like it that invited his feet. He leaned back, feet up, eyes closed, and relished the comfort of being away from the smells, the cries, the disorientation, and death that permeated the hospital in these waning days of summer.

It was on the tip of his tongue to pray for an early frost—how long had it been since he'd prayed?—but he was asleep before any words took shape.

"Oh! I'm sorry, I didn't see you in the dark."

For a moment Cal was convinced he must be dreaming, though his eyes had been closed only a moment ago. Now he was fully awake. Standing before him, of all people, was Miss Van de Klerk! But instead of the chiffon and linens of the latest fashion, she wore plain, dark garb covered by the white cotton apron of a nurse. The hair that had been so elaborately entwined with ribbons and lace when he'd first met her was now pulled out of the way as if it were an inconvenience and not something with which to draw a man's eye. Worse than any of that, instead of the scent of flowers she carried with her the same noxious odor he suspected he carried himself, remnants of treating yellow fever victims.

"Miss Van de Klerk?"

She'd already turned away but stopped upon hearing his voice. "Yes, it's me. I'm sorry to have disturbed you."

Then he heard the soft footfalls of a slippered retreat. How did she know to wear the traditional leather soles to avoid disturbing the patients?

There was little chance of sleep now as he asked himself what she was doing here. Despite all the evidence, he could hardly believe she was tending patients. Not the frothy, beribboned and bejeweled society maiden who talked only of silly books, worthless theater, and pretty uniforms. Surely he'd dreamed her appearance, though he could not guess why.

It was well into the evening, and he'd been there since shortly after dawn. There was so much to do Cal was tempted to stay again, but he reminded himself he was better off healthy. So rather than settling for the bed of two chairs, he headed for home in search of a much-needed bath, fresh set of clothing, and a few hours' rest.

"I plan to leave later this morning," said Early to Cal, after Cal had bathed and changed into odor-free clothing then slept the rest of the night.

"And Mindia's mother is aware of this invitation to the Pipperday country house?"

He held up a slip of gold-rimmed paper. "Sealed and delivered with her signature. I shouldn't be so proud of myself because I'm beholden to Mindia, but this will be my first portrait. And I couldn't imagine a subject I'm more interested in painting."

Cal wanted to caution his young cousin, since caution about love came so easily. Instead, he smiled and wished Early the best. Perhaps if Mindia's mother liked the portrait enough, it would not only garner Early more commissions, but pave the way for her approval of his intentions toward her daughter.

In any case, it would get them out of a city rife with fever, and for that Cal could only be grateful.

"Father, how could you not have told me? The fevers are far worse than last summer or the summer before that."

They'd met at the top of the stairs before going down, just the way they always had when their clocks directed them to the breakfast table if they were both at home.

He frowned. "I didn't keep it from you, daughter. I've just been too busy tending my patients. You've always understood our lapses in communication in the past."

"But this! I'd have come at once if I'd known how much I was needed."

"I haven't given permission for you to come home, and I'd prefer you return to Mindia's. Her family is likely going to the country once news of the fevers reaches the papers."

She didn't mention she'd received a note that morning from Mindia, saying they were leaving that very afternoon. "I have no intention of fleeing when I'm needed here."

He now looked at her curiously, as if her words took time to register. Though he led the way downstairs, he asked, "What do you mean?"

She sucked in a deep breath. "I went looking for you at the hospital yesterday."

His frown deepened, but he said nothing.

"They fairly begged me to stay and help, and so I'll be working there until this passes."

"Ah, so it's come to that, has it?"

"Yes, Father." She looped her arm through his as they entered the dining room. "Even with all the fever victims, the hospital may be safer than various neighborhoods—some of the places you visit every day. If the patients are any indication, Battery Park and other low areas have been the worst hit. Please, Father, come up to the hospital. The air is foul inside, but with the windows open, it's not nearly as bad as some of the spots you visit too often."

"I'll go with you this morning," he said, "which is what I'd planned doing anyway. But if I cannot convince you to go with Mindia, I'd rather you were home. You should be planning the dinner for me to meet your Reverend Mr. Lebsock, remember?"

"Father, how can you believe for a moment that I would stay home when I know there are so few people helping at the hospital? Half of the staff has fled if they have someplace else to go."

He sighed heavily. "Then as you say, at least it is up ground. I will be there when I can, but I'll not abandon my circuit, no matter how foul." He managed a wink, conjuring her image of the cheerful man hiding beneath too heavy a load these days. "You see, I am every bit as stubborn as you."

"Yes, you've modeled that trait well."

"Miss Van de Klerk is here often," said Miss Pasario to Cal after he'd inquired about her. "She was here nearly all day yesterday, and I expect her to be back. She often works with her father, but everyone on staff knows she has an open door here whenever her father can spare her."

She works with her father? The vapid girl who read nothing of more importance than a novel of seduction? That same girl?

He was half-tempted to repeat the name, just to make sure they spoke of one and the same. But the lingering memory of seeing her face the night before, albeit in a darkened hallway, confirmed the truth. He would make a point of acknowledging her today, if only to witness the miracle of transformation from society girl to one of true value.

He soon found not only Abigail Van de Klerk at the bedside of his weakest patient, but her father as well. Dr. Van de Klerk looked pleased to see him, despite Cal's abandonment of his practice.

"Ah, Dr. Tallery! Have they been keeping you as busy as I suspect?"

"There is nothing like calamity to offer opportunity for great responsibility," he said, his gaze traveling easily from father to daughter. He hadn't noticed they were nearly the same height, making Miss Van de Klerk taller than he recalled. Nor had he ever observed such a sedate look on her face as she gently swabbed away the foul sweat from the delirious patient. She showed not a trace of repugnance over the task.

"I didn't know your daughter had any interest in your work, Dr. Van de Klerk," he said, still watching her, although she seemed to be making a point of looking anywhere but at him.

"Keeping that a secret was by design," Van de Klerk said, as if he were a bit embarrassed. "She's quite talented in medicine, but such a gift isn't often accepted when first meeting someone."

He could have told them he'd not only have welcomed knowing such a thing about her but extolled such knowledge. Yet it hardly seemed appropriate, given his previous reluctance to befriend either one of them. What, really, had changed? That he was relieved Van de Klerk hadn't sired a dull daughter? He must still keep to his own company if he was to honor the barriers he'd so carefully erected to protect himself from the kind of loss he was too tired of experiencing.

Somehow, though, keeping such a distance didn't seem quite as easy as it had been before.

Chapter Eleven

After her father left her to see to patients on another floor, Abigail belatedly stopped at the nurses' office to let them know she was reporting for duty. To her disappointment, instead of returning to Dr. Tallery's ward, she was sent across the hall. They were short two nurses and could use her help.

Abigail's shoes could have been made of rocks for all the trouble she had moving her feet. Most fevers, especially yellow fever, were hard to tend. But Dr. Dawson's poisoning and purging, bleeding and blistering seemed only to add torture to an already sick patient.

By midmorning, if it weren't for the suffering she hoped to relieve as best she could, Abigail might have been tempted to leave with or without Dr. Dawson's permission. Though she'd hardly needed it, he'd instructed her on how to properly bleed a patient—a technique her father had grown to abhor in recent years. He'd come to reject so many of the ancient ways, far preferring anything to help the body naturally heal itself if it could.

When Dr. Dawson was otherwise occupied and no longer monitoring her every move, she brought in warm broth rather than administering poisons like mercury or dogwood bark. It was no less than insubordination not to follow his orders, but she doubted they would ask her to leave. Considering the procedure was being carried out right across the hall, she had plenty of reason for her boldness. Dr. Dawson may not be losing more patients than other wards, but it didn't take a trained eye to see which contained more suffering.

At least they agreed on fresh air, and for once there was a breeze—hot as it was. She welcomed the puff of air as she spoon-fed one of the patients.

"Nurse Van de Klerk." Dr. Dawson's reproachful tone was clear in the brief address, but he used it so often it could mean nothing more than a request for her to help him bleed another patient. Again. "I will see you in the hall as soon as you've finished here." He glanced at the near-empty bowl. "Which I assume to be within the next minute."

Then he turned on his heel. Whispering apologies for not staying a moment longer than necessary once the broth was finished, Abigail followed Dr. Dawson's path to the hall.

"Like your father, I believe every illness has a cure," he began, giving her his profile, chin lifted, brows high. "I've done a considerable amount of study regarding fevers, and for this one in particular when it's obvious the stomach must be filling with blood, it's my opinion that bleeding is—"

She was as exasperated as she was tired. "I beg your pardon, Dr. Dawson, but I'm sure the books you've read about such techniques are outdated. You can see your method isn't curing anyone any better than other, more palatable treatments."

Now he turned to face her, his brows gathering over eyes filling with anger. "Despite my respect for your father, girl, I have no intention of standing here to be questioned by his offspring. You'll do as I tell you or I'll have you arrested for endangering my patients."

"Endangering! By giving them broth instead of poison? I'm here to alleviate suffering, Doctor, not to add to it."

"I'll not stand for this kind of insolence—"

"Well, then," came a voice from the other side of the hall, a surprisingly friendly tone. When Abigail turned to see that it was none other than Dr. Calvin Tallery, she was sure her surprise over his congeniality nearly matched Dr. Dawson's astonishment at the interruption. "I'll gladly invite Nurse Van de Klerk to my ward, where her practices are most welcome."

He looked from Dr. Dawson to Abigail, to whom he extended an open palm inviting her into the room behind him.

"Now just a minute, Tallery," said Dr. Dawson, "I've already had enough of your interference when it comes to how we ought to manage this summer's fevers. First your insistence that this is yellow fever, when it could be any number of others: camp fever or perhaps just as easily autumnal fever. You, a newcomer—perhaps from the very ship that brought this plague to our city!"

Dr. Tallery's eyes narrowed. "This hospital and its committee asked me to help deal with an unusually high number of fever patients. I'm happy to do so because I've served where tropical fevers lurk year-round. I have no obligation, however, to listen to you or to allow you to redirect the staff of my choosing. Good day, Dr. Dawson."

Then, far more gently than she'd expected from the harsh tone in his voice, Dr. Tallery took Abigail by the elbow and directed her inside the ward he'd been assigned.

Once they were well away from the openmouthed but silent doctor, Abigail faced Dr. Tallery. If he thought she would be grateful for his coming to her defense, he was mistaken. Did he still think of her as the society maiden she'd mistakenly presented herself to be? In need of his heroics? "Dr. Tallery, in case you didn't notice, I was in the process of explaining to Dr. Dawson that his methods are outdated. I did not need, nor did I welcome, your effort to act the knight in shining armor."

Heart pounding harder than she thought it could, she spun around and went back to work. She returned to Dr. Dawson's side of the hall, convinced she ought to stay there as long as she could stand it, at least to spare whomever she could from the old ten-and-ten.

Abigail had little time the rest of the day to contemplate whether or not she'd been unfair to Dr. Tallery. It simply didn't matter. He'd made clear he had no interest in getting to know her, and just because she'd proved herself capable of a little hard work didn't change the person she was inside. Someone he'd never expressed an interest in spending time with.

Only the most serious cases of illness came to the hospital these days. If only they knew what caused such a fever! She'd seen doctors and nurses fall ill at the side of some patients they visited in their homes, while others, even family members, were untouched by whatever air or agent carried the dreaded disease. She felt as healthy as ever, and Nurse Pasario certainly wasn't slowing down despite the fact she was old enough to be Abigail's mother. What protected them from catching it?

The air was distressingly fouled by the various symptoms that came along with the illness. Though they kept the linens and walls and floors as clean as possible, left each and every window open to move the air, the heaviness of illness couldn't be hidden. Neither vinegar-soaked rags nor the residue of gunpowder following the boom of a nearby cannon—much to the dismay of resting patients—could clean the air sufficiently. Perhaps the cannons reminded older patients of the not-too-distant past when those cannons roared for far deadlier reasons.

After a quick lunch shared with Miss Pasario, they returned inside the hospital. Just as they were about to take opposite directions to the two different wards being used for fever victims, Abigail spotted Dr. Dawson approaching from a nearby hall window, almost as if he'd been waiting for her. She threw a good-bye glance at Miss Pasario then prepared herself for another confrontation.

"I do not want you working in my ward," he said, his usually sonorous voice now hushed yet not a bit less intimidating. "I'll not have you undermining my methods right under my nose."

Without waiting for a reply, he strode past her toward the ward where she'd previously been headed.

Abigail was used to being ordered about, questioned because she was a woman often doing what only men were allowed to do. Knowing she was right, however, was balm enough for being exiled. So after a prayer for Dr. Dawson to abandon old practices, she reported to the nursing office to let them know she would not be working where they'd sent her that morning. She'd much rather suffer Dr. Tallery's presence—a reminder of his rejection—than work under Dr. Dawson's antiquated ways.

Back in the ward with Dr. Tallery, she was relieved they were both too busy to pay each other any attention. She grew unaware of the time as she delivered yet another cup of warm broth to a patient. This one was a sailor, echoing Dr. Dawson's accusation that the fever had arrived on a ship. She'd noticed Dr. Tallery had spent considerable time at this particular patient's side when he had first arrived, so perhaps it shouldn't have surprised her when Dr. Tallery approached while the patient was awake.

"Good afternoon, seaman," Dr. Tallery greeted the man. The friendly tone of voice surprised Abigail again, since she'd seen for herself that Miss Pasario had been accurate in describing his normally formal behavior as he went about his work.

"Ah, so I didn't dream it after all," said the sailor. "None other than my friend from Saint Kitts."

Friend? Other than Early Goodwin, who was also a cousin, Abigail had convinced herself the man didn't have any friends.

Nonetheless, Dr. Tallery smiled just then, and to her annoyance she couldn't help but notice it only multiplied his attractiveness. "Nurse Van de Klerk, this is Felix Brown, better known to his shipmates as Bulldog." He then looked at the seaman curiously. "I'm surprised you're still in New York, Bulldog. I would have thought the *Fair Winds* sailed back to the Indies weeks ago."

"And so it did. I'm assigned to sail on a sister ship expected up here in November." He gazed around at the hospital ward. "Only I didn't know my visit would be in a place such as this. I'm on the mend, though, I can feel it. The aches and pains I arrived with are nearly gone—well, except for the kind I've gotten used to with age. The good Lord warns us when it's time to go on, sort of easing us along the way to heaven."

Abigail exchanged glances with Dr. Tallery, noting he didn't encourage the man's optimism. Likely Dr. Tallery had seen even more cases than she when a fever victim appeared to be on the brink of recovery only to be struck down in the next day or two, far worse than before.

He reached behind the sailor to shift the pillow to a better position for sitting while Bulldog took up the broth Abigail had just handed to him. "We'd like to keep you here a bit longer, just to be sure all's well."

Bulldog saluted with his free hand. "Aye-aye, sir. Only I hate to take up a bed if I'm well enough to go on my way."

"We just want to make sure, sailor."

"For anyone who is up to it," Abigail said lightly, "I've asked another patient who feels as well as you do to entertain us with a reading from Thomson's *The Seasons*." She spared a narrowed glance at Dr. Tallery, wondering if he would object to her effort to bring some of society's art into a hospital ward. She might not be a debutante, but Mindia had taught Abigail enough to convince her that one lurked inside. She wasn't about to hide anything now, not her work nor even her readiness to dance the next time she had the opportunity. "The reading starts with autumn, since we're all looking forward to that now that summer is waning."

To her surprise, Dr. Tallery's brows lifted with approval, enhancing the second smile she'd ever seen on his face.

Chapter Twelve

The sun had long since set, and Cal knew he ought to go home. It wouldn't take yellow fever for him to collapse if he let fatigue get the best of him. But despite knowing another doctor had volunteered for night duty, he was reluctant to leave. Instead, he found himself searching for Bulldog. The older sailor had been moved with healthier patients to a corner of the ward screened off from the weaker patients, with the belief that the foul air from the sickest patients was best avoided by those who seemed so close to recovery.

Cal had been anything but friendly during their voyage to New York, yet Bulldog possessed one of those irrepressibly optimistic dispositions that wouldn't be swayed no matter how others resisted him. Cal had vowed not to care about anyone beyond those he already, irreversibly, held in affection, like Early and the rest of his remaining family. Somehow Bulldog had slipped past the fence, only Cal hadn't recognized it until the man showed up at the hospital.

"If I answer your question, you must answer mine."

Cal stopped behind the cotton wall, hidden by a mere curtain suspended from a string pulled taut from wall to wall. He recognized Abigail Van de Klerk's voice. Cal used to consider eavesdropping unethical, but during recent years he'd found it an effective means to gather information, particularly when patients were more comfortable talking about symptoms to someone other than a doctor who might suggest surgery.

"Very well, young lady," came Bulldog's crusty voice. "Let's set our questions out like a hand at cards, then decide."

"Mine is harmless enough. Why are you called Bulldog?"

"Ha!" He laughed a familiar high-pitched grunt. "An easy one. I'm not sure the question I have for you is as easily answered. Why isn't a pretty young woman such as yourself already married?"

"Hmmm." She followed that with a little chuckle that reminded Cal of how she sounded at a society party. He'd nearly forgotten those images of her; they'd been replaced by absolute admiration for the work she'd done here. No matter how repulsive the task, she addressed every need that crossed her busy path. He appreciated this version of Abigail far more than he ever could the woman he'd first thought her to be. "Perhaps I ought to get two of my questions answered in exchange for that one, especially since you've admitted mine is so easily answered."

"Go ahead and offer two, Bulldog," came another voice from behind the curtain. Evidently Cal wasn't the only one listening in on this conversation.

"I can tell you why that old coot is called Bulldog," rang someone else, "and you don't even have to answer a question from me in return." The men talking might not be guests at one of those society parties she obviously liked to attend, but it sounded like she'd drawn a flock of admirers right here. "Look at 'im. If he don't resemble one of those little dogs trained to bite the heel of a bull, I don't know what else he looks like."

There were a few titters at that, and in the generally cheerful mood surrounding the exchange Cal decided to join the group.

"Uh-oh," said Bulldog, "looks like we're in trouble for prattling too late into the night."

"Not at all," he said. "I'm glad to see so many of you in high spirits." Although he didn't say so, their chatter was far preferable to the cries coming from those who were bound to their beds for safety's sake, just as many of these had been so recently. He was sure Miss Van de Klerk didn't need—or want—rescuing again, but he was fully prepared to spare her from having to answer Bulldog's question. "However, Nurse Van de Klerk has been at the hospital today for nearly as long as I have, and it's high time she went home for a good sleep." Over a few moans, not of pain but of protest, he added, "You don't want her to get sick, do you?"

She'd been sitting on a stool pulled to Bulldog's bedside, though it could have been a throne for all the loyalty on exhibition from those around her. Nonetheless, she stood but hesitated at the foot of Bulldog's bed. "I want you to know I don't believe for a minute you resemble a bulldog."

He winked at her, the wrinkles around his eyes all the more prevalent, even under the meager light of the nearby oil lamp. "Believe it, miss, because that's the truth of it. Now let Dr. Tallery take you home. You've both earned a good night's rest."

Cal found himself delighted at the suggestion, even as he was assailed with doubt she'd want his company. Besides, spending any time outside of working together violated his vow to keep everyone who wasn't family at a fair distance. That especially included this woman and her father.

He couldn't tell if she planned to follow Bulldog's advice about letting Cal see her home, since she didn't acknowledge or even look at him. But she did leave the ward, and he followed. He knew she must stop at the nurses' office to tell them she was leaving and to turn in her cap and apron for proper laundering. Instead of parting ways, with the hospital exit one way and the nursing office the other, he took her by the elbow and led her to the office.

If she had any objections, he was glad she didn't raise any.

Abigail's heart thumped. Was he truly intent on seeing her home, just as Bulldog had suggested?

Resentment popped up alongside her confusion. She was suddenly worthy of his company because she'd spent her day in a way most people in Mindia's circle would find unexpected? Yet she couldn't deny anticipation was overtaking her thoughts.

"You needn't see me home, Dr. Tallery," she said as they stepped out into the warm night air. Her words were automatic, spurred by the resentment she'd thought gone. "My home isn't far, and there's usually a hack at the end of the block. My father and I know the driver. He's almost always there to take me home, or if not, I don't have long to wait."

"That must be the hack I've hired myself these last few nights. We'll let him transport us both, then, if you have no objections. I'm sure your father would thank me."

She should insist he go on his own way, but she didn't. What was she doing, letting her heart behave in such a way? Mindia's tutelage this summer had already produced its fruit. Hadn't Abigail told her father about Ordell? Perhaps more importantly, she'd led Ordell to think she was receptive to his attention. And she was. Wasn't she? Although nothing was official, and although sharing a hack with Dr. Tallery for the sake of convenience was hardly scandalous, if Ordell knew how jittery she felt at this moment, he would hardly approve of her spending time in this man's company.

"I wanted to speak to you about some of the patients," he said, "and this will give us that opportunity."

His businesslike tone cooled the excitement all too eager to take root, but nonetheless her step was considerably lighter than expected after such a long day of toiling.

"I can see you're well versed in caring for the sick," said Dr. Tallery, "but I wanted to warn you about the future of some of the patients you were just sitting with. Some of them—perhaps up to half, in fact—might be moved right back to the other side of that curtain, in worse condition than they were when they first came in."

She sighed. "Yes, I'm afraid I've already seen that happen. That's why I was with them tonight. I wonder how many of them suspect what might be in store, or why we're keeping them in the hospital when they seem to be improving. I know they converse among themselves, but I wanted to make sure the topics would be lighter than what might be on their minds."

Though she looked ahead, intent on keeping an eye on the path in front of them, she could feel his lingering glance. Mustering the boldness to catch a look from him, she saw something like admiration on his face. "I commend you," he said in a tone that confirmed what she saw—words so gentle they felt like a caress.

She snapped her gaze back, seeing the end of the block was empty. Under the glow of the street's whale-oil lamp, the intervals between lighted posts looked darker than ever.

"Now I'm certain I was meant to see you home," Dr. Tallery said, more politely now, erasing any hint of intimacy she might have imagined. "It's not only your father who would worry about you waiting alone at this hour. Those society matrons who watch over the parties you like to attend wouldn't approve of you being out at this time of night."

She wished she could summon a light retort, laced with the sort of carefree, amusing timbre she'd learned so well by mimicking Mindia. But somehow Abigail's brain was working as if coated in molasses. She could confess to Dr. Tallery that her father had always been too lenient when it came to her behavior; she could admit she'd driven their carriage home all by herself from the homes of various patients at hours even later than this. But she was too uncertain. To her own shame, the source of her indecision wasn't loyalty to dear Ordell. Rather, she wasn't sure Dr. Tallery would welcome the truth about her ways. That it mattered should certainly be a source of concern, whether or not Ordell would appreciate her hesitations.

In that moment she knew her best behavior must also be honest. Why pretend to be part of a social set she had no intention of frequenting, at least on a regular basis? Dr. Tallery still had no interest in her personally. He'd taken the opportunity to act a gentleman by seeing her out, but he was not only concerned about what she knew of their patients, he had a vested interest in seeing her home for a good night's rest. The hospital couldn't bear the loss of any more nurses.

She must let him know she was neither a society maiden nor exactly a nurse. Once these fevers passed, as they were sure to do, if he returned to work at her father's side, he ought to know it would be at her side as well.

Glancing first one way down the street then the other, she saw no sign of the expected hack. They had at least a few more minutes to wait. "Doctor, I believe I should tell you something about myself that might not be clear, especially given what you could easily have assumed upon our first meeting."

He appeared to stiffen, as if surprised the conversation was taking a more personal direction. She nearly changed her mind.

"You met me under circumstances that were rather disingenuous." She was speaking more quickly than gracefully but didn't know how to slow herself. "My father was worried that I needed to do more with myself than work with him, so he sent me to Mindia's with the hope of securing personal happiness. She taught me as much as she could, considering my inadequate social education. While I admit enjoying myself more than I expected, the truth is I am more than a nurse. I work with my father, doing as little—or as much—as our patients will allow me to do for them. I am, for all practical purposes, a doctor myself. Without the title, without, I admit, the respect that goes along with it, but a doctor all the same." She met his gaze. "I thought you should know all of this if you still plan to work with my father when the summer fevers pass."

He held her gaze, looking far less surprised than she expected. In fact, he looked nearly. . .pleased. But he broke the gaze before she knew for sure. Looking down the street, he asked, "And have you?"

"Have I. . .?"

"Secured your personal happiness."

It wasn't the question she expected. What of the bigger matter, that of working beside a woman, respecting her work, her opinion? But then Ordell came to mind, and she knew she had to speak of him. "Yes, I have."

He looked at her again now, one of his brows dipping. "Yours will be a most unconventional marriage, then." His tone was gentle, the way it had been earlier.

"Yes, that's what Mindia says, too."

The carriage pulled up just then, and Dr. Tallery stepped forward. He waved to the driver up top, opened the door for Abigail, and then helped her to board before following her inside. Settling opposite her, he smiled with a peculiarly unfamiliar look in his eye, visible in the swinging light suspended on the coach just outside its window. "You've just answered the question Bulldog posed, Miss Van de Klerk, about why you've remained unmarried so far."

The blood in her veins heated as if she herself had the fever, only with no ill effects. "Then what about you, Dr. Tallery?" The question came out before she could catch it. "Why is it you've never married?"

Chapter Thirteen

Cal looked at Miss Van de Klerk, indeed had no trouble staring into her charming eyes. But between them in the close confines of this carriage was a crumbling wall. Brick by brick toppled with each passing moment, leaving him entirely exposed. How had this happened in the course of a few short days of working beside her? He must explore that at a future date. But it was irrefutably true, and likely irreversible. Perhaps he hadn't erected that wall as effectively as he had thought.

And she with her happiness secure! A marriage in the not-too-distant future. All he could be was her friend, but even that was more than he should allow, particularly in view of how easily he'd taken to working with her father. Cal had promised to keep to himself after he lost his family. Then he'd been adopted, so to speak, by Charles—only to lose him, too. And so he'd rebuilt that wall. But hadn't affection for Bulldog somehow grown on that voyage? And once back home in New York, hadn't Early reminded him how easy it was to care for another human being, in spite of any wish not to?

Perhaps the biggest chink in the wall occurred when he'd first set eyes on Abigail Van de Klerk all those weeks ago; she might not have been in his presence often since then, but the strike against the barrier must have been so strategically placed as to have rendered it weak ever since.

"Haven't you guessed why I'm unmarried, Miss Van de Klerk? Like you, I've dedicated my time to medicine. But unlike you, at least what I've seen while you've been working at the hospital, I've done my duty by technique and not heart. A doctor's goal, as you've claimed, is to alleviate suffering. Sometimes that's nothing more than standing at the bedside, offering comfort the way you did with those patients tonight. With cheerful conversation, your smile, your hope for tomorrow. I'm a bit surprised you haven't had a patient propose marriage to you already. I, on the other hand, would stir no such interest from my female patients because I offer medicine only in the form of technique. Without a heart."

She eyed him as if skeptical. "I wonder how a doctor can be without a heart. Not when the goal is to help others. I've seen you working tirelessly these past few days. That's certainly more than technique."

He shrugged, tearing his gaze from hers to look out the window. The moment this conversation had begun he'd sensed it taking him in a direction he wasn't prepared to follow. Yes, she was beautiful. He'd recognized that from the moment he saw her. Now that he knew she wasn't as shallow as a butterfly, he was all the more susceptible to her charms. He still wanted to fight it, to resist, to remind himself death always lurked every time he came to care for someone.

But it was no use. He couldn't deny his heart still beat inside, that the breath he breathed was given to him by God, who the Bible claimed was the very embodiment of love. He'd created people to love, hadn't He? Cal had spent so much time shaking his fist at God he'd forgotten there were other elements of life than death. There was love, or at least the possibility of it. That made all the rest bearable.

Yet with her about to marry someone else, all he could owe her was gratitude for reminding him he might be able to care for someone, after all.

"Let's just say," he whispered, "that I've kept my compassion to a minimum."

"My father has always said a doctor's heart must be made of India gum—soft, serviceable, but able to erase what it must to go on and help the next patient. Keeping what we learn along the way, erasing what we can of the losses."

He caught her gaze. "Does India gum not have the tendency to crumble, though?"

She held her own eyes steady with his. "Only when overused, not under."

Cal couldn't have looked away from her even if he'd commanded himself to do so. Whatever was left of that crumbling wall had just been swept away.

Chapter Fourteen

Abigail was ready to set off from home for another day at the hospital, but she lingered in her father's company after they'd breakfasted. She had so little opportunity to spend time with him these days. Even so, she was quiet as she sipped her coffee, wishing she could share her strange mix of reluctance and eagerness for the duties ahead.

Somehow, even with its horrors, the hospital had transformed to a place Abigail wanted to be—not only because she felt so useful, but because she could work at Dr. Tallery's side. He served fever patients tirelessly, but if he was called to assist cases in other wards, he never complained. Those who worked with him spoke only of his knowledge, and few complained about his lack of warmth. They were too grateful for his experience.

"I'm going to the health commissioner's office this morning," Father said, pulling her attention back to the present. "Do you know they still haven't issued a warning for the public to clean out their yards, to empty damp cellars? They must make sure the city scavengers are more diligent about sweeping the streets."

"I've been so isolated at the hospital I haven't been reading the papers lately," she admitted. "But I noticed there was little being written about the fevers."

"That's true," he said with a heavy sigh. "So far they've been more effective at ignoring so many cases than warning people away from the sinks and damp. They hope to avoid panic—yes, I understand. They don't want everyone who has somewhere else to go to abandon the city. But economic reasons over health? It's shameful."

"Father, you go every day to the areas you're warning people about. Won't you stay up here instead? In the medicine room, or even go to the hospital?"

He stood, tugging his waistcoat down over what had once been a more rounded middle. She was sure he was losing weight. "Now, darling, you're not to worry. I'm seldom in one place for very long. Oh, and I've forgotten to speak to you about something that's rather important. Bromley tells me Reverend Ordell has left his calling card at the house three times this week, but you have yet to see him."

A wave of guilt washed over her. "Yes, I must speak to him, but I've been so busy."

"I'm still looking forward to meeting the man who's stirred your interest. He must be quite extraordinary."

She averted her gaze, afraid of what his sharp eye might detect. The truth was she hadn't thought of Ordell in the last few days, except once in the carriage with Dr. Tallery.

She stood and would have led the way from the dining room, but her father's voice detained her. "Abigail?"

The single word confirmed he'd guessed anyway what she'd tried hiding. Still, she couldn't very well talk about her confusion concerning Ordell. She needed to speak to Ordell first, to see if he'd considered their last conversation and what conclusions he might have drawn.

"You haven't plunged yourself so thoroughly back into work that you're forgetting the future again, have you?"

"No, Father."

He drew her close with one arm about her shoulders. "I can see something is on your mind, and I won't press you if you're not ready to confide in me. I'm just a foolish old man wanting to see my daughter happy and not left alone after I'm gone. You can forgive me of that, can't you?"

She patted his chest. "You still have plenty of time to see my future secured."

After a kiss to her forehead, he chuckled. "May God be willing, my dear."

As he walked beside her out of the dining room, she couldn't help but notice his gait was slower, his shoulders more rounded. She wasn't accustomed to seeing his age, but somehow he was growing old in spite of her wish otherwise. He should be slowing down. She considered sending for one of her brothers, but even if their country circuits had no fever victims, they were still likely busy. That was the one surety in life: wherever there were people, sickness would abound.

When Abigail arrived at the hospital a short time later, her gaze naturally sought Dr. Tallery. But when she found him, she drew in a sharp breath. He was at Bulldog's bedside, who was back among the weakest of the fever patients.

Cal wiped the blood from the corner of Bulldog's mouth. The sailor was in the last stages of the disease, with yellow skin and eyes, blood oozing from his nose and mouth. He now vomited black blood over a tongue that was brown and dry. Worse, his pulse seemed to grow weaker by the minute even as he alternated between complete coherence and delirium.

He hadn't wanted to restrain the man, but the fever madness had him thrashing with far more strength than Cal thought Bulldog possessed. One of the straps had loosened, and Cal bent to retie it.

"Oh, Mr. Bulldog."

The greeting came from a source Cal both welcomed and wished away. It was difficult not to worry over Abigail Van de Klerk, despite her competency. It was easy to catch the back of a hand or worse from a patient in the throes of the fever, and he feared for her safety.

Even as he dreaded losing Bulldog, Cal tried to rationalize his concern for her. The hospital couldn't spare anyone willing to work these days. It was, however, growing sillier by the day to refuse admitting the truth. He suspected she might be right about his India gum heart being overused, because it was certainly involved whenever he thought of her.

"He's exhausted," Cal said to her as she approached the other side of the cot. He let her stay there, only because he was sure the binding on that side was secure. "Sleep is what he needs most."

"Don't want to," came the surprisingly clear response from the patient himself. "Been waiting for you to get here, miss."

"Me, Mr. Bulldog?" Abigail prompted.

Bulldog nodded, looking from one to the other. He tried to move, and Cal stiffened to see the man's amber eyes widen. But Bulldog let his arms fall back to his side as he tried sitting up, looking for something. "My bag," he said. "Where is it?"

"It's here," said Abigail, and she pulled up the seabag that had been stored beneath the bedside table.

"There's a bottle—"

Cal wouldn't protest if Bulldog wanted a strong drink, though he wondered what Abigail would do. She was, by all accounts, not only a woman of faith, but recently of the fruit-punch circle in polite society.

"If you're thirsty, I can find a glass for you," she offered, leaving Cal wondering if she'd fill that glass with whatever was in Bulldog's bottle, or water.

"No, it's. . .not that kind of bottle," Bulldog said. "It may be worth nothin' but what the bronze could be melted for. Still, it's priceless to me. I'd like to see it again."

Abigail offered the bag to him, evidently forgetting for the moment that Bulldog was still bound to the bed frame. Cal hoped Bulldog wouldn't ask her to free him, regardless of his present state of cognizance.

"It's tucked along the side."

One of her hands disappeared inside the seabag. He'd admired her hands before today, how slender and yet strong they were, graceful yet competent. In a moment she pulled the thing out. It was old and likely worthless, Bulldog was right about that. The dark bronze cask was dented here and there, with more than a few scratches. The cap was tightly sealed with some kind of wax. But even with all its wear, an elegant engraving graced its neck: a design or letters. It was hard to tell at first glance.

Bulldog lifted his head to better see it then lay back on the pillow with a smile of satisfaction on his leathery face, as if reunited with a long-lost friend. "Do you see it? What's written there, on the neck?"

The old, battered bottle was curved but not thick, shaped almost like a flask. Abigail held it high, aiming toward the light from the window. "Letters," Abigail said. "A word. Let's see. . . . An *S* is clear, along with a *P*. . . Oh! It's *S-P-E-R-O*. That's Latin, isn't it? For 'hope'?"

Bulldog's serene smile deepened. "It is. Do you know, I always thought I might want to have a look inside that bottle at a time such as this."

"I can open it for you if you like," Abigail offered.

"It—it already gave me what I needed." He seemed to bask in whatever notions the bottle conjured for him, staring ahead as if neither Cal nor Abigail were there. But then he came out of it, looking at Cal. "I want you to have the bottle. A young man needs something like this, some reminder that we oughtn't lose hope. I kept waiting for the moment I thought I'd need to look inside for more than just that word. But the reminder was always enough. Like it is now. I wouldn't hold it against ya if you want to know the contents, but maybe all you need is what's written there."

He coughed again, and this time Abigail was quicker with a cloth. It was just as well; the cotton Cal carried was nearly soaked through.

"You decide whether or not to open it, Bulldog," Cal said. "It's your bottle."

"Maybe after you've rested we can open it," Abigail suggested.

Bulldog didn't seem to hear her. "It's paper in there—I guessed from the flutter when I used to shake it. Maybe a parchment from a king. A love letter? Orders from a general. A note from a shipwrecked sailor. Or a banknote." He closed his eyes. "I could have been owner of a fortune, but my imagination was likely more real. That word—*hope*—was reminder enough from God Himself."

"You need to rest now," said Cal. "I've seen cases like yours recover, so you have every right to claim the hope you've just been reminded about."

Bulldog opened his eyes again, looking at Cal. "No, sir. I'm ready to go on. But one more thing, and then I'll go to sleep and I hope never to wake up, not on this earth, anyway. I'm giving that bottle to you on one condition." Then he shifted his gaze to Abigail. "I waited for you as witness. The time will come when this doctor should be reminded of hope. You will do that for him, miss, won't you? You can even tell him to look inside if he wants. There's no crime in it. And then if he wants to someday, he can pass it along to give someone else hope, the way it's done for me."

Cal looked instantly to Abigail, saw her blush. No matter how generous of Bulldog, how thoughtful, it was the most inappropriate sort of gift. It tied a woman about to be married to someone else to an unmarried man when their only association should be in their profession. But when she caught his eye, he couldn't have been more pleased when she nodded.

"I will, Bulldog. I'll remind him."

Chapter Fifteen

Abigail wasn't sure why she didn't leave that night, although as usual there were plenty of patients to tend. But she kept her eye on Bulldog. She'd seen death far too many times, and not just from a fever that killed half its victims. Though Bulldog was certainly among her most pleasant patients, she stayed because she didn't want to leave Dr. Tallery—who wouldn't leave Bulldog.

He was at Bulldog's side when the old sailor died. Afterward, the doctor revealed no outward sign of grief: he filled out the appropriate form for the hospital and health commission and stood by as the body was collected. The only difference came when he directed the ward assistant to send the body to a funeral director Abigail recognized: one who tended to the needs of the best families in New York.

"That was good of you, Doctor," Abigail said as she approached his side while two attendants took Bulldog out on a stretcher. "To stay with him, and now to pay for a proper burial."

It was certainly more than any other sailor far from his own home port would have received. She wasn't even sure Bulldog had a home.

Dr. Tallery's gaze followed Bulldog all the way to the door. "He was kind to me when I didn't deserve it." Then, Bulldog gone, he pulled out his pocket watch. "It's past midnight, Miss Van de Klerk. We both ought to go home."

She nodded. "Yes, you're right. I'm surprised my father didn't stop in on his way home. He said he might, if only to drag me along."

"Then I'll see you home, to vouch for your dedication. Although," he added, "I'm sure your father doesn't need anyone speaking on your behalf."

She averted her gaze and murmured a thank-you then went about the normal procedure to let the staff know she would be leaving at last and would return later than usual in the morning. When she found Dr. Tallery still at the hospital doors, she was too tired to either explain or fight her delight over the notion that he'd been true to his word and waited.

But seeing his empty hands, she looked back at the ward. "Aren't you forgetting something, Doctor?"

He looked at her, obviously perplexed.

"The bottle. I was assigned to make sure you took proper ownership of it, and to remind you of it now and then."

A slow smile formed on his face, but one that quickly turned grim. "I'm not sure he ought to have given it to me."

"I think he knew exactly what he was doing, particularly if you need reminding. I'll get it."

She found the seabag just where she'd left it, beneath the bedside table that had belonged to Bulldog only a little while ago. She'd already stripped the sheets, and the bed now awaited Bulldog's replacement.

There was proper procedure for personal items brought in by patients without family, and so Abigail retraced her steps to the nursing office. She stayed only long enough to remove the bottle, to report she was taking it to Dr. Tallery who had been bequeathed the item in her presence. They would record it and any other items in the bag that would likely be given to the only heir Bulldog had named: Dr. Tallery.

As she approached him once again, she held out the bottle. His hand brushed hers as he accepted the item, and once again she hadn't the energy to quell her reaction. For Ordell's sake, she ought to see herself home and not spend a moment longer than necessary in the company of a man whose mere touch could spin her heart. But she simply couldn't resist his company.

It was such an odd hour, the normal hack wasn't at the corner. Another soon appeared, and Dr. Tallery helped her inside.

Perhaps they were both too tired; perhaps it was the sadness over losing Bulldog. Neither spoke as the carriage rambled along, horse's hooves clattering to break the silence. She wondered if he was thinking about the bottle, wondering where it had been and what was inside, the way his thumb went over the single word etched near its opening.

"Will you open it?" she asked at last.

"I don't care what's inside. That bottle didn't do Bulldog any good against the fever, did it?" He offered the bottle to her. "Would you like it?"

She gasped. "Oh, no! He meant for it to be yours, Dr. Tallery, at least longer than an hour. How could you even think to give it away so soon?"

He looked at it again, brows sinking as if somewhat abashed. "It's because of that word."

He spoke so quietly she wasn't sure she'd heard him. Perhaps he hadn't meant for her to hear. "Hope?"

He nodded. "I've forgotten how."

Abigail was tempted to abandon her seat to squeeze herself beside him, to draw him into her arms and assure him there must always be hope. What else had Christ come for, but that? This time, however, even in her fatigue she pushed away the idea of being so close to him. She couldn't be so bold, whether or not Ordell would object. Instead, she whispered, "I think that's exactly why Bulldog wanted you to have the bottle. To help you remember."

The silence between them resumed, and after a few moments she wondered if the exchange had even happened. There was something undeniably intimate about the words he'd shared, as if baring part of his soul. Perhaps she'd fallen asleep right inside this carriage and had dreamed it. In a way, she almost hoped she had, and it had nothing to do with guilt over sharing a meaningful moment with another man who was not Ordell. She could only feel as if she'd failed to encourage him. Dr. Tallery was likely every bit as exhausted as she, which was probably why the grief that hadn't shown earlier at the hospital was now absolutely clear.

"Bulldog was right to give it to you," she said at last, knowing the carriage would soon stop at her home and she must leave him. She couldn't do so without offering what little more she could. "And right now, he is in paradise. He wouldn't come back even if he could."

Then the carriage did stop, just as she'd expected. She remained still, though she would have to go inside now, claim much-needed rest. Perhaps rest was what he needed, too, every bit as much as a reminder of hope.

Dr. Tallery pulled open the carriage door, alighting to assist her before the coachman could.

But to her surprise, before she could even say good night, she heard the rapid tap of shoes against the stones leading from her house. Bromley stopped a few feet from them, a look of utter horror on his old, familiar face.

"It's your father, miss."

Chapter Sixteen

Abigail scrambled from the coach, at first not aware that Dr. Tallery followed. But as she rushed inside and up the stairs, she was more than a little relieved to hear not only Bromley's steps echoing hers, but Dr. Tallery's, as well.

"What happened?" She called the question over her shoulder.

"He collapsed when he got home," Bromley said, his words coming in spurts between gasps for air. "He came in just a short time ago—but then I didn't hear footsteps on the stairs. So I came to check and found him inside the door."

Myriad thoughts clamored in Abigail's brain as she tiptoed into the room nearest the top of the stairs. It was dim, just one lamp lit beside the bed. The windows were open, but no breeze stirred the curtains. She stopped at her father's bedside, where Bromley had already supplied a bowl for her father's sickness—something he'd already been using.

"Oh! Father!"

Bromley and Dr. Tallery went to the opposite side of the bed. She made no objection when Dr. Tallery set aside the bronze bottle he'd carried then touched her father's forehead just as she checked his neck to assess just how high the fever might be.

"Now, now." She'd thought Father sleeping, but his grumbled voice was clear and coherent.

Vaguely, she heard Dr. Tallery giving orders to Bromley. Cool drinks of barley water interchanged with apple water to bring down the fever. Red wine with laudanum to help him sleep. A good supply of damp cloths to minister to face and hands and arms. Everything she might have said had she not been gripped with tears and fear.

"How long have you been ill?"

"I'm not so sick," Father said, but then his body denied the words as he retched again into the bowl. Abigail went to the washstand in the corner of the room, returning with a dampened towel to wipe his face and hands.

"I'll stay with you until you're better," she promised. "But now you must sleep."

"I'll sleep if you do, daughter," he said, his eyes fluttering.

She offered a cheerless smile. "Yes, Father. I will, right here."

There was a padded chair in Father's room, which Dr. Tallery was already shoving closer to the bedside. One of the pillows hung unused near the edge of the mattress, and he grabbed that, too, then stood by as if inviting Abigail to the spot.

"Thank you," she whispered.

"I'll stay," he said, two words that increased the tears in her eyes.

But she couldn't accept. "No, Doctor. You need rest, too."

"Bromley will be back with the barley water soon. I can help you with that."

"I'll manage."

If he was offended by her rejection, Abigail couldn't tell. But how could she accept, knowing he'd been awake as long or longer than she had? Nonetheless, he stayed until Bromley entered a few minutes later with the broth then quietly slipped from the room.

Her gaze fell on the bottle at her father's bedside table, and she nearly called to remind him about it. But she caught her own words.

She guessed Dr. Tallery had purposely left the bottle with the single word facing her:

Hope.

Cal went no farther than down the stairs. He could sleep here as easily as he could at his own home—empty now since Early had left for the Pipperday country house.

Even as Cal removed his shoes and loosened the cravat at his throat to settle upon the long, padded couch in the Van de Klerk parlor, he called himself a fool. He'd vowed not to befriend these people. But even during the time he'd worked with Dr. Van de Klerk, the older man had charmed him as easily as he obviously charmed his patients. He was kindness and calmness and wisdom and experience all in one, and anyone within the radius of his voice rarely wanted to leave it.

How could Cal *not* care? His heart would surely have to be as dead as he'd hoped it to be. The only foolish notion had been believing it was.

He had little trouble falling asleep but woke before feeling rested. He looked out the window: still dark. Perhaps his unusual surroundings were to blame for his fitfulness, although it was true he'd learned to snatch sleep wherever and whenever he could.

Then he heard something from the hall. Someone was coming down the stairs. Cal sat up. With moonlight filtering in from the high windows above the front door, he could easily see the staircase through the wide archway leading from parlor to vestibule. It was Abigail, bowl in hand.

Cal left the couch, calling softly so as not to startle her. "How is he?"

She must have been accustomed to the dark, since even though he'd removed his shoes and had walked soundlessly to the archway, she had little trouble directing her gaze his way.

"No worse," she said. "But no better."

He approached her at the foot of the stairs. "I've slept. Why don't you let me watch over him for a while so you can rest?"

She shook her head, though he saw the hint of a grateful smile. "I slept a little, too. Chairs can be comfortable enough."

"Yes, I know."

She nodded again, eying him. "Thank you for staying, Doctor. Though you needn't. I'm sure you'll want to go back to the hospital in the morning. Will you explain for me that I won't be there until my father is better?"

He wondered if she believed he would recover. Cal saw in a moment her confidence was false. The dim light wasn't enough to hide a quiver to her lips, the sag to her shoulders. He stepped closer, taking the bowl from her hands and setting it on a stair behind them.

"Abigail," he whispered, and for a moment he was unsure what to say next. How could he offer hope when he knew it to be a cruel friend? So he said nothing, only took her into his arms.

She sobbed then, tears mixing with words he soon recognized as a prayer. For the first time in longer than he could remember, Cal added his own prayers to hers.

He wasn't sure how long they stood like that, praying softly together. The embrace was too natural, too needed to be wrong or unexpected. But eventually he knew he must let go. He retrieved the bowl, walked to what he assumed was the way to the kitchen where she must have been headed. There, he directed her to a chair while he went to the pump at the sink. He washed out the bowl, rinsed the rags. Looked through drawers before she directed him to one with more linens, then supplied what she needed before escorting her back to the stairs.

He was half-tempted to go up with her but didn't. He wasn't needed. He did hope he'd given her some comfort—enough to see her through the rest of the night.

But rather than going home, he returned to the Van de Klerk parlor.

This time a persistent tapping woke him. Cal opened his eyes, for a moment wondering where he was. Dreams of the islands haunted him, reliving his bedside vigil next to Charles so that now, almost awake, he was deeply aware of a sense of dread.

Then he remembered where he was, and why. He stood, intending to check on Daniel Van de Klerk even as another dream came to mind, of comforting a crying Abigail. More wondrous than that, praying with her. Was it a dream? Repeated tapping interrupted the vivid recollection. Someone was at the front door.

Cal was barely aware of his own disheveled appearance as he pulled on the door handle, but upon seeing a gentleman impeccably dressed—white collar in stark contrast to his black frock coat—the difference between their attire couldn't have been more obvious.

"Isn't this. . .that is, I *am* at the Van de Klerk's?"

Cal knew immediately who the man must be: Abigail's soon-to-be-announced fiancé. Guilt erupted, accusing him of taking advantage of Abigail during the midnight hours when she'd been distraught. He shouldn't have held her so close; he could have let her pass the parlor for the kitchen without even letting her know he was there.

The other man looked confused enough to turn away, but his eye caught the medicine room sign identifying the correct address, so he faced Cal again.

"My apologies," Cal said. "The household is in some distress this morning, which must include the staff. Come in."

He stepped aside, and the man entered, looking around as if more evidence was needed that he'd arrived at the right place.

"I know it's early, barely eleven, but is Abigail Van de Klerk at home?"

"Yes, she's upstairs with her father. He's taken ill." It occurred to Cal that he ought to explain his presence, but he decided to let the man assume the truth: that he'd stayed out of concern for the patient. That was mostly the case.

He was about to invite him to wait when Bromley appeared at the top of the stairs. He was fully dressed, though his usually impeccable jacket was rumpled and his vest askew. Hurrying down the stairs, he apologized as he approached.

"My apologies, Reverend Lebsock. I'm terribly sorry I wasn't here to open the door."

Cal perused the new arrival. He'd witnessed the sad observation that too few priests or pastors came to the hospital recently, either to comfort the sick or to be at the side of a dying parishioner. He ought not hope for cowardice in this man but found himself looking for fault anyway, at least enough to pronounce him unworthy of Abigail.

"I don't wish to intrude if her father wishes privacy, but please let Miss Van de Klerk know I'm here if either she—or her father—would like me to visit with them."

"Right away," said Bromley then retraced his steps up the stairs.

The reverend had removed his white summer straw hat but twirled it awkwardly through his fingertips. His gaze first avoided then settled on Cal.

"I'm Dr. Tallery," Cal said.

"Ah, the doctor from the islands? Dr. Van de Klerk's new partner?"

It sounded so simple from his lips, so innocent. Cal nodded.

"Abigail—that is, Miss Van de Klerk, has wanted me to meet her father for some time now. I never envisioned it in such a way, with him possibly on his death—" He cut himself off. "You've been tending him, I suppose. How is he?"

"Abigail—Miss Van de Klerk—stayed with him through the night. I haven't yet seen him this morning. But last night he appeared to have all the signs of yellow fever."

The man closed his eyes as if he'd received a blow, until Cal realized he was praying. As hard as he'd hoped, Cal couldn't find fault with him so far. Besides, even Cal himself had succumbed in a moment of confused weakness to praying for the man. He was tempted to announce it would do no good, that he had all the evidence he needed against prayer saving anyone. His brothers; his father; his mother; Charles; Bulldog. And now, he feared, Dr. Van de Klerk, too.

In that moment, assessing the man surely worthy of Abigail, Cal told himself again that caring led to loss. He could tend the sick at the hospital, those strangers whose loss was great only in number. He mustn't stay here, not where he wasn't needed and where, if he stayed, it threatened to make him care. Abigail's future was clearly secure. Daniel Van de Klerk, if he survived, didn't need Cal, and Cal didn't need him.

So he politely excused himself, retrieved his coat, put on his shoes, and found his way out.

Chapter Seventeen

Abigail woke to Bromley's voice.

"Reverend Lebsock has arrived, miss. He offered to visit with your father if you like."

Ordell! Here, now? Only a moment ago—in her dreams?—she'd been with Calvin Tallery. She glanced at the window, seeing the sun was high.

Thankfully, Bromley's hushed tone hadn't wakened her father. The laudanum-laced wine was clearly working, and she clung to hope her father would make a full recovery. It had been hours since he'd last vomited; his forehead was cooler, his pulse strong.

"I hadn't anticipated Ordell meeting Father in such a way," she said. "I'm not sure Father will appreciate it, once he's more himself. Will you ask Dr. Tallery to come up instead? I'll see Ordell in a moment."

Alone again with her sleeping father, Abigail couldn't stop her thoughts from straying to Dr. Tallery. Calvin. Cal, she'd heard Early Goodwin call him. Was that how he referred to himself? Cal. . .

She was vastly more interested in seeing Dr. Tallery than seeing Ordell, and wondered at her lack of shame. Clearly her heart wasn't cooperating in the plans she'd made for her future. Perhaps having Ordell arrive now was the opportunity she needed to let him know she was having second thoughts.

Even with such serious pondering, she couldn't help but smile. Perhaps she could still have the future her father wanted for her. Remembering Calvin's arms about her last night—and more importantly, the soft cadence of his voice as he'd prayed—her hopes deepened. They multiplied when her gaze fell again on the bronze bottle he'd left for her and her father.

Hope!

In a moment, the door opened and she caught back her breath, but she was disappointed to see Bromley.

"I'm afraid Dr. Tallery has left, miss."

"Left?" *Without a word? Without checking on Father?*

"Likely returned to the hospital, if he's anything like you and your father."

Abigail nodded automatically, even as her heart sank.

Bromley neared the bedside as if to take over the vigil. "I'll come for you if he wakes."

"Hmm? Oh, yes." She checked her father's forehead once again, relieved at its coolness. "I'll see the reverend now."

Then she made her way downstairs, without even bothering to check her appearance in Father's mirror.

Ordell offered all the right words. He promised prayers for her father's quick recovery, for her strength in caring for him. He spoke of admiration that she was so well equipped to supply what her father needed. But she only half listened. On the floor between the parlor and the foyer, she spotted a dropped handkerchief, as if its owner had left in a hurry.

While listening to Ordell tell of yet another funeral he was helping to plan—she was sick nearly to death of death itself—she left her chair to retrieve the abandoned item. Sure enough, she spotted the initials *CT* embroidered in purple. She tucked it in a pocket, wondering when she would have the opportunity to return it and if she wanted to. Why had he left? It was forgivable that he'd gone without a word to her—he might, after all, regret having taken a woman into his arms under the intimacy of the night when she'd told him she belonged to another. But to leave without asking after her father was something else altogether.

"And so I was hoping you might attend the service, even though you didn't know the deceased. It'll help you to get used to my work, because once I have my own church, where I'm preaching every Sunday, you'll be every bit my helpmate."

"Attend the funeral? Of. . .someone I don't know? Won't the family think me— well, unnecessary at best, an intruder at worst?"

With the strain to keep her attention on Ordell came the blatant, definite realization she lacked devotion to him; she barely thought of him when they were apart. She'd been wrong to believe they would make a compatible, effective team.

"If they understand you're to be my wife, it will be perfectly acceptable."

"But, Ordell, I would no more expect you to be at the side of the patients I tend—at least unless they were near death—than I would expect to be at your side when you're carrying out your duties."

His lips pursed. "I'd hoped you wouldn't compare my duties to yours, Abigail, that you'd come to the same conclusion I have." He glanced to the ceiling, as if seeing her father. "Besides, once he's. . . Well, after he's gone, even if he fully recovers this very day, you won't have a circuit the way he does, or run a medicine room without a doctor. Your future is likely to be very different once your father is no longer with you."

"How can you even speak of—even hint that he might die? You haven't seen him. I have every reason to believe he has only a slight case and will make a full recovery."

"Of course!" He took her hand, patting it. "I didn't mean—I spoke without thought."

She pulled her hand from his. "I realize no one lives forever, and I haven't forgotten my father's age. However, there are a great number of people who have trusted me because they know my father has trained me well. Besides, this house will be mine. My brothers don't want to live here. I do. I see no reason why I wouldn't continue to operate the medicine room myself."

"You? Alone?"

"Is that such a shock?"

"I thought that was the reason your father was taking on a partner? To take over. . . Well, as you say, your father is older and must plan to leave his medicine room to Dr. Tallery."

Pure anger filled her, half at Ordell's assumptions and half at her own fear that he might be right. Surely her father had been entirely honest when he'd said he only wanted her to marry because he feared for her future? That he'd considered working with Dr. Tallery because the opportunity presented itself, not because he'd planned for Dr. Tallery to take over?

She stood, her mind awhirl. "Ordell," she began, keeping her back to him. Words failed her, so she took in a deep breath. "I think we both fear the same thing—that we cannot continue." She spun around, certain she would recognize on his face what she felt inside. Sorrow, certainly. But relief, too? "Isn't it best to realize our mistake before anyone else knows we've made it?"

Instead of agreement he looked confused. He stood, searching her face now, too, perhaps hoping she didn't mean what seemed obvious. "It isn't a mistake. I've prayed ceaselessly about it. Our marriage still makes sense to me."

She held his gaze. "But it doesn't to me. I'm sorry."

Chapter Eighteen

Before going to the hospital, Cal stopped at home to freshen and change clothes. He even ate a small lunch, though his stomach simultaneously yearned and turned at the thought of food. Fortunately, it wasn't the kind of stomach ailment that came with the fever.

Although he forced himself to focus on each task at hand, his mind returned to the Van de Klerks. How was the doctor faring? How was Abigail coping? Such thoughts were like a rope, pulling Cal from the hospital and to their home.

By six in the evening, he could ignore it no longer. He must go back, no matter how much he tried to resist. It was too late not to suffer if Daniel Van de Klerk succumbed to the fever—if not on Abigail's behalf and the undeniable love he knew he held for her, but for the respect and admiration her father had earned from him even before Cal had come back to New York. He must do all he could to prevent such a loss, or offer whatever commiseration he could if the feeble attempts of medicine failed.

Abigail collapsed into the chair at her father's bedside, heart still pounding from the ordeal she and Bromley had just suffered. Even now, tears welled in her eyes to see the bindings she and the butler had been forced to apply to her father's surprisingly strong limbs: evidence that the fever held him in a deeper grip than she wanted to believe.

She hadn't wanted to restrain him, but she still felt the sting along her jaw from where the back of her father's hand had caught her. He hadn't meant to do it. If he were coherent, as he was surely bound to be any moment now, he would be horrified. As soon as she regained control of herself, she must go to the mirror and make sure there was no evidence of the strike. She should apply a cold cloth—a challenge considering the summer's heat had melted the last bit of ice they'd stored in the yard's ice pit—then go to the medicine room for some comfrey for a warm compress.

She collected herself, taking her gaze from Father only to glance once again at the bottle. *Hope.*

Bromley stood by, no longer wearing his usual coat. Considering the indignity brought to her father by his illness, any sort of protocol seemed downright silly. As grateful as she was for the faithful servant, she'd never felt so alone just then. Her father had forced her to deepen her friendship with Mindia, but Mindia was safely in the country. Without Father himself to lean on, Abigail had no one.

With Father asleep again, it was easy to escape the room in an attempt to abandon her thoughts as well. Unfortunately but not unexpectedly, an image of Cal followed. She wished, not for the first time, that he was here with her. His absence might be a roundabout compliment, evidence he thought her entirely competent to give her father the best care. Nonetheless, she couldn't help feeling abandoned when she and her father needed him most.

The clock in the foyer chimed half past six just as she reached the bottom step. She'd miss another meal, although Marta was no doubt preparing something anyway in between her constant scrubbing. She suspected the cook's loyalty had been tested since Father came home with the contagion, but so far loyalty was winning.

Just then, Abigail saw a shadow pass the window near the door. She'd sent a messenger to her brothers, asking them both to come home, but it was too soon for either to have traveled all the way here. Curious, she opened the door before whoever was there had a chance to knock.

Cal stood before her, a grim yet reassuring look on his face. For a moment she wished she could cast aside protocol here, too, and throw herself into his arms out of sheer gratitude and relief. Caution held her back. He might be polite enough to make a house call, but that didn't mean he'd come to support her. Besides, a new germ of resentment hovered in her mind. He might be her father's replacement, a role she'd always envisioned for herself.

"How is he?"

The lack of greeting neither surprised nor upset her. Without waiting for an invitation, he stepped inside. As he passed her she heard his breathing stop, and one of his hands rose to her face, tilting it so he could better peer at the very spot she'd intended to treat.

"Do you have any parsley?" he asked.

She was glad he hadn't made an issue of the bruise. A doctor like Dawson might have castigated her for not binding a fever patient before it came to that. "I was just going for a cool cloth, though we don't have any ice left."

"Not many places do this summer."

He was fully inside now, closing the door when she forgot.

"Which would you like me to do?" he asked. "See about your bruise, or go straight to your father? I've let the hospital know I'm here to relieve you and won't return until your father is on the mend."

"You'll stay?" she asked, nearly breathless with hope and fear.

"If you'll let me, after having run away this morning. That is," he added, "if your reverend won't mind having someone working at your side who holds you in far greater regard than any mere colleague should."

Abigail nearly cried with happy relief, a stark contrast to the horror of the past few hours. Before she could sort her thoughts, Cal put a hand on each of her shoulders.

"Abigail, this isn't the time for me to clutter your mind with my confessions, but you ought to know your intended isn't the only man in love with you. Let me stay, no matter how you feel about me. I know you're fully capable of giving your father the best care, but I can relieve you. Will you let me?"

She nearly fell against him and was grateful when he took her into his arms. "Yes, Cal, absolutely yes."

Chapter Nineteen

Dr. Van de Klerk's fever fell but rose again in defiance of Cal's best efforts. Despite his presence, Abigail never left. She sat but did not sleep, even after sending Bromley for much-needed rest.

Night came again, and neither spoke of what had happened downstairs. Cal didn't regret his confession, especially when his gaze occasionally met Abigail's. He saw nothing there to dissuade his love for her.

But that could be because she was filled with gratitude for his help. He knew this night would see resolution: either her father's fever would break, or it would be the end of him. Cal found himself praying more than once, knowing Abigail did, too.

Although there was another chair, the one Bromley had used while he'd helped care for the doctor, Cal rarely used it. Instead he sat on the edge of the bed, if only to prevent Abigail from doing so. He held the bowl for the blackened vomit, wiped at the doctor's chin, administered all the aid they knew to give. For the last hour her father appeared too worn even to vomit.

Not for the first time, Cal's tired gaze fell on Abigail. She was awake but was looking at neither her father nor Cal. Instead, she stared at the bottle.

"Open it," he said, low. "We can all use what it claims to hold."

To his relief, her brows rose with interest. She'd looked so downhearted he was convinced she was losing confidence, even the pretense of it. At least this, if only an exercise, would occupy her mind for a while.

Slowly but without hesitation, she picked up the bottle. The seal was waxen, ancient, partly cracked but still intact. It took little more than a pinch to break what wax remained, but the stopper beneath was sunk deep. She stood, going to a medical bag that probably belonged to her father and pulling out a surgical knife—long and sleek. But her hand trembled, so he offered his. She gave the bottle to him.

In a moment he flipped it open, but rather than emptying it, he returned it to Abigail. She turned it upside down, and a small scroll tumbled out, tightly bound so not to catch at the narrow mouth.

Abigail looked at Cal, as if for his permission to read it. He nodded, at the same time turning up the wick on the bedside lamp.

The scroll was old but not brittle, not even faded since no light had touched it in some time.

"Oh, Cal," she whispered, and he knew for certain his heart wasn't dead because it leaped at his name on her lips. "It's from the Bible. I know some of these verses."

Instead of reading from the scroll, she handed it to Cal so her hands were free to search a shelf beneath the bedside table. In a moment she brought a Bible to light.

"From Isaiah. . . 'Sing. . .and be joyful. . . . The Lord hath comforted his people. . . .' And John"—she turned the pages again—"about the many mansions He's preparing for us, so where He is, we can be."

Cal looked at the list, neatly written in bold, masculine English scrawl. "Matthew 22:31 and 32."

She rifled the pages again, reading aloud with a quavering voice about God not being the God of the dead, but of the living. Next on the list was from Revelation, promising no more death nor sorrow nor crying or pain, the former things having passed away.

"You said when Bulldog died that he went to paradise," Cal reminded her. "That even if he could he wouldn't want to come back. All of these verses say it's true."

Tears sparkled in her lovely blue eyes. "Is it selfish of me to want to keep my father here a bit longer?"

Cal shook his head then looked at the last verse on the list. This handwriting was different from the rest. Softly feminine, practiced, and as elegant as the engraving on the bottle's exterior. "This last one from the thirtieth Psalm is likely filled with praise. There is hope in praise, Abigail."

She smiled in spite of her tears. "So the bottle does offer what it claims?"

"Indeed."

Abigail read the last of the verses aloud, of turning mourning into dancing, being girded with gladness. She looked at her father as she spoke the final words, torn between faith and need. She knew in her heart his life was in God's hands, but even as she ended the quote she burst into tears, pleading God's mercy would extend to her in her weakness over the thought of going on without him.

"Now, now. None of that."

Abigail didn't know why she was weeping, whether from gratitude over the bottle's reminder or fear that such verses were meant to usher her father into heaven with God's promises still echoing in his ears. But the words stopped her. Had they been spoken aloud, or only in her mind? Because surely the voice was not Cal's.

Cal's surprised gaze met hers, confirming he'd heard it, too. She fell to her knees at the bedside, where her hand met Cal's at her father's forehead.

Cool!

As if to fortify Abigail's hopes, her father opened his eyes. "I believe I've had enough rest, my dear."

"Oh! Father!"

Then she wept again, hugging him, feeling his hand reach feebly to pat her hair.

Abigail was almost afraid to leave him but knew Bromley would fetch her if anything changed. She went downstairs with Cal to the parlor, where the air was a trifle cooler.

"No fever for eight hours," Cal whispered, as if reading her mind. "He kept the barley water down, too. He'll be fine."

How had Cal known those were the words she needed to hear, in spite of telling herself the same thing? Whether it was pure exhaustion or that she was finished fighting any resistance to him, Abigail let herself fall against Cal. He accepted her into his embrace.

"I ought not take advantage of your weariness," Cal whispered, holding her close, "but I don't want to let go."

"Perhaps I'm taking advantage of you." She pulled away just far enough to look into his eyes, smiling. "Since I clearly demanded you hold me."

His gaze was steady. "And what of your reverend?"

"He's not mine," she admitted, suddenly feeling more invigorated than she had in days. "We weren't well suited, and I told him so."

Cal's brows rose in what she hoped was delight. "Then. . .I may kiss you without stealing another man's bride-to-be?"

"You may kiss me," she said, nearly adding she hoped she might still be a bride-to-be. Someday.

He bent his head, but before completing the kiss, he held back with a grin. "In fact, I prefer kissing a bride-to-be. My own, if you'll have me."

"Thank you for reading my mind, Calvin Tallery. I'm sure my father would say I should allow a kiss only if it's accompanied by the best of intentions."

Then his mouth came down on hers, and Abigail's hope for the future was complete.

Chapter Twenty

Abigail reveled in the chilly weather. After such a hot, horrendous summer, she vowed not to complain about the cold this winter. Frosts stopped the spread of fevers, and this fall was no exception. This morning as she waited in the parlor, she took a moment to praise God, knowing He always put a limit on suffering, even if those limits were tested.

It had been several weeks since the last fever victim had come to the hospital, two weeks since she'd returned to her father's medicine room. Father was still weak, despite his excellent recovery, and asked Cal to help Abigail with his patient circuit. It had always been too much for just one doctor, and because of that, they all knew Abigail wouldn't be able to easily take it over on her own.

She was surprisingly grateful for Cal's aid on the circuit. Besides her work, it was a consuming endeavor to plan not a single but a double wedding. Ever since Mrs. Pipperday had seen Early Goodwin's talent as an artist when he painted Mindia's portrait, she'd not only launched his reputation into the best circles of the city, but welcomed him into the family.

Abigail waited for Cal, looking forward to the day they would be united in marriage and live under this same roof. Now that Early had the promise of a steadier income, he'd offered to buy Cal's home as soon as he was able. Cal had asked Abigail if she had a preference as to where they should live, and she'd confessed she'd always wanted to live in her own home, where their patients were used to coming. So with Father no longer traveling farther than the medicine room itself, Cal and Abigail traveled the neighborhood on the days they weren't working in the office or at the hospital.

Father had asked about the bottle he'd found at his bedside, and Abigail told him how it delivered exactly what it promised when she'd needed it most. Cal had made a gift of it to her, and she'd accepted only because she knew it would be his again after they married. The bottle held a prominent place on the parlor mantel, where it reminded her often of the meaning of real hope.

Each and every time Abigail's gaze fell upon the bottle, as now, she longed for her wedding day, only weeks away at last. Just the evening before, Mindia had arrived with a copy of the invitations requesting guests for the joyous occasion of joining in matrimony not only Miss Mindia Pipperday to Mr. Early Goodwin but also Miss Abigail Van de Klerk to Dr. Calvin Tallery. It promised to be New York's social event of the blessedly welcome new season.

Abigail caught a glimpse of Cal's shadow as he made his way to the front door. They'd made a habit of greeting each other in the foyer every morning, a far more private place to begin the day—and so many more to come—with a kiss.

Abigail hurried to open the door.

Maureen Lang writes stories inspired by a love of history and romance. An avid reader herself, she's figured out a way to write the stories she feels like reading. Maureen's inspirationals have earned various writing distinctions including the Inspirational Reader's Choice Contest, a HOLT Medallion, and the Selah Award, as well as being a finalist for the Rita, Christy, and Carol Awards. In addition to investigating various eras in history (such as Victorian England, First World War, and America's Gilded Age), Maureen loves taking research trips to get a feel for the settings of her novels. She lives in the Chicago area with her family and has been blessed to be the primary caregiver to her adult disabled son.

A River between Us

by Jocelyn Green

Chapter One

Roswell, Georgia
July 6, 1864

Water roared over the dam behind her, an echo of the blood rushing in her ears. Dropping to her knees, Cora Mae Stewart plunged her spade into the earth. The Yankees were coming. Everyone knew it, since the Southern army had burned the bridge over the Chattahoochee River yesterday and retreated south. The few valuables she and her mother possessed she would not see into their pillaging hands.

In dawn's watery light, Cora Mae carved away enough soil to make room for a cigar box wrapped in oiled paper. Inside the box nestled some dented silverware, jewelry, and tintypes of her father and brother in their Confederate uniforms.

Heart thundering, she tucked the box down deep and refilled the hole. Spray from the waterfall beaded on her pinned-up hair. Rising, she made a passing attempt to brush the dirt off her apron. Her bare feet, however, were hopelessly coated with mud.

Movement flickered in the corner of her eye. She whirled toward it, her spade thrust out. Poor defense against a Yankee marauder, indeed. "Hello?"

A man stepped from between the trees and doffed his hat.

Relief rushed through her at the sight of her father's friend. "Why, Mr. Ferguson!"

"I do wish you'd call me Horace." But at forty years old, he was twice her age, and a loom boss.

"I was just—"

"I saw. Getting ready for the bluebellies, that so?"

She began walking toward the cotton mill just beyond the dam that powered it. "I aim to get to work on time." She persuaded a steadiness into her voice. "Mama's feeling poorly today, but she'll be back just as soon as she can."

He matched her stride. "Sorry to hear it. That's the second time in two weeks, ain't it?"

It was. More than twenty years of inhaling cotton dust and lint took its toll. Her gaze scaled the red bricks of the four-story factory as she approached.

"Hate to say it, but Matilda may lose her spot at the mill. She don't have much work left in her, God bless her. I'm sorry about it, and I'm sorry you lost your pap and brother in this danged war. You've gone from four wage earners in the family to just you."

Pausing in front of the factory, Cora Mae wiped her hands on the apron that covered her hoopless, homespun dress. "Then I best not be late."

"Being on time won't answer your troubles." Mr. Ferguson touched her elbow and beckoned her to the side of the building until they were half in shadows again. As other mill girls filed into the building, they stared and whispered behind their hands. "I told your pap I'd look out for you and Matilda. This here's the best way I know how. Do you have an answer for me yet?"

She curled her toes beneath the fraying hem of her skirt. Words stuck in her chest like dry corn bread.

"I checked with the company storekeeper, Cora Mae. You're deeper in debt than your pap ever was, God rest him. If you marry me, we'll combine our wages, and we can all live in my cottage on Mill Street together. Me and you, Matilda, and June."

Cora Mae had forgotten about June. The little girl had started working at the mill the day her mother, Mavis, had married Mr. Ferguson last year.

"Since June's mother died a few months back, she's as lost as can be. She needs a new mother, truth be told, and you surely do need a man's wages on your account."

The bell tower in the mill yard sounded, and she bolted toward the door.

"Won't you answer me?" he called after her.

"I will." The bell chimed again.

"Today!"

She was inside the mill, dashing up the stairs as the bell finished calling out the hour. For now, she had to concentrate on her work or risk an accident. In the weaving room, she hurried to her place at the table where she drew patterns for Confederate uniforms on the special gray cloth.

As she worked, the millhouse rattled and boomed with its own kind of battle noise. Up on the fourth floor, spinning girls spun thread from raw cotton. Their machines whirred so loudly that bobbin girls like June had to watch for hand signals alerting them it was time to deliver another empty bobbin or take away a full one. Brass-tipped shuttles fired across looms to weave the dyed thread into cloth, and of course the mill wheel on Vickery Creek chugged with the power of a locomotive.

The floor shook beneath Cora Mae's bare feet as she worked, and the table trembled beneath the cloth she drew and cut. Her limbs thrummed with the reverberations. Her stooped back ached, but the Confederacy needed the uniforms, tents, and rope the Roswell mill produced. Their instructions were to stay and work until Yankee soldiers drove them out.

By half past six, the sun had lifted its bright head in the sky. Thirty minutes later, the bell rang for the breakfast break, and with a lurch, the mill shut down. She fell in line with the other girls trickling outside and then hurried back up to her apartment on Factory Hill.

With a sharp tug, the back door unstuck from its frame, and she entered their kitchen. Mama was already at the table with a glass of milk and a plate of corn bread. As Cora Mae sat, Mama coughed into her handkerchief, staining the unbleached linen brown. Her smile seemed brave. "Grace, please."

The two bowed their heads, and Cora Mae thanked God for the daily corn bread in her own Southern rendition of the Lord's Prayer. "Amen."

Mama broke off a small piece of bread and ate it. "You look troubled."

Wind blew under the door and ruffled Cora Mae's skirt over her feet. "Mr. Ferguson talked to me again this morning."

"Faithful Mr. Ferguson." Mama smiled. "Remember the corn and sowbelly he left on our doorstep when we most needed it?"

Cora Mae nodded. "He's asking me to marry him. Says we can both move in with him and his stepdaughter on Mill Street."

Blanching, Mama stopped chewing for a moment. Her fingertips rippled over the persimmon seed buttons on her bodice, the way they always did when she was surprised. The irregular shapes spotted the unevenly black fabric Mama had dyed for mourning Pap and Wade. "My land. How very fine."

Cora Mae lost her appetite. "Yes, ma'am, it's very fine."

Mama cleared her throat. "You ain't pleased."

"Pleased enough, I reckon." She dredged up something akin to a smile and prayed her mother had forgotten everything Cora Mae had ever said about wanting to quit the mill and move away. "We sorely need the help, Mama. Just as Pap knew we would." Maybe in time she would grow fond of Mr. Ferguson, the way a wife should. But at the moment, she barely felt anything at all, excepting the grit between her toes.

"Oh, darlin'." Mama placed one hand on the side of Cora Mae's face. Her blue eyes crinkled at the edges. "Before Pap left for the war, he told me that if he should die, I should let Mr. Ferguson—still a bachelor at the time—head our home. It's what he wanted."

Tears stung Cora Mae's throat as she clasped Mama's hand and leaned into it. "It solves our worries." Refusing the offer would be foolhardy.

Mama nodded. "I'll see to the dishes."

"Yes, ma'am." Her chest constricting, Cora Mae rose and pressed a kiss to the top of Mama's silvery-blond hair.

When she returned to the mill, she was not surprised to find Mr. Ferguson waiting for her at the front gate. This time, June was with him, dressed in brown plaid homespun. Her hair, pulled into a bun high on her head, glinted in the sun like a dark copper kettle. Cora Mae smiled down at her.

"Why, you're quite the little Junebug, aren't you?"

The girl's molasses-brown eyes rounded in heart-shaped face. "That's what my ma calls—called me. Did you know?"

Cora Mae tilted her head. "No, but I can see why she did. I'll bet you miss her at least as much as I miss my own pap and brother."

June's brow furrowed. "You lost them?"

"In the war."

Her little hand slipped into Cora Mae's. "You gonna come live with us, then?"

Cora Mae glanced at Mr. Ferguson in time to see him swipe the straw hat from his head and smooth his thinning black hair. "Here, step away a bit." He led her and June away from the gate, where mill girls were streaming back from breakfast. He stopped near the dam on Vickery Creek, within sight of the small mound she'd made at the foot of a tree that dawn.

"Well?" Mr. Ferguson half shouted over the roaring creek. "What do you say?"

Water tumbled down thirty feet before crashing into the creek below. The spray misted her face, and she licked it off her lips. "Yes," she called out.

His eyes brightened. He laid one rough hand against her cheek. "It's for the best. For all of us."

She simply nodded. It was the right thing to do.

"Let's marry today, after work. I'll find a preacher. You can wear Mavis's wedding dress."

Cora Mae reeled. "Tonight!" she gasped. Over the rushing water, the mill bell echoed the alarm in her spirit.

But he had already turned back toward the mill, pulling her behind him over the water-slicked, rocky path. She grasped June's hand as they both struggled to keep from slipping.

Chapter Two

Back at her post at the drawing table, the reverberations of the mill seemed to shake Cora Mae from the inside out. She couldn't stop her hands from trembling. The fact that Horace had been a friend to the Stewarts did nothing to dispel the dread knotting her middle at the thought of the night ahead.

Suddenly, the mill heaved then stopped. Straightening, she turned toward the door to the stairs just as a blue-uniformed officer came striding through it. "Everybody out."

All around her, wide-eyed mill girls looked askance before following the order. Fear cycled up and down Cora Mae's spine as she progressed down the stairs.

Once outside, she stood in the dappled sunshine and listened to the eerie silence of a factory stilled during work hours. The sound of the rushing water pulsed in her ears as she watched the rest of the four hundred workers stream outside. When June appeared, she waved to her, and the little girl scurried over to hold her hand.

Two Yankees fled from the nearby storehouse with cans of oil in their hands then turned back to watch. Crackling flames sounded from the top floor, their fiery-orange tongues lashing out the windows. Timber creaked then crashed as the top floor fell into the one below it.

A woman next to Cora Mae swiped tears from her cheeks, while one behind her laughed bitterly, cursing the well-to-do patriarchs of the city who had fled Roswell weeks ago. Another set of soldiers had gone into the cotton mill building, and from the smell of smoke billowing from those windows, it would soon be up in flames as well.

Instinctively, Cora Mae wrapped her arms around June. The entire world shifted then collapsed right before their eyes.

Yankee soldiers, some mounted on sleek black horses, began filtering in and among the mill hands. "Clear on out of here," one called out. "Every last one of you is to come to the town square within the hour for further instructions."

Half the girls broke into a run as smoke and soot blackened the sky. Yankees followed them, making it clear they were under guard even now. Cora Mae stood rooted into place, craning her neck to find Horace as his stepdaughter fairly melted into her skirt.

He lunged through the crowd to reach them. "You'll not see me again for a spell."

"What?"

A fierceness took hold of his eyes. "I heard talk of treason. I'm not sticking around to be arrested. I'll send for you when I've got a new home somewhere safe." He knelt before June. "Stay with Miss Stewart. She's your new mama now. Or right close to it."

"Horace! How will you—" An idea sparked. "When you're ready, send word through the preacher if you can't get back yourself. We'll find a way. I'll get June back to you, I promise."

Rising, Horace kissed her on the cheek and June on the forehead, as if they were both his daughters. He blended back into the current of mill hands flowing from the mill yard, past the tannery, past the picking and dyeing buildings, out the front gate, and toward their homes.

The row of apartments on Factory Hill swarmed with Yankees and panicked mill workers by the time Cora Mae and June arrived. In and out of slamming doors, the Union soldiers marched, their faces tanned and their sky-blue trousers freckled with fine red dust. They carried bolts of gray cloth with "CSA" stamped into the weave.

Holding fast to June's hand, she pushed past some soldiers and entered her home to find it already occupied by the enemy.

"You live here?" she heard one of the soldiers say.

Ignoring him, she hoisted the hem of her skirts and bounded up the stairs. "Mama?"

June followed Cora Mae into the bedroom where Mama sat, white faced, in her rocker, her fingers clutching its arms. "Yankees?" Mama whispered. "In my house?"

Cora Mae nodded. June whimpered. "June, this is my mama. Mama, this here is June, and she's going to be with us from now on."

"You all just came from the mill?" The soldier from downstairs entered the room.

Trouble pressed in around Cora Mae until she thought it would squeeze the air right out of her. She glanced at Mama. "She didn't."

"Then she can stay."

"What are you doing in my home?" Mama's breathing rattled in her chest before she coughed something fierce into her handkerchief.

The soldier's face softened. "This row of apartments is a Union hospital now. You two mill girls are to report to the town square."

"What will you do with them?"

"I'm just following orders, ma'am. If you give me any trouble, I've got orders to deal with that, too."

Cora Mae's gaze settled on the pistol at his hip.

"Now say your good-byes." He left.

She swept to Mama's side and knelt by the rocker. "We'll come back just as soon's we can."

Mama's smile wavered. "You hold on to hope, child." She cleared her throat. "June, I'm real sorry to not have more time with you just yet. I'll be praying you both home, you hear?"

Cora Mae embraced Mama, inhaling the chinaberry soap scent of her hair, and turned to go.

"Cora Mae." Mama's voice was stern now. "I know you're powerful scared. Don't let it turn into hate. The good Lord says we are to love our enemies and pray for those who bring us pain."

"I recall that, Mama. Come on, June. We best scoot."

Her feet felt leaden on the short walk to the square. A ring of bluecoats parted to let her and June slip inside the already packed area. The noonday sun beat down, and her scalp burned where she'd parted her hair.

"Let's find a spot to sit," she said to June.

"Right in the dirt?"

"If they're going to pen us in like hogs, we may as well act like hogs to keep cool."

June managed to giggle at that as they claimed a small patch of the square.

Whimpers and cries mingled in the air with fool-headed, girlish nonsense. Cora Mae couldn't decide if those girls thought they'd fare better by flirting with their captors, or if they really didn't understand that they were being held hostage by the enemy that had killed so many of their fathers, brothers, and husbands.

Time seeped by at the pace of cold molasses, while smoke from torched buildings choked the air. Some folk in the square fainted from the heat, and so did a few of the soldiers standing guard. Those who needed to use the privy did so with a Yankee escort, who yelled at them to hurry up. Some sorely mistaken girls shouted that brave Confederate soldiers would come rescue them at any moment. If the Roswell Battalion had stayed to defend them instead of skedaddling right after burning the bridge, they'd buckle against this force. Cora Mae couldn't count them all, but she'd heard there were some three thousand men here, with their horses.

"Ain't we gonna go home before bed?" June asked.

Cora Mae licked her dry lips, tasting smoke. "At this point, I don't reckon we will."

Twilight faded into an ashy gray night. Northern accents barbed her from all sides. "Next stop, Atlanta!" one of the soldiers hooted. "But did you ever see so many girls all in one place before than this? Think I might see about keeping one or two of 'em warm!"

The bright notes of a harmonica rose up under Yankees singing:

"Right down upon the ranks of rebels,
Tramp them underfoot like pebbles,
March away! March away! Away! Victory's band!"

Lying flat in the dirt, with nothing but insults to cover them, Cora Mae let a tear slip free. Listening to mothers hush their crying children, she wondered how Mama fared. Beside her, June sniffed, and she recalled she was standing in for the little girl's mother, near strangers though they were.

"Junebug," she whispered. "I'm glad you're keeping me company. You're right courageous."

"Well, I'm eight years old now."

Cora Mae smiled at the girl's solemn nod. "And just as brave as you ever could be." She stretched out her arm, and June nestled into it, curling into her side.

The next day, everyone in the square was damp with dew, sore, and hungry, though the soldiers did pass around corn bread. But when one Yankee made an announcement later that day, Cora Mae wished she'd left her stomach empty.

"By order of General Sherman," he hollered, "commanding officer of the United States Army, you are all under arrest for making cloth and rope for the Confederacy. Aiding the rebels with this wartime manufacturing is treason, making each of you traitors to your rightful government. You will all be deported to Indiana, where you can no longer assist the Rebellion!"

Stunned silence. Then a wail rose up from the crowd that made June cover her ears. Cora Mae felt as if she was going to be sick. Indiana? How would she ever get back home now?

"You'll be taken by wagon to Marietta and continue your journey from there."

If he said anything else after that, Cora Mae didn't hear it. Dropping to her knees, she clutched June to her and felt the girl's arms wrap around her neck. "We'll stick together. We'll hold on to hope." But on the inside, she felt herself unraveling.

Chapter Three

The wagons didn't come that day, or for the next three, but more Yankees did. Cora Mae and June and close to four hundred others spent the rest of that week in the town square, shading their heads with aprons and forcing themselves to eat the rations. On Saturday evening, a few army wagons came to carry off some mill hands toward Marietta, but neither Cora Mae nor June were on them.

That night, a thunderstorm soaked everyone to their bones. By morning, the square was a quagmire of red clay with barely any grass left underfoot, and the damp clothes steamed in the fresh heat of a new day. The limbo was unbearable.

Then, on Sunday, a Yankee general congratulated his troops with whiskey, and new devilment wormed into the square. Unclaimed rations were quickly guzzled by those who'd already had their fill. Cora Mae shuddered as she watched the demon alcohol do its work. Guards previously content with ogling the mill girls now came in among them, all hands.

"I can do what I want with you, spoils of war!" One soldier reached for a girl a yard from Cora Mae. The girl stomped on his foot and tried running off, and he stumbled after her.

Drunken Yankees hooted and hollered as if they were watching a greased pig chase before joining in. Cora Mae hunched her shoulders, trying to be less visible. Cupping June's shoulders to keep her close, she backed away from the space where the bluecoats mixed with drab and dusty homespun.

"*Oof!*" She bumped into something solid and turned to find a bearded soldier with red-veined eyes leering down at her.

"Well, make it easy on me, Secesh!" His chortle reeked of whiskey. The top buttons of his coat were unfastened, his undershirt plastered to his sweating chest.

Cora Mae's heart jumped into her throat. She turned around and pulled June away with her.

"Well, looky what we have here!" He tramped after June. "Ain't she a beauty!"

"Don't touch her." Her voice was a growl, her heartbeat a drum against her ribs. In a flash, her hand slipped into her apron pocket and grasped the handle of the trowel that had been there since she'd buried her box by the dam. When the soldier moved closer, she whipped it out and pointed it at his gut.

"Who do you think you are?" He lunged for her, and she darted from him. June slipped away, out of sight, out of reach.

"June!" she cried out. "June!" Her head yanked back, her hair pulling at her scalp. Some soldier had gripped the knot of her bound-up hair and clasped her around the middle. His breath was hot in her ear, but the alcohol slurred his words to an unrecognizable mess. The fury of a wildcat flooded her then, and she jammed her elbows into his ribs to push away. "Let me go!" she shouted and heard the same refrain echoing from all over the square. *Lord, have mercy!*

Galloping thundered in the distance. *More Yankees?* She groaned aloud at the thought. But when the cavalry came crashing into the square, they whipped their sharp tones not at the mill hands, but at the drunken soldiers among them. Scabbards and bridles jangled amid the pounding hoofbeats, and in the commotion, she broke away from her pursuer. Wildly, she spun around, calling for June, but she could barely hear her own voice.

Then she saw the little girl, rising up out of the crowd. A mounted soldier had pulled her up onto his dark bay horse, seating her in front of him.

The spade dropped from her grip. "June!" Cora Mae screamed, frantically elbowing against panic-stricken girls and intoxicated Yankees. "June! June!" All was confusion as the red-haired soldier began carrying her away. All over the square, mill hands were being swept up on horses.

"Take my hand." The baritone voice turned Cora Mae's head. His speech didn't have the same edge as the other Yankees. "My name is Sergeant Ethan Howard, Seventy-Second Indiana Mounted Infantry. I'm here to take care of you. Come on." Green eyes pierced hers. Sun flashed on the gold crossed sabers above the brim of his black forage cap.

She grabbed his forearm. He gripped under her elbow. Almost before she knew what was happening, she was straddling a dapple gray horse, tucking her skirts around her legs with one hand while she wrapped her other arm around his midsection.

"Hiyah!" The horse lunged forward, and she flung her other arm around Sergeant Howard, clutching the leather cross belt over his chest to keep from falling off the backside. Through his blue wool uniform, heat radiated from his body and into hers.

Pulse throbbing against her skull, she looked around. June bounced in the saddle, terror in her eyes. "June!" Cora Mae chanced to let go and wave before clasping her hands above her soldier's belt buckle once again. "Hang on tight! It's all right!"

But it wasn't. Heading west, every step took her farther from everything she knew. As they rode past the white-columned homes of Roswell's wealthy families, Cora Mae bristled. Those residents had all gone somewhere safe weeks ago, and they could all come back when they chose to. But when, and how, would she ever get home now?

On the rust-colored dirt road outside of town, the horses slowed and formed two columns. Close to two hundred of them, by her estimate, carried Roswell girls along with their Yankee riders. The air was thick with dust and hoofbeats. She released her hold on Sergeant Howard and gripped the back of his saddle instead. All around her, bedraggled girls cried or scolded or moaned, while others simply stared blankly. On the other side of the road, riding parallel to her, June slumped in front of her Yankee, the one with shoulder-length, fiery hair.

Sergeant Howard nodded toward the pair. "Ease your mind about the girl. Lieutenant Dooley's a good man. He'll not see harm come to her."

She eyed the soldier who had taken June, and he saluted her. Beneath the brim of his hat, his blue eyes sparkled, and boyishly round cheeks flushed almost as bright as his wild hair. His stirrups stretched lower than most to accommodate his tall frame.

"Where are you taking us?" Cora Mae asked.

Sergeant Howard coughed then turned his head to the side to speak. "Marietta." He smelled of coffee and leather and balsam. "Where you should have been taken as soon as the order was given."

"The order should not have been given at all." She braced herself for a speech about her treasonous activity.

"This is the army. We have to follow orders, even the ones we dislike." A muscle bunched in his jaw.

"Even when it hurts women and children?"

Sergeant Howard faced forward once again. "Even then."

She strained to hear him over the din of two hundred distraught mill hands. Dust rose in great clouds from the road, fading the green of the trees, the blue of the sky. "You and Lieutenant Dooley turn around and take us home." Before and behind her, other girls on horseback echoed Cora Mae, pleading with their captors to be free.

"You know I can't do that, Miss—"

"Stewart. I know you won't do it. That's not the same as can't."

He twisted in his saddle to look her in the eyes. "The mills are gone. The Yankees are encamped all over the place, and not all of them as well behaved as yours truly. So tell me, what would you do?"

She leveled her gaze at him. "We'd see to my sick mother. Instead of a daughter bringing her comfort in her illness, she has an enemy under her roof. The same enemy as killed her husband and son."

Ethan trapped a curse for Sherman in his throat. He shook his head, searched for something to say. But with Miss Stewart staring at him, a fire lit behind those hazel eyes, words dropped into his belly like hardtack. He knew what it was to care for an ailing parent, to watch a loved one suffocate right before his eyes. He could only imagine what it must feel like for Miss Stewart to be absent when her mother needed her most.

"As you say, the mills are gone." Venom flavored her tone. "What harm could we possibly bring you Yankees by staying with our families?"

Ethan caught Lt. Seamus Dooley's eye, but the Irishman only shrugged and glanced at the small charge astride his Morgan horse, clearly at a loss, as well. Looking ahead once again, Ethan shifted the reins in his hands. "I'm real sorry about your parents and brother." He coughed again, the dust in the air irritating the coal dust still in his lungs.

Swinging his leg over the pommel in front of him so as not to kick Miss Stewart, he dismounted and patted the saddle. "Have a seat." He looked the opposite direction while she maneuvered herself onto the saddle. "We've got sixteen miles to put behind us before we get to Marietta. Just thought I'd give Reckless here a break." Up and down the mounted infantry columns, other soldiers did the same.

Lifting her chin, Miss Stewart straightened her spine, though her walnut-brown hair hung in an unkempt braid down her back, and mud caked her dress and apron. Dangling above the stirrups, her bare feet, too, were stained red with the land she might never see again. The ache in her eyes knotted his chest.

She didn't deserve this. She was only doing her job for the company that kept her family alive. Fumbling a bit, Ethan drew a handkerchief from his pocket and wet it with water from his canteen.

"Truce?" He offered it up to her, a soggy white flag, and the mill workers in line ahead of him whipped around to glare at him. One of them cursed at him with as much skill as any soldier he'd met.

Miss Stewart gasped. "For shame, Cynthia!" She glanced at Ethan with a quick, disapproving shake of her head, surprising him far more than the cussing.

"Yankee lover!" the girl spat. "I reckon this is a real dream come true for you, Cora Mae. You finally get to leave Roswell." She turned back around in a huff.

Miss Stewart reddened beneath Ethan's curious gaze. After a moment's hesitation, she took his handkerchief and wiped her face and neck then used the other side to wipe her hands and her arms before laying it over the pommel to dry. "Doesn't make us friends."

"Noted." He cleared his throat. "Care to explain that very interesting remark? You *wanted* to leave Roswell?"

"Not like this." She motioned to the columns of homespun-clad mill workers and Union soldiers curving around the road ahead in ribbons of brown and blue.

Ethan let the matter drop. Between sweat-lathered horses, heat from the midafternoon sun undulated in waves off the road. He felt as though he were baking inside his scratchy wool uniform. Unslinging his canteen from over his shoulder, he held it up. "Thirsty?"

With a whisper of thanks, she drank. After handing it back to him, she cast another glance toward June, who he could only guess was her sister. *Cora Mae and June.* If their parents had another daughter, Ethan wondered if they'd name her April.

Guilt coated him like a paste of dust and sweat. These were no frivolous planter's daughters, waited on by slaves. Sunburn bloomed on Miss Stewart's skin, but other mill hands who'd brought sunbonnets had sickly pale complexions, bearing witness to long hours of indoor work. Before the war, his skin was just as untouched by the sun as theirs, his world just as limited.

Pine trees scrubbed the sky. A mile passed, maybe two. All around them, shrill complaints jabbed the humid air and lower-pitched voices barked after them, yet Ethan's mind drifted. "I lost my brothers, too." He didn't know why he said it, for he didn't expect her to care. He and his two brothers had survived a decade of coal mining together and three years of war. At twenty-five years old now, Ethan went from being the oldest brother to the only one left.

Reins in his right hand, he rubbed the heel of his left over his stinging eyes. "I'm not saying I know how you feel." He hazarded a glance at Miss Stewart.

She nodded. "Your loss is still loss." She could have praised the Rebels that killed his brothers. Yet she didn't.

Reckless slowed his pace. Across the road, Dooley took notice and matched Toledo's gait to keep June near Miss Stewart. The horses had reason to be worn out, and as they were in no hurry to get back to Marietta, Ethan let other mounted infantrymen and their charges pass ahead of them. When Reckless began limping, however, he halted completely.

"What's wrong?" Miss Stewart asked.

"We'll see. But come on down first." He reached up for her.

Careful to keep her hoopless skirts tucked modestly around her legs, she leaned down and let him help her to the ground.

"Mind holding the reins?" Ethan handed them to her then laid his buckskin gloves across the saddle. Facing the rear, he slid his hand down Reckless's front leg, pinching the back tendon. "Pick up your hoof." Reckless bent his knee. His shoe was clogged with mud that had dried into rock-hard dirt. One hand cradling the hoof, Ethan drew his jackknife from his pocket, opened it, and picked out the mud from beneath the shoe. A loose nail would need to be fixed at Marietta. When he came to a rock wedged near the frog, he knew he'd found the source of the horse's limping. He dislodged it and let Reckless place his hoof back down.

"Dooley," he called over Reckless's back. "Check Toledo's shoes, just in case."

"Aye," Dooley grunted. "Already doing it."

For good measure, Ethan cleaned the rest of Reckless's hooves and shoes. "That should do it." He patted the horse's powerful haunch and put his gloves back on, and then he took the reins from Miss Stewart.

She scanned the road. "We're at the rear of the line."

"So we are. But we'll catch up. Reckless is in good shape now." He offered his hand to help her back up into the saddle.

She didn't take it. Instead, she walked around the front of Reckless, over to June, and took her hand. "If you won't take us home, just let us go. No one will notice."

Ethan tossed his reins to Dooley, who stood between the two horses. In three strides, he stood before Miss Stewart and her sister. "I can't let you go."

The two mill workers backed away from him, putting distance between themselves and the horses. "What does it matter to you?" Miss Stewart asked.

He approached as he would a skittish horse, calm, but firm, searching for words likely to persuade. This entire matter left a rotten taste in his mouth, but it was out of his hands completely. "I told you. Orders are orders." *Elegant speech, Howard,* he chided himself.

"My mother needs me!" Wind ruffled Miss Stewart's skirt about her legs and her hair around her face. She backed farther down the road, one slow step at a time, with wide-eyed June at her side. She had to know that if they ran, he'd catch them both.

"Come on!" June yanked on Miss Stewart's hand, pulling her off balance. In trying to catch herself, the woman's bare foot came down hard on the side of a wagon wheel rut, twisting that ankle. Sucking in a breath, she winced and hopped on the other foot.

"I'm sorry!" June covered her mouth. "Oh no, I didn't mean to!"

Miss Stewart paled. "I know you didn't." She tried some weight on it, muffled a groan, and stood on one leg.

"Well. That's that, then." Ethan slipped one arm around her willow-reed waist and the other beneath her knees and scooped her up. "It doesn't seem quite right, does it, for all these horses to have four shoes each, when you mill hands have none."

June pointed at Reckless's legs. "He even has four white socks!"

"Aye, so he does, lassie." Chuckling, Dooley swept her back up into his saddle then rubbed the white strip on Toledo's nose.

Ethan helped Miss Stewart mount Reckless once again, confident the Thoroughbred-Arab mix would not tire from her thistledown weight. With long strides, he led Reckless to close the gap between them and the rest of the cavalry.

Dooley traveled next to him with Toledo and June.

Shuttering the sunlight, the pines spiced the air with their sap. The journey that should have taken four hours stretched into five, and they still weren't in sight of Marietta.

As shadows lengthened, Ethan glanced up to find Miss Stewart dozing, listing to one side in the saddle. He considered waking her before she fell then stopped himself. She'd been sleeping on the ground for four nights, and there'd be no feather bed awaiting her in Marietta. If she could sleep sitting up, she should.

With an apology to Reckless for the extra weight, Ethan stepped into the stirrup and mounted the horse, reins still in hand. Sitting behind the saddle, he reached around Miss Stewart, guarding her from toppling over the side. She swayed then nestled back against him. Unbidden, a protective instinct flared within his chest.

Chapter Four

Marietta, Georgia
July 10, 1864

With a start, Cora Mae awoke to find herself braced between Sergeant Howard's arms. Embarrassed, she sat bolt upright, and he dismounted to walk alongside her. A few yards from her, Dooley walked Toledo, with June quietly in the saddle.

They passed through Yankee guards to enter Marietta. It didn't suit. She'd heard this was a charming resort town, with natural springs and fancy hotels. The homes along the road they traveled had Greek-style pillars on breezy porches, or gingerbread trim and picket fences. She could easily imagine Southern belles who lived there, dressed in frothy dresses over wide hoops to dance with cadets from the nearby Georgia Military Institute.

But as the street broadened, and they approached the center of town, all she saw and heard was Yankees. Sidewalks crowded with crates of ammunition, hardtack, and blue uniforms. The smell of manure and sweat-soaked wool overpowered her. Soldiers and horses tramped through the street, some of them pausing in the shade of maple and oak trees to stare at the Roswell girls now among them.

Still at the rear of the Seventy-Second Indiana columns, Cora Mae and June were the last to reach the southeast corner of the town square, defended by a gleaming Union cannon. The square was packed with white army tents and with more Yankees swarming over the red clay mud between them. Covered army wagons lumbered through the street, and other tents crowded up against a drugstore, Cole Hotel, a three-story Masonic Hall, and other buildings so obscured she couldn't tell what they were.

"We're here." Sergeant Howard's hands encircled her waist, helping her down. Pain still pulsing in her ankle, she was mindful to favor it.

Lieutenant Dooley, face ruddy from the day's heat, lifted June down from the saddle. The girl hurried to Cora Mae's side.

The sergeant cleared his throat and pointed behind them. "This is the Cobb County Courthouse, where you'll be staying until you continue the journey north." The brick building rose up on the east edge of the square, facing the lowering sun. The Stars and Stripes snapped from the pole at its top.

With June's hand in hers, Cora Mae climbed the building's steps. Sergeant

Howard and Lieutenant Dooley tied their horses to the hitching post at the street's edge then followed them up the stairs.

"What are all these for?" June pointed to the tents.

"Those in the square are where the Second Ohio Cavalry and the Twentieth Connecticut Infantry are camped," Dooley offered. Snatching his hat from his head, he raked a freckled hand through his red hair and mopped his brow with a handkerchief. He pointed to the tents surrounding the buildings on the outside edge of the square. "All of these are hospital tents. For the sick and wounded."

June wrinkled her nose. "There must be a hundred of them!"

Sergeant Howard chuckled as he surveyed the grounds. His short, dark blond hair curled at the nape of his neck. "Try a thousand. There are five Union army corps here in Marietta, with more than four thousand sick and wounded. They've taken the churches and hotels for the patients, but obviously, that's not enough room."

The courthouse's double doors swung open, and a bearded Yankee in spectacles strode through them. "All right, men, I'll take over from here. Inside, all you girls." He motioned to the mill girls still lingering on the street.

"We'll sleep inside tonight, Junebug." Cora Mae forged a smile as a gust of wind, still laden with heat, swept over her.

"As long as I stay with you."

"You Secesh will go where I say you go." The provost guard rocked back on his heels.

Sergeant Howard and Dooley looked at each other, brows furrowed. "These two stay together," said Sergeant Howard.

"Says who?"

"Says decency," Dooley chimed in, jamming his hat back on. "Ain't no cause for separating kinfolk just to prove you can."

The provost guard grunted. "Come on, let's get you locked up." Other Roswell girls straggled up the steps and into the courthouse as he spoke. "You'll find combs, soap, and tooth powder inside, compliments of the Christian Commission that's set itself up here in Marietta."

Sergeant Howard touched Cora Mae's sleeve, so lightly she almost didn't notice. "Do you need a doctor? For your ankle?"

"No." She didn't care to see any more bluecoats than she had to. "It'll mend quick enough."

"I pray it does."

When she frowned, he added, "Didn't anyone tell you? Not all Yankees are devils." Something akin to a smile slanted his lips as he tipped his hat to her then trotted down the stairs, along with Dooley, to their waiting horses.

The room to which Cora Mae was assigned was crammed with girls, and not much else. The mill hands took turns at pails of water set in the corner, eagerly using the soap, and pocketing the new combs. For dinner, they broke Yankee hardtack.

June tugged a piece of hair from her braid and sucked the end of it. "I been chewin' on something. Do you reckon I ought to call you Mama, seeing as you almost are? Weren't you fixin' to marry Mr. Ferguson before he had to run off? The mean Yankees might keep us together if they think we're relations."

Cora Mae's nose pinched. She still couldn't quite imagine being married to Horace. But she could surely imagine loving this little girl as though she were her own. "Call me Mama if you like," she whispered.

As the girls claimed patches of the hard wooden floor and one blanket each, guards paced outside the windows. There was even a pair standing watch at the door to the hallway.

"I never did see so much blue in all my life," June whispered.

A snatch of a psalm scrolled through Cora Mae's mind. "Have you ever heard this verse? 'Thou hast beset me behind and before, and laid thine hand upon me.'"

"I can't say. What does it mean?"

"Preacher said it means the Lord is hemming us in. He's in front of us, and He's behind us. He's even got His hand directly on us."

"Well, that sounds like the Yankees sure enough! They're everywhere!"

Cora Mae smiled. "I think so, too. Let's play a game. Every time we see a blue-coat, let's say or think to ourselves, 'God's there.' Because He is!"

From somewhere outside, campfire smoke wafted into the courthouse, along with the Northern twang of Union soldiers swapping tales.

June sucked in her breath. "God's out there." Then she giggled.

Cora Mae savored the rare sound.

Rolling onto her side, June yawned. "I like it. Thank you." Her breathing grew slow and steady.

Thank You, Lord. Hem us in now, and my own mama, too. Bring us back together again.

Sighing, Cora Mae let her gaze drift to the window. Outside, twilight banked the blazing sun, taking the fever from the air. Every few seconds, a soldier with a musket on his shoulder paced by, dissolving any plan to sneak out and run away.

"*Psst.* Miss Stewart." A whisper sounded at the window. "It's Sergeant Howard. I've got news for you."

She rose and went to him.

"You weren't sleeping, were you?"

"Not yet," she said, leaning on the windowsill. "What do you want?"

He straightened his hat. "General Dodge—the Union general commanding the sixteenth corps here—he thinks Sherman's order is absurd."

Hope flickered. "So will he let us go home?"

"I told you. You can't go home, not yet." His sharp tone needled her.

"Well, then, what use is Dodge's opinion for us?"

"Dodge told the chief surgeon here to hire as many of you girls as he can. You could be a nurse, paid in greenbacks, with rations to eat, all while you stay here in Marietta."

She held his unblinking gaze. The sharp smells of illness and ammonia drifted from tents and trenches outside. "Work for Yankees."

"Stay here in Georgia," he countered. "A half day's journey from Roswell. You'd be as close to your mother as you could possibly hope to be."

"Could I visit her?"

The sergeant shifted his rifle to his other shoulder. "You'd have to stay here, or go where the army goes. Do you think you could nurse wounded Yankee soldiers, Miss Stewart?"

Fireflies blinked against the lavender sky. She cupped one in her hands, and its yellow glow pulsed from between her fingers. "So they could heal up and go on out and kill more Johnny Rebs?" Her heart throbbed against the notion.

"It's the only way to stay."

She opened her hands and let the firefly take wing. "I can't do it," she whispered as she watched its flight. "I can't support the Yankee army."

"You're looking at it backward. Let the Yankee army support you."

Cora Mae shook her head, incredulous. "I can't understand why you care."

Ethan leaned his rifle against the outside of the courthouse, swiped his forage cap off his head, and crushed it onto the windowsill. "Look past my uniform for one second and recognize that I'm not your enemy."

She raised an eyebrow. "I don't hate you, you know." Her tone lost its black-coffee bitterness.

"Don't you?"

She blew an exaggerated sigh from her lips. "Not allowed. 'Love your enemies.' Heard of it?" The corner of her mouth curved in a half grin, and a dimple pressed into her cheek.

Caught off guard by the tease in her eyes, Ethan stifled a laugh. "Just so happens I have. Didn't notice?"

A strand of hair blew in front of her eyes, and she tucked it behind her ear. "I still won't stay and nurse." She looked away, and his gaze skimmed her silhouette, from her bristly lashes to the tip of her delicate nose, over lips shaped like cupid's bow, and down her slender throat. He swallowed and wondered if she knew how beautiful she was, even with sun-browned skin and dusty hair. Coughing into his elbow, he silently cursed the dust in his lungs.

Miss Stewart watched him with wide, inquisitive eyes. "That sounds familiar."

"Coal," he explained simply. But that wasn't what he wanted to discuss. "Miss Stewart, what did that mill hand mean when she said leaving Roswell was a dream come true for you?"

She crossed her arms on the windowsill. A white-winged moth fluttered between them before flitting into the courthouse. "It was a long time ago."

"What was a long time ago?"

Cicadas ticked and whirred above the moans of the sick nearby. She looked beyond him, and he suspected she saw more than the hospital tents spilling into the street. "By the time I was fifteen, I'd already pined for years to be anywhere else but Roswell. All I knew was the inside of the cotton mill, my family's apartment, and the path between the two. Then a textile engineer from New York came to fiddle with our machinery. When he talked about places he'd been, I longed to see it all for myself. The ocean. Mountains. Snowdrifts higher than my head. A menagerie full of animals from all over the world."

Her voice grew smooth and warm as she lovingly spoke each dream. A smile, slow and beautiful, broke over her face like a sunrise.

"The more I realized I was stuck in Roswell, the stronger my urge to leave." Tears glimmered in her hazel eyes. "I just felt—" She spread her hands.

"Trapped," Ethan finished for her. "I know."

Crickets chirped in her hesitation. Miss Stewart peered at him, head tilted. "Do you?"

"For me, it was books." It wasn't easy, learning to read while working in the coal mines, but once he did, the world opened up to him and beckoned. "Every place I read about, I wanted to visit. An impossible dream."

"Like mine." The hint of a smile on her lips, she waited for him to continue.

Raucous laughter turned Ethan's head toward soldiers passing into the square. He waited until their footsteps receded before facing Miss Stewart again. "I was twelve when my mother died of cholera. My father couldn't bear anything that reminded him of her, so he moved us from Kentucky to a town in Indiana, where he and my two brothers and I found work in a coal mine. Samuel and Andrew were ten and eight. We broke the mined coal into pieces by hand and separated the coal we wanted from whatever we didn't, like rock, slate, clay, and soil. The coal dust was so thick sometimes we could barely see what we were doing. I hated it. But we couldn't leave. In the end, my father was the one who left us. Black lung."

Ridges lined her brow. "I'm sorry." Wind rattled the trees above the courthouse, and she chafed her arms, though the night was still warm. "Do you have other siblings? Besides the two brothers killed in the war?"

Ethan fought the sorrow expanding in his chest. "Just Sam and Andrew." Ethan hadn't even been with them when they died. They were killed in battle while he was delirious with typhoid fever in a field hospital away from the fighting. And they'd been his responsibility. "You're blessed to have June, you know. And your mother, too." Eager to change the subject, he asked, "You told your friends you wanted to explore?"

She didn't respond right away. Then with her fingertip, she traced a crack in the sill's white paint. "They laughed at my foolishness. So I stopped talking about it and just worked at the mill like everyone else. Even if I had the means to leave, I wouldn't have abandoned my family."

"I understand." For hadn't he done the same, year after year, until an army recruiter showed him the way out of life underground? In her soulful eyes, he saw himself: loyalty to family; commitment to provide; and deep down, the rare spark of hope for a better life. He knew the ache of forfeited dreams, the sting of wishing for something different when everyone else is content with the same. "Do you still dream, Miss Stewart?"

"I really shouldn't." Her voice trembled. "My family needs me. God has a plan for my life, and I aim to hold tight to that hope."

Such faith, even now. "He does. Don't give up on that." An owl gurgled in the deepening night. Darkness closed in around them, blotting out Marietta and its thousands of troops and horses. For a fleeting moment, even the war fell away. All he saw was Miss Stewart's moonlit face. When a tear traced a silver path down her cheek, he covered her hand, his wool sleeve catching on the brick wall between them. "I understand you," he said again. "We're not so different, you and I."

A sad smile bent her lips. "Said the guard to his prisoner." Withdrawing her hand from beneath his, she picked up his forage cap and placed it on his head in a gesture so endearing, he hardly knew what to make of it. "Good night, Sergeant Howard," she whispered. Her Southern drawl gentled his name.

"Miss Stewart—if it weren't for the war, we'd get along just fine."

"I reckon we would." A smile bloomed then wilted, and her dimples disappeared. "But there is a war. And we're on different sides." She tapped the windowsill that barred them from each other.

"I'm on *your* side." A revelation, even to himself.

Miss Stewart's gaze narrowed. "You mean *our* side—all of us mill girls? Feeling guilty?"

He shifted his weight and accidentally knocked his rifle to the ground. Snatching it up, he slung his weapon over his shoulder and lowered his voice. "I mean you. You and June."

"Why?" A whisper this time. She leaned forward, braid swinging in the musky breeze.

Why, indeed? Any guilt was eclipsed by something more. Hearing her talk had been like looking at his own reflection, the recognition so complete, it was like coming home. The woman he captured just this morning was now seizing his heart instead.

With his rifle against his back, and words lodged in his throat, he made a terrible Romeo. He didn't tell her that she was brave and strong, that when she looked at him an ache throbbed in his chest. He didn't tell her he admired her for her faith, for daring to dream, and that she shouldn't stop. All he could say was, "Sweet dreams."

Her wistful smile told him she understood.

Chapter Five

July 15

Beneath full-bellied clouds that threatened rain, humidity licked Ethan's skin. His palms grew slick on his Spencer rifle as he escorted the Roswell mill hands across the muddy town square, between the Second Ohio Cavalry and Twentieth Connecticut Infantry camps. His gaze roved, alert to soldiers eager to molest the girls he guarded. Keeping them away for five days had been no easy task.

Limping ever so slightly, Miss Stewart trudged beside him, holding June's hand. He didn't need to glance at her to see her sun-kissed face in his mind. Nor did she need to speak for him to hear her honeyed voice talk of dreams and faith and hope, though she was a prisoner and homeless. She had softened toward him after their talk the first night at the courthouse. Since then, and between guard duty, he'd read *Harper's Weekly* to her and June through the window to pass the time, and she gifted him with unhurried smiles. *"You've stopped scolding me,"* he pointed out yesterday. *"On account of I'm a very good Christian,"* she replied solemnly then flashed a dazzling, teasing grin. His spirit resonated with hers in a way he'd never known with another.

And she was leaving. The speech he'd rehearsed into his shaving-kit mirror now lodged in his chest like unmined coal.

The tramping of boots and the gentle plodding of bare feet filled his ears as they passed the brick depot building and into the yard of the Western & Atlantic Railroad half a block beyond it. Sherman's headquarters, the four-story Fletcher House, towered over the tracks, with a US flag shuddering from its roof. Odors of straw and livestock wafted from open doors of two long trains, hinting at their most recent use.

Mill workers from Sweetwater Creek and New Manchester, billeted at the Georgia Military Institute, joined the Roswell hands at the depot, bringing their number to eighteen hundred souls. They jostled and tripped over each other, pressing toward the train in an unruly mass.

The gray sky lowered, pressing down like a lid over the simmering summer day. Ethan put his hand on Cora Mae's shoulder, and she turned to him with red-rimmed eyes. It took all his restraint to keep from wrapping her in his arms. "Cora Mae."

At the sound of her Christian name, her lips parted in surprise.

He took her hand. "You can't leave like this. You get on that train, and they'll take you up to Louisville and dump you on the north side of the river, and that's it."

"What do you mean?" She glanced at June then back at him.

"No one knows what to do with all of you. Sherman's order is to send you away and drop you off. You think Indiana townsfolk will take to hundreds of devout Confederates suddenly in the streets? You think there will be enough jobs for all of you? Just what do beautiful young women do when they're desperate to survive?"

"Stop," she gasped. Fear pooled in her eyes. "Why are you telling me this?"

Mill hands swept around them like a river around a stone. "Marry me."

"What?" Eyes suddenly wild, she stepped back.

Ethan stepped forward, pulled her close enough to hear what he had to say. "Sign the papers and marry me. Don't get on that train. I've got no family left; my paychecks can go to you while I serve in the army. You'll be provided for while you stay here in Marietta. If I die in the war, you'll be paid by the US government for the rest of your life. You won't have to work at the mill. If I don't die by the end of the war and you decide you're better off without me, we can annul it before we—"

Her cheeks flamed red.

He cleared his throat. "You understand. This war—it won't last forever. When all this is over with, would it be so bad to have a partner in this world, someone who truly understands you? Dare to imagine a different life than the one you got used to expecting. I know you can." *Dream, Cora Mae.*

The train whistle shrieked, and Cora Mae jolted. She started to turn toward the sound, but Ethan caught her against him. "Don't do it. Let it go without you."

She didn't pull away. "Sergeant Howard, I—"

He was losing her. Without thinking, he bent his head to hers, his hands on the back of her neck and the hollow of her waist, and took her lips in the kiss he'd been dreaming of. Her body stiffened then relaxed against his.

Cora Mae should have pushed him away. But heaven help her, she didn't. For one urgent, fleeting moment, she forgot he was a Yankee and she a Rebel, forgot to blame him for following Sherman's orders just as her own menfolk had followed Johnston's. For the span of a few racing heartbeats, Ethan Howard was just a man, and she was just the woman in his arms.

"Mama?"

And then she remembered everything.

Jumping back, she pressed her hands to her cheeks and looked from June to Sergeant Howard.

Shock registered in his eyes. His chest rose and fell with deep breaths. "I've missed something. 'Mama'?"

"Close enough," piped up June. "She's gonna marry my step-pa, Mr. Ferguson!"

"You're engaged?" Sergeant Howard's tanned complexion flushed scarlet, and she read regret in the fine lines framing his eyes and mouth.

"She's going to be my mama," June said. "So I reckon that makes us kin enough already."

Cora Mae placed her hand over her wildly beating heart, as if to keep it in its cage. She could barely think, let alone speak. Her feet grew roots into the ground, but time marched relentlessly on.

"All aboard!" a conductor called above the humming crowd. Steel-gray locomotive steam rose under wool-gray clouds, the sky having lost all color.

Sergeant Howard cleared his throat. Kneeling, he chucked June's chin. "Don't you worry. I'm not about to take her from you. You keep each other safe until you get back to Mr. Ferguson, all right?" Rising, he grasped the hilt of the sword at his hip. "If you can get to Cannelton, Indiana, there's a cotton mill there. Godspeed." After quickly tipping his hat, he disappeared in the teeming rail yard.

Cora Mae touched her fingertips to her lips, where his kiss still burned. Wind scented with the coming rain sighed over her as she climbed the ladder into the boxcar, accepted a bag with nine days' rations in it, and squeezed onto a bench in the steamy, foul-smelling car.

"Did I speak out of turn?" June asked, looking repentant.

Cora Mae gathered her onto her lap. "You were right. I'm engaged to Mr. Ferguson, who we will find just as soon as. . ." Her voice trailed away. As soon as what? There was no timetable for her return to Roswell, or for his. Still. . . "You and I belong together. That much I know is true." She would not abandon June, come what may.

"But what did the sergeant mean about not finding work? You're a good worker. Mr. Ferguson said so. So am I. Why wouldn't we get jobs?"

More mill hands loaded into the boxcar. Some of them sat cross-legged on the straw-covered floor. Soon the air became almost too thick to breathe, and this was only one car. The entire train was just as full. There was a second train, too, devoted entirely to mill hands.

"So many," Cora Mae whispered.

"So many what?"

"So many of us." Fear trickled through her. "The sergeant was saying there are so many of us, from three different mill towns, he doesn't see how we'll all find work in factories once we get across the river." She scanned the hungry faces around her, her pulse quickening. Once they came to the end of the journey, these girls would no longer be fellow sojourners. They'd be competitors for a decent wage.

The train whistle screamed again, clawing at her ears. Cora Mae's stomach turned. The locomotive belched sooty black smoke right before the Yankee in her boxcar slid the door closed almost all the way.

"Next stop, Chattanooga," he said.

"It's not going to work," she said under her breath. She couldn't marry that reckless Yankee, but he was right. She was a fool to think they'd survive the North with nothing but a Yankee general's order to be exiled from the South.

"Get up," she said to June, who slipped off her lap. "Stop the train!" She squeezed past gaping girls and to the guard at the door.

"Ain't no way." The Yankee laughed at her.

"We're getting off. General Dodge ordered the chief surgeon to hire some of us as nurses, didn't he?"

"What of it?"

"I'm going to do it. We're going to do it." She wrapped her arm around June's shoulders.

"Traitors!" a woman cried out from the shadows.

"Yankee-lovin' cowards!" Another voice, a slap against her ears.

The wheels chugged beneath the floorboards. Through the narrowly open door, she watched the tracks begin to move slowly by.

The guard yawned. "Too late."

Stooping down, Cora Mae hissed into June's ear. The girl's eyes rounded, but she nodded.

"Oh, Billy Yank," a mill hand called from the corner. "There's a seat by me if you get tired of standin'." Her singsong voice was an invitation, and he took it.

As soon as the Yankee was out of reach, Cora Mae threw her weight against the rusty door to shove it farther open. Before the train picked up any more speed, she scrambled to sit at the edge, pulling June to sit beside her. In one breath, Cora Mae told her, "I'll help you down, be ready." Skirts bunched in one hand, she jumped to the dusty platform below.

Ignoring the pain in her ankle, she whirled back to the boxcar and hurried alongside it to catch up to June. The little girl leaned forward, and Cora Mae reached under her outstretched arms. "I've got you!" she cried and, with a great heave, pulled a screaming June off the train.

Chapter Six

Stumbling under June's weight, Cora Mae fell back onto bags of feed corn stacked on the platform. Ankle throbbing and heart racing, she kissed the top of June's copper hair. "Anything broken?"

June stood, waving her hands in the air and walking in place. "Not a thing!" Behind her, hundreds of factory workers who hadn't fit on the train still milled about the yard.

Hot waves of coal-flavored air blew over Cora Mae as the train rolled by. A gust of wind swirled dirt and dust into her eyes. Blinking furiously, she rose and shook straw from her skirt as an older man approached. Her eyes watered, and she wiped her cheeks with trembling hands.

"Found yourselves on the wrong train, did you?" The twinkle in his blue eyes disarmed her, despite the Union blue of his coat. White whiskers fluffed about his cheeks and jaw like cotton.

"We've got no cause to go north, you see." The damp wind strengthened, whipping her dress about her legs.

"I'm afraid General Sherman says otherwise, my dears." He bent on one knee and offered his hand to June. "I'm Theodore Littleton, a chaplain."

"I'm June." She shook his hand. "A Georgian."

Chuckling, he rose stiffly and shook Cora Mae's hand as well.

"Cora Mae Stewart, sir. And we aim to stay. The surgeon still needs nurses, I reckon."

Chaplain Littleton eyed her. "I haven't heard anything at all about using mill hands to fill those slots. There are plenty of convalescent nurses doing the job."

A second train screeched onto the still-warm tracks. They could still be thrown onto this one. "Please, sir." She raised her voice to be heard over the officers calling for order. "It was General Dodge who said we could. We need to stay here in Georgia." She craned her neck to see if she could spot Sergeant Howard. Surely he would confirm this. But all she saw beneath the glowering sky were strained faces of women and children and the backs of Yankees she didn't know. "I wouldn't lie to you, Chaplain. Please. Don't put us on that train."

Chaplain Littleton squinted at her, lips tight in thought. "I'll take you to the provost marshal."

Pebbles pressing the soles of Cora Mae's feet, she and June followed him through the rail yard to the Fletcher House as the first drops of rain splashed her face. Crates of Union army supplies stacked up just outside the double doors of the hotel, smelling of damp leather and wool and gunpowder. Just inside in the high-ceilinged lobby, they waited while Chaplain Littleton, with a slight hitch in his gait, climbed a broad staircase of polished cherrywood. The sweet scent of tobacco puddled in the heavy air.

Rain drummed against many-paned windows, streaming down in braided rivulets. Beneath the ragged hem of her skirt, Cora Mae curled her dusty toes into the plush red carpet, wishing she could hide her bare feet. June's brown eyes widened as she took in the sconces on the papered walls. Opposite the staircase, Yankees lounged in crimson armchairs between doily-topped tables. Deep voices mingled behind newspapers that rattled open and shut. Two soldiers burst through the front door, rain spilling from the brims of their hats. Scabbards swinging at their lean hips, they trudged up the stairs.

"Think they're going to meet with Gen'ral Sherman?" June whispered, face paling above her soot-streaked brown dress. "Think they're planning new devilment for Georgia?"

"Hush, now." If they were going to stay here, they best not give cause for reprimand.

"I just wondered if Mr. Ferguson might have found that safe place he was talking of." Her voice quavered. "Or if maybe there's no safe place left."

A sigh feathered Cora Mae's lips. "I wonder, too."

In the next moment, the chaplain came down the stairs with another man in Yankee uniform. "Miss Stewart, this is the provost marshal."

"How do you do." She dropped a curtsy, though it galled her. "This is June. She's a hard worker. She can carry water or boil it, or whatever the patients need. I want to nurse."

"So I've heard." He peered over his spectacles at her. "You understand these are Union patients."

"Yes, sir."

"And I understand you and your town have suffered, from your perspective, under Union hands."

She held her tongue and gave June a silencing look as well. It would do no good to reveal their feelings now. "Sir, the suffering on both sides need care."

The provost marshal's eyes were hard as he stared at her. "We need that in writing. From both of you. You need to sign the oath so we know we can trust your loyalty." He produced two slips of paper and a pen and motioned for them to follow him to the reception desk.

Thunder rumbled outside. June stood on tiptoe, her hands on the brass handrail encircling the desk. "I get to make my mark, too? I know my first name. Will that do?"

"Fine. But first, raise your right hands. The both of you. You will repeat after me. 'I do solemnly swear, in the presence of almighty God. . .that I will henceforth faithfully support and defend the Constitution of the United States and the Union of the States. . . .'"

Cora Mae's right hand shook with the weight of the moment. Her pulse quickened as she repeated the words with faltering voice. Outside, the train hissed and shrieked, drowning out the provost marshal, but she did her best to follow along and move her lips after he did. Then it was over. He lowered his right hand, and they did the same.

June took the pen first. The tip of her tongue poked out from between her lips, and her brow furrowed in evident concentration. Then she smiled at the large, uneven letters of her name.

"Now, Miss Stewart, if you please." He slid a small piece of paper toward her, inked the pen for her, and gave it to her.

She licked her lips as she took it. "I sign this, and I'll be paid, and given rations, isn't that right?"

"If you work, you'll surely be paid."

She hesitated before slowly, awkwardly writing her name on the blank line. Exhaling, she looked at the rest of the writing all swirled together on the page. Her letters didn't look anything like those fancy loops and dips.

The provost added his name to the document and waved it in the air to dry the ink.

"What was all that other writing?" she asked.

"The text of the oath you just took," Chaplain Littleton said.

June grasped the brass railing and leaned back as far as she could go. "I didn't understand a lick of all that."

"Stand up straight," Cora Mae hissed.

"It was the Oath of Allegiance, young lady." The provost marshal tucked both their papers into a folder. "It means you're a true and loyal citizen of the Union. You're not a Confederate anymore."

June's chin quivered, and her eyes grew glossy. "What?"

Cora Mae squeezed her shoulder. "It means we can stay and nurse." But her voice quaked as she said it, and a tear trickled accusingly down her cheek. "We're still here, still together. That's what matters."

July 19, Georgia Railroad Line near Decatur, Georgia

Already roasting inside his wool jacket, Ethan stared into the flames crackling from the wooden cross ties and felt an intimate sympathy for the iron rails laid over the top. He still burned with embarrassment for playing the fool at the Marietta depot with Cora Mae. He shook his head at his own recklessness. She was gone now, God help her, and he had a job to do.

General Sherman's Special Field Order No. 37 instructed General Garrard's cavalry units to destroy the Georgia Railroad. The rails were to be heated in the middle then bent or twisted so they couldn't be used again without being hauled away, melted down again, and reforged, which the Confederacy was in no position to do. With the railroad destroyed, Lee wouldn't be able to send reinforcements for the battle that would soon come to Atlanta, now that the Confederates' beloved General Johnston had been replaced by General Hood. The one-legged general was a fighting man, and likely ready to brawl. The fall of Atlanta would mean a huge loss to the South in manufacturing power and transportation, and Hood wouldn't easily give it up.

Ethan and his fellow cavalrymen started several fires along this stretch of track, at fifteen-minute intervals. Stepping away from the black smoke and the undulating heat, Ethan scanned the open land surrounding them. Picketed away from the bonfires, cavalry horses swished their tails against the flies while they waited for their riders to need them. On one side of the tracks, a sparse thicket of pines screened a frame house and its outbuildings. In the distance, Stone Mountain rose up from the landscape, as bald as Garrard, who remained mounted, trotting up and down the railroad line with a spyglass. If he heard or saw anything that hinted of battle, the cavalrymen would drop their special mission and gallop to reinforce McPherson's army.

Ambling back to the fires, Ethan counted heads and came up two short. "Where are Riley and Weston?"

Someone pointed, and he followed the direction with his gaze until it landed on two figures sneaking away into the woods toward private property.

"Riley! Weston! Get back here. We need every man!"

"He got us! It's all over!" Riley shouted. Childishly they feigned being shot and dropped to the ground before popping up again, laughing maniacally. When they were close enough for Ethan to box their ears, he could smell corn liquor on their breath.

"Drunk? In the middle of the day. While on duty." Ethan's blood boiled. "I realize your enlistments are almost up, but that's no excuse for this behavior."

"A feller gets thirsty, Sergeant." Weston's sloppy grin and watery eyes held no respect for authority. As far as Ethan was concerned, the sooner the two men left the unit, the better.

"Rail's hot!" Dooley called.

General Garrard trotted closer to the fire. "All right, men. Five to each end of the rail."

Ethan walked to one end and wrapped his hands around the iron bar.

"Every other man facing opposite directions. On the count of three. One, two, three!"

With a heave, the ten men lifted the thirty-foot-long, five-hundred-pound rail.

"Walk it!" Garrard called, and the men obeyed.

Dust rose in clay-colored clouds as the men shuffled along the ground and over to a dead pine tree. As soon as the red-hot center of the rail was positioned against the trunk, the men walked their ends toward each other until the rail was bent completely in half.

"Cross the ends!" Garrard shouted.

The dry, dead wood of the pine smoked and flared where the rail looped around it. The iron was already beginning to cool. Sweat spilled between Ethan's shoulder blades as he strained to push one end of the rail over the top of the other then pull the opposite end back toward him. When the ends of the rail had been pulled as tight as they could, the men dropped it to the ground.

With a brief reprieve to wipe the sweat from their palms and stretch their backs, the men went back for the rail's twin and repeated the process.

Afterward, Ethan walked over to Reckless while the next bonfire was still heating its rails. He rubbed the horse on his nose then took a swig from his canteen.

"Howard!"

Ethan turned at the sound of Garrard's voice. "Sir?"

"Get those men in line!" he growled, pointing after Weston and Riley. The two delinquents were running back into the woods. This time, they had their rifles and satchels, which Ethan could only imagine they meant to fill with plunder.

"Yes, sir." Blood simmering, he grabbed his rifle. It was little wonder so many Southern women were terrified of Yankees. Fools like these two gave them reason.

Pinecones crunched beneath his boots as he followed them through the woods. Sunlight fell in narrow slanting shafts through the trees. "Weston! Riley!" he shouted. "Do not trespass that private property!" He double-timed his march and emerged into a clearing a short distance from the house in time to see them slip inside the front door.

A woman screamed. Two soldiers laughed. Ethan took off running.

His boots clambered over the porch. At the front door, he shouted, "Ma'am, my name is Sergeant Ethan Howard, and I'm coming in to fetch the two scoundrels who just broke into your home."

With the toe of his boot, he nudged the door open farther, his hands firmly on his rifle. Not wanting to alarm the woman more than necessary, he kept it lowered as he entered.

"Don't hurt me, please! Oh Lord, have mercy!" an old woman gasped from a rocking chair in the corner.

"I'm not here to hurt you." He lifted his gaze to the creaking ceiling. "They went up there?"

She pointed straight up. "Ain't we poor enough already? You gotta tear up the railroad, too? It's not just soldiers you're keepin' away. It's food. It's medicine. It's anything worth havin'."

Drunken laughter tumbled down the stairs.

"They can have my money. I got wheelbarrows full of Confederate dollars out back. But if they steal the only things that mean somethin' to me..."

"They won't." Ethan bounded up the stairs.

At the top, he caught a glimpse of a round black barrel and felt his heartbeat suspend in his chest. Time slowed then skipped a beat. There was no chance to shout, or to duck, or to raise his own weapon and fire a shot in self-defense. All he could do was watch the spark and smoke spew from the rifle's mouth.

Fire combusted below his right elbow. His rifle clattered down the stairs, though Ethan didn't feel his hand dropping it. Stunned, he stumbled backward, lost his balance. He felt himself falling, but his arm refused to catch himself. His body crashed against the hard edges of the steps, his head slammed on the side of the wall. His right hand useless, he pushed himself up with his left. Leaning against the wall in the stairwell, he looked from the blood soaking his sleeve to the white faces staring down at him from above.

"You idiot!" Weston hissed.

"I thought he was a Reb coming up to kill us!"

The pain was a hatchet to his flesh, a torch to his nerves. A hammer to his bone. Clamping his hand over the hole in his arm, Ethan watched his fingers grow crimson with blood. The sickly sweet metallic smell filled his nostrils and turned his stomach. "Get. Out."

Their rifles slung over their shoulders, Weston and Riley squeezed around him on the stairs. The last thing Ethan heard was the slam of the door behind them, and the woman weeping from her chair.

Chapter Seven

Marietta

In the Methodist church turned hospital, Cora Mae walked down the aisle between wounded men held aloft by planks resting atop the pews. It was a gruesome distortion, she thought, of the stained-glass window depicting Moses walking through the Red Sea. But in the three days she had been nursing here, while June helped in the cooking tent west of the square, the helpless condition of these patients had made it easier to ignore that they were Yankees. They didn't mock her. They needed her.

The men were placed side by side across the pews, with a narrow width between each row. Beginning her rounds with the patients closest to the altar, she climbed onto the front pew, dipped her sponge in her pail, and then squeezed it over each patient's wound to keep moist the lint the doctor had packed inside. When she was done with one row, she hopped to the floor, walked five pews up the aisle, and climbed on that one to repeat the process. Other nurses worked here, too, but most of them were soldiers recovering from illness or injury. They needed frequent breaks, still being weak themselves.

"You're doing well, Cora Mae." The soft voice of Anne Littleton, the chaplain's wife, drifted from the side aisle, where she paused with a tray, recently emptied of its corn bread. "We're most grateful for your help. I hope you know that if they were Southern boys, I'd still work alongside you to care for them just the same."

"Thank you." Cora Mae finished wetting one more patient's wound then climbed down from the pew and walked up to the next. She smoothed her apron over the calico dress Anne had insisted on giving her.

Anne walked with her, peering over her shoulder to confirm the patients in earshot were sleeping. "I suppose you have relations in the war yourself?" she whispered.

Cora Mae paused before climbing back up onto a pew. "My pa and older brother, Wade, were killed at First Manassas, way back at the start." And she was not done grieving them.

"Merciful heavens." Anne rested her blue-veined hands on top of Cora Mae's. "And now here you are." She shook her head. "What a fine Christian woman you are to nurse our men."

Cora Mae bit her lip. "I do aim to be. But truth is, I just didn't want to go north."

Anne fanned the flies off the patient closest to her. "I don't blame you one bit. This is your home. You want to be near where your mother is, just like I want to be wherever my husband is."

"That's a fact." Cora Mae mopped her brow with her apron hem and stepped onto the pew, plunged her sponge into the tepid water, and squeezed it out over the next wound. "Is June doing all right in the cooking tent?"

"She's doing real fine." Anne smiled. "I best get back there now." Tray in hand, she glided out of the church.

Moments later, the church doors burst open again. "Miss Stewart!" The tone in the doctor's voice lassoed her.

"Coming!" Leaving her pail and sponge aside, she jumped into the center aisle and hastened to assist. The table that once held the sacraments held a bleeding patient instead, another sacrifice on war's altar. Some of the patients looked over at the injured man, while others groaned and turned their heads away.

Dr. Wilcox held a napkin folded into a cone over the man's nose and mouth. His lips were moving silently, and she guessed he was counting. He touched the patient's eyelids with his fingertip and, apparently satisfied at the reaction, took the cone away.

She sucked in her breath. Her mind whirred. *Ethan.* "What happened? What do we do?" Blood dripped from a balled-up uniform jacket and rolled off the table to the straw below.

"He was shot in the forearm at close range. Bones shattered." He handed her a pair of scissors. "We need his shirt and jacket off, straightaway. You can do this. Consider it practice; there will be more than you can count once the battles begin."

She took the scissors from the doctor and slipped a blade under the fabric at his right wrist. *It's just another uniform I'm cutting out,* she told herself. *Just a pair of blades on wool, but blue instead of gray.* Quickly, she cut from the wrist to the place where the sleeve had already been blown away. Bits of bone could be seen in the gaping, ragged hole above his wrist. Clamping down on the urge to gag, she began cutting again, from above the wound all the way up to his shoulder until they could peel the material completely away from his arm.

"If there was no battle, how did this happen?" she whispered.

"Keep cutting. We need his entire chest bare so we can monitor his breathing through his chest wall."

Her own pulse hammered. Swallowing, she pulled his shirttails up from his waistband and cut up through the chest, and over to both shoulders. The sight of his bare chest squeezed her heart as she remembered melting against it in his strong embrace not ten days earlier. Laying down the scissors, she stripped the fabric down and away from his body. His right forearm was destroyed. The hand that had cradled her head as he kissed her was bloodied and useless. Above it, shards of bone thrust out from shredded muscle and skin, a wretched contrast to his healthy, chiseled torso.

"Watch his face." He pulled Ethan's arm out until it was at a right angle to his body. "His tongue could slip back into his throat and choke him before we realize he's in danger. If he turns gray, you must reach in and pull the tongue forward."

Obediently, Cora Mae watched his face, fighting to master her emotions. In the corner of her vision, Dr. Wilcox threaded a tourniquet strap around Ethan's arm then turned a screw to tighten it, and she felt her own chest constricting. "Must you really?"

"There's no repairing it. He'd die of infection in days."

The air left her lungs. "I can't do this to him!" she gasped.

"Young lady, you will help me save this man's life." His gaze arrested her for a fraction of a second. Then, "We begin."

Oh God! Tears glazed her eyes, filled her throat. She stared hard at Ethan's face, watching for a change in color, and thought she saw a twinge across his features. "Can he feel it? Is he aware?" Horror spiraled through her.

"Not if I hurry. Hold these."

She grasped two linen straps and pulled them snugly with one hand, retracting the muscle tissue away from the bone.

The sound of metal teeth rasping on bone clawed at her ears and turned her knees to jelly. She leaned against the table with one hand, while the other still held the retractor strips, watching Ethan's face. A grimace stole across his countenance, and she nearly came undone. The possibility that he could hear, could feel, that he knew what was happening, was too terrible to accept.

Back and forth, the saw ground away, shaking the table. Then, almost as quickly as it began, it stopped.

Ethan's right hand was no longer a part of him. The operation was over. Cora Mae dropped the retractor strips, and the doctor pulled them away.

After working needle and thread for what seemed an eternity, Dr. Wilcox asked for a wad of lint, then for adhesive strips from his kit to be dunked in a pail of water. She scrambled to fetch her bucket from the pew. At last, he wiped his hands on his apron and pulled a pocket watch from his vest. "Eight minutes."

"Pardon me?" She dashed the tears from her face with the back of her hand.

"From start to finish, that took eight minutes. We'll need to get it down to five."

"I don't understand."

"Once the battles begin, we'll have more amputation cases than you can imagine. Minutes shaved are lives saved." He wiped the flat of his saw and knife blades against his apron and put them back in the case.

Ethan's neck tightened in his sleep. With the danger of suffocation over, Cora Mae's fingernails dug into her palms and straw crunched beneath her steps as she hastened out of the church and down the steps, where she collapsed on the ground and wept.

Chapter Eight

The burning in Ethan's right hand pulled him back to consciousness. Even before he could lift his leaden eyelids, he groaned through gritted teeth and reached instinctively for the pain.

He couldn't find it.

Heart lurching, he opened his eyes. A bandaged stump ended just below his elbow. His hand wasn't even there, though he could feel it as vividly as he felt his left. Revulsion twisted his gut. Breath rattling in his chest, he fought to control his spiraling pulse. He'd known the moment he saw his mangled forearm that he'd already lost it, but there was no way to prepare for this.

With his left hand, he pushed himself to sit up on the straw-covered door beneath his back. The blood rushed to the end of his severed limb with such force, he cried out in pain then collapsed. Sweat coated his bare chest. There were other patients in the sanctuary, but he could scarcely hear their own groans of agony over the throbbing in his nerves. Throwing his left arm over his eyes, he tried to bear up under it, but he feared the moaning in his ears was his own.

Then, relief trickled over the scorching pain. Breath suspended, he lowered his arm to see someone's hands squeezing water from a sponge over his dressings. Remarkably, it cooled his right, no-longer-there hand.

"Does it help?" the doctor asked.

Ethan exhaled. "Yes, some."

"I'm Dr. Wilcox. The first few days are critical. You must lie still and not exert pressure or you'll disrupt the healing. Understood?"

"The healing," he repeated, dully.

"The operation was a success, no matter how it feels to you now. You will heal, a little lighter in the arm, but no less a man than you ever were."

But the only words Ethan grasped were *less a man*. They clung to him like leeches, sucking away his pride.

The doctor's retreating footsteps shook the pew beneath Ethan's wooden bed. Closing his eyes, he prayed for sleep to take him.

Cora Mae's face filtered through his semiconscious state. It was well indeed that she'd refused his proposal. She deserved more of a man than he. It was this train of thought that carried him into slumber.

Vivid images scrolled across his tormented mind, terrible pictures of war and death, until he fought to swim back to wakefulness. The drone of cavalry faded, until he realized it was only the buzzing of flies he heard.

Then it stopped. A miraculous coolness covered his brow, and his eyelids fluttered open. At the sight of Cora Mae leaning over him, he wondered if he was still dreaming.

"You're awake." Her smile unfurling, dimples starred her cheeks as she wrung out a rag over a pail and began wiping the sweat from his skin.

Her velvet voice yanked all his senses to attention. "Are you—really here?" With his left hand, he touched her wrist as she passed her cloth over the depression in his chest. Watched a tendril of her hair sway near her cheek.

"I really am." Her hazel eyes glistened.

Inwardly, he reeled, rebelling against the pity he read there. He hadn't dreamed he would see her again. Certainly not like this. Never like this. "I thought you got on the train." His voice was hoarse. Weak. He hated himself for that.

"You persuaded me otherwise." She swiped the rag from his neck over his left shoulder and down his arm. The cool cloth moved to his cheek, so soothing he couldn't help but close his eyes. "Can you tell me what happened?"

Ethan licked his dry lips and turned his head to cough. "Two soldiers disobeyed orders and entered a private home with obvious intent to plunder. I went after them to stop them, and one of them shot me. Said he thought I was a Rebel coming to kill them both." Anger and pain rippled his brow.

"You were shot by your own man?"

He coughed again, his flat position making his lungs work harder for breath. When he opened his eyes, he caught her looking at his bandages. Humiliation seared him. "You can go, Miss Stewart. I don't need you here."

She flinched. "But I—"

His nostrils flared. "Nothing you can do will fix me up so I can go out again and fight. A relief to you, yes? So please go. I don't *want* you here."

Cora Mae's face reddened; her lips grew thin and tight. *Good. Let her be angry.* Maybe then she'd leave him in peace.

"Did you see him?" June fairly pounced on Cora Mae as soon as she entered the small tent where the few female nurses slept. "Does the sergeant know his arm's cut short?"

"He knows." A knot formed in her chest as she eased herself onto her cot and pulled her shoes—another gift from Anne—from her swollen feet.

"Well, what did he say?"

Anne sat on June's cot, rubbing her back. In a secondhand nightdress bleached white, the little girl looked pure and fresh and altogether too young for a war.

"I reckon he's doing all right." She sighed.

June's forehead furrowed, but she closed her eyes.

When she had drifted off to sleep, Anne rose and wrapped her arm around Cora Mae's shoulders. "Do you know how long the spirit takes to heal?" the older woman asked.

"Much longer than skin and bone."

"Give him time, dear." She paused. "I didn't realize you were friends."

Cora Mae sniffed, chuckling. "He brought me and June out of Roswell and kept us prisoner at the courthouse." Inexplicably, she confided in Anne about the rail yard proposal, and Mr. Ferguson, and jumping off the train. She did not, however, tell her about his kiss. That, she kept hidden in her heart for her memory alone.

"Merciful heavens!" Anne fanned herself when the tale was told. "Little wonder that you care!"

"But I shouldn't, you see. Not any more than I care about the other patients. My future is in Georgia, wherever Mr. Ferguson finds us another mill, and Sergeant Howard's is in the North. There's a river between us, and I'm not just talking about the Ohio."

"That may be so. But the wonderful thing about rivers, Cora Mae, is that they can be crossed. Even after the bridges have been burned." She kissed her forehead and bade her good night.

The next day, there was no time to think of Ethan or rivers or trains. On the twentieth day of July, there was a battle at Peachtree Creek, outside Atlanta, and the wounded poured into Marietta like rain down a waterspout in a storm.

The church filled with broken, battered men bleeding into the straw so quickly that the freedmen and women who were tasked with changing it could not keep up with the work.

The tents bordering the square nearly burst with patients, too. Ambulance drivers crammed wounded men together under patches of shade that couldn't stretch to cover them all. The screams that rent the air seemed loud enough to be heard in Roswell.

"You stay away from the square, June, do you hear me?" Cora Mae knelt and grasped June's shoulders, staring her in the eyes something fierce. "Do not go near them, no matter what. I don't want you in any of the hospitals, either." No little girl should see or hear what was going on inside.

Nodding, June agreed to help Anne in the cooking tent.

Convalescent nurses labored to keep up with the mere forty-five Union doctors wearing blood-smeared aprons and sun-bronzed brows. Dr. Wilcox pulled Cora Mae from the Methodist church to assist his operations beneath a tent at the edge of the town square. While he amputated, she stood with him, her apron spotting scarlet as she held mangled limbs in her hands. The amputations took seven minutes now. Then six. Now five. They could not be done any quicker without unspeakable barbarity.

Day melted into night. Fireflies and moths fluttered against the lantern Cora Mae held while Dr. Wilcox performed his work in the jaundiced glow.

"No more," the doctor finally said at midnight. "We must rest." He wiped his saw back and forth on his apron as she splashed a bucket of water over the door on which the surgeries took place, sluicing the blood into the red-stained grass.

After four hours of sleep that felt like none, she awoke with muscles as sore as her heart.

"Good morning, dear." Anne smiled down at her. "I hate to rush you, but Dr. Wilcox has already sent for you. He needs you straightaway."

Covering a yawn, Cora Mae nodded and stiffly rose from the cot. "How is June?" She bent and kissed the girl's tangled hair as she slept.

"She's getting along, but it's all so much for her to take in. I keep her close, so don't you worry."

"That's a comfort to me. Thank you." There was more to say but no time to even begin. Instead, she raked her fingers through her hair and bound it up again at the nape of her neck.

The walk to the square was bewildering. Wind sighed mournfully through the oak trees while songbirds trilled cheerfully from their branches. Overhead, a cloudless blue sky hung over scenes of incredible anguish. White hospital tents flapped in the breeze like angel wings, shielding the men from the sun, and perhaps the heavens from the hell below.

When Cora Mae found Dr. Wilcox at his table, two freedmen were already with him, looking to be in their early twenties and strong.

"Miss Stewart, this is Joshua and Titus. They'll be assisting us today."

Cora Mae nodded to each of them. "Good morning." She turned to the doctor. "Do you still need me, then?"

"I need all of you. The fellows we'll be operating on today may put up a fight, and Joshua and Titus will need to hold them still."

She frowned. "Won't they be unconscious for the operation?"

"Too much time has passed since their injuries." He waved to the freedmen to bring the next patient to the table.

"But how can you! With nothing for the men!" Shock sharpened her tone.

"Do not pretend to care more for them than I do. If we put them under at this point, they very likely will not wake. Feel sorry about it later, but now we must do the work."

Disbelief paralyzed her as a young man was helped onto the table.

"Don't take my hand! Don't take it off! Oh God, help me! Get away from me, you old sawbones!" His brown eyes were wild with terror, his hand already crushed to an unrecognizable pulp. Joshua and Titus flanked him, laying their broad, dark hands on his body.

"Miss Stewart!" Dr. Wilcox's voice snapped her back to attention. Bags drooped beneath his eyes as if he hadn't slept in a week.

Drawing a deep breath of air, she plunged into her work. "Hello, soldier, my name is Cora Mae Stewart." She took the scissors and began cutting up his sleeve. "What's your name?"

"M—Morris. James Morris the third."

She cut the sleeve from his arm all the way up to his elbow. "Where are you from, James?"

"Chicago. Illinois." His speech slowed, likely because he'd lost so much blood already. "Please—stop."

"What's Chicago like? You have family there?" She held his gaze as Dr. Wilcox threaded the tourniquet band under his arm.

He looked at her, puzzled for the briefest of moments, and she offered a soft smile, even as she noticed Dr. Wilcox set knife to flesh from the corner of her eye.

She placed a hand on James's elbow while the freedmen stabilized his arm and legs. "Look at me, James. Keep looking at me. You will get through this."

"Oh no, oh no no—" He struggled under their hands.

"Try not to move. It will be over soon." She watched his face turn beet red, and then his eyes rolled back in his head. He had passed out from the pain, but he was still breathing.

When Dr. Wilcox finished minutes later, Joshua and Titus carried him off the door and laid him under a tent.

"Next!" The doctor called, and she prayed that God Himself would be her strength, and the doctor's, too.

Every operation bruised her. The screams she would carry in her mind forever, she thought. But Dr. Wilcox didn't flag, and neither did she, until at the end of the day, he pronounced them finished. "I've had no time for rounds." He pushed his splattered spectacles up the bridge of his nose. "In the morning, I'll need you to change whichever dressings are three days old. Then come back to me."

For the second night in a row, Cora Mae slept in her clothes.

Chapter Nine

July 22

Pail in her hand, and heart in her throat, Cora Mae entered the Methodist church. The smell nearly knocked her back, but her determined feet walked over the soiled hay anyway. Most of the men crowded onto the pews would only need their dressings moistened. There were only a few whose bandages needed to be completely changed. Ethan Howard was one of them.

Flies peppered the foul air, along with voices invoking God's name such as this place of worship had likely never heard before. Sorrow threatened to drown her to see so much suffering in one place. She felt no rejoicing that Confederate soldiers had caused it, nor was she unaware that Yankee soldiers had likely dispatched the same amount of anguish. *How long, Lord? When will this wretched war end?*

Pushing a strand of hair off her forehead, she squinted again at the sea of faces. There at the end of a pew, she spotted Ethan and went to him, bracing herself for his protests.

As she drew near, however, alarm bells clanged inside her. His blond hair was dark with sweat. His complexion was so altered, he barely looked himself. She placed her hand to his brow and quickly drew it away. His skin was scorching hot. Quickly, she wiped a cool, wet cloth over his face, neck, and torso.

"Sergeant Howard? Ethan."

He didn't stir.

Glancing at his bandaged arm, she pulled fresh linens and lint from her apron pockets and laid them on the pew. While cradling his elbow in one hand, she unwound the dressings until only the adhesive strips were left. With a sponge, she soaked those until they loosened. Holding her breath, she removed the sodden strips—and the ball of soiled lint tucked inside—until his skin was bare, and she set them aside. Odor assaulted her senses.

Choking back a sob, she looked at the seam where Dr. Wilcox had fused the skin back together at the end of his abbreviated forearm. It was so swollen, she was sure it was the cause of his fever. A bright red hue crept upward toward his elbow. Was the unchanged dressing the cause? She couldn't help but wonder as she sponged his arm clean.

With nimble fingers, she took a pinch of lint, wadded it into a dense pack, and held it against the seam at the end of his arm. Then she wrapped it snugly into place with fresh strips, winding the bandage around and around until she finally tied a knot below his elbow.

Ethan's eyelids fluttered. "Cora Mae? Am I dreaming?" He didn't sound like himself. "This is no place for you." His chest rose and fell with his breath.

And he was gone again, deep into a fevered sleep.

She said a prayer and moved on to the next patient in need of fresh dressings, more troubled than she cared to admit.

Wagonloads of casualties came pouring in again, this time bearing wounded from the Battle of Atlanta. While Anne kept watch of June, Cora Mae steeled her nerves against the screams of shattered men and helped Dr. Wilcox do his job in the sweltering tents.

Surely a callus had formed over her heart, for she no longer quaked at every rasp of the saw, every snapping of bone. Only sweat, not tears, now wet her face as she understood Dr. Wilcox's efficiency was not cruel, but merciful.

But once another twenty-four hours passed from the time of the battle, the anesthesia was necessarily put away, and operations performed without it. Cora Mae never would get used to this. She reckoned the doctor felt the same, for all his brusque demeanor. The terror, the thrashing about, the begging and pleading to take life rather than limb—it was enough to shake a cedar tree from the ground.

"Enough," Dr. Wilcox declared at last. "Clean up, eat something, get some rest."

She rinsed the ruined door. "Will there be more battles soon?" She could not imagine how many more men the Union had to spare.

"More battles, yes. Soon? I don't know."

Wearily, she nodded and parted ways with the doctor she'd come to respect.

As she threaded her way between the hospital tents, wounded men stared at her from their sultry shade. "Dirty Secesh!" The words cut through the air. "She's a Secesh! And a butcher!"

Cora Mae whirled around, in search of her accuser. James Morris III came stumbling from beneath his tent, waving his handless arm in the air.

"You didn't tell me you were one of the exiled Roswell hands with an ax to grind—or should I say a bone saw!" Eyes blazing, he shouted, gesturing wildly to other amputees. "Held me down without anesthesia while the doc cut off my hand!"

"Aw, shut up and leave her alone." A voice came to her defense from somewhere in the tent's shadows. "She's a saint for nursing the likes of us, especially after what we did to her homeland."

"No, no, Morris is right! She did the same to me!" called another man. "Held me down, gave me nothing for the pain. Didn't seem troubled a bit as I felt the blade slice through me."

James came and waved his bandaged forearm in her face. "How would you like to know what it feels like?"

"Please." Her voice was hoarse with fear. "You'll rupture your stitches. You need to rest. Go back and lie down."

A smile slid over his face. "How's about you come with me!" In a flash, he had both arms around her and tripped her so she fell to the ground on top of him.

She screamed, and he laughed harshly, grinding her against him.

"Let her go, Morris!" Whoever yelled it apparently couldn't do more than that. "You're a disgrace, you fool!"

"Hey, what say you roll her this way when you're done with her!"

Terror cut through Cora Mae. In their eyes, she was their enemy still and had deliberately caused them pain. What wouldn't they do for revenge? Her voice utterly useless, she rammed her knee as hard as she could between Morris's legs, but succeeding only in bruising the ground.

"Woo! Feisty little Secesh, ain't ye?"

A shot cracked through the air overhead, the force of it shuddering through her.

"Unhand her, you rat, or the next bullet will be for your head." Dr. Wilcox's voice boomed above them. Morris relaxed his grip, and she rolled away from him, mortified. Standing, she dashed behind the doctor, who still had his pistol trained on Morris. Once the young man slinked away, Dr. Wilcox escorted her all the way to her sleeping tent.

"Coming back to work tomorrow, I hope?" he asked gently.

Cora Mae put on a smile. "Of course." She was pleased that her voice did not shake.

The sun was high in the cotton-tufted sky the next day before she found him at the square. "How is Ethan Howard? Have you checked on him yet?" A basket of dressing supplies swung from her elbow, and a pail of water hung from her hand.

"Ah, Miss Stewart." His eyes sparked with something she couldn't read. "I'm afraid you won't be needing those anymore." He took the pail and basket from her and set them on the ground. "Walk with me."

She followed him from the hospital tent into shade cast by the three-story Masonic Hall. "How is Sergeant Howard?"

"I'm afraid there's been a change. He's no longer your concern."

Her breath hitched. "I beg your pardon? You can't mean—he isn't—"

"You won't be nursing anymore." He wiped his brow with his handkerchief then stuffed it back into his pocket.

She stared, waiting for an explanation. "I don't understand."

Sighing, the doctor rubbed his hand over his unshaven jaw. "Word travels fast, even when the messengers don't have both feet, as it happens. News of your incident yesterday evening with Private Morris reached Sherman's ears. He called me in to explain, which I did to the best of my ability. Turns out, he never authorized the chief surgeon to hire any mill hands to stay on as nurses."

"No, it was General Dodge."

"Sherman outranks him." He squinted at her. "He says this disorder among the men must end. That he can't have doctors spending time guarding Southern nurses, or patients interrupting their healing to lash out at you, or other patients growing sympathetic to the plight of Southern civilians because of you."

Her head ached with concentration. "What are you saying?"

"Not me. Sherman." His apologetic tone unnerved her. "He's ordered you north, just like all the other mill hands. You and the girl in your care will be given two tickets and passes to get you through. The train leaves. . ." He consulted his pocket watch. "In thirty minutes. You'll both be on it."

"No."

"I realize you've not yet been paid. Take this." He stuffed a roll of greenbacks in her hand, along with two documents. "Your oaths, and a letter of recommendation. It should help you find gainful employment. Lieutenant McDowell's enlistment is up, and he's agreed to escort you as far as Louisville." Chin to his chest, he muttered, "Blast this war." Then he signaled to someone, turned, and walked away.

In a daze, she watched him from the sidewalk, and then her gaze drifted to soldiers she'd met and cared for over the last several days. It was not a role she'd aspired to, but now that she was stripped of it, she hardly felt relief. *Go north? Today?* The gears of her mind turned so laboriously to grasp this, she was breathless with the effort.

A touch on her elbow, and she turned to find a soldier waiting for her. "I'm Lieutenant McDowell, ma'am. Here's your tickets and passes. I'll be riding with you. I'll make sure nothing happens to you on the journey."

Stunned, she took in the earnestness in his brown eyes. "What will I do in Louisville?" she wondered aloud.

"Papers say there's a women's refugee center a block from the depot. A thousand mill hands are there. You could find shelter and rations there, I wager." He scratched through his charcoal-colored beard. "But some reporters say there's not enough beds or blankets. Still, they have to stay there because they won't take the Oath of Allegiance to the Union."

She blinked. "You mean this?" She showed him her oath.

"Yes, that's the one. If you've signed that, you won't need to sit out the war in prison. But you'll need to find your own work and lodging."

"Cannelton." The word burst from her. "In Indiana. There's a mill there, Sergeant Howard said. Can you help me get there?"

"That's on the Ohio River. Once we get to Louisville, I'll see you onto a steamboat, and it'll be up to you to get off at the right dock. But we better hurry now."

Still reeling, she marched past him and headed toward the tent she'd called home. When she reached it, June was outside folding linens with some freedwomen. Anne was nowhere to be found.

"What is it?" June asked when she saw Lieutenant McDowell at Cora Mae's side.

"Get your things, June. And mine, too, please." She turned to McDowell. "I want to look for Mrs. Littleton. I want to say good-bye." And if she could catch a glimpse of Ethan, too, it sure would set her mind more at ease.

The train whistled from a few blocks away.

"No." McDowell looked in the direction of the depot. "We're going, now."

Shock numbed her. Even good-byes were stolen from her, just as they had been at Roswell. Without another word, she plunged into the tent and looked frantically for a paper and pencil to leave a note for Anne. Finding none, she took a tin of talcum powder and dashed a thin layer across a folding table. With her fingertip, she traced her farewell: *Thay sent us north.*

Chapter Ten

July 26

Above Ethan, a crystal chandelier caught the light and threw miniature rainbows against whitewashed walls. The air was thick with heat and flies and with the smell of wounded men. Turning his head, he stared hard at the bouquet of bandages beneath his elbow, until his sight overrode the sensation that his right hand was attached to his stump.

Finally, the uncanny feeling receded, and mere pain took its place. Sweat filmed his brow as he gritted his teeth against it. Then a pitiful moan filled his ears. On the plank next to him lay a patient with one leg.

"Water," he rasped. "Oh for the love of God! Bring me water!"

Ethan pushed himself up and scanned the sanctuary crammed full of men. Not a nurse or doctor was among them. "What's your name, soldier?"

The patient opened his eyes. "Joseph Parker." His gaze flitted to Ethan's right arm. "You?"

"Ethan Howard." And although he had but one arm, he still had two legs for walking. "Let me see about that water. I'm mighty thirsty myself." Cautiously, he swung his legs over the side of his plank and jumped down onto the straw-covered aisle.

Light-headedness slowed his pace, and the sun nearly blinded him when he stepped outside and sneezed. But he was up and moving. It felt like a victory. Ache throbbed beneath his bandages, but he shoved that aside as he focused on the pump. Surely he could work it with one hand.

Just before he reached it, a short, plump woman swept toward him, a pail and dipper swinging from her fist. "Hello there!" A wisp of black hair sprung from her bun and coiled beside her wilting collar. "You need some water, honey? Let me get it!"

Warmth flooded him. "Much obliged, ma'am." He nodded to her, and he wondered if seeing his bare chest and reduced arm made her as uncomfortable as he was. "But would you mind if I pump it myself?"

"Oh, there's no call for that, dear, I can manage it."

He rubbed his hand over his face and was surprised to find a week's worth of beard. "I don't want to sound ungrateful. But I'm itching to use the muscles I still have."

"Oh! Well!" Her cheeks flamed red. "Of course, I just—" Apparently giving up on her speech, she set the pail beneath the spout.

"What day is it, anyway?" He grasped the iron handle in his left hand, felt the chipping paint beneath his palm.

"Twenty-sixth of July."

Ethan plunged the handle up and down, waiting for water to gush forth. "Then it's been more than a week since my injury." The fever must have erased a few days' time from his memory.

"And we've had two battles since then. I'm so sorry you had to come looking for water yourself. But there are many, many more for us to tend to now."

With a gurgle, the water flowed into the pail in a clear braided stream. He wondered if he'd see Cora Mae again after the way he'd sent her away. Part of him longed to make things right with her, but toward what end? She was spoken for. And Ethan didn't think he could bear her pity.

He blew out a sigh and felt the familiar tickle in his lungs. He turned his head to cough into his elbow.

"I'm Anne Littleton, by the way. Chaplain Littleton's wife."

"Pleased to meet you. I'm Ethan Howard."

"Sergeant Howard!" She clapped her hands together.

"Have we met?"

"No, no. Cora Mae was so concerned when you were laid low with the fever recently. She'd have been so pleased to see you up." A shadow passed over her face.

Perhaps it was merely a reflection of his own. "Well, you can tell her not to worry next time you see her."

Her expression drooped. "I'm afraid I can't."

Ethan shoved the pump's handle down one last time. "What do you mean?"

"She was sent north, dear. Cora Mae and little June both. Yesterday."

"Are you sure?" Surely she was mistaken.

"Quite so, I'm afraid. They're headed to Louisville now."

The news shouldn't have mattered to him at all. She was engaged. He was an amputee. Yet the knowledge of her absence carved away at him. Angry that his heart was so drawn to a woman he couldn't have, he hoisted the pail and returned to Joseph Parker in the church.

"Sit up, will you?" Ethan walked between the pews and stood over Joseph. "I'm not putting this dipper to your lips for you. Couldn't if I wanted to."

Joseph squinted up at him then sat up on his plank. "I see that. It's hard knocks, eh, Howard?"

"For you and me both." He lowered the pail into Joseph's lap, and Joseph took the dipper for his drink. "Thank you." Sighing, he laid back down.

"Bring it here!" A voice called to Ethan's right. "Please! Water!"

"I want some, too!" From his left.

All over the sanctuary, hands and voices beckoned him. So Ethan went to them and helped them quench their thirst.

When the men had finally had their fill, he brought the pail and dipper back to the well, far more fatigued than he cared to admit, even to himself. He paused to lean on the handle. "Now what?" he said aloud.

"Now, you rest a spell with an old man who could use some company." Chaplain Littleton appeared beside him and clapped him on the back. "But cover up first. I'm blushing." He handed him a clean shirt.

Ethan slipped the loose-fitting garment on over his head, threaded his arms through the sleeves, and then sat beside him on a bench in the shade of a magnolia tree.

"I've got something for you, son." He pulled from his haversack a round, greenish-gray bottle that tapered into a narrow neck.

"That's quite a flask, Chaplain. You thirsty, too?"

Chaplain Littleton laughed. "Actually, yes. But for something far more satisfying." He popped off the cork and turned the bottle up, until a small scroll slid into his hand. Setting the bottle aside, he pulled a loop of twine of one end of the scroll, and a small booklet unfurled in his brown-spotted hands. THE SOLDIER'S PRAYER AND HYMN BOOK was printed in block type on its cover. The chaplain flipped it open and began to read. "My soul thirsteth for God, for the living God. . . . My tears have been my meat day and night, while they continually say unto me, Where is thy God?" He closed the booklet and looked Ethan in the eyes. "Put thy trust in God."

Nodding, Ethan picked up a dark green magnolia leaf and rubbed his thumb over its glossy surface. "The forty-second psalm."

Seams creased Chaplain Littleton's face as he smiled. "You know it."

"I believe in God. I'm a sheep in His fold." Ethan's half-empty sleeve waved in summer's hot breeze. "But right now, my soul is thirsty, and somehow, I can't seem to get a drink. I don't expect you to understand."

"Really? I'd like to tell you a story." He pulled up the hem of his trousers, exposing a wooden leg.

Ethan's eyebrow lifted, and the chaplain let the faded cloth fall back into place.

"I wasn't always a chaplain, you know. I was a soldier once, like yourself."

"Mexican War?"

"Right. That was nearly twenty years ago. During one battle, a friend of mine was hurt badly. He had this bottle on him, with letters for his wife inside it. Right there on the field, he handed this to me, and just before he died, I promised him I'd deliver the letters to his wife. Tucked this bottle into my uniform jacket and kept fighting. It wasn't long till I was hit, too."

"In your leg."

"And lost it. But I kept my promise to my friend."

"You delivered the letters to his widow?"

"Yes." Mischief flashed in his eyes. "And then I married her."

"You did?" Ethan laughed in surprise. "Mrs. Littleton was your friend's widow?"

He nodded gently.

Ethan pointed to a crunched dent near the bottom of the bottle. "What happened there?"

"I don't know. Not sure my friend did, either, but look at this." He pointed to the letters carved into its neck. "*Spero*. It's a Latin word. It means 'hope.'"

"Hope." Ethan gazed at the script. "Well, I sure could use a dose of that."

"Who can do without it?" Sweat glittered on the chaplain's brow. He rolled up the prayer book and slid the twine over it before slipping it back into the bottle. "*Hope* is on the inside. Even if the vessel is battered and scarred. Hope can still live within." He turned the bottle over in his hands, smiling. "This bottle has served me well. It's high time it brings hope to someone else." He placed it in Ethan's hand. "Be ever hopeful, son."

Ethan searched Chaplain Littleton's eyes. "You would give this to me?"

"I just did."

"Thank you." The words seemed so inadequate. When the chaplain stood, Ethan remained on the bench, studying the gift he cradled in his hand. *Lord, fill me with hope. Satisfy me with Your living water. Help me trust You for Cora Mae's care and focus on what You would have me do right here. Use this vessel for Your work.*

August 2, Cannelton, Indiana

"This is it!" Cora Mae told June, who was leaning over the railing watching the stern-wheel steamboat paddle white ruffles into the river.

The last two days on the steamboat had been a welcome reprieve after five days of train travel. They'd retraced Sherman's path up through north Georgia, where lone chimneys stood mourning the ruins of their homes. Chattanooga was entirely surrounded by white Union tents camped out upon the mountain slopes. Nashville, too, was crawling with Yankees. Louisville had been as sooty and crowded as she'd imagined a dumping ground for exiled Southerners would be. It had seemed to Cora Mae that the entire world had turned Union blue, when just a month ago, her whole life had been wrapped in Confederate gray.

"Ready to set foot in the North?" She poured all the calm into her voice she could muster. *Please God, let me find work.*

The steamboat docked. Slinging her satchel over her shoulder, she walked with

June down a wooden plank and onto the north side of the Ohio River. People and horses and wagons flowed past her in a great hurry, and for a moment she felt like a sapling at the edge of a stream. The women's gowns swayed like bells around their footsteps, a marked contrast to the hoopless calico dresses Cora Mae and June wore.

"Now what?" June kicked at a rock in the road.

A breeze swished through birch trees and swept over Cora Mae's skin. Shielding her eyes from the sun with one hand, she looked up and down the river. "There. Do you see it?" The four-story building with two pointed towers loomed large, even from this distance.

"It's a mill!" June cried. "Just like Sergeant Howard said!"

It didn't take long to walk there. As they neared it, the familiar clanging and thudding sounds grew louder. The building was made of gray stone, not the red brick of Roswell's mills, but the windows looked larger and cleaner. As they reached the front gate, a bell rang from one of the steeples, and the thwacking inside grew silent.

"Quitting time, I reckon." Inhaling deeply, Cora Mae tucked loose strands of hair behind her ears and fished Dr. Wilcox's letter from her satchel. Girls in crisp blue muslin dresses with white collars and aprons streamed out of the front doors, chatting to one another. Mostly, their words twanged in the Northern way, but some of them talked more like Dooley, and a few spoke a language Cora Mae had never before heard. Then came a man wearing a dark suit and bowler hat.

"Here we go. Best behavior now, June." She felt more like her mother with each passing day and sounded like it, too. Drawing herself up as straight as a spindle, she marched toward the man in his Sunday best, stopping him on the sidewalk.

"Excuse me, sir. You work at the mill?"

"Yes, I do." His gray eyes appraised her. A neatly trimmed black beard and mustache shadowed his pockmarked face.

"Who would we talk to about employment?"

"You're talking to him. But we're not hiring." He tipped his bowler hat to her. "Good day."

"I have a letter from a Union surgeon." She thrust it out, awkward and uncomfortable in her desperation. Swallowing her dismay, she tried again. "My name is Cora Mae Stewart, and this here is June. I've worked at a cotton mill for ten years, and I truly would appreciate a job at yours."

Perhaps it was only curiosity that made the man reach for the letter. But as he read it, his brow furrowed, and his lips pinched together. "What sort of work do you do?"

"I'm a drawing girl." The faint smell of burning coal stuck to the warm wind swirling between them, hinting at the massive mill's source of power. In the corner of her vision, a few more young women whisked out of the building, bright spots of blue and white against the drab limestone.

He nodded slowly. Handing the letter back to her, he crossed his arms. "It's a real shame what happened to you and the other mill workers in Georgia. But I'm afraid we almost have more workers than work as it is. Our cotton supply is drying up. As you can imagine."

Cora Mae's stomach dropped. June squeezed her hand. The moment stretched long, while horses clopped and buggies trundled over the road beside them. "This is all I know, sir. I don't mean to tell you how to run your fine factory, but I sure would appreciate the chance to work for you."

His mustache twitched. Eyebrows plunged, he took the letter back from her hand and read it once more. With a great sigh, he finally met her gaze. "The little one is too young to work here, but if you're looking for extra income, try Mrs. Beasley's boardinghouse. She's looking for help with cleaning and odd chores." Returning the doctor's letter to her once more, he gave directions to the establishment.

"Thank you kindly." She waited while the gentleman tapped his whiskered chin.

"See you in the morning." He tipped his hat to her and sauntered away.

As she watched him go, she slowly exhaled.

"Does this mean we're going to be all right, Mama?" June's small voice lifted.

Suddenly dizzy with relief, Cora Mae knelt on the sidewalk and wrapped her arms around the little girl. "Yes, Junebug, I reckon it does."

"I wish we could tell Sergeant Howard thank you for telling us about this place."

"I wish we could, too." Her throat grew tight. *Lord, thank You. Thank You for Ethan, and please be with him now. Heal him, body and soul.*

"Are we real Yankees now?" June whispered.

Cora Mae leaned back, holding June by the shoulders. "You and I are the same people as we ever were." But she wasn't. The war had changed her. It changed everything.

That night, at Mrs. Beasley's boardinghouse, she and June slept in real beds for the first time in almost a month. In the morning, they had pancakes and sausage for breakfast. June stayed at the boardinghouse to sweep and dust, while Cora Mae worked at the mill.

The staircases at the Cannelton mill were wider than those in Roswell, and the machines were powered by steam power from coal instead of water. Gas jets lit the rooms when sunlight wasn't enough, and at mealtimes, vents suctioned the extra lint from the air.

Other than that, the work was the same. Only Cora Mae worked with blue cloth now instead of gray, and she wore a new muslin dress rather than her old homespun. Her days fell into the familiar rhythm she had grown up with, and that was a comfort.

As the weeks stretched into months, drying leaves shivered and fell from their limbs. News came that Sherman had captured Atlanta, and she filled up to over-flowing with thoughts of home.

Then in October, the mill stopped running, and there was no more work, once again.

Chapter Eleven

Marietta
November 3

L ookin' good, laddie!"

Ethan looked up to find Lt. Seamus Dooley striding down the aisle between the pews of the Methodist church, his red hair brushing his shoulders. He smiled at his old friend, just returned from Atlanta, then schooled his features into a more serious expression. "I could really use a hand."

Dooley's eyes widened, and his freckled cheeks puffed out. "'Tis a wee joke, then, is it?"

Ethan hesitated just long enough to watch Dooley squirm, and then he laughed. "Afraid so." He may never win a sword fight now or load another musket, but after three months of nursing in this church hospital, there were few tasks he could not accomplish.

Carefully, he placed glass bottles of laudanum, quinine, and chloroform into a medicine chest. The patients had already been cleared out, according to Sherman's order. The army—all sixty thousand troops—was preparing to move south.

"Will you be coming with us on the march through Georgia?"

Ethan shook his head. "This is as far as I go with Uncle Billy. It's time for me to move on."

"Back to Indiana? What'll you do?"

"Pay a debt, for one. But something tells me the Cannel Coal Company won't be eager to hire any one-handed miners."

"So." Dooley paused dramatically. "What'll you do?"

"Think I'll take Lincoln up on his Homestead Act. Get myself some land. I sure have taken to life aboveground since I joined the army."

"Aye, but farming? How can you—" Dooley reddened.

"Oh, I expect a challenge. But after all, there's only one 'arm' in 'farm.'" His grin tipped sideways.

Dooley looked scandalized for a moment before guffawing. "I bet you'll find the 'ow' in 'plow'!"

Ethan laughed, and Dooley hooted until tears pooled in his eyes.

"Hoo-ee!" Dooley swiped off his hat and ran his hand over his hair. "Come on out front, now. Somebody is waiting for you who I think you'll want to see." He scratched his scalp before tugging his hat back onto his head.

Ethan stared at him. "You tease."

"Nope. Wouldn't do that to you." He motioned him to follow.

Ethan's heart thunked against his ribs. Who did he want to see but Cora Mae Stewart? Leaving the medicine cabinet on the end of a pew, he trailed Dooley down the aisle and through the wooden doors of the church.

"Behold your visitor!" Dooley said with a flourish.

Ethan smiled as he walked down the steps, but his heart sank quickly back into place. "Hello, Reckless." As he stroked the horse's dapple gray nose, a wave of nostalgia washed over him. Reckless had been with him for everything that mattered, from his first charge in battle to the raid on the Georgia Railroad, and everything in between. Including the Roswell rescue of Cora Mae. If only he could erect fortifications around his memory to keep thoughts of her away. He cleared his throat and ran his hand over Reckless's withers, checking for the white hair that grows over scars from ill-fitting tack. "He hasn't been ridden too hard, has he?"

"His new rider takes good care of him. But tell me, why do you seem disappointed to see him? Who'd you think I brought here instead?"

Ethan raised one eyebrow, almost apologetically.

"Oh, laddie. Still pining over Miss Stewart?"

A sigh escaped him as his gaze followed columns of marching soldiers on their way toward the square. Down the street, a cannon fired, likely to test a new shipment of shells, and crows exploded from a nearby tree. "Dooley, I can't get her out of my mind."

The smell of saltpeter soured the air. "You're being discharged. Go after her! Do you know where she is?"

"Maybe she's in Louisville still, but according to the papers, she could have been taken to New Albany, or Jeffersonville just north of the Ohio River. Some mill workers were taken to Cincinnati, or Indianapolis, or even to Cairo, Illinois." He shook his head. "But I did tell her there was a mill in Cannelton."

"Cannelton, Indiana. Your hometown?"

"Yes, but I don't know if she would have remembered that."

"Howard! She could be there right now! Why are you still here?"

"Cora Mae is engaged to another man. What would I say to her even if I found her?"

"You'll think of something."

Cannelton, Indiana, November 15

Wind whistled through the hole in the only window the attic had. Shivering, Cora Mae scooped up the rag that had dropped to the floor and stuffed it back in.

On the bed, June pulled her quilt tighter up under her chin, though it wasn't nearly time to sleep. "Why couldn't we keep our old room? Is it because we're from the South? Did Mrs. Beasley get vexed with us because her son died at Atlanta?" She sucked the end of a strand of her hair.

"No, I'm sure she doesn't blame us for that, any more than we would blame her for what Sherman did to us."

"Then why?"

Cora Mae sighed. "We can't pay what we used to for a regular room. This is what we can afford." The mill had been shut down for a month now, because there just wasn't enough cotton coming from the South to mill. And even though she and June did help with the cleaning, it was only when one of the maids couldn't work.

"I liked the other room better. It was warmer. And prettier."

"Let's try to be grateful for the roof over our heads, Junebug." A dripping sounded in the corner, where rain leaked into a pail. "Even if there are holes in it." Surely the women's prison in Louisville where most of the mill hands remained was far worse than this.

June turned on her side and coughed; then she huddled deeper under the covers.

The coughing was getting worse, and though Cora Mae knew it wasn't the same illness caused by decades of breathing in cotton lint, the sound of it filled her with the same sense of helplessness she felt for Mama, who she prayed was still waiting for her return after four and a half months.

Snatching up a stack of newspapers Mrs. Beasley had given her, Cora Mae returned to the window and felt for drafts coming in between the panes. When she found one, she tore the headline of Lincoln's reelection from the newspaper, folded it in half, and wedged it into place to block the cold air from seeping through.

Then she stopped. She brought the paper over to the kerosene lamp and slanted the tiny columns of print into its glow. Words jumped out at her: *Marietta. Sherman. Burned.* She tried sounding out the rest of the words, but it was taking far too long.

"I'll be back in a minute, June." Straightening her hair, she left the attic, paper in hand.

Downstairs in the dining room, two gentlemen were just pushing back from the table at the end of the dinner hour. She'd seen them before, and they'd been civil. She took a deep breath. "Pardon me, but I'm having trouble making this out. Could you—would you mind? What does this say about Marietta?" She held out the paper.

"Can't read, eh?" one of the men muttered, twisting the ends of his mustache back into their points.

"Not quick enough to suit me."

"Pay him no mind," the younger of the two men said. He took the paper from her and scanned the text. "Says here that Sherman's troops voted via absentee ballot for Lincoln on November 8, probably winning the election for him, so the war goes on."

"But what does it say about Marietta? Did something burn?"

He ran his finger down the page. "Ah. Sherman's sixty thousand troops evacuated Marietta by November 13. . . . Sherman began destroying the railroad behind him. . . . He had the Union army set fire to the buildings around Marietta Square, too. They're marching south through Georgia."

"So there are no more Yankees in Marietta?"

"Looks that way." He handed the paper back to her. "You're awfully lucky to be up here and not down in his path."

As Cora Mae climbed back up the stairs and slipped into the garret, she didn't feel lucky at all. How could she rejoice in her own safety when her homeland was being laid waste?

Chapter Twelve

November 20

Even as Ethan had traveled via train and steamboat from Marietta to get here, he knew the chances of finding Cora Mae were slim. Now, standing before the massive but silent Indiana Cotton Mill, hope guttered altogether. While he stalled on the edge of the street, pedestrians and wagons passed him by, gazing a little too long at the sleeve hanging empty below his right elbow.

Turning his collar up against the wind, he crossed the mill yard and stood on the bank of the Ohio River, looking south and thinking of Georgia. Cannelton no longer felt much like home. In the two days since he'd been back, he'd gone to the coal company that powered the mill to tell, or rather show, that he'd not be returning to work. Then he'd paid a visit to the doctor who had tended his father in his losing battle with black lung, to pay him the debt he owed for those services. With the mill not operating, there was nothing else here to do.

Rubbing his hand over his jaw, he could still smell the balsam shaving soap he'd used right before coming here. Sunset gilded the river as steamboats paddled by. He should be on one of them, heading west. Tomorrow, he'd book his passage.

A knock at the garret door sounded feebly amid June's coughing. "Miss Stewart?"

Cora Mae left the girl's side and opened the door. "Mrs. Beasley."

"Such a racket!" The woman's nose wrinkled as she peered around Cora Mae. "Myra Johnson is ill today, so I need you to clean room six." She handed Cora Mae a key and a bucket with rag and duster inside.

"I'll do it right away."

"See that you do, and do it well." In a rustle of plum taffeta, Mrs. Beasley descended the stairs.

After tying an apron over her dress, Cora Mae went down to room six and let herself in. The room smelled faintly of boot black and balsam. Inhaling deeply of it, a longing ripped open inside her for the man she'd tried so hard to forget. If she closed her eyes, she could believe she was wrapped not just in his essence, but in his arms.

Guilt stirred as she dusted the furniture. Soon the war would end, and she'd return to Mr. Ferguson. She'd best not think of another. Kneeling at the hearth, she took the small shovel and scooped ashes into a pail. After sweeping the hearth clean, she trimmed the wicks in the kerosene lamps and wiped soot from inside their glass chimneys. At last, she straightened the counterpane over the bed, swept the floor, and shook the rug outside the window. With her bucket of supplies and the pail of ashes in her hands, she stood with her back to the door, surveying her work.

Suddenly, the door opened, knocking her forward. As she stumbled, her pails slipped from her hands and clattered to the floor, peppering it with ash. "Oh, no!" she cried and reached for the hearth broom to sweep the mess back into a pile. "I'm so sorry!"

"No, I should have noticed the door was already ajar. I was careless, forgive me." The boarder knelt beside her and replaced the rags and feather duster back in her bucket.

Embarrassment scorched her. "Please don't tell Mrs. Beasley what I've done," she whispered, unwilling to peek at his face. "I can't lose this job."

The man's hand stilled on his knee for a moment. Then he took the broom from her and set it on the floor. "Yes, you can."

Startled, she looked at him fully for the first time. And gasped. Tears sprang to her eyes, and words refused to come. She could only stare. His green eyes seemed to drink her in, though she knelt in a pile of ashes. His lips slowly slanted in a lop-sided smile as he rose and offered his hand. She took it and stood with trembling knees. He was every bit the man she remembered him to be, no less masculine or commanding for his shortened right arm. The way he looked at her now... She felt herself unraveling. Realized after a moment that her hand was still in his.

"In case you've forgotten, my name is Ethan Howard. And I'm here to take you home."

Tears spilled down her cheeks. Overcome, she covered her face with her hands and bent her head against his shoulder. Everything in her yearned to embrace him. His arms went around her, cinching her against him.

"I won't steal another kiss from you, Miss Stewart," he said into her ear. "But I do want to keep you from falling."

Laughter broke through her sobs, and her shoulders shook as she nodded.

"You still want to go home, don't you?"

She leaned back and looked at him. "With all my heart. But June's sick. Her cough is something awful. I don't know if she should travel just yet."

Furrows lined his brow. "Where is she?"

"In our room in the attic."

"May I see her?"

Leaving the ashes on the floor behind them, Cora Mae led the way up the stairs and into the chilled garret. "June, I have someone here who wants to see you."

"Who?"

Ethan grabbed a chair by its back and set it down next to her bed. "Hi there, little lady." He sat beside her.

At the sound of his voice, June turned. "Mr. Howard!" The word caught in her throat, and she began coughing again.

Ethan shook his head. "That's too big a cough to come from you."

She reached up, and he leaned down, clasping her to himself before gently releasing her. "Are you feeling better?" she asked. "Is your arm sore?"

Cora Mae cringed, but Ethan didn't seem bothered. "I'm feeling much better, thank you."

"Where you been all this time?"

He laughed. "Expecting me sooner, were you? I was busy getting healed up and then nursing other sick men down in Marietta. But I'm done with the army now."

"That means you can do whatever you want instead of always following silly old orders?"

"It means I can do whatever I think is best." He tapped her on the nose. "And do you know what I think is best right now?"

"No."

Ethan stood and walked around the room, feeling the draft come in through the window and roof, despite the newspapers and rags stuffed in the cracks and holes. "The best thing we can do is to trade rooms. You'll be doing me a favor really. Mine is filthy, ashes all over the floor." He winked at Cora Mae.

"Do you mean it? Mama, did you hear that?"

"I mean it." With a few long strides, he crossed the small space to Cora Mae. "Why are you up here in the first place?"

With a sigh, she explained it to him.

"She'll never get better in this room, and you're liable to fall ill yourself. I won't let that happen. You'll take my room, and I'll stay here."

"For how long?" June called out. She was already climbing out of bed.

"Until you're well enough to go home."

June clapped her hands and then fell into a gasping cough once again.

Cora Mae met Ethan's gaze, and he put his hand on her shoulder. "I know you're worried," he said, too calmly.

"Yes, I'm worried." She cut her voice low, so June wouldn't overhear. "My mother sounded like that, and she's dying of brown lung."

"And my father died of black lung. But little June has neither. She's sick from the air, and we're changing that. Do you have use of the kitchen?"

She nodded.

"Why don't you make some tea while I move her to room six, and bring my own things up here. There's a crack in one of my windowpanes, but it's nothing compared to this."

Cora Mae reckoned that to be polite she should argue with him. But she was so eager for June to be well again, and it felt so good to be taken care of, that she simply agreed to make tea.

By the time she brought a tray of tea up to room six, June was beaming in the bed, her hair hanging in two coppery plaits over her nightdress. The ashes had been swept from the floor, and Ethan was on one knee, building a fire in the hearth. She set the tray on a small table before joining him at the fireplace. "I can't believe you found us."

He stood and rolled his shoulders back. "I very nearly didn't. I went to the mill today to look for you, and when I saw it wasn't operating, I figured I'd never see you again." He smiled. "Never been so glad to be wrong."

She felt herself blushing and quickly moved to bring June her tea. "Sit up, please. It's hot. Little sips."

"Yes, Mama."

"For me?" Ethan pointed to the third cup of tea.

"Please. Sit." In the corner of the room opposite the bed where June rested, Cora Mae sat across from Ethan and focused on the steam curling up from her cup, suddenly at a loss for what to say.

He stirred a lump of sugar into his tea then took a sip. Leaning in, he murmured low enough so June wouldn't hear, "How long has she been calling you 'Mama'?"

She swallowed. "Since Marietta. She thought that would make us more likely to stay together. It sounded strange at first, but it seems to fit now. When her step-pa skedaddled, I agreed to take care of June as though she were my own. And now I feel as if she is."

"She is. In all the ways that matter. Now, this man you'll be marrying. Is he a good man?"

"He was my father's friend. He offered to marry me and provide for me and my mother." Just as Ethan had offered to marry and provide for her. Glancing at June, she was relieved to find she'd set her tea on the stand and had settled down to sleep.

His gaze bore into Cora Mae. "Do you love him?"

Her face growing warm, she looked away. The fire Ethan had built hissed and popped while she searched for words to say. "I respect him. My mother and I owe him a debt for the kindness he's shown in Pap's absence." Stifling a sigh, she traced her finger around the rim of her porcelain cup. "It's a practical arrangement."

"I see."

She wondered if he truly did. "Do you recall I told you about a textile engineer who came to Roswell?" He was rich, and handsome, and very persuasive.

"I remember."

Cora Mae nodded. "I didn't tell you that he took a shine to me. Promised to take me up to New York and marry me, and take me every place I had a hankerin' to see."

Ethan's eyebrows raised beneath a wave of dark blond hair. "And?"

"He broke his word." She swallowed. "Because he already had a wife."

He let out a low whistle, leaned back in his chair. "Filthy, lying cheat."

She shrugged, as if her heart had not been crushed. "He told me I was too common to be his wife, but that I could be his—" Her cheeks burned. Her longing for romance and escape had almost cost her honor. "I said no, of course, and stayed at the mill. Mr. Ferguson is nothing like Charles Hampton. He's a good man, and loyal. I'll not break my promise to him the way Mr. Hampton broke his promise to me. I aim to be honorable, Mr. Howard."

Ethan coughed into his elbow then drank the rest of his tea, brow furrowed in thought. "All right," he said at last. "I respect that. And I'll do my best to help you keep your word. Sherman once said, 'War is cruelty,' and he was right. But I still believe God has our good in mind, both for your life and for mine." He pulled his haversack from where it hung on the back of his chair and set it in his lap. Flipping open the top, he withdrew an odd gray bottle. Grasping the neck, he popped the cork out of it with his thumb then tipped it up until a scroll came out. "Would you mind turning to hymn number twelve?"

Cora Mae took the scroll, pulled the twine off it, and flipped through it. "What is this?"

"It's a Soldier's Prayer and Hymn Book Chaplain Littleton gave me in Marietta. But the truths inside aren't just for soldiers. I'd like to read some of this to you."

Relieved that he wasn't asking her to read, she handed the open booklet to him.

"Listen," he said. " 'God moves in a mysterious way, His wonders to perform; He plants His footsteps in the sea, He rides upon the storm.' And then verse three: 'His purposes will ripen fast, unfolding every hour: the bud may have a bitter taste, but sweet will be the flower.' "

"May that be true," Cora Mae whispered.

"Be ever hopeful." His smile warmed her to her toes. "And now I'll take my leave so you ladies can get some rest." Ethan went over to June and tucked the quilt around her little body until she couldn't move an inch. "Look at that! Snug as a Junebug in a rug." He kissed her forehead, and Cora Mae's breath caught in her throat at his tenderness.

"You know something?" June yawned. "You weren't too bad for a Yankee. But you're even better as just our friend. Don't you think so, Mama?"

A bittersweet smile curved her lips. "A very good friend, indeed."

November 22

Ethan could hear June coughing from the end of the hall as he made his way toward room six. Only two days after he'd given up his room, he didn't expect her to be well yet. But her rasping still scraped at him.

He knocked at the door and stood back, gaze drifting to the Chinese-patterned wallpaper peeling away at the ceiling. A large patch had been stripped away from the wall, revealing spidery cracks in the plaster beneath. He wasn't surprised that even the boardinghouse's corridor was in disrepair.

Cora Mae opened the door. Sunlight from the west-facing window behind her glinted on the thick braid coiled around her head. "Getting cold in the garret yet?"

He wouldn't admit that his fingers still tingled from the attic's chill. "Actually, Mrs. Beasley told me if I was so concerned about the crack in your window, I could fix it myself." He held up a thin sheet of wood. "So here I am. If you don't mind."

She opened the door wider to him, and he stepped past her. Birch branches shook just outside the window, so that when she faced him, light and shadow played across her face. "Are you sure?"

"Of course. Hello, June!" Ethan strode to where she sat at the table playing with paper dolls cut from newspaper and kissed the little girl on her silky hair. He coughed, and then so did she. "It's not a competition, you know," he teased.

Her laughter brought a smile to his lips. "What's that for?" She pointed.

"To cover that windowpane, so wind can't get through anymore." He nodded to the cracked glass.

"Oh, it's just a tiny smidge of wind."

Removing his jacket, Ethan strode to the window in his shirtsleeves. "No smidges allowed." Tucking the plank under his right arm, he drew several nails from his pocket and held them between his lips before unhooking the hammer from his belt. His tool pressed to his palm with two fingers, he grasped the plank and placed it over the glass. Angling his body, he pinned the wood in place with the end of his right forearm, and froze.

In the next instant, Cora Mae appeared at his side. "May I?"

"I think you'd better," he said around the nails poking from his mouth like pins from a cushion.

Hazel eyes dancing, dimples popped into her cheeks as she reached up and wiggled a nail from between his lips. "Where do you want it?"

"There." Hammer still in hand, Ethan pointed to a spot on the plank.

Pinching the nail, she held it in place and squeezed her eyes shut.

"Don't miss!" June piped up from the bed, laughing.

Ethan chuckled. With a sure hand, he tapped the nail into the wood until Cora Mae could release her grip. Then, with a few solid swings, he drove it into the existing wooden frame beneath. "Next," he said around the nails.

"Oh, stop it." She laughed, holding out her hand. "Let me have them."

Bending his head, he dropped the nails into her palm. "Thought you'd never ask." He grinned.

Together, they drove several more nails into place all around the pane, until the cracked square of glass was completely sealed. "Done." Ethan stood back and nodded with satisfaction. "Matches the rest of the decor around here, don't you think?"

She laughed. "Thank you."

He bowed to her. "Thank you." She already knew he couldn't have accomplished the task without her. He straightened. "And now I have a favor to ask. I hear you have some experience drawing patterns. And perhaps with needle and thread?"

Her eyebrows arched. "Yes?"

"I find myself in need of a new shirt. If I supplied the material, would you sew it for me?"

The corner of her lips tipped up. "I would."

"And if I should happen to come across a bolt of fine green wool, the kind that makes warm dresses for ladies and girls in the winter—would you know what to do with that, too?"

She smoothed her hands over the thin calico dress he'd seen her wear in Marietta. The threadbare fabric was no good for winter. "I couldn't pay for it."

Moving to the hearth, Ethan positioned the fireplace pan on the floor before grasping the broom and sweeping the ashes into it. "Never mind the cost. You and June need clothing more suited to the weather. And for traveling." He knelt and stacked more logs upon the dying flames then crushed newspaper pages and stuffed them in the chinks. "And I need to get the fabric out of the attic where it's doing no earthly good."

"You already purchased it?" Her voice was laced with disbelief.

Rising, he turned to face her. "Please. Make something for yourself. Make a shirt for me, too, and I'll consider it a fair trade. Any extra white linen, you can use for yourselves."

"A new dress? For me, too?" June grinned, accentuating the point of her small chin.

Cora Mae's nose pinked as she looked at the little girl. "Well, then. I reckon I better get busy." The smile she turned on Ethan held far more than a mere thank-you. "Do you know your measurements?"

He reached into his pocket and withdrew a measuring tape. "Figured you'd do it right."

With a few steps across the small room, she took it. She circled around him and pressed one end of the tape to the back of his neck. A shiver swept over him as her fingertip slid over his spine, stopping at his waist. Next, she held the tape shoulder to shoulder across his back.

"Need to write it down?" he asked.

"I'll remember." She came back to face him. The faint scent of rosewater filled the space between them. "Hold out your arms, please."

Heat flashed over his face as he raised only his left arm and gazed through the partially boarded window. Beyond it, leaves fell in a blizzard of brown and gold.

"Mr. Howard," she murmured gently as she measured from shoulder to wrist. "Wouldn't you like both your sleeves to fit you properly? It's up to you, of course. But I think you'd be more comfortable with a perfect fit."

He looked at her then, his perfect fit, a wistful smile curving his lips. "Yes, I would." His throat tightened as he struggled to swallow his longing. Still holding her gaze, he spread both arms wide and felt the weight of the emptiness they held.

Her cheeks bloomed pink.

His eyes closed while her tender touch trailed from his shoulder to the end of his arm, where the fabric had grown thin and torn.

"Good," she breathed, and he lowered his arms. "I just need one more measurement." Pressing her lips together, she lifted the tape over his head and drew it snugly around his neck, her fingertips cool as they brushed his skin and feathered his hair just above his collar. The flush in her face matched the heat in his own. She was close enough to hear his hammering heart.

"When will my dress be done, Mama?" June asked, a welcome distraction.

Cora Mae placed the measuring tape into Ethan's palm without taking the time to roll it back up. "Patience, Junebug." Whirling around, she brought the backs of her hands to her cheeks.

As June improved in health and spirits, Cora Mae's hands stayed busy with needle and thread. Every stitch she made on Ethan's seams seemed to bind her heart closer to him, though she knew the end was coming. A knot would form, and the thread would finally be cut.

Snow fell in great white flakes, coating the trees outside the window in frosty, delicate crystals and casting a silvery glow into the room. At last, the dresses were made, the shirt was complete, and June had all but stopped coughing. When Ethan purchased three tickets for the steamboat to Louisville, Cora Mae felt the threads that bound them pull taut. After the coming journey was over, the strands that tied them would snap.

Chapter Thirteen

December 14

Rain pelted the windows like shrapnel as the train hurtled between Louisville and Nashville. Cora Mae braced her hands against the corridor in the passenger car as she slowly made her way back to her own compartment on the rocking train. If there was any other way to get home, she would have taken it. If there was any way to be near him without wanting him, she had to find it. How could she give herself to Mr. Ferguson while dreaming of Ethan Howard? No, it would never do.

Resolved to steel her heart, she opened the door to their compartment and promptly failed. In her new, green wool dress, June had curled herself between Ethan's arm and his chest, her braids all askew. The little girl looked so peaceful, Cora Mae feared she might break the spell as she latched the door closed. Noiselessly, she seated herself across from the dozing pair.

Wind roared past the train as they rushed into the night. Shadows quivered across the compartment as she picked up her sewing and began stitching again. If she could concentrate, June's new apron would be finished by the time they reached Nashville.

But the straight seams didn't require much focus, so her thoughts drifted stubbornly away. They weren't a comfort. Sighing, she dipped her needle in and out of the white cotton and then carelessly pricked her finger. She glared at the drop of blood on her fingertip then wiped it quickly on a scrap of fabric in her basket.

"The light's too dim for that kind of work, maybe," Ethan offered.

She met his gaze. "I see just fine." When she saw that June didn't wake up, she spoke again. "I see my little Junebug is quite attached to you."

He squeezed June's shoulder, smiling down at her. "She is, isn't she? Quite latched on."

"That's not what I meant. She's so fond of you."

"Good taste in men." His green eyes sparkled. "I'm fond of her, too."

Cora Mae stabbed her needle through the corner of June's apron pocket and pulled it through the other side. "I'm pondering whether she's too attached. You're not going to be around for much longer, you know. If you keep being so wonderful with her, it'll only make it harder when she says good-bye."

His eyebrows raised. "Should I pinch her?"

She swallowed the laughter that threatened. "You're impossible." Lips pressed together, she turned to the window. Once they arrived in Roswell, she would not be able to keep June and Ethan both.

"We're stopping," he murmured as the chugging slowed, rousing the little girl from her sleep. "Stay close to me once we get off. Nashville is glutted with Yankees."

"So I recall." The iron wheels screeched to a halt, and steam hissed and belched from the funnel as they climbed down the narrow steps. "Button your coat," she told June, wrapping the green-and-red-plaid shawl over the child's head before tying her own tartan flannel beneath her chin.

Ethan offered his arm. "So I don't lose you."

Cora Mae took it, holding June's hand on the other side, and followed him as he weaved through the crowded platform to the depot where they'd purchase fare for the next stretch of the journey.

"Two adults and one child for Chattanooga, please." Ethan's breath steamed against the glass above the ticket counter for the Nashville & Chattanooga Railroad line.

The man behind the counter shook his head. "No passage for civilians."

Dread drizzled over Cora Mae. She rubbed June's hands in her own to keep them warm.

Ethan glanced at them before turning back to the counter. "But I was just on this railroad a month ago coming the other way."

"A lot's changed in a month."

"Such as?" Ethan stuffed his fist into his pocket.

"Such as Sherman diving down south and General Hood making a dash at us while he's away. After Hood got walloped at the battle at Franklin—that's near twenty miles south of here—he's not giving up. The line between Nashville and Chattanooga is to be kept clear for military use only right now. Sorry."

Cora Mae studied Ethan's face as he led them away from the counter. For a moment he didn't look at her, scanning the crowd instead. Outside the depot, carriages and wagons rattled over the street, and horses stomped and nickered.

"Well, Mr. Howard?" she tried, tentatively. "What do we do now?"

When he turned to face her, his jaw was set. "We improvise."

Chapter Fourteen

South of Nashville
December 15

A knight in shining armor, Ethan had never claimed to be. But as he walked between June and Samson, a worn-out artillery horse he'd procured in Nashville yesterday, he couldn't help but feel just how far he fell from the ideal rescuer.

Looking over his shoulder at the Union embankments they'd just crossed through, he prayed they wouldn't all need rescuing before the day was through. Those soldiers had been ready for battle. Ethan wasn't. So when one of the Yankees tipped him off that Hood's army had gathered to the southeast of town, Ethan decided to travel west of it in a wide arc before cutting east to the Nashville & Chattanooga Railroad track. They might not be allowed on the train, but they could follow the rails south.

"A little looser with the reins, Miss Stewart," he called up. "Samson is mouth-sore and won't appreciate pressure on his bit. Remember, reins are for steering, not for balance. Keep your weight squarely in the saddle and stirrups."

Cora Mae nodded, her face tight and pale. The gray cloak he'd bought her draped over the Percheron's black haunches, hiding the moss-green riding skirt she wore. The double black ribbons she'd sewn to its edge resembled Confederate officer's stripes.

Walking beside Ethan, June shivered in her knee-length cloak. "Are we going to walk all the way to Roswell?"

"I might," Ethan said. "But you and Miss Stewart can share Samson just as soon as those two get to know each other better." Samson wasn't up to hauling any more cannons for the Union army, but he could carry both Cora Mae and June at once for spells.

The roads were rutted and glazed with ice, so both man and beast had to choose their path carefully. Ethan called instructions to Cora Mae, quite content for her to learn some horsemanship while he hoofed it on solid ground. Poor Samson surely wouldn't know what to do with a one-armed rider at the reins.

When thunder rolled, Ethan glanced at the heavens. There wasn't a cloud in the sky.

"June, ready to ride?" He nodded to Cora Mae, whose serious eyes reflected the urgency he felt. "Miss Stewart, want some company up there?"

"Whoa." She drew rein, and Samson stopped.

Ethan took a knee, and June used him to climb into the saddle in front of Cora Mae. "Careful not to kick your heels into his belly, now, June. He might be ticklish." The smile he pasted on his face felt counterfeit. It didn't seem to fool Cora Mae.

"That's. . .some thunder," she said coolly. "What do we do?"

"We keep going. We're headed away from it, if we can trust that Yankee's word." She raised an eyebrow, as if to say, *What if we can't?*

He swallowed the answer to her unspoken question. "We go southwest until it stops. Then we'll turn east and carry on until we reach the Nashville & Chattanooga Railroad. We're going to follow that south and retrace the journey you took north in August. When we come to the place where Sherman had the railroad torn up, we'll follow the ripped-up land that's left all the way home. Do you understand?"

A boom shook the ground beneath their feet, and another closely followed. Cora Mae's wide eyes scanned the perimeter. "Yes. I understand."

The galloping grew louder behind them. Dust rose up in great billowing clouds from the winter-silvered land. With a jolt, Ethan realized the Union cavalry was flanking Hood and headed straight toward them. *If Hood heads this way, too. . .*

His heart pounded to the rhythm of the hoofbeats in the distance. "You need to get out of here."

June twisted around to see him. "What about you?"

"Remember the plan. Ride until you can't hear it anymore; then head for the tracks."

"No!" June wailed. "Mama, we can't leave him here!"

"Hush!" Cora Mae scolded, but her face was pale as cotton, her knuckles white on the reins.

Ethan slapped Samson's flank. "Git!" The horse loped into a trot, kicking up icy mud behind him.

Pulse rushing in her ears, Cora Mae rose up in her stirrups and clucked her tongue to Samson.

"Ow!" June bounced painfully, her hands clutching the pommel. "Slow down!"

She didn't. Every step, she hoped, was a step toward safety, and while she couldn't very well gallop with June wedged into the saddle, she dared not slow their pace from a trot.

Cold penetrated her fingers that were wrapped around the reins. The shawl slipped down the back of her head, and the wind knifed through her hair.

The thunder crescendoed behind them, louder and louder. *It's only the cotton mill clanging and banging*, she thought, trying to lie to herself. But the truth was too obvious to deny. The war was right here, right now.

Movement flashed in the corner of her vision, and she turned her head, careful not to turn the horse as well. A current of bluecoats flowed over the road Samson had trod mere minutes ago, and into the field to the left. Thousands upon thousands of them poured by. The cavalry pounded the earth, their shining leather boots squeezing the sides of their sleek mounts. The sky-blue trousers of the infantry marched together, the sunlight bouncing off their rifles and the brass buttons of their dark blue coats.

June turned to see them, too. "They're like water over the Vickery Creek dam!"

They were too many to count. Too powerful to stop. Too purposeful to change their course—unless the battle turned and they were driven back.

They couldn't be here if that happened. Cora Mae urged Samson into a quicker trot, and they continued their path. Minutes later, from some place unseen, a bugle sounded bright and bold. Then the Rebel cry split the air, slicing straight to her heart. Musketry rattled, and the ground shook with cannon fire. Smoke knit together in a blanket of haze that smelled like rotten eggs, obscuring the view but not the sound.

The air cracked, over and again, with a force she'd never imagined possible. But worse than that were the cries of men hurtling themselves into the fray, and of men struck down. A gust of wind carried gun smoke to Cora Mae, and she coughed at the terrible smell of battle. She looked left and saw the cloud of smoke light up in snatches but could only guess at the carnage that lay beneath.

Minutes dragged as she prodded Samson along the road, and away, she hoped, from danger. The sun held no warmth as it peered down on the fighting below. June no longer looked anywhere but right between Samson's ears. Reaching down, she patted his neck with one hand.

Fixing her gaze once more on the shredded road ahead of her, Cora Mae steered him away from the worst ruts. Suddenly, his foot faltered in a mud puddle, and June swung to the right. She dropped the rein and lashed her arm around the girl's body, pushing her back up straight again. Samson wheeled left, off the road.

"Mama!" June yelled over the roar of battle.

Frantic, Cora Mae looked over her shoulder and saw the road shrink to a dingy ribbon behind her. Smoke rose from the ground to her left, but the air was clear to the right. If she was lucky, she'd already passed the edge of the battle, though the clamor still rang in her ears. Truly, if she waited until she could no longer hear it, she'd ride miles upon miles away from where she wanted to be.

She dug her heels into Samson's flanks, and he broke into a gallop. It was all she could do to stay upright and keep June from vaulting off Samson's back. With all her might, she squeezed her legs around the horse's middle and urged June to do the same.

Hoofbeats pounded. As she looked left, her heart leaped to her throat. A mounted soldier in a pitiful excuse for a uniform headed straight for her.

"Halt!" he cried and thrust his thin gray horse in front of Samson.

Muskets popped, cannons boomed, and the air shuddered in cold waves. Cora Mae drew rein, but Samson only turned, skirting the Confederate horseman, unaware she wanted him to slow.

The ragged rider came alongside and grabbed Samson by the bridle, forcing him to slow. "Just what in God's green earth are you doing here, miss? Don't you know you're on the edge of a battlefield?" His eyes were too large for his thin, gaunt face. "Where are you trying to get to?"

"Home!" June cried out. "We want to get home to Roswell!"

"Mill workers, eh? I heard tell about that. But you're not getting anywhere if you don't get off this field lickety-split."

The high-pitched Rebel yell pierced the air from somewhere beneath the smoke, sending a chill down Cora Mae's spine. "We're headed for the railroad to follow to Chattanooga."

"Traveling alone? All the way to Roswell?" He narrowed his eyes. "It don't seem fitting. There's rogues everywhere. Have you got a gun, at least?"

She didn't. But she suddenly felt uneasy about admitting it. "I thank you for your help." Heels to her horse, she urged Samson onward.

"I'm Jedidiah Colbert, a Confederate scout. I'll escort you a piece, just to make sure you get shed of this field." He positioned his horse between the fighting and Samson, and led the way on a horse so scrawny she could scarcely see how he bore his rider.

One mile followed another as they covered fields where the grass had turned to jelly. Icy water splashed Cora Mae's ankles as Samson plunged into and out of shallow creeks. Overhead, clouds brocaded a blue silk sky. But artillery and gun smoke blotted the sky to the north, and the smell of sulfur thickened in her nostrils and throat.

At last, Colbert turned to face her. "That's the end of the field, I reckon. Head another four or five miles straight that way, you'll run smack-dab into the tracks you want. Godspeed!"

"Thank you!" She watched him ride west again and sent a prayer heavenward for his safety.

After she'd put three more miles between them and the battlefield, she slipped down from Samson and led him while June occupied the saddle alone. For stretches of time, the child sat directly on Samson's haunches, drawing heat from the horse's body. The sounds of battle grew dimmer, but every crack and roar shook her core.

Two more miles later, they came to the tracks.

Leaning forward, June buried her hands in Samson's mane. "Mr. Howard will get here soon." She nodded confidently. "He'll get here."

Pine trees standing sentinel cast shadows as long as city streets. Wind scraped Cora Mae's cheeks raw and buffeted her ears through her shawl. Spying a stiff patch of faded grass, she led Samson to it, helped June down, and picketed the horse.

The air crackled with cold. "We'll camp here for the night." Cora Mae unstrapped the bedroll from Samson's back and brought it closer to the pines, where fallen needles softened the cold ground. After she unfurled the India rubber sheet and wool army blanket, June scrambled between them, groaning about her sore seat from the day's ride. Her teeth chattered as she curled herself into a ball.

Hands almost numb with cold, Cora Mae broke hardtack and peeled the lid from a tin of meat for their dinner. Purple velvet twilight melted into gunmetal gray, and stars poked through like saber points. As night dropped its veil, she coaxed a small fire to life. With several handfuls of pine needles and a few pinecones, the flames lapped higher into the dark.

June stared listlessly at the pluming smoke. "I wish Mr. Howard would hustle."

The fire snapped and writhed, and sparks turned to ash in the air. "Why don't I read to you? It'll pass the time."

"Yes!" Throwing her blanket back, June sprang from the ground and fetched the old bottle Ethan had tucked into the saddlebag, for it contained the only reading material they had. By the time she skipped back to the fire, she had popped off the cork and tipped it up until the scroll fell into her little hand. "Here you go!"

"Thank you." Cora Mae took the booklet and the bottle both, slipped the cork inside her pocket, and burrowed the bottle under the ashes. "We'll heat it up while I read, and then we can take turns warming our hands on it."

Firelight danced on the open pages of the Soldier's Prayer and Hymn Book as she turned to Hymn 177. The words came slowly at first, as she sounded them out, but the discovery of the meaning made up for it. "Guide me, O thou great Jehovah, pilgrim through this barren land." Recognizing the hymn from church, she recited the rest from memory. "I am weak, but thou art mighty; hold me with thy powerful hand. . . . Feed me with the heavenly manna in this barren wilderness; be my sword, and shield, and banner; be the Lord my righteousness."

June yawned beside her then tucked herself under the wool blanket. "That's a mighty good prayer for us this night, isn't it?"

"I reckon it is." Cora Mae dug the bottle from the ashes, wiped it clean with the edge of her petticoat, and handed it to June to hold.

Hoofbeats pounded the ground, riveting their attention. A deserter? A guerrilla? Ethan? Cora Mae stood and waited.

Ethan's pulse galloped faster than the Confederate horse that carried him alongside the railroad. The danger of the battle was behind him, but guerrilla raiders might yet be between him and Cora Mae. They roamed Tennessee and north Georgia, plundering homes, burning houses, and brutalizing anyone they pleased. A woman alone with a young child would be far too easy a target for such men to resist.

A small fire beckoned him, and he rose up in his stirrups as he charged toward it. Easing back into the saddle, he squeezed his legs around his mount's flanks and pulled back on the reins as evenly as he could with one in his left hand, and the other in a loop over his right elbow. "Miss Stewart? June?"

"We're here!" Cora Mae called out.

"Whoa, Johnny." Halting the gaunt Kentucky Saddler, he slipped the rein off his elbow, awkwardly dismounted, and then rushed toward the fire whose glow had been his guiding light. "Are you hurt? You're all right? Both of you?"

"We're fine." Stepping forward, Cora Mae reached out to him then just as quickly pulled back, crossing her arms instead.

"Thank God." Exhaling relief, Ethan knelt, and June clambered onto his lap. He draped his arm protectively around her waist.

"Don't you leave us again, Mr. Howard! Not ever!" At that, June took Ethan's face between her small hands.

"Why aren't your hands cold?" he asked in wonder.

Cora Mae's cloak fanned about her as she sank to the ground beside them. She pressed his bottle into his palm. "We warmed it in the ashes." Wrapping his fingers around it, warmth flowed into his skin.

With Spero in his grip, Ethan bowed his head and studied June's earnest face, from her dirt-smudged cheeks, to her deep velvet eyes, to the determined set of her little chin. She nestled against his chest again, her hair snagging on his stubbled jaw. A lump forming in his throat, he looked up and locked eyes with Cora Mae.

She wiped at the tears streaking her face. "How did you manage?"

"Stayed out of the way, mostly." And felt for all the world like a cowardly skulker as he'd watched Union troops defend Nashville without him. He pointed to his pitiful new mount. "Found Johnny Reb there caught in a bramble at the edge of the battlefield. His rider no longer had need of him." The Confederate cavalry officer had stared up at Ethan from the bloodied ground, unseeing, his mouth frozen agape in a silent scream. He shook his head to dislodge the image from his mind. "I'd have been here sooner, but it took Johnny and me a while to get used to one another." The horse was fifteen and a half hands high, and mounting him without a right hand was only the first hurdle. Handling the reins was the other.

Freezing raindrops pattered through the branches above them, spitting and sizzling into the fire. He rose, listening for thunder. "We'll not stay here this night."

After packing up the bedroll and his bottle, Cora Mae helped June into the saddle and then seated herself behind her. Ethan took Johnny's reins and a thatch of mane in his left hand, and with an ungraceful, lopsided heave, mounted the horse and took the lead.

Lightning stabbed the night. The rain drove harder, its icy chill spilling down his neck and between his shoulder blades. Beneath the flashing sky, he found what he was looking for. Wrapped in shadows, the abandoned cabin leaned drunkenly like others he'd come across on the Chickamauga campaign through Tennessee to Georgia. It offered some protection, however scant.

Ethan dismounted and picketed the horses, wishing he had a dry stable for them instead. As he slung his haversack over his shoulder and slid the saddlebags from Samson, Cora Mae pulled the bedrolls from their backs.

Once inside the cabin, he pulled a lucifer and candle from his haversack before letting his bags drop to the ground. They nested in his hand, mocking him, just as the battle had. "I cannot hold this candle and light it, too." The confession cost him.

The walls shuddered. Cora Mae's silhouette was barely visible as she reached for him. "Let me." When she swept her hand over his jacket to find his sleeve, and ran her fingers down his arm to his hand, she could not know the ache she left in her wake. Her skin was cold on his palm as she laid her hand over his.

When he felt the slight weight of the wax leave his hand, he struck the match, and watched the wick dip into its flame, chasing the shadows away. As she held the light, Ethan shoved the door back into its frame and scanned the barren space. Not a stick of furniture remained. He spread out the bedroll, and June caught the end of it to help lay it on the floor, away from the rain that sprayed through the walls.

"Can't we have a fire?" June pointed to the fireplace. Wind moaned through its chimney, stirring ashes and leaves over the dirt floor.

"Wood's too wet," Ethan explained.

June scuttled under the blanket. "It's so dark and scary."

"We'll let this burn for a while." He took the candle from Cora Mae's hand. Stooping, he burrowed the taper into the dirt floor until it stood upright and then pulled the saddlebags and his haversack with him as he lowered himself to sit. "I'm not tired, so I'm going to stay up anyway. Get some rest."

Weariness rested in blue shadows beneath Cora Mae's eyes. "Thank you."

"Miss Stewart, before you retire. . ." He motioned for her to sit next to him and then wet a handkerchief with water from his canteen.

Hesitantly, she accepted the linen and used it to wipe her face clean before giving it back to him. "We've done this before," she said, and memory washed over him, bringing him back to that red-hot day in July when he first met her.

"Ah, yes. And you told me we wouldn't be friends." He smiled. "Not that I blamed you."

Candlelight flickering over her shining face, she held his gaze. "I was wrong." A raw, wet wind swirled about them. Her arresting gaze slid to June, asleep under the blanket, then back to him. "You're more than that." The words dangled in the air.

"Excuse me?"

Rain pounded against the warped planks, sharpening the sweet smell of rotting wood. "I reckon you're missing that right hand of yours, and I'm sorry for the pain and trials losing it has caused you. But you have what's more important by far. The last time I saw Mama, she told me to love my enemies. It was a bitter pill to swallow to even say I'd try after what you Yankees did to me and my town. But you—" She pressed her lips together.

He braced himself, even as the damp cold began to numb his senses. The candle's struggling flame was no match for Cora Mae's hazel eyes.

"I know you had your orders to follow, just like every soldier on both sides. Now I don't know exactly what you were like before I met you, but it sure seems to me you've been getting better ever since. You loved your enemy when you told me how to stay in Georgia. You loved your enemy when you chased after those scoundrels invading that lady's home. You hate what that injury did to your body, and rightly so. But when I see you, I see a man who knows how to love his enemy. You're still doing it, every step of this journey back to Roswell."

The truth sat on his tongue until it burned, and he had no choice but to admit: "You were never my enemy."

She shivered, chafing her arms. "Then what am I?" she whispered. The tip of her nose was pink with cold. "Ethan?" A lock of hair blew across her face, bronzed by the candle's glow. She pinned him with her gaze. Waiting.

"The keeper of my heart," he admitted. "You stole it away from me, and I've never been able to get it back."

Her composure crumbled. A tear traced her cheek as she drew a ragged breath.

Outside the battered cabin, rain crescendoed to a low roar. "I shouldn't have said it." He swallowed, at a loss. "I'm sorry, Cora—Miss Stewart."

"Oh don't, please don't call me that. Not tonight. Not right now."

The pleading in her eyes lanced his heart. He wiped the tear from her face with the pad of his thumb then let his fingers slide into her silky hair. "If I could take your sorrow away, I would. Every trouble, every heartache. Gladly would I shoulder every burden you bear."

"I know." Her words were a whisper. She covered his cheek with her hand in a gesture so tender, he could barely hear his conscience over the pounding of his heart.

Wind churned through the cabin from between the chinks in the wall, snuffing out the candle, leaving only the scent of melted wax behind. Darkness blanketed Ethan and the woman he loved.

Stifling a groan, he denied his impulse to claim her with a kiss that would heat them both. Instead, "Come here." His left hand found her shoulder and guided her to sit in front of him on the floor. She leaned back against his chest, and he wrapped his arms around her shoulders to warm her shaking body.

In the dark, she reached up and touched his arm. "You are everything a man should be, and more."

Disoriented, Ethan could form no response.

Shifting slightly, Cora Mae rested her head on his shoulder, her forehead against his cheek. The weight of her body warmed him.

"I can't do this." Nor should he. He released her, and rain gusted into the space between them. "You aren't mine to hold."

A rustling sound told him that she was already moving away. As Cora Mae curled up next to June under the blanket, Ethan settled on the dirt floor near the door with nothing but cold to cover him.

When dawn came, Cora Mae still ached with a longing she could not—would not—name. Her heart was as divided and ravaged as the land they traveled, one portion loyal to the South and to the promise she'd made Mr. Ferguson, June, and Mama. The promise Pap himself had wanted her to keep. The other portion beat only for Ethan.

The days were bitter and short as they traveled deeper into the South. Near Chattanooga, mountains rose in bristly mounds, their trees a delicate black embroidery on the hem of a slate-blue sky. As they crossed the state line, snow powdered horses and travelers alike, but the flakes melted as soon as they landed, so that Georgia was laid bare.

It was desolate. Sherman's destruction blighted the land with a savagery that stole Cora Mae's breath. The Union armies had scorched fields of golden wheat and snow-white cotton to nothing but blackened stubble. Poor folk who gave her, Ethan, and June a place to sleep warned of nationless bushwhackers claiming to be Wheeler's Confederate cavalry. Also called guerrillas, they'd ransacked neighbors' homes—looking for deserters, they'd said. But the scoundrels ravaged women and stole their last pigs before setting their houses aflame.

Iron rails ripped from the railroad tracks lay forlornly on the ground, twisted into spirals or looped and crossed like neckties. The scars left in the landscape made the trail they followed to Roswell—where their journey began, and would end.

All sense told Cora Mae she should not love a man who'd helped ruin the South, even if she hadn't promised to marry Mr. Ferguson. But even as she rode in the wake of destruction, the thought of bidding him good-bye carved a hollow inside her that threatened to swallow her whole.

Chapter Fifteen

Roswell, Georgia
December 27

Cora Mae should have been prepared for the shell that Roswell had become and for the memories that rose up to haunt her. Samson and Johnny Reb plodded quietly through the town square that was now only dirt, and beyond it to the mill village.

Ethan looked over his shoulder. "Let's get there," he murmured.

Clucking her tongue, she urged Samson into a trot that took her to Factory Hill. Weeds spread and mounded erratically, reclaiming the yards, choking the paths to the apartments. She dismounted the horse, reached down, and furiously yanked a clump of weeds from the path that led to Mama's door.

"You gonna go in?" June came and held her hand.

"I'm going." Casting the weeds aside, Cora Mae brushed off her hands and glanced at Ethan, who offered her a half smile.

Then she heard it. Coughing.

Bounding up the porch stairs with June in tow, she rushed into her old home, fisted her cloak and skirts, and took the stairs two at a time to reach the top.

"Mama, I'm here! We're home!" She burst into the bedroom, tearing the shawl from about her head.

"Darlin'?" Mama gasped from her rocking chair and spread wide her arms.

Cora Mae fell into them, weeping. "Oh, how I missed you!" Only then did she notice the walls and floor had all been whitewashed, and remember it had been a Yankee hospital. The only color in the room was the patchwork quilt on the bed and the braided rag rug at her feet.

Footsteps sounded heavily on the stairs before stomping into the room behind her. "What the devil?"

Rising, Cora Mae wheeled around. Each heartbeat was a blow against her breastbone.

Dust danced in the sunbeams streaming between the window's homespun curtains. Striped with light, Mr. Ferguson gaped, and the mismatched teacup and saucer in his hands listed to one side.

Quickly, she rushed to take it from him and set it on the table beside the rocker.

"You've come home to us." He kissed June on her head and engulfed Cora Mae in a father's embrace for a prodigal child. He was thinner than she remembered. So was Mama.

"You've been looking after Mama?" She wiped her palms on her cloak then kneaded them together.

"As much as she'd let me." The smile he gave Matilda was tender. His scant black hair had grayed noticeably since July, and the lines about his mouth carved deeper. "There's no work for me in Roswell, so I found a job in my widowed sister's town, a day's journey from here. But I come here regular to see she has enough food. It's been a stretch, I'll tell you, especially on account of the rogues who came by and cleaned out our stores. Been working on Matilda to come live with me and Opal, but she insisted on staying to wait for you."

"Have any others returned?" Cora Mae asked. Roswell mill girls marched through her mind.

"Not one." Mama squeezed her hand. "How did you manage it?" She beckoned June, who ran to hug her.

"Our Yankee, Mr. Howard, brought us back," June quipped. "Same one as took us away."

Mr. Ferguson frowned, deepening the seams from his mouth to his chin. "A bluebelly?"

Mama waved the term away. "I'd like to meet him."

June skipped toward the door. "He's not a bluebelly anymore, he's just Mr. Howard. I'll fetch him here and stay with the horses myself. Mr. Howard's worried about horse thieves," she added.

Moments later, Ethan entered the room alone and doffed his cap, tapping it against his thigh. Mr. Ferguson crossed his arms, eyeing him.

"Mama, this is Ethan Howard, the man who brought me home." Finality weighted the statement. He had done what he set out to do. It was over. "Mr. Howard, this is my mother, Matilda Stewart, and this here is—this is Mr. Horace Ferguson. He's been looking after her." Tears bit Cora Mae's eyes.

"It's my very great pleasure to meet you." He bowed slightly to each of them, his face a mask of good manners.

"Come here, son."

Striding toward Mama, he tucked his hat under his arm and filled her outstretched right hand with his left.

"God bless you, young man." Tears traced her cheeks. "Thank you for my daughter, and for June. Thank you."

"It was my pleasure." Ethan cleared his throat then opened his mouth as if to say more before pressing his lips flat. Blinking in the slanting rays, he simply bowed again and replaced his hat on head. "I'll take my leave. Miss Stewart, one last word, if you please."

She met him in the hall, where the sunlight couldn't reach. "Mr. Howard, I—" Speech abandoned her.

"I have something for you." His voice was gravelly. From inside his jacket, he drew his old, beat-up bottle, the housing for his prayer book. He tapped the scroll-work on its neck. "Did I ever tell you this word is Latin for 'hope'?"

She shook her head. A floorboard creaked beneath her boots.

"I want you to have it."

"Hope?" She peered at him, memorizing the sweep of his hair across his brow, the green of his eyes, the faint lines that fanned from them when he smiled. Her vision blurred.

"Yes. Hope. The bottle. All of it." He held it out to her, and she grasped the cold metal. "If you should feel hopeless, look inside." At that, he tipped his hat to her and whispered, "It's time for me to go."

Words froze in her chest as she watched him descend the stairs.

The screen door banged behind Ethan. "Well, June. . ." Hoofbeats cut him off. Standing on the front porch, he shielded his eyes against the sun's stark glare and watched a cloud of dust rise from the road. Dread snaked through his middle. Three houses they'd passed in north Georgia were smoldering heaps. It wasn't Yankees who'd torched them.

June hurried to him. "Comin' fast," she whispered. "Who do you think it is?"

"Get inside," he told her, and she immediately obeyed.

The horse pounded over the hill, barreled up the street, and halted right in front of the Stewarts' apartment. Long black hair streamed from beneath the rider's hat and over the shoulders of his oiled deerskin cloak. When he dismounted, the sun glinted on the pistol at his hip and on the musket in his hands.

"Can I help you, Mr. . . ?"

"Walker." The man spit syrupy brown juice on the bottom porch step then grinned, a tobacco plug bulging inside his cheek. "And I aim to help myself." In one leap, he topped the stairs.

Ethan splayed his hand against Walker's chest. "No, you won't." The man was a guerilla, a vulture come to pick Roswell clean. "There's nothing for you inside."

Before Walker could shoulder the musket, Ethan shoved him off balance, and he crashed down the steps. Pushing himself up from the weed-snarled ground, Walker aimed his rifle at Ethan. "If you was a deserter, I'd have every right to kill you where you stand."

"I'm not." Ethan met him on the ground, planting himself between Walker and the apartment.

"Sound like a Yankee." The gleam in his brown eye was the devil's own as he lit upon Ethan's shortened right sleeve. "Even better."

"I'm a civilian. You have no business here." His pulse quickened. In his mind, he rehearsed lunging, dodging, disarming Walker. Saw himself fumbling the musket with just one hand and a nub of a forearm. Could he shoulder it? Could he aim and fire it, if he had to? Sweat beaded and chilled his skin.

The door burst open behind Ethan, and two sets of footsteps sounded on the porch.

"We haven't got much. Take it and leave." Mr. Ferguson and Cora Mae descended the steps and passed Ethan as they approached the bandit. Each of them held a full sack of food.

They'd go hungry without provisions. "Don't give him a kernel," Ethan advised. "He's a thief." Alarm licked through his veins. He could barely defend himself, let alone two more souls.

"And you ain't?" Walker sneered. "What do you call what Sherman's army's been up to all the way through Georgia? I'm through with Yankees." He cocked the hammer.

"No! Don't shoot!" Cora Mae jumped in front of Ethan.

A shot blasted the air, and then another, and one more.

Cora Mae fell back at an angle, corn spilling from a hole in the burlap sack she held. Instinctively, Ethan lunged to catch her with his right arm, in vain. With a sickening crack, her skull hit the corner of the porch step. Horror seized him as he knelt and scooped her head into his lap. *Not this, not now. Not after everything we've been through.* Anguish swelled in his throat.

Vaguely, he was aware of Walker dropping his gun and collapsing, of blood pouring from two holes in his chest. Mr. Ferguson bent over his betrothed, face ashen, with a smoking pistol in his shaking right hand and the sack of peanuts he'd hid it behind still in his left.

"Cora Mae," Ethan called, her name bittersweet on his lips.

Her eyelids fluttered, and her hands released their grip. The corn slid off her waist, golden pebbles pooling in the gray folds of her cloak. A frayed hole next to the buttons sent a shock coursing through Ethan.

"Give her to me." Mr. Ferguson's voice quaked. "You've done your part. I'll take it from here."

Chapter Sixteen

A throbbing headache pulled Cora Mae awake. She opened her eyes and scanned the bare white room. "Where's Ethan?"

Sitting in the chair by the bed, Mama smoothed the hair back from her cheek just as Mr. Ferguson and June came rushing in. "You're awake!" June clasped her hand.

"She's delirious." Mr. Ferguson peered into her eyes. "You took a nasty spill."

Holding her breath, she reached under the quilt to sweep her hand over her middle, and found it miraculously whole. "Wasn't I shot?" She pushed herself up to sit on the thin bed tick.

"Yes, darlin'." Mama handed her Ethan's bottle.

She took it, the cold metal drawing the heat from her skin. A few inches below the neck, the thick, aged bronze was deeply dented in the shape of a bullet. With a prayer of thanks and wonder for the treasure she'd tucked into her cloak, her fingertip dipped into the space.

"I shot that rat first, and it turned his aim so it wasn't dead on," Mr. Ferguson explained. "He fired at an angle, and the corn slowed the bullet some before it came to rest in that tin. Then I finished him, but you fell and hit your head. Oh, what a scare you gave us."

"You been sleeping for hours," June said. "You been calling out for Ethan."

"Delirious," Mr. Ferguson said again, his leathery palm coming to rest on her brow. "She ain't well just yet."

"I'm not delirious. Where is he?" With one hand resting on the bottle in her lap, the other nervously picked at the yellow stitching on Mama's quilt.

"Mr. Howard's fine, likely thanks to you. I told him to go. Weren't no cause for the Yankee to stay, now that you're with kin."

As though in a fog, Cora Mae's gaze drifted from Mr. Ferguson's face to June's and Mama's. Wincing, she touched the ache at the base of her skull, but the searing pain in her chest could not be reached.

"Now that you're home, we'll all go and live with my sister Opal. We best get moving, lest Walker's friends come looking for him. Between his horse, mine, and Samson, we'll have a mount for each adult, and June can ride with you."

His words blurred into nonsense. All she could think of was Ethan. *If you're hopeless, look inside,* he'd told her. Uncorking the bottle, she tipped it, and the prayer book slid out. Around the scroll this time, was wrapped another piece of paper. A note. Throat tight, Cora Mae slowly read:

> *Dear Miss Stewart,*
>
>   *I pray that your new life with Mr. Ferguson and June brings you great joy and peace and that you will both be loved the way you deserve. I'm going west to cultivate the land instead of ravage it, but first I'll rest Johnny Reb in Marietta a few days. You'll forgive me for thinking of you when I enter that town, for I have thought of little else since we rode into it together. But know that with each thought, I'll say a prayer for your family.*
>
>   *Good-bye,*
>   *Your Yankee*

She read it once more. Longing wrenched her. Decision resounded within her.

"Mr. Ferguson. Mama." She looked from one to the other, desperate that both should understand. "I've got somewhere else to be. With your blessing," she added for Mama, whose gaze dropped to Ethan's note. But her mind was made up.

Mr. Ferguson frowned. "She ain't well, Millie."

But Mama smiled, her blue eyes twinkling with recognition. "Oh, yes she is. But she'll be powerful better just as soon as she reunites with the man she loves."

"What in tarnation are you talkin' about?"

Cora Mae grasped her mother's hand and turned her gaze on Mr. Ferguson. "You always been good to us. Pap couldn't have asked for a better friend. But Mama's right. I belong with Ethan Howard."

Suddenly, his face darkened. "Did that bluebelly violate you? You in the family way, Cora Mae?"

"No, no. We never—no," she said. "I love him with all my heart. I been bottling it up, trying to do what's honorable by my family. But he's my family, or could be. So is June."

"I want to come!" June cried. "Mama, take me with you!"

Tears lined her lashes as Cora Mae absorbed Mr. Ferguson's bewildered stare. "I love her as my own. Since neither of us are her blood relatives, don't you think we ought to let June choose?"

Confusion carved his brow. "That's a mighty big choice for a child to make."

"Horace." Matilda turned a warm smile on him. "The child has been in Cora Mae's care almost as long as she'd been in yours. Let her go with the young folks."

"Please." June rested her hand on Cora Mae's shoulder as she turned toward Horace. "I want to go with Mama."

A sigh heaved from Mr. Ferguson, and his shoulders slumped as he rubbed his chin. "I'm supposed to provide for you all. I promised Mavis. And I promised Asa." He looked soulfully at Cora Mae.

Mama laid her hand on his arm. "You have, and you'll keep on providing for me. But the Lord has provided for Cora Mae."

Doubt dimmed his eyes. "It don't suit. Asa wouldn't have stood for her taking up with a Yankee, and I'll be buggered if I need to spell out why." He rubbed a blue-veined hand over his sagging jaw. "Ah, Asa." Such weight in those two small words.

Still in her green wool dress, Cora Mae pushed back the quilt and stood beside the bed. "He would have wanted me to be well cared for, and well loved."

"We love you, don't we? Ain't I got a plan to care for you, too?" Dismay cracked his voice.

Compassion surged for this weary man, loyal to Pap to the end. "Mr. Ferguson, I've got to go." She laid her decision gently upon him. "And if June wants to join me, you ought not stop her."

Mama rounded the bed and enfolded Cora Mae in her soft arms. "Go on, dar-lin'," she whispered in her ear. "If there's a way, take it. I'll be fine, knowing you are. You give my new son my love, you hear?"

Squeezing her eyes shut, Cora Mae dampened her mother's shoulder with her tears. As she hugged the woman who'd raised her, she embraced, too, the memory of Pap and Wade, things familiar, and the life that had disappeared when the mills burned to the ground.

And then, she let her go.

Chapter Seventeen

Marietta
December 30

amson was lathered with sweat by the time Cora Mae and June galloped into Marietta's town square. Horace Ferguson rode beside her on his thin chestnut bay, insisting on escorting them before spurring his steed back to Roswell to spirit Mama away to Opal's home. This ride in the opposite direction would have been too much for the woman when another journey awaited. They'd seen her safely into the preacher's care until Mr. Ferguson's return, unwilling for her to be alone.

The reins firm in her hands, Cora Mae trotted Samson around the square's perimeter, barely recognizing the place. The Cobb County Courthouse was mere rubble, along with most of the other buildings skirting the square. Where a thousand white tents had stood was now an expanse of fire-charred ground.

"Are we too late?" June cried. "Did he go west without us?"

"I don't know. We'll keep looking." Her palms grew damp on the reins. *Please, God.*

"Mr. Howard!" June began shouting. "Mr. Howard!"

Eyes shadowed by the brim of his hat, Mr. Ferguson shook his head but clucked to his mount to keep apace with Samson.

Wind nipped Cora Mae's nose and cheeks. Her throat squeezed as she shielded her eyes from the harsh winter sun and scanned the square. No one else was there.

Crossing into the rail yard, they passed the once-grand Fletcher House, now soot stained and missing its fourth floor. No trains in sight, and tracks torn asunder, the yard was eerily silent. Wisps of cloud rolled by like ghosts of engine steam from days gone by. Weariness and memory pressing down on her, she dismounted and helped June down as well, while Mr. Ferguson stayed quietly in his saddle.

June leaned on her, looking into the distance. In the next moment, she took off running down the platform at full tilt, her shawl slipping from her hair to her back.

"June!" Cora Mae's breath stalled in her lungs.

At the end of the platform, Ethan knelt, and the girl threw herself against him, clinging with all her might.

"Well, I'll be." Mr. Ferguson's voice drifted from behind. "Go on, then."

Heart thudding as loudly as her footsteps, Cora Mae approached, and Ethan stood.

"Thank God," he breathed. "I stayed until after Mr. Ferguson had brought you inside. He told me the bullet didn't penetrate, but—"

Smiling, she pulled the bottle from the folds of her cloak and pointed to the dent. "It didn't." A moment passed before she tucked it inside her cloak once more and stepped closer to him, pulse racing. "I ended the engagement with Mr. Ferguson. It was never love for him that kept me from you. It was commitment to honor and honesty, the same commitment I know you hold dear. I've loved you, Ethan, more than I could bring myself to admit—until now. If you'll still have me."

His eyes misting, a slow smile curved on his face. He pulled her to himself, cradling her head as she melted into him, and swayed his warm lips against hers in an answer more eloquent than any words could be.

Remembering June, she pulled back and laughed at her wrinkled nose.

Still on his horse, Mr. Ferguson ambled over to them, and Ethan reached up to shake his hand. "Good to see you, sir."

Mr. Ferguson tipped his hat and grunted. "Cora Mae here says she loves you, and you love her and can take care of her and June both. That so?"

Ethan took off his hat. "Yes, sir."

"You gonna ask her to marry you?"

Memories of Ethan's first proposal—near this very spot—rushed at her.

His eyebrows arched over sparkling green eyes. "All due respect, sir. I'll take it from here." Bending on one knee, he brought her hand to his lips. "Cora Mae Stewart, I love you. I love your integrity, your faith, your strength. Will you do me the honor of becoming my wife? Would you build a life with me where the air is sweet and the land is unmarred by war? I'm not saying it will be easy, but if we're together, well—" He swallowed. "I'll do right by you, Cora Mae. You are my perfect fit."

Joy shuddered deliciously through her. "Yes," she whispered. "Yes."

June shouted with glee, and Ethan stood, wrapping them both into an embrace. "And you, Junebug, would you do me the honor of being my daughter?"

"Yes, Daddy." Her chestnut hair shimmered in the sunlight as she beamed up at him.

With her beloved's arm still about her shoulders, Cora Mae gazed up at Mr. Ferguson. "You're the best friend Pap ever had. Thank you for caring for Mama." Gratitude thickened her voice.

Tears glossed his red-rimmed eyes as he bobbed his head. "Be well, all of you." He turned his horse around and softly plodded away.

As the hoofbeats faded, Ethan laid his hand on June's head and kissed Cora Mae once more, and her heart overflowed with hope.

Jocelyn Green inspires faith and courage as the author of more than a dozen books to date, including *The Mark of the King;* the award-winning Heroines behind the War Civil War series, which includes *Wedded to War*, a Christy Award finalist in 2013; *Widow of Gettysburg; Yankee in Atlanta*; and *Spy of Richmond.* She also co-authored *The 5 Love Languages Military Edition* with bestselling author Dr. Gary Chapman. A former military wife herself, her passion for military families informs all of her writing as well as her numerous speaking opportunities. Jocelyn graduated from Taylor University with a BA in English and now lives with her husband and two children in Iowa. Visit her at www.jocelyngreen.com.

The Swelling Sea

by Joanne Bischof

Chapter One

C old water slid across his body, the dip and rise of the swell bringing challenge to his course. Jonas plunged his arms in forward strokes, heard his breath quicken over the rustle of water—felt his pulse pounding in his chest, burning in his legs and back. Most often this single sacred hour at dawn found him outdoors, though normally, instead of swimming in California coastal waters, he would have been rowing near the grounds of Stanford University.

But thanks to three of his friends, he'd traded in a single-man rowboat for ten days that held something much grander. A quest. A bond of brotherhood. A feat they were soon to face in a four-man scull designed for two-thousand-meter races. And so they'd come south to this grand resort, their sights on both their past and their future, which meant yet another attempt across the bay that would be anything but easy.

Jonas didn't want to push his crew too hard, too quickly, so with them sleeping in after mumbling something about *enjoying* the first day of their holiday on Coronado Island, he had opted for a different kind of release.

The water grew warmer. The shore close, he dipped down and let the tide swallow him up as he swam into the shallows. He rose with a gasp, lungs on fire. Salt water dripped down his face. The familiar tang of it on his lips. His feet struck loamy sand, and with waves crashing behind, he took the dogged, leg-weary walk to dry beach. Up ahead loomed the massive Hotel del Coronado, glinting in the sunrise with its white corridors and gables, all topped with sprawling, brick-red rooftops. As if it all belonged in a fairy tale and not on the coast of California.

Fondly known as just the del, the seaside resort had opened the summer of 1888, but Jonas could remember a time, three years prior to that grand event, when this resort island had been covered with little more than shrub brush and quail. And among that, four defeated lads about to give up on a dream.

He glanced back across the bay—those memories of old colliding into him.

Sinking to the ground, Jonas pulled a hotel towel into his lap and ran it over his face. The shorts of his black bathing suit clung to his thighs, and the tank covering his torso stuck to his chest like a chilled, second skin. He drew in careful, steady breaths. With asthma a black spot on his athletic career, he knew how far to push himself, but lately he'd taken to challenging himself harder than ever to see if he couldn't increase his stamina. Jonas watched the water for a few minutes as his heart rate slowed. When he was more than ready to warm up with a hot bath and a change of clothes, he rose in the light of the brightening dawn.

Something glinting a few meters down the shoreline caught his attention. Scrubbing the towel against his hair, Jonas tossed it aside and started that way. A crash, and foam rushed over his feet. Realizing that the glinting was a metal bottle sticking up from the sand, he broke into a light jog as it disappeared from sight. The wave twirled back where it came from, and the bottle caught the glare again, this time buried a little deeper. Jonas reached it and gave a tug, but it was wedged in firm. Before another wave could come, he knelt and began to dig.

Tiny sand crabs scurried out of the way, burrowing from sight, only to be unearthed again by his efforts. A small wave came, bubbling and swirling against his legs. Fingers numb, Jonas gripped the bottle neck and tugged, finally winning. He rose just as a wave slammed into him. The bottle looked old. Was dented in several spots and scuffed in others. Maybe not worth much, but he was curious all the same, especially when he noticed a flash of filigree etched along the top. Jonas squinted and ran his thumb over the wet metal. Filigree and. . .Latin? The latter he'd studied plenty of at Stanford, but he would have to clean the bottle up before he could begin to decipher each letter.

Jonas turned and trudged along drier sand toward his things. Salt water dripped from his hair, and he ran his face against his upper arm.

"Oh, no you don't!" A young woman's voice made him turn.

Clad in a cloak, the hidden little figure yanked at the bottle, claiming it from his slick, sandy hands. Jonas froze. Her black hood fell away and a mass of white-blond hair tumbled free, barely bound in a braid as thick as any sailor's knot and just as sturdy, he discovered, when she spun away and it whipped him in the face.

He winced. "I beg your pardon!"

She strutted off.

"Excuse me, miss. That's mine." He jogged to match her pace.

"Is not." Wide-set eyes, as pale blue as the rising dawn, flashed in his direction—vulnerability and anger clashing in every blink.

"Excuse me?"

"Request granted." She brushed past him.

He jogged forward then walked backward to face her. "Is something the matter with you?"

The young woman slammed to a halt and, gripping the bottle by the neck, hitched the butt of it closer to his face. "You poachers come all the time to glean treasures from these shores, and I'm done with being trounced by fellows who have no real appreciation for the sacredness you discover."

Eyes widening, he raised his hands peaceably. Was she insane? He looked at the bottle, which she yanked down into the folds of her skirt.

"Let's begin again." He forced an even tone. "You see, I was standing there. Right there on the beach." He pointed the way they'd come. "I happened to look down, saw the bottle half-buried, and used these very hands to free it." He raised ten sandy fingers.

She shook her head. "No. *I've* been coming here every morning *waiting* for this bottle."

"Waiting for a bottle to be washed ashore?"

She rolled her eyes. "This is mine."

"Actually it's mine because I found it." He went to pluck it from her, but she stepped back.

"No. You just scavenged where you didn't belong."

"Which qualifies as finding first." Were they really having this conversation? There was no way this young woman could be serious. But as ridiculous as this was, two years of studying law made it impossible to stand down. "Let's take a moment to go over what's occurred: one minute ago I felt rather victorious in my discovery—the evidence in question being of course the bottle—and I took no care to check behind me in preparation for you to swoop in and snatch it." Maybe not the greatest plead, but it was what popped out.

The wide-eyed look she was giving him triggered something in his mind.

Jonas tipped his head. She seemed familiar somehow. "Don't you work at the hotel?" He tried to picture her in a maid's uniform, but truly, he hadn't been at the hotel long enough to have a good impression of any of the resort's staff. Still, he remembered seeing hair that color in the hallway last night. This very face. He was sure of it now.

"What of it?"

Aside from the fact that he could now have her fired?

She eyed his sopping wet and rumpled appearance; then her gaze slid over to his things, the plush hotel towel lying there. She was a fair thing, but he was certain she just grew a shade paler as her gaze slowly lifted back to him.

"McIntosh," she whispered, "3323."

His eyebrows lifted. "That's the one."

"You're here with those other young men. The ones with the boat."

"Yes, and—"

"You're all on Mr. Babcock's tab."

One of the hotel founders who had taken an interest in their insane endeavor? "Right again." And now for the apology she owed him.

But she just set her mouth and, though she was surely near to his own age, looked at him with blue eyes that held the solemnity of an old soul. "I apologize for my rudeness," she said softly. "And for calling you a poacher." But she tucked the bottle farther against her skirt.

He eyed the scuffed relic, then her face. Noted the gentle pinch to her brows that confessed what they both knew to be true: she had much more to lose from this encounter than he. She took a small step back, gripping tight to their discovery. A fierce hope that made him more than willing to let her have it.

He was quite finished here anyway. "Enjoy your treasure, miss." He touched the brim of an invisible hat and started toward his things.

Reaching the towel, Jonas snatched it up and draped it over a shoulder. Next he grabbed his book and watch with its chain. Without looking back, he headed for the oceanfront access of the hotel. He looked back just once. Just once over his shoulder in time to see the young woman doing the same as she neared the servants' entrance. The distance proved too far to read her expression as the sun pierced over the red peaked roof and she disappeared from sight.

Chapter Two

Jonas crossed through the carpeted lobby just as a porter was greeting departing guests. "Let me see these to the carriage for you," the uniformed man said. "I hope you enjoyed your stay at the del."

Striding around them, Jonas headed up the stairs to the third floor and, after rounding the corner of the hallway, let himself into room 3323. He paced to the far windows and flung back the curtains, sending a trio of groans around the room. "Wake up, little children."

His cousin Oliver, with his pumpkin-orange hair, rolled over and peered through one eye. "What's wrong with you?" He flopped a freckled hand around on his nightstand, groping for his pocket watch. "It's not even. . ." He squinted at the round plate. "Seven o'clock."

"Right. All the more reason you should be awake by now. We wasted an entire morning of practice. The water will be swarming with people within the hour." Pinching that freckled cheek, Jonas rattled it.

"It's called a vacation, Jonas." Thomas Oakes—just Oakes to the four of them— sat up and rubbed his eyes. "Most people vacate."

"You don't even know what that means."

Oakes scowled all the way to a sitting position. "Oh I'm sorry, *magna cum laude*. I forgot you know everything."

Jonas shot him a look, and Oakes fired one right back. An hourly occurrence between the pair of them, and a type of normal that still had them the best of friends.

Jonas peeled off his damp tank while the others shoved blankets aside and sat up. Most of the rooms weren't designed to accommodate four bachelors, but wanting to squeak value out of the pricey resort and the generosity of the hotel owner, they'd committed to sharing a room. As that girl on the beach had put it—they *were* on Mr. Babcock's tab. But not wanting to take advantage, they'd all agreed to a rotation with two sleeping abed, the other two dozing on rickety cots. Jonas had gotten a bed last night; Oliver, too. Which was probably why Oakes and Dexter—the long, lean stroke man—were both eying him as if they had a crick in the neck.

Nothing good could come of a grumpy middle oarsman, so Jonas ran his hands down his face and sat on the edge of the unmade bed. He didn't mean to be short with them, but that girl from the beach had been his undoing this morning. Already exhausted from his swim, the last thing he'd needed was a confrontation that had propelled a nice little blow to his ego. Probably best that none of his friends had witnessed that. Maybe there was something to be said for them sleeping in.

Oliver stepped behind the dressing screen and, by the sound of his stomping about, was swapping nightshirt for pants.

Dexter, as red in hair but not nearly as modest, stripped down to his shorts in the center of the room, grumbling about a hot cup of coffee. Oakes, too, but instead of grumbling for coffee, he reminded Jonas that the bay wasn't all that big. That they were all older now. "Nothing to it."

Jonas wasn't so certain. He rose and moved to the table near the window where rested a map of the island. He studied the pencil line they'd drawn when they'd all been around fourteen years old. The rough line that led from the beach just in front of the resort, out into the bay, and around the rocky lighthouse point, then around to the other side. "It's more than being older. I'm not sure that we're prepared for this—"

"We're *prepared*." Dexter flexed a sinewy bicep and kissed the muscle.

Oakes smirked. "That wasn't very comforting."

And Jonas didn't want to let on how much the swim alone had taken out of him. Was he truly up to this? He'd spent his entire life on the water, feeling the burn of oars against the tide as it grew him into a man, but when it came down to the bottom line—his lungs, well. . .

There was a reason he'd chosen a university that had yet to develop a rowing team.

He looked at the three young men before him. Each of whom had signed up for this crazy adventure, once again. They exchanged glances, and Jonas wondered if anyone else was thinking of that summer day in '85 when they'd rowed out beyond their boyhood playground of sagebrush and jackrabbits. Far away from the safety of this beach.

They'd set off in an old skiff, intent on being the first boys to row from one end of Coronado harbor to the other. Or so they'd imagined. They walked away from that day with a near drowning and four battered spirits. The boat, smashed to pieces. But that day they'd made a pact to try again when wounds were healed and backs were stronger.

Now five years later, they'd pooled their resources for ten days at the hotel with sights set a little higher than rowing across the bay. A five-mile route around the lighthouse. A journey past waves and rocks that, as far as they knew, had never been attempted by a four-man scull designed for sprinting.

Jonas looked at his friends, who all wore pinched brows and sober expressions.

Rushing to mind was the memory of their skiff unable to make it past the break.

Only to crack apart among the rough waves. They struggled to swim amid it all. And all bore the scars from that day. Oliver on his left leg, and Oakes, a thin white strip along the side of his jaw, which the ladies always fussed and swooned over. Dexter had a dozen healed cuts across the bases of his palms. And Jonas's right shoulder and forearms still tingled with the scars he bore. From the minutes they'd been tossed in the rush of the bay, being pummeled by waves and the broken fragments of their own boat. Though healed and faded, he'd carry the scars of that day with him forever. Just as they all would.

Realizing he should get dressed himself, Jonas threw on dry clothes while his roommates set about shaving. He needed to look halfway decent to dine at the hotel, so Jonas buttoned up a vest over his pressed shirt then finished with a few tugs of his collar. Some pomade overrode the briny feel of his hair. As his stomach grumbled for breakfast, he followed his comrades out into the sunroom that would lead them to the courtyard stairwell.

The long, window-lined corridor was quiet until Oliver elbowed Dexter. "Did anyone order more towels?"

"I did it because none of you cream puffs can seem to do anything." Oakes's quip was met by a couple of shoves. Chuckling, he pulled out a comb and fixed his hair. "They said they'd send some up." He started down the stairs, and the rest of them followed.

Famished, Jonas trailed his friends beneath a bright sun. Two maids were starting up the stark white staircase, clutching stacks of clean linens—towels, sheets. Jonas and his friends formed a single file, and not a one of them kept their eyes down as the two ladies passed. Jonas slowed when he spotted the second maid. In a black dress with a white apron and cap over her pale blond hair, it was the girl from the beach. Her gaze rested on the steps ahead, but when she glanced to Jonas, her feet slowed.

She was so easy on the eyes that he nearly smiled, but remembering what a pest she was, he checked it. They passed one another without a word. At the bottom of the steps, Jonas glanced over his shoulder, but his friends nudged him onto the courtyard path and toward the nearest café. Once there, they settled at a table by the windows that overlooked the seaside.

Surrounded by diners feasting on puddings and sausages, the four of them ordered humble fare of orange juice and hash, the latter not even being on the menu. While they ate, Jonas tried not to think of the girl or the way she'd boldly stood in front of him, lit by the cool gray of dawn, but his gaze kept wandering that way.

By the time they finished eating, Dexter suggested a warm-up row on Glorietta Bay, one of the calmer, smaller bodies of water nestled against Coronado Island.

Jonas seconded that notion. A glance through the polished glass showed that the main beach was filling with vacationers and their striped umbrellas. The water beyond, dotted with bathers in swim costumes that offered both modesty and an opportunity to enjoy the waters and seaside air that were rumored to offer comfort for anything from rheumatism, to tuberculosis, to his very own asthma.

With it his turn to pay, Jonas downed the last of his juice, dropped enough cash for their meal and a tip, and then led the way from the café. Starting back up the stairs, he slowed when Dexter slapped a hand over his chest and squeezed past.

"How did the windpipes treat you this morning?"

"So-so," Jonas answered.

"Then we've got our work cut out for us."

Jonas chuckled, and by the time they were back in their room, he was genuinely surprised to spot a stack of fresh towels on one of the newly made beds. The maid. The towels. . .

The little bottle thief. Why hadn't he realized sooner?

Maybe he should check his drawers. Just to be sure she didn't steal anything else of his.

"What's that?" Oliver asked.

"What's what?" Jonas turned in the direction his cousin was looking.

"That."

His eyes found the bottle on the table beneath the window. Jonas stepped closer. With the young maid's face flashing across his mind, he picked the metal vessel up and turned it over. It was clean and dry. While certainly weathered and corroded, she'd taken some care with the metal that he now realized was bronze. He touched the cork top. It was wedged snug in a way that said she hadn't opened it. The cork, though sealing things well, seemed out of place. Not fitting the age of the rest of the antique, as if someone had forced it into the opening out of necessity. He tipped the bottle toward the light to check the inscription again. *S–P–E*. . .what looked like an *R* trailed by an *O*, or maybe it was a *Q*. Jonas squinted and turned it ever so slightly. No he'd had it right the first time. *Spero.*

Hope.

He knew the word from a banner hanging in a corridor of the Stanford library. It was one he couldn't forget. His very life summed up in three words: *Dum Spiro Spero.* "While I breathe, I hope."

Resting where the bottle had sat was a small square of card stock that bore the hotel's logo. Jonas picked it up and read the two words that couldn't have been anyone else's but hers: *I'm sorry.*

Chapter Three

Rosie ran the feather duster along the length of the windowsill in room 3345. She looked out the glass panes to the beach below. There, the family from this suite was settling in for a day of sea breezes in several lounge chairs. The father struggled with angling a hotel-issued umbrella just right, while the wife held up the hem of her dark skirt and chased their toddler girl along the edge of the water.

Smiling, Rosie watched the scene. She glanced back to the father's antics, the way his older children were gathered around to help him. For a single, pinging moment, she envied what it would be like to know one's father and mother.

To remember one's early childhood.

Focusing back to her work, Rosie wiped toddler-sized fingerprints from all the windows, emptied the waste bin, and then left to begin the next room. The clock in the lobby chimed one, which meant the next room would have to wait. She pushed the housekeeping cart into the storage closet then started down the corridor for her meeting on the first floor. Mrs. Kline, the head housekeeper, gave her the half hour off twice a week—doctor's orders.

Their meetings used to be monthly, but with Rosie's increasing headaches and the doctor's increased research, he'd upped the frequency, hopeful they were near a breakthrough.

Just outside of a ladies' powder room, Rosie stepped aside for a trail of hotel patrons then let herself into a small storage room where she always met with Dr. Brooke. The silver-haired gentleman looked up from his notebook and smiled. Pen in hand, he stood next to an abandoned pool table where she always sat during the exams. Well respected throughout San Diego, Dr. Brooke had been her friend since she was ten years old. Since the night Rosie had been found in the water in front of where this very hotel now stood and was then taken to the hospital inland. Now, eight years later, they were perhaps a few steps closer to understanding what her time in the water and the loss of oxygen to her brain had rendered irreversible. Rosie glimpsed the top page of notes in the doctor's book. The one that listed her original symptoms:

Loss of memory

Lack of proper function in right hand and right leg
Fear of the sea
Headaches

Headaches she could endure. She'd even come to grips with being afraid of the bay, but to not remember precious years spent with her adoptive grandparents—Abner and Esther Graham—it was all she could do to not give into tears afresh.

Now in this room, with afternoon light streaming through an upper window and banquet chairs stacked along one wall, Rosie walked over to the doctor smoothly and easily—a product of years of therapy. She sat on the edge of the pool table, liking this hour because the sun shone through the windows, making a discarded chandelier glitter, and because Dr. Brooke was always so kind to her.

Rosie folded her hands in her lap.

His mustache lifted in a smile. "Good afternoon, Miss Rosie."

"Good afternoon, Dr. Brooke."

He exchanged a few pleasantries with her then flipped forward in his notes and leaned closer to her.

Pressing his thumb to her left brow, he peered carefully into that eye, and then the other. "How are your headaches?"

"Worse in the mornings, or when I'm out by the water. I'm afraid one made me irritable this morning."

"Irritable? That's not like you. Let's revisit that before we finish today." He jotted something down then read his past notes in silence. Finally he looked up at her. "Can you tell me the first city you remember living in?" His questions were always different.

"The first I remember is living on the Point Loma peninsula, just across the bay."

"Can you tell me the name of your parents?"

"I've never known that, Dr. Brooke."

"I'm sorry, Rosie, but these questions are important to circle back to. Do you have any brothers and sisters?"

He was so kind, so gentle with her that at the impossibility of the question, she had to fight a smile as she pressed her hands between her knees. "I don't know. Do I?"

The doctor angled his book away and gently touched her arm. "Will you close your eyes for me?"

She did as he asked, and he was quiet for several moments.

"If you think back. . .try to go as far back as you can. . .what is the first memory you recall? What comes to mind?"

"Seeing your face for the first time." It was nothing but the truth. She opened her eyes. "I also recall an old man."

"Yes, he was there at the hospital. But use his name, since you know it. And since he and his wife raised you almost your entire life."

"Abner Graham. Keeper of the lighthouse out on the point." And the dearest soul he was. Her attention veered to Dr. Brooke's hands as he shuffled through small bottles of medicine. She hoped none were for her this week. "How is your book coming along?" she asked.

"Fresh off the press and I got word from the publisher that they were shipped last week."

"Oh, that's wonderful. I'll be the first to buy a copy. What title did you come up with?"

"Um. . ." He paused in his search, looking flustered, likely not as used to questions as she was. "Well, I decided upon *The Western American Journal of Psychology*." When she scrunched her nose, he looked genuinely concerned. "No good?"

"It's rather boring."

He chuckled. "That tends to be the way with medical journals."

"I think *A Brief History into the Mind of Rosemund Graham* would have been so much more romantic."

"That does have a nice ring to it. Except *your* name is Rosie."

Yes, but she was just trying another on for size to see if it triggered something. She said as much, and he laughed. Then she assured him that she truly was grateful for the name the Grahams had given her when she was two and they had adopted her. When she was too young and frightened to give them any name of her own.

After listening to her heartbeat, Dr. Brooke slid his stethoscope around his neck and felt the glands just below her jaw. "Anything new that you want to tell me?"

"I learned how to carry a tray with ten glasses on it."

"That's quite an accomplishment."

"I'm rather proud of it. But girls aren't allowed to work in the dining room. Only men can be waiters." She opened her mouth farther when he held a tiny wooden paddle to her tongue. "I'm not thick," she mumbled around it.

"You never are, my dear. You're fit as a fiddle. I still need to be thorough, though." Taking her by the wrist, he quietly took her pulse. Rosie let her gaze drift to the window where people walked past, no doubt heading for the front entrance and check-in desks. Porters hustled bags and trunks to and from carriages.

"How often are you using headache powders?" he asked.

"As little as possible. Once a week at most."

He touched the lower right side of her skull. "And the pain is still often here?"

"Always there. Sometimes there's also pain right behind my eyes." Still perched on the edge of the pool table, she swung her legs gently. "But maybe I just need glasses."

He glanced to his notes, looking doubtful. Then he smirked and studied her swinging feet. "And your age, Rosie Graham?"

"Same as it was last time. Eighteen."

"Then why the schoolgirl wiggles?" His brown eyes twinkled.

"I'm sorry." She stilled her feet, linking her ankles demurely. As the doctor occasionally reminded her, just because she lost her memory at ten did not mean she was meant to *stay* ten. She didn't mean to, but certain qualities, certain things a young lady was taught, often felt snagged and stuck. As if rules and remembrances were sometimes buried under a mound of fisherman's netting and she was still struggling to untangle it.

"You're doing well," he said. "And all the social graces you've been working on, you're growing into them steadily. I'm very proud of you." He paused to make a notation in his notebook.

"Are you writing down that I was wiggling?"

He nodded softly. Rosie shot a breath, and his amused eyes landed on her. He had her best interest in mind, that she knew, but did he have to document *everything* she did?

"What will you be doing to help that along?" he asked.

She slid her gaze back to the abandoned chandelier, knowing the simple lesson by heart, so often he'd been teaching it to her. "Observe those around me. That will help me understand the rules, restrictions and *polite-ities* of society."

He smiled at her made-up word. "Very good. And. . . ?"

Rosie bit her lip. Her mind suddenly felt like a long hallway with no doors. She could run her hand along the walls, but nothing existed other than flat, smooth, emptiness. "Brush my teeth?"

With a chuckle, the doctor snapped his bag closed. "No. Though hygiene is always encouraged."

"I can't remember, then."

"To enjoy the life that you've been given. Exactly as it is." He took her hand and patted it. "We've only got one turn at this life, and while you're waiting for your past to return to you, and for certain perceptions and understandings to redevelop, be sure and enjoy the very special future that's ahead of you."

"Why are you so nice to me?" Rosie pulled her small notebook from her apron pocket, followed by the little pencil she always toted alongside it.

The doctor's mustache bowed upward. "Because it's not every day that a mermaid washes ashore. And that I get to be her friend." He tipped her chin like a father would.

Peering down, she turned her black shoes from side to side.

"Yes, no fin, Rosie. That was a metaphor."

She winked and he chuckled.

Sobering, she watched the doctor add a few more notations to his journal, and while he did, she made a note to enjoy life in her notebook. The place she jotted down all the things she aimed to remember. But there was something she wished to forget. "He acted as if I was insane."

"Who?"

"The young man I met this morning. When I was irritable."

"And what do you think of that?"

"I'm not insane." Mr. McIntosh's handsome face and steady gaze flashed through her mind, and Rosie tried to blink it away because it only reminded her of her behavior toward him—something she sorely regretted.

"I think you're remarkable," Dr. Brooke said kindly.

"But you also believe that I won't ever fully recover."

Slowly, he sighed. "You're making great strides in so many areas. But recovery in the fullest textbook sense may not be what we're aiming for now."

A cool brush of sadness spread over her.

"For your memory loss, brain trauma has been the only explanation, Rosie. Amnesia is highly unlikely. That lasts days, not years. Your head showed no kind of physical injury, and because you were found unconscious and in a state of not breathing, the lack of oxygen to your brain for those minutes is the best explanation for the changes you've experienced. But look at what you've accomplished." He tossed his pen to her, aiming for the right side, and she caught it.

The doctor grinned and Rosie joined him.

"You couldn't do that a few years ago."

"No." And he'd helped her every step of the way. "Do you think I'll ever be as I should? That I'll behave as a young lady ought to? Maybe even remember things from when I was smaller?"

"We're going to take it one day at a time."

"But you believe me. That I'm doing my best."

"I've always believed you, and I'll continue to." Dr. Brooke pulled something from his satchel. A small piece of driftwood carved in the shape of a coiling shell.

Rosie gasped. "Did you make this?"

He nodded.

She fingered it carefully. "You're getting better and better."

"Thank you for encouraging me to keep practicing."

"I'll put this with all the others."

"I'd be honored."

He finished a few notations, asked her several final questions, and then promised to meet her again in a few days. He placed his hat on his head and tipped it to her. "Until then, Miss Graham."

"Good-bye, Dr. Brooke." Rosie hopped down from the table and nabbed her feather duster. Time to go fetch her cart from storage and get back to work.

Out in the hallway, she hurried past a stretch of windows and glanced briefly out to the glittering bay just beyond the lush hotel grounds. A late-afternoon sun made the water shimmer. Sailboats dotted the dock, bobbing gently with the current, and beyond that, a long, narrow boat holding four rowers skimmed across the open gray. Rosie peered closer, noting that two of the men had brown hair; the other two, red locks. Which meant they were the young men from 3323.

She studied the rower in the third seat and decided that it was Jonas McIntosh. Something about his athletic build and determined strokes—both of which she'd noted earlier that morning before their colorful conversation when he wouldn't have known she'd been watching him. And she not realizing that the young sportsman was the one with the plight that Mr. Babcock, one of the hotel owners, had taken an interest in.

"Rosie, where have you been?"

Rosie spun to see Mrs. Kline bustling past. "I'm so sorry. It was my afternoon to meet with the doctor. I'll get back to work straightaway."

"The third floor is nearly done now, so either start in 3321 and make up the crib in there, or change out the pillowcases and sheets in this one." She nudged a door open with her elbow. "Or just down the hall, I've left a pile of sheets that need to be gathered."

"I'll do it all." Rosie hurried down the hall and fetched the sheets out of the way. She tucked them into a canvas bag on the bottom of the cart. In the next room, she made quick work with the baby's crib. Mrs. Kline had already made the other beds and freshened up soap and towels at the washstand. Rosie gathered and tucked the sheets carefully to keep the little one safe then folded a silky blue blanket that must have been brought from the family's home. She draped it with care over the crib railing, tossed a scrap of paper into the waste bin, and then took quick note that the room was in tip-top shape.

"Rosie!" came a hasty whisper.

"Coming!" She slipped out, snatched up the pile of fresh pillowcases Mrs. Kline held out, and slipped into room 3323.

She yanked off pillowcases and slid on new ones, piling everything to be taken to the laundry in the center of the room. Sheets went next and she swiftly creased folds and angles—making neat work of the linens just as the housekeeper had shown her over the year of working here.

Finished, Rosie gathered up a discarded coat, hanging it on a chair. She was just turning away from the desk near the window when her gaze filtered across the bottle. The antique vessel looked just as she'd last seen it. Battered and unopened and sitting atop a note.

A note?

Written on the same type of card stock as her own. She leaned closer and read the masculine script without touching it.

At the observatory—2100

Chapter Four

Grateful it was empty, Jonas strode through the grand ballroom and toward the stairs that curved up the wall to the overhead balconies. Beneath glistening chandeliers and a domed ceiling, he climbed several flights, tired legs sorer than ever as he passed the first catwalk and then the second—his sights not on the ballroom with its circular seating designed for plays and concerts, but on the narrow, winding stairs that would lead to the observatory. The tiny cap of lookout tower that was the highest point of the del.

He knew how many flights he could go before his lungs gave him trouble, so it was on the last bend of creaking steps that he slowed and made himself draw easy, calming breaths.

The twisting stairwell pinched in tighter and tighter, and he had to turn sideways as he reached the top. Though there were no windows to peer out just yet, he could feel how high up he was. It was a dizzying sensation, and combined with the tight space, one that spurred him to climb onward. Reaching the top landing of the lookout brought both relief and a burst of fresh air thanks to a window that rested ajar. Had he not been up here before, he would have been struck dumb by the scope of the 360-degree view.

Nearly ten stories up now, Jonas paused to catch his breath even as he wondered if Rosie would have understood that the note he left was for her. Not wanting to pace or think through alternate scenarios, he settled down on one of the bench seats and simply watched the doorway.

He checked his pocket watch. With the night in full swing, he was grateful for the lights strung from different levels of rooftops that lit the resort, giving even this tiny room a soft glow. Clearing his throat, Jonas shifted his feet and waited. The ballroom below had impressive acoustics, so he knew they'd alert him to any comings or goings. But all was silent. After a while, he checked his watch again. Twenty minutes past.

He glanced to the doorway. Maybe it was just as well if she didn't come, because this was a ridiculous idea. If she was to come and they were caught in this place together, it would spell much trouble for the both of them. Worse, likely, for her. That's when he heard something below. Footsteps? He stood quiet, listening.

Someone was there on the stair.

The person gently tap, tap, tapped higher; then the bowed head of a maid appeared as she rose into view. The young blond lifted her gaze, spotting him the moment he did her.

She panted out a breath. "I walked around for an eternity thinking of where room 2100 would be, but all the rooms in this hotel begin with *three*. It's a good thing you also mentioned the observatory."

Jonas hurried to take her hand as she navigated the last two steps.

Finished, he stepped back, any notion of greeting her suavely falling away. "What are you talking about?"

"Twenty-one hundred. I wasted so much time trying to figure out what you meant. I even asked one of the waiters if there was a room twenty-one hundred that I didn't know about."

"Twenty-one hundred means nine o'clock at night."

She blinked several times. "It does?"

"It's. . .it's from the twenty-four-hour clock. Something they use in astronomy." He took another step to the side and motioned for her to sit. "I'm sorry. It's a habit from school."

Her brow pursed and her cheeks flushed. She sat, looking disappointed in herself as she peered up at Jonas. "I fear this is something I should have known. Are there other hours of the day that have this astronomy time?"

"They all do."

Pulling a small notebook and pencil from her pocket, she went to write something but just looked overwhelmed. She tucked a curling ribbon of hair back under her maid's cap. Not the type of curls that bespoke hours with a hot iron, or curlers abed, but one that was from birth. A wild mass of hair that seemed barely contained.

Jonas settled a proper width away from her, bumping into the telescope as he did. "It's my fault. I shouldn't have been so vague on the note." He gave her a half smile, and she gave one back. Though she tucked the little notebook away, he could sense her uneasiness.

Best to get right to it.

"This"—he pulled forward the bottle, which he'd wrapped in a pillowcase—"you didn't need to give it to me. You keep it." He set it beside her.

"No, it was wrong of me." When she passed it back, her fingers brushed his.

Her eyes were wide, expression vulnerable, as if she hadn't a single secret. She was a pretty thing, this bottle thief.

But he needed to stop thinking of her as a thief. "Well one of us ought to take it, and I think it should be you. Or if you prefer, I can cast it back to sea."

"You would do that?"

"I'll do what you wish with it. You're certain you don't want it?"

"I'm certain. That bottle was destined for someone, but it wasn't me."

"It would have been, had I not come along."

"But you did come along." She was still watching him in that unnerving way—an unveiled watchfulness. Just as a child might who wasn't afraid of being caught staring. But she wasn't a child. She was a young woman with stunning eyes that were yet to leave his face.

"Yes, I suppose I did." He tipped the bottle and brushed at a few lingering flecks of sand. "Shall we open it and see what's inside?"

"I'd rather not. Not now, anyway."

As he tried to make sense of her words, Jonas made study of the cork set into the narrow neck of the bronze vessel. It looked relatively new. Untested. As if it hadn't been in the water very long. "So what do we do?" he asked.

She took the bottle and turned it slowly. Realizing he didn't know her name, he inquired gently.

"Rosie Graham." She settled the bottle in her lap. "At least for the time being."

"Pardon?"

"It's just a temporary name because I've forgotten my own."

Jonas blinked. Flexed his jaw just to keep it from falling. "Come again?" In the distance, the night waves crashed and swelled on the shoreline below.

She squinted sheepishly. "I shouldn't have said that."

"Miss Graham..."

"Mr. McIntosh."

Well she remembered his name at least. He shook his head to jar some sense back into it—into this conversation. Time to circle back to their purpose. He touched the cork. "This should be easy to open. Do take it, open it when you're ready."

"I'll be sure to let you know what's inside." She accepted it. "And I won't mix you up like I do the other young men you're with. You're the one I seem to find most easily because you have a very remarkable face." She clamped a hand over her mouth as if she shouldn't have said that, either.

Despite himself, he smiled. "Is that so?"

Hand still over her mouth, she nodded.

Easily the strangest creature he'd ever met. Yet everything about her seemed to bind together into what was nothing but endearing. All wrapped in the prettiest of packages with her eyes a winter blue—a color so soft and pale it was almost otherworldly. With skin and hair equally as fair, it only added to her mystique. Looking at her now, he was reminded of the fairies in the stories he'd read as a boy.

But something was markedly different about her than other young ladies he knew. Something he couldn't quite grasp hold of.

Truly, though, he hadn't the freedom to find out. They each had their places, and he would do well to remember his own before he caused her any trouble. With their business completed, Jonas cleared his throat, suddenly uncomfortable that he'd brought her here to the highest tower of the del. This window to the stars that was filled with a cool, salty breeze.

"Miss Graham, thank you for meeting me." He pushed aside the telescope just enough to stand. "And thank you for your apology, but it's I who owe you one. Please keep this, and I hope it brings you pleasure."

She rose slowly, peering up at him without so much as a blink. "May I ask you a question?"

He gave a small nod.

"Why do you row your boat across the bay without ever going beyond it?"

Her question surprising him, he grasped for an answer. "It's. . .uh. It's practice. For my friends and me."

"Practice for what?"

"To row around the lighthouse." He motioned to where the great lantern was aglow across the giant bay. "The point." She was the first person he'd told this to. Well, apart from Babcock, but the hotel owner already knew everything about their quest.

"You wish to see something on the other side?"

"We're not aiming to see much, just to get there."

If that baffled her, he wouldn't blame her. Their plan made little sense without the full story to explain it. Inching nearer was the desire to detail it to her, but he stepped from that path of thinking. It was wisest to go now.

"Thanks again for meeting me." To edge by her, he brushed a hand to her side. Though he scarcely grazed the fabric of her black dress, he was struck with how much softer it was than the oars he'd gripped all day. "I'll see you around."

She peered up, and that was when he realized that rather than bafflement, her look was one of gladness. As if his declaration of their quest brought her joy. "I'd imagine you will. I'm the one who cleans your room, but I only clean it when you're not there. So if I do my job well, you won't see me."

Smiling again, Jonas finished stepping around her then scratched the back of his head. "All right, then."

"I wish you the best. In your boat."

"Thank you." He stepped toward the spiral staircase, and while he was pleased to see the cloth-wrapped bottle tucked in her grasp, he also realized that they should head down separately.

He went to motion her first then paused. "How did you forget your name?"

Her mouth parted as if she hadn't expected him to inquire. He regretted that it had taken him this long.

"Apparently they asked my name, but I didn't give one. Maybe I was too frightened." She glanced around the observatory, then back to him as if warring over how much to disclose. She gently pressed onward. "I'll never remember now because a few years later, I fell into the water and was found by morning fishermen. I was barely alive when they brought me in. I don't remember any of it. And the doctors said that something about the way I was found—not breathing—is the reason I lost other things." She touched the side of her head and looked at him with a hint of regret.

It was a look that pierced him, as if she was somewhat ashamed of that. "And you lost your name."

"In a most final sense, yes." She adjusted the draped pillowcase around the bottle, making slow work with the folds. "But I have tried not to ever worry about that. More urgent was forgetting who I was. Memories. I also lost what they tell me was once a love of the sea. I forgot about the people who I cared for—the Grahams." Though she smiled gently as if it hadn't taken long for that love to bloom anew.

Voices sounded from below, and, not wanting to give away their presence here, he stepped nearer to Rosie, speaking softly. "I'm so sorry."

When she tipped her head down, a curl that escaped from beneath her cap looked soft as a dove's feather. "It's all right. I'll get them back one day. The memories."

Then she glanced around, pulled out her notebook, and penciled something in. "I write things down that I mean not to forget. Notes for remembrance."

His watching her scribble something down must have made her wonder. . .

"Would you like one?"

He wet his lips. "Um. . .sure."

She flipped forward a few pages—seemed to take her time in deciding—then tore out a single slip. Rosie folded it and tucked it into his shirt pocket.

Jonas glanced down at it even as her nearness, the brush of her fingertips to his chest, unnerved him. He took a small step back. "Well, Miss Graham. It's been remarkable meeting you." He looked at her once more; if he were the sea, he'd be jealous to have lost her.

She tucked away her notebook, bid him good night, and slipped back down the stairs.

Standing there, dumbfounded, he didn't move for some time. When he finally did, it was to reach into his shirt pocket and pull out what she'd put there. He unfolded the slip of paper, more than a little curious to find out what it said. What she offered him to remember. But it simply said, *Be patient.*

Jonas glanced down the coiling stairwell before eyeing the paper again. He waited another few minutes then left the tower, thoughts on who was easily the most interesting girl he'd ever met.

Chapter Five

There was a reason they did a warm-up on the bay yesterday. While both Jonas and Oliver had spent years on various crew teams, Dexter was a rugby player, and Oakes's athletic career didn't expand beyond jogging to class when he overslept—or chasing pretty girls.

Jonas stood on the sand surrounding small Glorietta Bay, an early-morning sun blaring down on them, and studied his teammates. As eager as he was to be out on Coronado Bay just on the other side of the hotel, this little harbor had no waves and was calm as glass. Just the place for him and his friends to get their sea legs under them before facing the break again.

He swiped his hands against the sides of his bathing shorts then moved around the front of the quad, a racing shell built for four. "All right, Oakes, you're in the bow seat."

"In the back again?" Oakes tipped his chin up, ego showing.

Something Jonas was more than accustomed to handling. "Yeah, but we row backward so you'll cross the finish line first."

Morning light glinted on his slicked brown hair as Oakes smirked and climbed in. His seat slid back on its track, and he settled into place.

"Oliver, you and I are the powerhouse again." The middle rowers, this was the spot for the strongest team members. "And Dexter, right here at the stroke seat." Not only was Dexter strong, but he was calm and steady: a good leader, which made him born for one of the most important seats in the wooden shell.

"I've been wondering. . .what's this seat in front of me?" Dexter thumbed a portion of his black bathing tank and used it to swipe his jaw.

Jonas glanced to the stern of the boat. "That's the cox seat, but we don't have a coxswain so won't need to worry about that." As difficult as it was going to be, Jonas would have to make the calls.

"And what about you?" Oliver eyed him as Jonas fetched oars. "Any instructions for our noble leader?"

The words were light, but Jonas heard his cousin's warning. Really, a concern. "I'll be fine."

He'd brought a thermos of extra-strong coffee with him—something that worked in a pinch should his lungs need stimulation. Even as he thought it, he made sure the thermos was stashed against the floorboard. Oliver watched him, not seeming pleased.

Jonas straightened, and his cousin stepped nearer, concern tight in his freckled face. "You *waynough* when you need to, okay?"

"I really will be fine."

Looking doubtful, Oliver stepped away.

Standing beside the boat, Jonas held an oar out. He angled the paddle to face straight up and down for one more reminder to Oakes and Dexter. "Now remember, this is for the catch, offering the most resistance. But when you lift your oars, remember to feather." He turned the handle 25 percent so that the blade was flat, floating as a bird's wing above the sand. "Which will take the least resistance. Just like we practiced yesterday."

Oakes rubbed what had to be a sore shoulder, and Jonas and Dexter pushed the boat into the water. They climbed in, and when Jonas settled into his seat, he gripped the handles of his oars. The quad rocked and Jonas called over his shoulder, "Oakes, let us know when the bow is clear."

"Bow clear."

"Set ready," Jonas responded.

Everyone took their oars and dipped the shafts toward the water. The boat swayed gently, water lapping against the shell.

Time to straighten it. "Two rows starboard," Jonas said.

They followed his lead, and the boat lined up with the harbor—the bow pointing out toward smooth, open water.

"Set ready," he said again, and they all took a steadying breath. Water lapped against his oar, and he loosened mind, tightened body, and with a call for them to pull, they each dug deep. A second stroke and then a third. "Pull." He called it with each stroke, and they settled into a smooth rhythm.

"Place your blade with care, Oakes," Jonas said with a grunt. "You're the one keeping us balanced. And Oliver, give all the muscle you got."

"Sure thing," Oliver panted.

Catch, send. Catch, send. It was a slow, easy row. Just one to get the pace of working as a team. Though the water didn't churn here, it seemed to have a force all its own as they dug oars in and used that tension to power the boat across the water. In the distance, a fisherman paused with his nets to watch them pass.

"Easy, steady strokes, Dexter," Jonas panted. "We're following your lead."

Dexter nodded.

"Rotate. . .a little sooner. . .on the release, Oakes."

Oakes did and caught onto a smoother rhythm with the rest of them. The wooden shell skimmed in a smooth glide, and Jonas called out for them to all quicken the pace. Now was the time.

"Pull!" He said it louder—a cue to row harder.

They pulled as he did. Blades dipped for the catch. Then the burn of muscle for the drive—the force that pushed the boat along. The hardest part. Then the finish where the pain loosened. Finally the recovery—the feathering as they turned their blades to skim back across the water, seats sliding forward. All in the blink of an eye before they sunk oars in for the next catch. At the drive, Jonas panted out, "Pull," but already it was getting hard to breathe. Drive. Finish.

Recover.

"Pull." Drive. Finish.

Recover.

Catch. Jonas stayed quiet as they slid into the drive. He grunted at the finish with the others then feathered his oar back, the four of them in perfect synchronization. He smiled. The feeling of this overriding any tension blooming between his ribs.

It was just them and the sound of screeching seagulls. The pull of water against wood and the creak of a boat that had borne rowers—always four at a time. Four souls. Four panting beings who knew that the burn would be worth it in the end. That the pain they were feeling now as their bodies stretched and coiled and complained would all be worth it at the finish line.

Regardless of how peculiar that finish line might be.

In front of him, Oliver's arms worked in perfect rhythm with Dexter's, and Jonas kept the metronome, knowing that by the sound of Oakes's breathing behind him, their bowman was synched, too. Catch and drive and finish.

His lungs were slowly beginning to tighten. Jonas tried to ignore it.

On the recovery, he called that they had less than a hundred meters left to go.

The July sun steamed the air. Sweat slid down the front of his chest, slicked his shoulders. Feeling their rhythm weakening, his directions slipped into panting words.

And with his last call to pull, that was all he had as he gasped for air. Fifty meters to go. Jonas's lungs were on fire. He coughed. In his mind, he kept the tempo, but even that was starting to falter as his body struggled for air that was suddenly coming too thin, too shallow.

"We're sprinting too fast," Oliver gasped between breaths.

Jonas set a slower pace, but even then, he could hear himself wheezing.

"Waynough, Jonas!" Oliver called over his shoulder before sliding into the recovery.

But Jonas plunged his blades again. He was fine.

"Way *enough*!" Still panting, Oliver carefully enunciated the command for him to rest his oars.

Jonas's lungs pinched tighter, but still he dipped at the catch and pulled with all his might. With the others. They were a team, and he was going to bear his own weight.

Thirty meters to go.

But he was gasping now. Oliver hollered out something, but Jonas couldn't hear it.

Dagnabit, he couldn't breathe. Jonas set his oars and bent forward, his body fighting for air. Maybe he was strong in build, but he was still the weakest link. He'd always be the weakest.

Tilting his face to the sky expanded his chest enough to suck in a sliver of air, but panic was taking over. He couldn't breathe. Upright. He needed to sit upright. It was nearly impossible with his constricted chest screaming at him, but he straightened and gasped for another breath. Stay calm. He had to stay calm. Even though he was drowning above the water, he couldn't panic. A breath in, a breath out.

The boat slowed and the others doubled over, panting. The finish line, then.

The sight of his teammates blurring, Jonas groped against the floorboard for the thermos. It had rolled out of his reach. Panic shot through him and relief fought forward as Oliver angled toward him, thermos in hand. Jonas unscrewed the lid and gulped down tepid coffee. His hands shook as he tried to keep the container still. The wet warmth made it easier to take a thin breath and another and within a few minutes, the caffeine would stimulate his airway. That was his hope. It hadn't failed him yet, but there was always a first for everything. Jonas swiped the back of his hand over his mouth. Tipped his jaw toward the sky and drew in all the air he could.

It wasn't much. He could hear his wheezing, and as a few minutes passed—and with his determination to stay calm—it began to slow.

"That was too fast," Oliver said. "We sprinted too fast." He looked to the others, brows clamped in frustration. "Not again. This isn't the Harvard–Yale Regatta. I don't care if it takes us a week to get around that lighthouse, we're going to go slower." As Jonas ran a hand down his face, Oliver added, "If you die, it's going to ruin everything."

Oakes snorted and Dexter chuckled. Despite everything, Jonas smirked.

He heaved in a breath. "I'm not gonna die." He reached for his oars when the others did but could scarcely row as they made their way back to their starting point. Jonas took the time—the simplicity of retreat—to steady himself. To recover in the fullest sense.

When they finally reached the shore of the bay, Dexter hopped out and tugged the quad farther onto the sand.

Jonas climbed out and walked away a few feet before sinking to his knees. The humility of not being able to stand lessened as his friends settled in the sand around him. Or maybe, just maybe, the humility deepened.

He looked at them in turn, his spirit awash with both gratitude and regret for this group of young men who had been willing—no, eager—to brave this scheme once again. These friends who understood his need to be a part of this.

They gave him plenty of time, and when Oliver finally said, "Should we head back to the boathouse?" Jonas was able to stand with the rest of them. They circled around the quad, and at Jonas's nod for Oliver to take the lead, the young man said, "All hold."

Then, "To shoulders. . ." They lifted the vessel. "Over heads."

Arms up, they hefted the shell above their heads. With it steadied, they walked up the beach and toward the boathouse. Jonas was certain his teammates were as exhausted as he was, but no one complained. It was just part of it. A responsibility that every oarsman had to bear for this sport. A reverent reminder that the journey down the water was only half the trip. They carried the shell to the boathouse, which was an exact mirror of the del itself—the same red roof, even a small tower up top for viewing the island.

By the time they headed back to the hotel for baths and a change of clothes, it was well into the lunch hour. Starving, Jonas buttoned up a clean shirt and had nothing on his mind but a hearty meal. Or two. He'd never been so hungry in his life.

When a knock sounded against the door, Oliver rose stiffly and answered it.

Jonas heard a gentle voice from the hallway. "Is Mr. McIntosh here?"

Eyebrows raised, Oliver looked back over his shoulder.

"I'm here." Jonas stood, recognizing that voice. His own still felt weak, but he sounded enough like himself that no one seemed to notice.

Suddenly Rosie ducked under Oliver's arm. "I have a question of utmost importance."

"Hi, Rosie. I'm all ears. But I think we should step out into the hallway."

"No, if we're spotted talking I'll get in trouble."

"If you're spotted in our room you'll get in trouble."

She glanced around as if she hadn't thought of that. "We could speak out on the roof?"

Jonas leaned toward her and said gently, "How about we just talk fast?"

She leaned near as well, smelling of the same fresh soap as the sheets, the towels. "Will you take me for a ride in your boat?"

She wanted to. . .what?

Jonas glanced to Oliver, who shrugged a shoulder, then to Oakes, who was gawking at her as if he'd never seen a pretty girl before. Dexter was gaping just as much, so Jonas took that as affirmative.

His brows pinched as he glanced back to Rosie. "Why?"

With a crook of her finger, she motioned him nearer. Jonas dipped his head beside hers.

She whispered against his ear, and he was certain that in her voice, he heard a spark of hope. Of bravery toward the waters she confessed to fearing. "Because I think I remember something."

Chapter Six

Surrounded by the observatory's whitewashed walls and snugly closed windows, the air felt strangely still to Rosie. With only a few stolen moments to speak before she needed to hurry out of his room, Jonas had asked her to meet him up in the lookout tower once more. So here she sat, short hours later, thoughts of him and the sea she was daring to brave all spinning in her mind.

The air thick and heavy, she thought about opening the door that led out to the balcony encircling the tower, but that would only alert passersby to her presence here, which seemed unwise. Also unwise would be for them to climb the narrow, winding stair together, so she'd slipped up here a few minutes before he was due to arrive.

But as Rosie looked back to the door, she had a glimmer of worry as to what might happen if they were discovered together. For a staff member and a hotel guest to be alone was unseemly. No, scandalous.

Pinching a bit of her bottom lip between her teeth, she crossed her ankles together and kept a keen eye on the closed door. Beside her, the telescope all but beckoned its visitors to squint an eye and press it to the round bit of glass that would lead all imaginings to the stars above, but she stayed still and unmoving until she heard footsteps on the stairs. Her heart pulsed away each steady *thud-thud-thud* until the door creaked open and Jonas appeared. It was an inquiring look, him yet a few steps down—a look that rose up to meet her with brown eyes that were nearly asking for her.

A slow smile lifted Rosie's lips, and she felt a wash of nervousness of a different kind. Though not as broad of shoulder as the sailors who waved to her and Abner along the point, his scholarly frame was strong. Athletic. The way he angled with ease into the small room, both unassuming and captivating.

He wore a brown tweed dinner jacket, and his deep-cocoa bowtie was slightly askew as if he'd just tugged at it. His hair was slicked to the side, yet a few stray hairs in the back didn't seem fond of his attempts with comb and pomade. He smelled of citrus and brandy as he stepped near, making her wonder how old he was. She asked the question before she could stop herself.

He settled on the angled bench a safe foot away from her. "Twenty."

"Oh."

With something in hand, he set down two bottles of root beer as if this were an early-evening rendezvous between old friends. Even sweethearts. But she couldn't be sure. Feeling lost, Rosie looked from the offering to his face—that steady, contemplative gaze he wore. "I don't know that this is a good idea."

"I overheard a maid saying it was suppertime for you. I didn't realize that when I suggested we meet now." He set a paper bag beside her, and she peeked inside to find a cheese danish bedecked with slivered almonds. Rosie looked at him in surprise.

Eyes amused, he pulled something from his pocket. "Straw?"

She took the paper straw, and he nudged one of the drinks closer to her. Using her thumb, she pushed the marble stopper down into the bottle, let the hiss of fizz escape, and then sipped.

Jonas didn't touch his own. "And what of you? Your age?"

"Eighteen, supposedly."

Like a blackbird across a sunset, confusion dipped over his eyes. "You're not certain."

"Not factually." Knowing she couldn't just leave it at that, she did her best to explain Dr. Brooke's estimates about her. Based on how and when she was found as a toddler on the lighthouse steps.

"So what are these theories?" he asked, dropping a straw into his own bottle.

Rosie broke off a piece of pastry and offered some toward him. He raised a hand, his conviction clear that he wished it for her.

"The doctor has pieced together his speculations about my past. He has pages of notes. They go something like this." She cleared her throat and squared her shoulders. "Parentage: uncertain. Background: decidedly American." She sipped her drink then hiccupped. "Moral standing: undetermined." She squinted over at Jonas. "What do you suppose he meant by that?"

He smiled—his gaze warm as it skimmed over her face.

It was such an endearing look that she dropped her own attentions, fiddling instead with the edge of her white apron. Rosie adjusted it, wishing suddenly that she could wear something other than this starched, black-and-white uniform. When she glanced out the window, she saw women wandering below, their glamourous gowns and hats glimmering in the soft radiance of strings upon strings of electric lights. That same glow rose up toward the observatory, gently lighting the side of Jonas's face where her focus once again landed.

He cleared his throat. "Are you off shift after your supper?"

"No. We eat early so we can do turndown service while guests are having dinner. I'll have to head back in about ten minutes." Slowly she turned her straw, unnerved to be sitting here, making small talk with this man. Perhaps if she prompted him toward their purpose for being here. "What about you, Mr. McIntosh? What do you do when you're not out rowing your boat on holiday or sitting in the lookout tower questioning odd birds like me?"

His brow pinched as he turned his face toward the glow below. "I'm studying law at Stanford. Second year."

Law. Stanford.

That was very. . .upper class. But he would be nothing but, not if he were staying at the resort. A week here cost more than she'd see in a year of service, and though she knew his trip was sponsored by Mr. Babcock, she sensed Jonas McIntosh could have secured a summer holiday here all on his own. Though the notion was never flaunted, he carried himself as if he came from money.

His look was regretful. As if he knew as well as she did that they shouldn't be sitting here together.

Then he said, "I'm not terribly fond of it."

"No?"

He shook his head. "It's my father's dream for me, but I. . ."

When he fell silent, she pressed the matter gently, but he just shook his head again.

"Never mind. It's a good career and will make a good life." Jonas rubbed a thumb across his palm, looking lost in thought.

He was holding something back, but she could see that he wished to change the subject.

"About the boat," she began.

"Yes." His brow eased. "That's what I wanted to explain." He smoothed his hands together, and they sounded rough and calloused. "It will be best to do it very early in the morning. Before sunup, when the sea is the most calm. Day after tomorrow all right for you? That will give us one more day to iron out some kinks."

"It's perfect." Rosie gave him a soft smile. One she meant with her whole heart. "Thank you." The trip to the lighthouse always took half a day by carriage. A cost she could scarcely afford but one she splurged on the last Saturday of every month to spend a little time at home with Abner.

To simply row across the harbor still needled fear into her. Ever since that night. But something was changing. A memory, perhaps. One worth fighting for. And she wouldn't know if she didn't try.

Rosie described to Jonas how she needed to go just to the base of the lighthouse cliffs where there was a little dock and a set of stairs. The place where she had been put into a rowboat that fateful night when she was ten. Placed there against her will.

How she remembered this, she didn't know.

Suddenly, voices drifted up from the stairwell. Jonas stood the same instant Rosie did. Her heart jolted, and she glanced around. Just the two of them, so near that they each took a step away from the other. Nowhere to hide.

Rosie thought fast. "Sit," she whispered, and when he did, she rolled her eyes. "Not there. Over there."

The voices drew closer, and Jonas moved to where she pointed. The place where moonlight puddled perfectly on a bench carved for two. She put the bottles of root beer beside him, tucking the half-empty one behind the full.

"Well, Mr. McIntosh," she said much too loudly. "If that's all you'll be needing, I'll get back to the kitchen. The chef is no doubt preparing your celebration feast now."

Jonas quirked a brow.

A couple stepped into the cupola, expressions expectant as if they'd heard her little speech from below. The man was dressed in dinner tails, and the woman on his arm wore a beaded gown and elbow-length gloves. They discreetly looked from Rosie to Jonas, and Rosie hoped they'd heard her.

She dipped a curtsy to Jonas. "I'll make sure everything is ready, and I hope your young lady is delighted by your engagement surprise." She clicked her tongue. "You've chosen quite a spot. And on a glorious night, as well. I wish you both the best, sir."

The newcomers fussed over this romantic revelation, and Rosie left a very wide-eyed Jonas to answer their queries about his mystery lady. She hurried out and grinned all the way down the winding staircase, through the empty ballroom. All the way out into the star-bright night where she peeked back up to the tower, and just as she imagined the couple doing this very moment, she silently wished Jonas well.

In the inner courtyard of the del, Jonas walked along the pathway. The four sides of the grand resort rose all around him, four floors of high-end rooms, all filled with polished wood paneling and ornate furniture. But here in the center of it all, it was a humble oasis beneath a night sky. Baby palms rustled in the crisp breeze; an owl hooted from a distant roofline.

Jonas carried the empty soda bottles, the thin necks fitting easily in one hand. A souvenir from his "engagement" night, he meant to hang on to these. It wasn't every day that a fella got to propose to the love of his life without having met her yet.

Bowing his head, Jonas started up the stairs that would take him to the third floor. A cot awaited him, and this late in the evening, having missed supper to sit and ponder things he should never have been pondering, he was ready to give in to sleep and see where his dreams might take him. Would they take him far from himself? Far from the standards of society that kept him bound to a future that had been set in motion before he could even crawl?

To be a lawyer—a noble career. But it was his father's insistence that Jonas take up such an occupation. Lay aside any notion of his boyish dreams.

As a lad, he'd wanted to be a carpenter, first. And then a seaman. When those notions collided into his father's frowning face, Jonas thought he might try and pursue a variety of other occupations—all that might keep him outdoors, out in the great, wide world that he'd loved. But those hopes died one by one against his father's insistence that Jonas take a position at a desk in an office. Something that didn't include physical labor. Something that wouldn't cause the breathing spells that had landed him in the hospital time and time again as a child.

The weakest of the McIntosh sons, Jonas had gone to Stanford, taken the exams. Begun the early days of what his family hoped would be a long and prosperous career in law. And Jonas knew his place: get high marks on the exams and make it into a good firm. Then begin the life he was raised for, right after he pursued an eligible young woman of amiable standing and good fortune.

Yet another dream that had never sat well with Jonas.

Shifting the empty glass bottles to his other hand, he watched the ground as he walked. Lifting his gaze, he took in the sight of the maids' quarters in the moon-light. It rose above the fourth floor as a large attic. The peaked roof was moonlit, and a window sat open as white curtains slipped out to play with the breeze. He paid attention not to the thin boards of the paneling or the closed little shutters. He imagined only Rosie somewhere there in one of the rooms.

And in that moment he wondered what she would think to know that as the adoring couple had inquired about his fiancée to be, Jonas had had nothing but a picture of *her* in his mind. Nothing but her face as he described who they believed to be his young lady. His love.

Chapter Seven

Crash. And cold. Jonas held his breath as he dived beneath a wave, the salty water chilling his skin since he had a habit of never letting himself acclimate. Just wade out and dive. Get it over with. It was always easier that way.

He rose for a breath then ducked under another wave just as it broke and foamed overhead. He surfaced and swam forward, taking a few strokes to find that smooth, easy rhythm, breaking it only to slip beneath the surface when a wave crashed and pounded. Stirring the sand, spurring him to swim beyond this place. Out into the great open where the sea was calmer, gentler. A feat that was always achieved by his strength and his strength alone.

As he worked his way away from the shore, risking to go only as far as he knew he could, he felt the open span of an early gray sky overhead and, for the first time in a long time, dared to question if perhaps he wasn't doing so well with his own strength.

His nursemaid had spent years teaching him that there was a place where greater strength could be found. When he was a boy, he assumed it had something to do with church pews and stained glass, but as he grew, he understood more deeply her meaning. Yet he'd wandered and strayed from that way of thinking. Something in him ached to return. To place his feet on the path that would carry him closer to the peace that had always lived in his nursemaid's gentle face. He could hear her afternoon prayers now. Remember the hymns she'd hummed as they'd walked hand in hand through the park.

But all that faded as he thought about how she'd chide him for swimming so far. If he'd had any strength to smile, he would have.

His body was tempered to the chill of the sea, and out in the deeps of this choppy bay, he had just enough fuel to make it back to shore. Jonas dipped and somersaulted, coming up again in a new direction, heading for land. His arms burned, and his back felt as if it hadn't a single stroke left when he finally touched sand again.

Wading toward dry beach, he looked around for his towel, spotting it the same moment he spotted Rosie. He'd be lying to himself if he didn't admit to having hoped she'd be here again, combing the beach for her treasures.

With her profile to him, she was bent over near the edge of the froth, perhaps twenty paces away. The hem of a skirt was bustled into her waistband, making makeshift pantaloons and showing bare calves and ankles. Her pale feet pressed small prints into the sand. She seemed to be searching for something as she walked, bending every few steps to pluck a pebble or shell, giving it careful study. A few items she slipped into a canvas satchel that hung from her shoulder. Others, she tossed back to the wet ground. Her hair was pulled back with a strip of ribbon, the gentle coils of it spinning about in the breeze.

Water still dripping down his face, Jonas ignored his towel to nab a perfectly whole shell from the gritty sand. He strode over without a word and dropped it into her bag. Rosie turned with a start. "Oh!" Upon seeing him, she pressed a hand to her heart. "Mr. McIntosh!"

He smiled. "Seeing as we're both showing so much skin, I think you can call me Jonas."

She chuckled, and it was so sweet, with her hand over her mouth, cheeks turning the shade of her name, that he finally had to chuckle as well.

Then he sobered gently and squinted at her. "I probably shouldn't have said that."

"I dare say you shouldn't have." She looked about to right her skirts, cover her bare ankles, but he stilled her hand with his own.

Gave a small shake of his head. "I promise not to look."

She smirked and tipped her head for them to walk on. Waves foamed about their feet, and low-hanging clouds kept the air cool even as dawn was breaking. He glanced over at her, content with this moment. When she crouched down and freed what looked like an old, rusted key, she turned it over in her hand. Rosie stood, and Jonas stepped a little closer, tipping his head nearer to her own.

"That looks like something worth holding on to," he said softly.

"Yes. Worth saving." She slipped it into her sack.

They settled in stride once more. He bent occasionally for shells that seemed pretty, and while they were all quite similar to him, she contemplated each one as if it were highly unique. She saved them all, but what she seemed to prefer the most were odds and ends that bespoke humanity. A coil of wire. A piece of an old pipe. A bead that might have been part of a necklace once.

"May I ask what you do with it all?" he said when she adjusted her sack to her other shoulder.

Rosie fiddled with the edge of the canvas bag. "I just tuck it away. Use it for remembering."

"Where you came from?"

She shook her head. "Not really. I don't know that I want to remember that."

He spoke the words as softly as he could. "Why not?"

Opening her mouth, she looked about to answer, then said, "Let's not worry about it now."

"Certainly."

He stepped on as she did, and when she glanced sideways, it was with a tinge of regret. "But I can tell you what I do wish to remember." Her voice was both steady and fragile. "I hold these treasures close to remind myself that there are others in the world. Others who are lost. Or who hurt. Or even who wonder. These waters. This sea. It's a bridge between us all. A reminder that we're not alone."

It took great effort to pull his gaze from her face, but Jonas did it briefly. Just long enough to glance at the sack draped over her shoulder. He nodded—the only response he could muster beneath the depth of her sentiment.

He hadn't thought of it that way in a long time. He'd learned to see the sea only as a foe. As something to wrestle against. Now he was thinking of stained-glass windows and the words she'd slipped into his pocket.

Be patient.

He glanced heavenward. For what? He thought of asking Rosie, but she mentioned that it was time for her to get back to the hotel. He stayed beside her as they headed toward the resort that now seemed tiny with the spread of open beach from here to there.

An easy silence settled about them. Rosie's face upturned toward the coming sun that surely wouldn't be brightening this day long, not with the storm clouds rolling in over the water. *Be patient.* He saw it in the way she turned over the shells he'd offered her. The way she studied the key with a pinched brow—as if there were an untold story there. As if she could reach out and hand it back, this treasure that someone lost.

Jonas glanced sideways at her, realizing afresh what she'd confessed to him to be true. That she'd lost something. The tender way she'd tapped the side of her head with both sorrow and grief. He must have contemplated this overlong, for she was asking him if he'd ever heard of a selkie.

"A what?"

"A selkie. Part human, part seal? It's old folklore."

He smiled at the oddity of that. "Can't say that I have."

She shrugged as if to lessen its importance. "Abner used to say that I was one."

Jonas tried to make sense of that, but then Rosie motioned up the beach some. "There, when I said I didn't want to remember where I came from."

"Yes." He bent for his towel when they reached it.

"That was the answer Abner used to give me. Whenever he'd tuck me in at night, he'd kiss the tip of my nose and ask me to stay a girl for one more night. That even though the sea yearned for me to come back, and I to it, to stay a girl a little longer or he'd be the worse for wear with missing me."

An ache rose inside Jonas.

"It's one of the few things I remember. He would say it after we prayed for him and Esther and myself. Thanking the Lord for the family that we were. Sometimes after, I'd ask why I didn't have parents to pray with me. Silly, I suppose. It's just a tale. An old Irish legend of sorts. Something we played at so I wouldn't be left to wonder." She was watching the water with eyes that thirsted for it. That thirsted for what was lost.

At the slight quake in her voice, he thought to cheer her. "So underneath all this"—he touched her chin for the briefest of moments—"you're just a seal."

Her face turned toward him, a smile brightening it. "If I'm ever gone, you'll know why."

"Then I'll hope as Abner did."

Surprise dawned in her expression.

"For you to stay a girl awhile longer."

Twisting her mouth to the side did little to hide her smile, but he could see how much she was trying to fight it. The sight of her that way, of her sweet inno-cence—all bathed in the sound and sentiment of her words—was so becoming that he forced himself to look elsewhere for the sheer need of it.

"There's something."

He glanced that way. Sure enough, wedged into the sand was a broken piece of green glass. Jonas fetched it for her. Though just a fragment, it felt weighty and right in the center of his palm. It was smooth as satin—every jagged edge rubbed away.

"That's very pretty," she said, peeking over his shoulder.

Jonas held the piece of glass up to the weak light. Then he offered it over.

"You keep it."

He dropped it into her satchel regardless. "But you spotted it."

She looked flustered. "I can't keep taking things from you." Pulling her bag around to her front, Rosie dug into it. "Not without. . .returning. . .the. . ." She scrunched one side of her face, still searching. "Favor." She held up a broken pair of spectacles then slid one earpiece into the front of his bathing tank.

"Very funny."

She laughed. "I find at least one pair a week. The bathers lose these all the time."

"Too bad they don't lose things of more interest."

"Oh, I found a ring once!" Rosie touched his arm in such a familiar way that Jonas glanced down at her hand, then back to her face.

"Yeah?"

"I gave it to the maître d', and he was able to locate its owner."

Jonas's brow furrowed. "That was kind of you."

"It was a ruby, I think." She held up the sea glass to the stormy sky again as if searching for light. He hadn't realized she'd still been holding it. "It wasn't as pretty as this, though."

He smiled at the sweetness of that. Of this girl.

Rosie glanced toward the hotel, and Jonas did as well. It stood bold and sprawling before them now.

"I should head in, or I'll be late for my shift," she said. "It would probably be best for me to go alone."

"Of course." He slowed to a stop.

"Thank you for your help." She slowly stepped onward.

"Anytime."

After turning the glass slowly between her fingers, she tucked it away. "You will be in my prayers tonight, Jonas McIntosh." With that, she gave him a small wave then headed off, leaving him to ponder the mysteries of this girl and the way she was working her way into his heart.

Chapter Eight

Rain pattered against the windows of the sunroom. Though a large room that ran the length of the hotel, filled with patrons stuck inside because of the weather, it was more than a little stuffy. Still, it was the brightest spot in the hotel, even on a day such as this. Jonas slipped his finger into his tie and loosened it.

Nearby, Oliver and Dexter were bent over a chessboard, a few children watching the game. A pawn was lost to a bishop, and one of the children leaned nearer. Oliver winked at the small boy. Oakes sat beneath the windows in the center of a wicker love seat. He was swathed in the rapt attention of two young ladies as he told a story from school that Jonas was certain was only half-true.

Newspaper in hand, Jonas read another column of the business section, his mind a million miles away. Hotel staff came and went, trying to keep guests comfortable and happy. Jonas ignored the grumbling from patrons over the fact that thunderheads had rolled into the midst of their holiday on the coast. Jonas and his teammates had lost a day of rowing, but that was often the way of it with the sport.

After reaching the end of another article, he glanced around. In the far corner, a man played an upbeat lick on a grand piano. Promenaders moved back and forth in front of the dewy windows, watching the sky. Children lay sprawled on the floor, spinning tops or dealing cards. Babies dozed in the arms of nursemaids, and women leaned toward one another, swapping gossip. Gentleman discussed business, some stepping out to smoke cigars or while away the afternoon in the billiard room. Jonas folded his paper, thinking nine-balls wasn't a bad idea just now.

"Some tea for you, ma'am?"

His ears perked at the sound of Rosie's voice just behind him. Still seated on his wicker bench, Jonas dipped his head and folded his paper once more.

"And some pastries?" Rosie said to whomever she was serving. "The macaroons are excellent."

"Oh, thank you," came a woman's reply.

Then Rosie's hurried whisper: "But don't take the ones on the left because I dropped those."

Jonas coughed to cover up a rising chuckle then saw a hint of a black dress and white apron just like all the others, except this time it was Rosie who edged among the crowded vacationers. She paused in front of Oliver and Dexter, and though her smile was for them, it swept all the stuffiness from the room.

"And something for you gentlemen?" she said respectfully. As if they hadn't met before. As if she hadn't ducked under Oliver's arm and into their room yesterday.

"Thanks." Oliver leaned forward and studied the delicacies on the silver tray that she lowered. Then he whispered, "Your left or our left?"

Jonas grinned, and Rosie quickly turned the tray so that only one end was in reach.

The redheads each took a miniature quiche, and she plucked up chocolate straws and handed them over as well.

"You can thank me later," she said.

"We'll thank you now," Dexter answered.

Her eyes were bright, smile almost bashful as she stepped away. Dexter lifted his gaze to Jonas, and Jonas gave him the warning look that suggested he find a different girl to flirt with. Dexter chuckled and went back to his chess. Smiling himself, Jonas rose.

Since sitting there watching Rosie would do no one any good, he headed out of the crowded sunroom. Best to keep busy.

Down the hall, he saw that the billiards room was packed and thick with smoke, the latter of which could send his lungs into a fit, so he continued onward, heading toward the south exit. Out on the covered steps, Jonas watched the rain tap the manicured lawns. Beat and ripple the leaves of exotic hedges. Birds called to one another just overhead, where they were perched beneath the del's logo, staying dry.

At the edge of the platform, still beneath the overhang, a valet stood arguing with a delivery boy about a stack of crates that, according to the valet, should have been dropped off at the back entrance. On each wooden box was stamped PYROTECHNICS.

"I see what you're sayin'," the delivery boy countered. "But these is the fireworks for the Fourth, and it was this or nothin'." He motioned around the awning with a tattered cap, then toward the rain now finally lessening. "I had to get them off that wagon right quick when these skies unleashed. So you can help me move them inside, or we can stand here arguing about it some more in the damp air and all your rich folk can just skip their big display."

The valet glanced around as if all those rich folk had overheard that. Since it was just Jonas, he gave a friendly nod and left the safety of the porch. Head bowed, Jonas strode in the direction of the boathouse. The rain, just a drizzle now, dampened his coat, his hair. Angling toward the sea, he kept his sights on the building in the distance that mimicked the hotel itself. The square building with its white walls and red roof fed into the bay by a long length of dock, all alive with the motion of men battening down hatches on sailboats or securing oars inside dinghies and skiffs.

Half-soaked, Jonas stepped inside and headed for the wooden quad that sat on its rack on the far wall. Near that hung netting and buoys. Two rental canoes sat parallel to one another. Jonas freed himself from both damp coat and vest then rolled back shirtsleeves to elbows. He ran an oar-calloused hand along the side of the hull of the quad, feeling salt and brine against the wood. His father's boat, it had borne the man and his teammates thirty years ago at Harvard. Jonas felt a fool, but he had the grain of each and every board memorized, he'd spent so much time in their boathouse as a boy, sitting in this very vessel. Dreaming that he might be strong enough. . .

In the storage closet, he filled a bucket with water, soap, and a clean rag. He dipped and wrung then smeared the rag along the lower boards. While the narrow shape of the boat was what he was accustomed to, the thin racing shell was a challenge out on this sea. Larger boats with higher sides would endure waves easier, but this was light, and any added weight would make the long distance more demanding.

With tomorrow in mind, he tried to think of what would be safest for Rosie. Since the boys were getting accustomed to this boat, it was probably best to stick with it. The shell had borne them well so far, and he was grateful.

He worked steadily, enjoying the cool, shifting air of the boathouse and the quiet it afforded. A few seafarers came and went, some tipping a cap to him, and Jonas returned the comradery. Sun glinted through the windows—clouds parting. Though he wasn't finished, Jonas dropped the rag in the bucket. He strode toward the door, ducking around a rack of life vests, and out onto the deck where he leaned forward on the railing. The water glittered and rippled. Fish jumped. Jonas inhaled the cool air, savoring the way it calmed his lungs as only a sea breeze could do.

In the distance lay the peninsula that stretched out, forming the bay. He could scarcely make out the shape of the lighthouse that rose at its tip. He squinted, trying to spot Rosie's dock, but the bluffs were mostly a blur. Still, it wouldn't take them long to get to the spot Rosie wished. It sounded as if this lighthouse keeper of hers made that trip now and again. And with the sun now showing its face, Jonas had a mind to see if the fellas weren't up for an evening practice.

Just to the lighthouse dock and back should be manageable enough, but a practice trip wouldn't hurt. And he meant to find a smoother course from the far end of the bay where an inlet would allow them to disembark more safely with Rosie. Even get them to the lighthouse quicker and easier.

Then in a few days, they'd face a different course entirely. One that would force them to face the break. If they managed to conquer that, the journey around the lighthouse itself would lead them past jagged rocks and open seas, a trip that took adventure—and danger—to new heights. Assuming his map was correct, it was three times the distance of even the longest collegiate race. A feat that no one had ever tried before because there was really no point. There was nothing to be gained in this trip they had plotted out.

Nothing other than restoring a little faith within the hearts of four boys. Boys who had grown into men and decided to keep trying.

Glancing up the dock, Jonas spotted a carriage pulling up to the front of the boathouse. Striding toward it was a prominent-looking businessman. Mr. Babcock. Jonas hadn't seen the man since that fateful day five years ago. Having so much to thank him for, Jonas started that way. He nearly called out to him, but that seemed coarse, so he broke into a jog.

A flash of rope whipped in front of his face, and he slammed to a halt. To his right, a middle-aged man was struggling with sails, trying to unfurl the jib and having no luck. Several children were at his feet, calling him Papa and asking when they would be able to set sail as promised.

After glancing once more to Mr. Babcock, Jonas looked to the children's father.

Bent above the rolled canvas, the man glanced over his shoulder as he tugged on a line. "Let a pal borrow this last week, and now it's a mess. I told him to take care not to flog the sails and, well. . ."

Three little faces peered from their father to Jonas, looking hopeful.

Jonas turned to see Mr. Babcock being greeted by the chauffeur.

Maybe if he just worked fast. . .

"Can I lend you a hand?" Seeing that the aft end of the sail had been pulled free, Jonas lunged aboard and bent to help. "Sounds like he didn't furl the jib tight enough."

"That and a few other things." The man gave a weary chuckle.

Jonas worked his fingers along the length of sail, and when it was set back to rights, the man unfurled it. The winch cranked, and the children cheered.

Jonas stepped off the boat and back onto the dock. Still trying to hurry, he wished the children and their father a fair wind. Turning, he looked to where Mr. Babcock had been standing, but the carriage was already driving down the lane, growing smaller until it turned the corner and was gone.

Chapter Nine

With the air all around still stained black as ink, Rosie stood on the beach. Dawn was near, she could feel it, but her heart was still a tumble as she clutched a lantern, all alone save the lullaby of waves on sand. It wasn't until she heard the gentle rhythm of footsteps that she turned in the direction of the distant boathouse.

The light from the lantern struck the young men. Lined up from stem to stern, they bore their boat overhead, hands gripping the hull strong and steady. They wore not their sportsmen's clothes, but instead, slacks and buttoned shirts. A set of sleeves rolled back here or there.

Jonas was in the middle, expression both sober and alert, and when his eyes found her, she sensed why. It was the way he bid her to walk with them—explaining in short, soft breaths, that they were going to embark from the far end of the bay where an inlet sheltered the water from any kind of waves.

Rosie carried the lantern quietly along, and when they finally reached the end of the beach, Jonas lowered the boat in time with his teammates. He motioned her nearer, and his tanned forearm skimmed her skirt as he settled an oar into place. "Are you sure you want to do this?" He rose.

"Yes."

"Then you'll sit right here in the cox seat."

"Hey, we finally have a coxswain," Oliver said.

Rosie settled in, and Jonas helped tuck her skirts about her ankles.

"What's that?" she whispered.

"It's the person who calls out the commands. But all you need to do is hold on, all right?"

He peered down at her with a pinch of worry. She had a sense it was for her sake and not in their abilities. That brought a surprise level of comfort. Chilled, Rosie pulled her cloak tighter. "Shall I hold the lantern?"

"If you'd like, but the sun will be up in a few minutes so it won't be dark for long."

She handed him the lantern, and Jonas set it higher up on the beach, where it would await their return. The boat wobbled as the four young men shoved it a few feet closer to the water. She nearly asked if she should help, but he'd already had her sit, so surely this was where he wanted her.

Water splashed against the wooden shell, dampening her fingers, which clung to the edges of the long, narrow boat. Rosie pulled her hands into her lap. The young men stood talking for a few brief minutes, plotting their course toward the lighthouse, which was still lit. Ripples from the bay splashed against the bow, and three of them climbed in. Each faced backward, looking toward the shore, but it was she who beheld a blackened sea.

"Do not be afraid," Rosie whispered to herself—the plea like a tattered ship's flag, one that heralded both glory and danger. She was not in this water. Not drowning. She was safe and all was well. *Do not be afraid.* A cry of heart, she repeated it over and over as her hands set to trembling.

Dexter gave a final nudge then lunged aboard. The tall, lanky redhead sat nearest her and had given the boat just enough of a push to slip it out away from shore. Behind him sat Oliver, who she now knew as Jonas's cousin. Just behind him was Jonas and at the farthest end of the boat, the lad they called Oakes, roguish enough to already be known by name among the maids. But it was Jonas and he alone who stole Rosie's attention.

He spoke some kind of starting command. His oars, resting on the edges of the boat, turned ever so slightly.

Like a well-oiled machine, six other oars followed suit. A thrill pulsed through Rosie. Should she hold on? When Jonas called out, "Pull," the boat lurched forward, and she gripped the edge to steady herself.

However did they manage this? Still one moment, then speeding across the water the next. A small wave splashed the bow, and a few stray drops struck her, cooling her skin, which was flushed with anxiousness now that they skimmed toward the frothy, churning bay.

"Pull." Jonas's voice kept a smooth rhythm with the oars. "Pull."

Or maybe it was the other way around.

"Pull."

Oars angled forward.

Rosie sat as still as she could and braced herself when another fading wave—cushioned by this inlet—sloshed against the bow of the boat, lifting the creaking wood onto its arcing surface. Though not harsh, this vessel was slim and lean, sides so low that some of the water sputtered over the edge. Cold seawater misted her skirt in splotches, dampened her boots. Fear settling about her, Rosie slammed her eyes closed, and above sounds of wood and men and sea, she searched only for the cadence of Jonas's voice. Finding it, she clung to his gentle words. Clung to the way his commands were leading this crew out into the open, vast water. Though waves didn't crash here, they rolled in, gusty and sure, making their task a heavy-laden one.

Jonas fell silent, his words replaced by the heavy breathing of four men—a different kind of rhythm—but just as steady. Out here, just as comforting.

She probably should have kept her eyes closed past the waves, but suddenly, she was awash with the thrill of this—the power of a vessel on the sea. Something sparked in her heart—her memory.

Something that *loved* this.

Even as she opened her eyes, tears stung. Rosie grasped for the answer. The truth behind this sensation, but all she saw were those long, quiet corridors in her mind. A hush as if a secret lay waiting and if she searched hard enough, long enough, she would find it. It was a strange uncertainty, but one that felt as if it ended in hope.

Suddenly, Rosie realized that the faintest traces of dawn were lighting the sky behind her; she could see the blooming of sunrise on glistening oars as each rose as one, wet and dripping from the water before plunging below. In perfect, practiced time, the young men dipped wooden blades. Tugged with a grunt. Then tipping their oars flat, pulled them back again, only to twist wrists and dig paddles beneath the glittering surface. Sunrise danced along it all.

"So now," Dexter panted. The freckle-faced man tipped his head toward her. "A good..." His voice was lost to a gasp for breath. "Coxswain knows all..." He panted again. "The right cues."

Eyes wide, Rosie nodded.

"What you can do..." He grimaced at the pull. "Is tell us what a good job we're doing."

Despite the fact that he looked near exhaustion, a smile tipped up the side of Jonas's mouth.

"Or..." Dexter breathed through the words. "Tell us how we can..." He grunted as he tugged his oar back. "Improve."

"You're all doing wonderfully," Rosie said, wishing for words to express this feeling.

She caught Jonas's eyes over his teammate's shoulder. Jonas's gaze was on her, and so very focused. As if it was she and she alone who was empowering him to dig and pull and dig and pull. The look was so settled, so unabashed and unmoving, that she dipped her head, overwhelmed.

Awash with a yearning she had no right to feel.

Rosie closed her eyes and felt the force of the boat and the way it glided smoothly and quickly. A breeze moved gently past her face, stirring her hair, and for the first time in a long time, she felt free. Something warm puddled against her neck—rays of a rising sun. She had felt it soft at first, but now it was stronger, brighter. Her eyelids fluttered open, and the sun brightened their faces, their strong shoulders. The water glittered.

"Where is this dock?" Oakes called, sounding winded.

Jonas—his eyes still on Rosie—spoke evenly. "Do you see it?"

Rosie craned her neck. "Nearly there."

"Anything else?"

It was as if he was willing her to remember. To hold on to this seed of a memory and let it take root. Rosie set her mouth, tried to soften the soil of her mind and cling to the traces of thought she had the other night while watching this very bay.

It was right there. Lowering her hand, she let her fingertips trail into the water. Breathed in the sweet, salty brine of this bay.

It was right there.

The call of seagulls snagged her attention, and she looked upward. There, near the lighthouse, stood Mr. Graham. Her grandfather. He tossed a handful of crumbs out over the water, and seagulls swooped and dived to catch them. It was a glorious flash of white feathers and bird cries.

Realizing the boat was no longer gliding, Rosie looked to Jonas. His oars rested in an easy position, and the young men spoke to one another, gently turning the wooden shell toward the small dock that rested against the cliff base. Rosie shifted to peer past four sets of shoulders, and it was there that she spotted it. The weathered boards that made up the quaint dock from her childhood. Jonas and Dexter reached for it, pulling them all nearer.

She nearly stuck out her hand to graze the faded wood but was suddenly pierced with uncertainty. Fear.

Why was she afraid?

No one—including herself—had ever known how she'd gotten into the water.

And the wondering that quaked her was feeling like she'd wanted to be in the water. Had wanted to sink below the surface. That something had frightened her there. Someone else—a stranger she didn't know. The reason why she was found in the bay at dawn.

A little girl without breath in her lungs until one of the fisherman helped her along. Coaxing her back from heaven's gates and into the Coronado sunrise. So near death that her brain hadn't wanted to work right. Not only with the loss of so many memories and understandings, but also with the inability to use her right leg and her right hand—both of which had slowly recovered with great practice.

A new kind of tears stung her eyes, and the hand that she finally pressed to the boards of the dock was unsteady.

Dexter climbed out and knelt. Reaching out to her, he gripped her beneath the arm. His other hand held one side of her waist as she stood and stepped onto the wooden platform. Flashed through her mind was the sensation of wearing boots much smaller than the ones she wore now. The cliffs seeming higher, the world around her larger. Of hitting the water hard and fast and sharp and sinking deep.

And so much fear.

A shudder coursed through her, and still holding on, Dexter must have felt it, too, in the way he glanced down.

"Thank you," she said softly.

The memory vanished as quickly as it had come. Rosie stood several moments without speaking. Just glanced around, trying to pull it back—but—nothing. Nothing more.

Her gaze skimmed from the young men to the bluffs rising above them all, where sandy clay was the bed for thick, dry shrubs. Wildflowers bloomed, and dusty earth shifted wherever lizards darted about on the steep, rough slope. Narrow, weather-beaten steps spliced into the hillside, meandering upward as they rose toward the sky. Made of stone, they were crumbling in certain places, and even as Rosie clutched up the front of her skirts, she hesitated.

A hand was to the small of her back, and she knew it was Jonas before he spoke. Could feel it in the surety of his touch, the gentle placement of his hand. "Can you make it up those stairs okay?" He surveyed the bluffs, and though the climb was perhaps twice that as the one to the observatory, there was no railing.

"Hey, look at that." Oakes pointed to something at his feet. "It says Rosie." Oakes knelt and fingered worn letters that had surely been carved years ago. R–O–S–I–E. The young man regarded her, then his friends.

Rosie glanced to Jonas, who held her gaze. Pushing aside her cloak, she climbed the first stone step, then another and another. Each embedded into the sandy bluffs. Upward they all went, Jonas never less than a step behind her, his hands at her waist the few times she stumbled.

Above them the brightening sky churned with seagulls, the crumbs all gone. And it was there in the shade of the lighthouse that her heart stood waiting in an old black coat and sailor's hat.

Chapter Ten

Jonas didn't know when he'd taken hold of her hand, but it was near the top of the cliff.

The place where the steps were the steepest, the most crumbled. Where he'd edged around her to pull her up.

Rosie clambered up the two remaining stones then brushed dust from her skirt. Jonas stood beside her and glanced back to be sure that the others were all right. Oliver and Oakes were right behind, and having tied off the boat, Dexter followed a few paces lower.

Jonas thought to let go of Rosie's hand but she released his first—a shade of pink brightening her cheeks. With a look of composed determination, she glanced around the dusty, shrub-laden yard that surrounded the lighthouse before striding toward the old man with the basket of bread. Graham's gray-blue eyes were filled with the sober honor of welcoming the lost home. And those eyes were trained right on Rosie.

Dipping his head in greeting, Jonas walked onward. If his friends noticed the fact that they were but meters from being able to see down the other side of the bluffs—their goal—they didn't let on. They seemed too awed by what was right before them. So different than the del's refined landscape, this was broad and flat. Humble. Sunlight glowed off a gravel path, and dried shrubs quaked in the sea breeze, wildflowers lilting about on their stems. A weathered skiff with peeling gray and blue paint sat at the far end of the lot, and a lizard seemed rather fascinated by the polish on Dexter's boots.

The yard that spread from one end of the broad bluff would have seemed desolate if it weren't for the lighthouse. Little more than a square cottage that looked to be whitewashed a few years ago, it boasted a smattering of small, dark windows, and was the sturdy base for the cupola that rose from the roof. Rimmed with an iron railing, the glass panes were no longer aglow, for above that, a dim blue sky was feathered with the pink of early dawn.

Standing just outside the gate was the keeper of it all. His gray, wiry beard brushed the collar of his shirt, which peeked out from beneath a worn and weathered coat. His eyes were jolly and his cheeks lifted in a smile. "It's not every day that a fine vessel pulls up to my dock bearing precious cargo." Those smiling eyes glanced back to Rosie. "I'm mighty glad you lads got your sea legs under you."

Rosie introduced each of them.

"Good morning, Mr. Graham. A pleasure to meet you," Jonas said.

A friendly nod, then Abner glanced to Oakes, Dexter, and Oliver in turn. "How about some breakfast?"

He led them up the gravelly path, his steps slow so they kept their own the same. Rosie fell in stride with her grandfather, resting her head on his shoulder for a silent moment. At the door, Abner pushed inside, and they followed. The house smelled of pipe smoke and coffee—all softened by the salty breeze that whistled through an open window. Split up the middle by the stairwell that rose to the light tower, the right side of the house held a small kitchen and the left, a parlor. Filled with windows, the snug parlor was flooded with morning glow. A rocker sat in the corner, draped with a faded quilt. Seashells lined the fireplace mantel above flames that crackled and popped. A rolltop desk looked scattered with unfinished business. Ink drops splattered the floorboards just beneath.

While Jonas's friends filled that room, Jonas stepped into the available space of the kitchen. The pantry door hung open, showing a small barrel of potatoes and a crock of mounded butter.

Abner offered a round of coffee, and everyone accepted except for Rosie.

"A cup of tea for you?" Abner asked.

At her soft thank-you, he moved a copper kettle to the top of the stove, and she plucked cups from a nearby cupboard. Next she assembled a tray with cream, sugar, and spoons. Jonas joined his friends in the parlor, and Rosie followed. Soon after, Abner brought over the coffee percolator to where Rosie had lined up cups. Abner filled each one with dark brew, his granddaughter at his side. Each task looked so comfortable, so compatible between them that Oliver and Dexter settled onto the sofa as if this were their home as well. Oakes wandered around the small room and paused to study an old map that hung on one wall.

Rosie stepped back into the kitchen, and when she had been gone for several minutes, Jonas glanced that way to see her mixing what looked like headache powders into a glass of water. She drank it down then set about fetching a loaf of crusty bread from a crate that bore the hotel's name.

Still roving, Oakes peered up at the winding center staircase. "Could we go up and see the lantern?"

A sturdy, wrinkled hand motioned the way. "All you wish."

As if suddenly boys and not men, Oakes, Dexter, and Oliver started up the twisting stairwell, voices hushed with reverence and barely veiled excitement. Jonas smiled. Rosie did as well, and when she waved him up, he gripped the smooth, curved handrail, starting after his friends.

The staircase coiled around as though it were the inside of a seashell. Jonas slowed on the tiny landing that was barely enough for him to stand on where a door led into a bedroom that was clearly the old man's. In a nearby corner, a sleeping, purring cat lay curled up. Jonas slid his hand over its head and the feather duster of a tail curved against his leg. To their right stood a bedroom that looked like it belonged to a lady. Judging by the combs and hairbrushes, a fashionable one. Through the open doorway, he glimpsed the folds of the soft quilt, the blouses and skirts peeking from a narrow cupboard, and the sun hat that draped from the curtain rod. Lace and ribbons. . .and Rosie.

He could imagine her here, growing up wild and free. It suited her. No doubt shaped her into who she was.

Climbing to the top, Jonas edged around the giant lantern and out onto the exterior walkway that circled around the glass panes. Cool air whipped at his shirt, and he gripped the iron railing.

Oakes was just tipping his chin toward the breeze. "I feel like I should have been born a sea captain."

"Aww." Dexter draped an arm around his shoulder. "You can grow up to be anything you want, little Oaksey."

Oakes shoved him off, and Jonas chuckled. Leaning forward on the iron railing, Jonas closed his eyes and let the crisp wind hit his face. Could they really be anything they wanted to be? Because if he had his choice. . .

Someone moved next to him, and Jonas looked over to see Oliver. He assumed the same resting position and kept his gaze on the water as he spoke. "A wise cousin would say, 'I hope you know what you're doing, Jonas.'"

"But. . ."

"I suppose I'm not that wise cousin."

"What do you mean?"

When Oliver dipped his head, the sun whipped across his red hair, knocking the thick locks about. "I mean you and Rosie." Oliver rested elbows to rail and interlocked his fingers. "She's a maid at the hotel." He looked over at Jonas. "You do realize that's going to pose some problems?"

Jonas nearly nodded, but he checked it. "Nothing is going to cause any problems. I'm just her friend. Nothing more."

Oliver's half smile was kind. "But that's the issue. I don't think you're even supposed to be her friend." Oliver straightened and clapped Jonas on his shoulder. "Not saying that I blame you. I just want to make sure you realize what you're doing. You're not supposed to know her name. Or where she lives or sleeps. Details about her life. It just doesn't work that way between. . ." He fell silent, but Jonas knew what he meant.

Between the classes.

"But *you* know her name," Jonas countered. "And you know where she sleeps."

Oliver's half smile bloomed to a grin. "Yeah." He straightened and took a step back. "But she doesn't look at me the way she looks at you."

Jonas dropped his gaze to the bluffs below. He stayed that way until Abner called them down for a breakfast of fried eggs and sausages. The hot, buttery bread that Rosie toasted for them all. They ate quietly, filled with thanks for the hearty fare and the kind generosity. Though the headache powders that Rosie had taken seemed to ease the crease in her brow, she was still awfully quiet.

When they had finished and Rosie was soon due for her shift, they bid farewell to her grandfather and headed back down to the little dock. Then it was less than a half hour of rowing and the skiff was sloshing up to the sands at the far end of the beach of the Hotel del Coronado.

Rosie was quiet all the way across the bay. Even when Dexter helped her out and the four of them lifted the boat overhead to carry it back to the boathouse. Certain she had to be chilled through, Jonas urged her to not wait for them, but she walked quietly beside him, across the sand and toward the square, squat building with its red roof. Inside the boathouse, they placed the quad with care onto its rack then headed back out.

The lads striding a few steps ahead, Jonas and Rosie trailed behind. As they neared the hotel, he finally spoke. "Did you find what you were looking for?" He climbed the three steps to the south entrance then opened the door.

But Rosie was still on the sidewalk, peering up at him. "I'll. . ." She glanced to the grand double doors, one of which was ajar for her. "I'll need to go in the other way."

Yes.

He'd forgotten.

She took a small step back, and he tried to think of something to say, but then a gaggle of women exited the open door, thanking him. By the time they passed by, Rosie was already striding down the sidewalk. He went to call her name, but with patrons now milling about, some even glancing between them, Jonas just ducked his head and stepped inside.

Chapter Eleven

With a newspaper clutched under her arm, Rosie strode down the sidewalk, pondering the various shop signs of Coronado Island businesses. A bank and then a milliner. A flower shop. Cafés that tempted with their strong aroma of hot coffee and baked treats. Such simple sights to ponder, but compared to the memories that had risen inside her on the water, the inviting storefronts were much easier to wrap her mind around.

She'd spent many sleepless hours last night trying to catch more of the past, but there was nothing else she could grab hold of. Even as she let out another sigh, Rosie spotted a rack of books ahead. *Bookseller.* She slipped around the rack and ducked into the snug shop. Inside smelled of paper and geraniums, the latter of which lined the windowsills, letting off a sweet, musky scent against the sun-warmed glass.

Stepping behind a nearby partition of children's stories, Rosie glanced again to the article in her newspaper. The two-day-old paper not only stated today as the first date the book would be available for purchase, but it had also given her enough time to secure the afternoon off by swapping shifts with a fellow maid. Now Rosie had the rest of the day and evening to herself and was just moments from standing face-to-face with Dr. Brooke's very own medical journal. All his hard work and efforts.

She perused the shelves, checking first the medical section before returning empty handed to the front of the store. There she spotted the thick text on display next to the register. She plucked a copy off the stack, slipping it carefully around the sign that read LOCAL AUTHOR.

Rosie tapped a small bell, and a friendly salesclerk strode from the back of the store. He tallied her total while she dug about in her reticule. After stating the sum, the middle-aged gentleman wrapped the book in paper and string. Rosie tried not to think too much about the cost as she slid most of that month's earnings across the wooden counter. She'd promised to be the first in line, and she had meant it. And since she would see the doctor this very afternoon, she was eager to have her copy signed. Not only because it would make the book all the more special, but because she knew what it would mean to her friend.

The transaction finished, Rosie thanked the clerk, clutched her parcel close, and slipped out into the sunshine. She strolled back up Orange Avenue, glancing about at shops that boasted maps or treasures from the coast. Palms and cypress ran down the center of the road in geometric perfection—illustrating the very spirit of this resort town that meant to please and awe its guests by drawing the eye to nature's beauty. Multilevel townhomes had their windows flung open to the breeze, and in yards, neatly trimmed hedges boasted exotic flowers. Rosie paused to smell a bud, and then another, making much out of her walk back to the hotel, so rare was a day off.

When she reached Ocean Boulevard, she crossed the street and followed the train tracks toward the south entrance of the hotel. Farther down the length of the resort, she slipped into the servants' entrance then climbed the stairs toward the fifth-floor attic, where her room was set on the far end of the hallway. The one she shared with two other maids, Jolene and Mary Anne.

Rosie let herself in and crossed to her narrow bed, where she sat and unlaced her shoes. After pulling her feet up, she leaned against the wall and tore into her new treasure. The book was thick, the heavy pages new and perfect. Rosie flipped through them and lowered her head to take in the comforting scent of freshly dried ink.

Returning to the beginning of the text, she read carefully and soon passed an hour as she read the introduction that Dr. Brooke had crafted. While some of the language and terminology was difficult to understand, Rosie could practically hear his voice. She smiled as she turned another page.

An opening paragraph caught her eye, and Rosie tilted her head to the side, reading further:

> In several of my studies, I have witnessed cases of memory loss due to brain hypoxia. Two cases were brought on by cardiac arrest, while the third was a lack of oxygen which resulted from a near drowning. It is the latter of these patients, one I have observed for nearly a decade at the writing of this text, who will be discussed in this section.

Rosie blinked across the room. That's about how long she'd known the doctor. Dropping her gaze, she continued reading:

> One of the factors that makes this case so unique is that, in addition to memory loss, the patient has also exhibited behavior that in some mannerisms would be considered childlike.

A little twinge tingled in her cheeks at the phrase, but it was nothing other than the truth she'd already known:

> *My initial conclusion was that this was merely a delay in development. The characteristics of innocence, confusion, wonder, and at times lack of propriety, however, despite repeated explanation and careful practice, has had occasion to continue into adulthood.*

The twinge turning to a flush, Rosie nearly closed the book, but the next line drew her attention back to the page:

> *The cause for this behavior is at no fault of the patient's but solely resulting from oxygen deprivation which occurred at the young age of ten, at which time the symptoms also affected the use of several limbs, not uncommon. While physical improvement has been shown to a high degree, several years of studying the patient has drawn the conclusion that the other elements of brain damage, thus far, have been irreversible. The following chapter will dissect these findings.*

Irreversible.

Brain damage.

That meant broken and there was no fixing it.

Lifting her gaze once more, Rosie caught sight of her reflection in the mirror. A pale face, wide blue eyes. *Childlike. Despite repeated explanation.*

She closed the book and set it aside, wishing very much to rise and leave this room, which was getting stuffier by the minute, but she couldn't bring herself to move. So she sat ever so still, memorizing the lines of the wood paneling beside her bed, repeating Dr. Brooke's words in her mind.

Small was the comfort that no one who read his text would know her identity. But even that tiny spark of relief was trampled down by the realization that she wasn't going to get better. She wasn't going to become the kind of young woman she wished to be. The kind that Dr. Brooke had made her *believe* she could be.

Irreversible.

The word churned her gut, souring every piece of hope she had.

The door burst open. "Rosie! There you are." Her roommate Jolene peeked around the door. "Your doctor friend is downstairs waiting. Mrs. Kline sent me up to fetch you."

"Coming." The word felt rushed and stiff as Rosie reached for her shoes. She slipped her feet in, tied up the laces. Looking to the book, she hesitated briefly then took it up and headed out. Down the hall she walked, not nearly as hurried as she might have been an hour earlier. When she reached the storage room, Rosie let herself in past the open door.

Dr. Brooke was just setting his medical bag on the pool table. "I came bearing gifts," he said. After opening the bag's clasp, he pulled out a small wrapped parcel and set it on the edge of the felt-covered table. His smiling face turned toward her, gaze falling quickly to the book she held in her hand, and his eyebrows lifted in surprise. "That's only just arrived in town."

She set it down slowly. "I was awful eager to get one."

His smile was full of pleasant surprise. "I'm honored by that."

She pushed herself up to sit on the pool table then crossed her ankles. It was with unsteady hands that she opened the cover and flipped to the pages she'd been reading. Rosie set the book down between them, not saying a word. Dr. Brooke looked to the text, skimming briefly, before lifting his gaze to her face.

All surprise—all manner of joy—gone. In its place was unveiled worry. "Rosie."

"This is true?"

"I mean only to write the truth."

"And this is how you think of me?" She motioned over the page before returning her hand to her lap.

"I think of you as remarkable. Because that's what you are."

She quoted him directly, and as the words he'd written about her fell between them, she felt anything but remarkable.

"This is nothing but what you've already known. I've shown you my notes. You've always been free to read through them at will."

Yes, and she'd done that multiple times.

He tugged out his leather-bound notebook, flipping toward the middle. "It's all right here," he said.

But his writing was nearly impossible to decipher. She said as much. "You write in riddles. In codes."

He squinted down at it as if trying to see it as she might. "This," he said, pointing to a section of the text he'd read, "is here. And this"—he pointed to another segment—"is here." He compared the two editions—his notes and his publication. Trying to show her they were very much the same.

Rosie glimpsed it all, trying to grasp the clarity, but it was lost to her. She covered her face with her hand, letting out an exasperated sigh. Perhaps this was what he meant by her being like a child. And here she had been thinking of herself as a grown woman. One perhaps worth the love of a young law student whose face she couldn't erase from her mind. What a fool she'd been. "I thought you were my friend. You made me believe I could trust you."

"You *can* trust me."

"You haven't been honest with me. . . ."

Dr. Brooke blinked at her slowly then shook his head. "Rosie."

"Stop calling me that."

"What would you like me to call you?"

For a single, fierce moment, she tried to conjure the name of the little girl standing on the Grahams' doorstep. Just two years old. Unwanted. But all she could see in her mind was a small lifetime spent with Abner and Esther. Bread crumbs floating down from the sky and flashes of white wings. The rush of the sea. Stories of ships and selkies at bedtime. Jonas's smiling face as he strode with her at sunrise.

Heart aching, Rosie pushed the doctor's gift aside, not wanting it. "I think we're done now," she said softly.

Dr. Brooke looked at her a quiet moment then gave a slow nod. He reached into his satchel and pulled out a small paper rectangle. His name and address were embossed on the front. Taking up the book that still lay between them, he licked his thumb and flipped forward two pages; then he eased the business card into the crease and closed the book.

He set it beside her and tapped the cover softly with the tips of his fingers. "If you should change your mind." Without another word, he slipped on his hat and left.

Chapter Twelve

From the Crown Restaurant came the gentle clatter of silverware and fine china. Waiters bustled about, and men wearing dinner tails leaned back in wicker chairs, sipping scotch and whiskey. Ladies fluttered fans, stirring the feathers in their hats. Jewelry graced ears and necklines, glinting in the electric lighting of the overhead chandeliers. Rosie glimpsed it all through the broad windows as she strode across the outside deck. At the stairs that led toward the beach, she shifted her gaze to the final, darkening threads of sunset.

She headed out toward the water, still feeling the gratitude of this evening all to herself. With the bronze bottle in hand, she carried it until she'd reached a place of solitude. There she settled down on the sand and placed the bottle beside her. She'd come here to toss it back to sea, but to hold on to it for a few moments more. . .

To remember him. That morning she first saw his face. Heard his voice. Saw the way the sun had glowed on his shoulders even as water dripped from his hair. And she in her haste had been pesky. So. . .childlike.

A tight throbbing in her chest, she pulled her feet in and gripped her ankles. Moonlight shone on the dark water, setting a glowing path. The froth glittered, and she could just barely make out the dips and rises of beach that led to the water's edge.

How many vacationers filled this spot during the day? How many dozens of blankets and chairs? Striped umbrellas? Children fashioning sand castles and collecting shells? Vacationers wading into the salty water to seek remedy from chronic ailments or to simply splash and play? Such silly wonderings—but they were easy. A safe trail of musings and her heart couldn't wander elsewhere just now. Yet the peace of such simplicity snapped at the sound of someone approaching. Rosie glanced behind her.

Jonas.

Her mouth parted. "What are you doing here? You're supposed to be attending the concert."

He settled down, his arm brushing hers. "I'm on holiday so I'm pretty sure my itinerary is wide open." He smiled; then his attention fell to the bottle. "May I?"

Rosie handed it over. Jonas tipped it upside down and ran his thumb along the base. Then he righted the vessel and studied the thick round of cork jammed into place.

"Have you opened it yet?" he asked.

"No."

"Would you like to?"

Rosie shook her head.

With a finger, he traced over the curves of the letters *S–P–E–R–O*.

"What does it mean?" she asked, sounding more teary than she wished.

Jonas eased the pad of his thumb over the etching. He looked to her, holding her gaze as he spoke. "It's Latin. It means 'hope.'"

Her mouth silently formed the word—*hope*. Then she glanced down at the carved word that looked centuries old. "How do you know?"

"I had to study a lot of Latin and Greek for university." He wet his lips then spoke a phrase she didn't understand.

She tried to repeat it. "Dum Spero. . .what?"

"Dum Spiro Spero. While I breathe, I hope."

The breeze stirred her hair, and Rosie clutched her arms about her waist, trying to block the night's deepening chill. "Do you have hope, Jonas?"

He seemed to notice that she was cold. He moved forward, settling in front of her, blocking the breeze some. She had a perfect view of his profile this way. A perfect view of his face as he tilted it down and said that he was trying to.

"What do you mean?"

He wet his lips again and smiled softly. Then he peered over at her. "This is going to sound really stupid."

"My standards are very low right now."

After a soft chuckle, he gave her another glance. "Haystacks."

"What?"

"Hope."

"You hope in haystacks?" It slipped out drier than she'd meant and he chuckled again.

"I thought you had low standards."

She rolled her hand forward. "Keep explaining. . . ."

Smirking, he angled to face her better and seemed to ponder what he wanted to say. "I'm thinking of that phrase. . .when you can't find something, how it's like looking for a needle in a haystack."

She nodded slowly.

"For each of us, our problems seem really big. But in reality, we're all just a needle in a haystack."

Rosie squinted at him.

"My problems and worries feel rather large. As do yours. As do the next person's.

We're each a needle, but really we're surrounded by a lot of straw."

"I thought it was hay."

"Close enough." He grinned. "We can spend a lot of time and energy worrying about our tiny sliver of the world. But if we look around ourselves, think beyond our fears and worries. . ."

"We're not alone," she whispered.

"Exactly." He pursed his lips, looking regretful. "I confess this isn't something I've been thinking about until you prompted me to look outside myself." He motioned up the beach where they had walked, hunting treasures together.

"You told me the other day that I would be in your prayers. Rosie, you've been in mine. And that's not something that comes easy."

Humbled, overwhelmed, she simply looked at him. He smiled softly, and she could see his depth of gratitude. She'd prompted him to think that way? She swallowed hard, awash by that. Then she sifted over his words again, his metaphor.

Everyone hurt in their own way.

She peered at Jonas, wondering what his hurts were. Wondering what he wasn't saying. What he'd been sparing her. He'd heard much of her story, but had she asked much of his? He always seemed so brave and so strong, but she feared that something more tender, more acute was resting just below the surface.

When he glanced back out to sea, his voice blended with the murmuring tide. "We all want hope to hold on to."

Bottle still in hand, he held it out to her, a needle in the haystack just as they were. Rosie held the bottle up to the moonlight, wondering how many people had touched it, held it. Growing was the desire to cast it out and pray it found a heart in need of comfort.

Dr. Brooke's face flashed through her mind, and Rosie swallowed hard. She thought on his expression when he'd spoken to her. The tender way he'd always been with her. His offer to help. To be her friend.

To be hope.

Rosie's throat thickened, but then Jonas was smoothing the back of his hand over her own. The lighting of the great lantern on the point could not have felt any brighter than that touch. Rosie's breath caught. He turned his wrist and covered her hand with his own. She thought of the way he gripped the oars as those calluses pressed a warm, perfect comfort against her skin.

When she looked up to his face, he was watching her mouth.

Before she could make sense of that, he was leaning closer.

"It would be best if you didn't kiss me," she whispered. Was that the right way to say it? She didn't know how to do this—let alone how to walk away from all the yearning she had for Jonas.

His voice was just as low. "Why is that?" He slid a hand behind her neck, and his bottom lip nearly brushed her own while flashing through her mind were pages upon pages of Dr. Brooke's notes on her. The codes and riddles that all amounted to the same thing. She was daft.

Rosie lifted her chin slightly and turned her head. The hint of Jonas's kiss fell away.

Embarrassment tinted the air between them as he straightened and cleared his throat. Feeling wretched, Rosie went to stand. She couldn't look at him as she did.

"I thank you for your kindness, Mr. McIntosh, but. . ." Swelling tears thickened her throat, and she took a step away, not bothering to fetch the bottle that sat beside him. "If you'll excuse me." Vision already blurring, she started off, leaving both her heart and hope sitting in the sand.

Chapter Thirteen

Jonas finished lifting the quad onto its rack with his teammates. One of his oars slipped out of place, and he shoved it back into the rowlock. He shoved another in as well, and Oakes stopped stretching his arms from side to side to slant a sharp look.

"Easy, Jonas."

Jonas reached for a dry rag and wiped the bow of the boat.

"Why are you acting like that was my fault?" Oakes asked.

"I'm not acting like it was anyone's fault."

"A wad of Benjamins nearly sinking to the bottom of the bay? I'd be upset, too," Dexter said, reaching for a rag all his own. "Still can't believe we almost sank."

Oliver leaned against a nearby windowsill, observing them all.

Oakes flung a hand toward Jonas. "Well if we almost sank it's because—"

Fresh light split the boathouse, and a sturdy figure entered. They all fell quiet. Jonas went back to drying the quad, assuming the visitor another seaman looking for gear.

But the man strode nearer, pulled off an old sailor's hat. At least seventy, his stance was uneven, but steady. Abner Graham. "I saw you boys turn back."

Frustrations mounting afresh, Jonas wiped two more boards then draped the rag over the frame.

Clad in shades of faded brown and black, Abner adjusted his stance, settling his weight on what seemed his better leg. "Didn't get very far this morning."

"Not exactly," came Oliver's easy reply.

"Had some troubles with the water," Dexter said.

"And our leadership," Oakes grumbled.

Jonas ducked his head—not contesting that. Rubbing fingers and thumb against his forehead, he tried to wipe the memory of Rosie and the night before from his mind.

With amusement in his wrinkled face, Abner glanced among them. "Came in early to have breakfast with my granddaughter. And now that I'm here, I think I might show you all a thing or two before I head back."

Jonas glanced to his teammates.

But Abner was looking only at him. "How about a little trip across the bay." He pointed the way he'd come. "And I mean in my boat."

"That old dinghy?" Oakes quipped.

The man smirked. "That *old dinghy* has traveled those waters more times than this little beauty." He smoothed a hand along the four-man scull, his gray eyes lit with clear admiration for its craftsmanship despite his jest.

"The water's too choppy today," Jonas countered.

Abner nudged one of the seats forward on its metal tracks then pushed it back to a resting position. He seemed to have never seen a racing shell. "You afraid of a little chop?"

Chop, wakes, and everything in between. It didn't take much to capsize a scull. This angry, churning sea was not going to think twice about dragging something under. "Do you see those waves?" Jonas motioned toward the window. "We'd never get past the break."

Abner stepped out and Jonas followed. All the way onto the dock where Jonas looked around for Abner's rowboat. The two-man dinghy with splintered wood and old fishermen's nets in the bottom. But he didn't see it. All he saw was a larger vessel resting in the sand. One with gray and blue peeling paint. The name *ESTHER* still legible on the bow, looking freshly touched up.

"Is this a skiff?" Oliver asked, circling around the boat that had to be more than twenty feet in length.

Abner answered with clear pride in his voice. "Fourern, 1837. Clinker constructed—fashioned after the ships of old. . .from Norway."

"Norway?" Oakes asked.

"Means it's got lines like a Viking ship," Jonas said.

Abner nodded, looking pleased.

Jonas strode around a long length of sweep-oar. The skiff boasted four of them—two starboard, two port. One to a man.

Jaw open, Dexter stepped closer. "Vikings."

Lifting his cap, Abner adjusted it. "Been out in force-six winds. Four-foot waves. She'll handle what you're looking to do out there."

Crouching, Jonas touched the peeling paint. Saw the stories living in the grain of the exposed boards.

"I suggest you get yourselves on in, young men." Abner strode around to the cox seat and spoke without looking up. "Or are you still afraid of the break?" He glanced toward the frothy waves then to each of them in turn, finishing with Jonas. He smiled, and his expression sparked with adventure. "That was always Rosie's favorite part."

Rosie turned on the electric lights of her room—the act still a novelty for a girl who grew up in a tiny cottage on the cliffs. Having finished her morning rounds in record time, she'd stolen up here for a few minutes before the staff meeting that was set for ten. There was something on her mind and heart that she couldn't shake. Well, two things.

First, the way Jonas had nearly kissed her last night and how she'd nearly let him. What was he thinking? He and her. . . It could never work.

Still, she fought a twinge of remorse. A wish that she'd simply let him kiss her. Though society deemed otherwise, both of them were free to place their hearts where they wished. Regret coiled in her middle, and, overwhelmed with what to do on that matter, she switched her attentions to the second reason she'd come upstairs.

Settling on the bed, she pulled Dr. Brooke's book into her lap. Studied the dark brown cover. Ran a fingertip over the embossed title then to the spine that bore his name. She eyed the business card that peeked out from the center—right where he'd tucked it.

With the slip of a finger, she opened the book to that spot and studied the small rectangle of card stock before setting it aside. She peered down at the open pages, and while a few words stood out to her, she meant not to read any. Yet something caught her eye. "While the brain is a fragile organ, the mind itself is a resilient part of the human makeup."

Resilient. Rosie squinted at the text and read on:

> *I have found in this particular patient that, despite hurdles and handicaps, she maintains a depth of character that is both captivating and caring. That though certain understandings may be lost permanently, they've appeared a hindrance of inconsequential amount when weighed in the balance of the scope of desired traits.*
>
> *All functions which would be deemed important to the quality of life and the fruits of the spirit are there in the fullest capacity. This patient's manner of being has been a continual striving within the very tenacity that supports life. In conclusion, it has been my finding to offer this study in support that we are both body and soul. And that united, they will triumph. It's my privilege to declare that I am changed as both a professional and a person for having witnessed this.*

The chapter went on to list footnotes for his studies, but Rosie couldn't read a thing, so blurry was her vision. She swiped at her eyes, blotting tears with the edge of a sleeve.

She pulled nearer the small, wrapped gift the doctor had brought her, and peeling back the paper revealed a box that also needed opening. First she discovered a voucher for passage to the mainland. Below that was a wooden carving. A small, roughly carved boat with two spindly oars. *Oh, Dr. Brooke.* He'd been trying to help her remember what she'd lost. A love she'd once had. Sniffing and swiping more tears, Rosie pulled his book closer and began to read. This time in full.

Exhausted from their afternoon of rowing amid the relentless break, Jonas and his friends made slow work of climbing the stairs from the resort courtyard to the third-floor landing. But when they finally made it into room 3323, they each settled in their respective spots.

"Well?" Oakes asked solemnly from the edge of one of the beds.

The cot Jonas was sitting on creaked when he shifted, and despite the fact that every part of him hurt, he allowed himself a small smile.

Dexter full on grinned. "Graham knows that bay."

Agreeing, Jonas glanced out the window. Abner knew the way the water swelled. He seemed to know when and how the boat would crash over the waves. Every eddy and shift in the current. The lighthouse keeper knew the rocks of the bluffs and the way the tide moved at different times of the day.

"So what does this mean?" Oliver asked. "What do we do?"

"We're going to make it around that point tomorrow," Dexter answered.

Jonas nodded, and he could see it in their faces. All lit up like they were fourteen years old again. But instead of scheming beneath a canvas tent with a lantern burning brightly between them, they were here in this hotel, both their past and their future crashing on the shore just beyond.

"I think we'll make it, too," Oliver said with a grin.

"But first we're going to need that bigger boat," Oakes added.

Jonas smiled—hope rising inside him. "And then we're going to need our new coxswain."

Chapter Fourteen

The line in the ferry house wasn't long, and as Rosie waited, she smoothed the front of her powder-blue blouse. Her gray skirt shifted soundlessly as she stepped forward for her turn, and her boot heels clicked to a standstill in front of the ticket window. She presented the voucher that Dr. Brooke had given her. The one that would provide passage for the twenty-five-cent round trip across the bay to and from San Diego. A kindness he so graciously extended despite her doubts. Her unkindness.

Finished, Rosie walked toward the windows and peered out over the water. Though dubbed an island, Coronado was in actuality a peninsula. A great many bays carved out its long, narrow shape that ran as a strip from north to south. The largest of those bays unfolded westward—where Jonas kept his dreams and where it drained out into the Pacific. A much smaller bay sat south of the hotel where boats harbored and Jonas and his friends had practiced. The body of water that spread eastward was what Rosie peered upon now. This was where the ferry scuttled passengers to and from the mainland of California. Even from this distance, Rosie could make out the shapes that made up the bustling city where Dr. Brooke worked and lived.

She'd waited but fifteen minutes when the ferry arrived and then watched with other passengers as buggies and horses were unloaded from the hundred-foot-long steam yacht aptly named the *Coronado*. Red, white, and blue bunting trimmed the banisters in celebration of this Fourth of July, and Rosie had no doubt the ferry would hold many people tonight wanting a water's view of the del's fireworks display. But for now, passengers filed aboard, and excitement buzzed in the air, particularly among the children. Little girls clutched ribboned hats to their heads, while boys scurried off to watch the embarking from the front deck.

As the paddles churned the water, driving the yacht toward the mainland, Rosie found a bench to settle on below deck. Beside her sat a gentleman. He had a shock of white hair, a hat resting upon his knee, and a magazine open in his lap. Rosie tucked her reticule against the folds of her skirt and clasped her gloved hands. She fiddled idly with the white lace, nerves tumbling as she thought over what she might say to the doctor.

The man next to her gave a soft chuckle. When he chuckled again, Rosie shifted a glance his way. "I think I might need to get one of those magazines."

He smirked, sending one side of his mustache upward. "It says here that the *S* in Ulysses S. Grant doesn't really stand for anything at all. But that at one point, he asked his future wife to pick a name to go with the initial since he didn't know what it stood for."

Rosie smiled. "This Mr. Grant, he is a friend of yours?"

The man's brows lifted. "He was. . .the. . .eighteenth president of the United States."

"Oh." Cheeks warming, she slid her gaze away, and when the man went back to his reading, she freed her notebook. She jotted that down, and a sideways glance verified her spelling correct.

The ferry ride was pleasant, and despite her embarrassment over the blunder— or maybe even because of it—the man beside her made friendly talk. When they reached San Diego, Rosie strode up the gangway with the rest of the passengers. With the business card in hand that bore Dr. Brooke's address, she followed the notes of streets and turns that she'd written down on her pad of paper. The sun was high overhead when she finally reached the four-story townhome. A brass plaque near the door read, INLAND INSTITUTE OF PSYCHOLOGY, HEROLD P. BROOKE, M.D.

Rosie drew a slow, steadying breath and let herself in. A small waiting room was cool and quiet. On one end of the room, three chairs were arranged near a window and, opposite those, a small desk. No one was in attendance, so Rosie gently tapped the bell on the desk's corner. Voices came from above, and she wondered how many patients filled the rooms.

Footsteps sounded down the dim hallway; then a woman of perhaps forty or so appeared. She took Rosie's name, assuring her that the wait would be only a few minutes. Rosie sat beneath the window and was just rehearsing what she might say when the receptionist returned, the doctor close on her heels.

He slid on his hat as he stepped forward. "I was just thinking it time for a break. Care to join me?"

Rosie stood.

He smiled at her, holding the door open as he did.

They strode back down the steps and onto the sunny sidewalk. After walking quietly for a length of several businesses, he paused at a small cart where a young man was scooping ice cream into a cone. The vendor handed the treat to a customer, and Dr. Brooke stepped forward. He requested pistachio and then glanced to Rosie. Realizing he meant her to choose a flavor, she eyed the canisters that filled the creamery cart. Rosie pointed to one that looked much like cherry and, when she took her first taste, was awful glad she'd chosen it. The vendor wished them a happy Fourth, and they returned the sentiment.

Dr. Brooke motioned for them to walk on as they ate their confection in companionable silence.

After a minute, Rosie slowed. "Why are you being so nice to me?"

"Because you're my friend."

"I don't think I make a very good friend."

"Certainly you do. Though I take it you haven't come for me to sign your book."

The back of her throat smarted. "In actuality that is one of the reasons I came." She pulled the text from her bag, along with a fountain pen.

His brows lifted in surprise, and when she insisted, he tucked the textbook under his arm and pocketed the pen. "Perhaps I should do away with this first." He took an oversized bite of his ice cream, and Rosie laughed softly.

"I'm in no hurry," she said.

They stood in the shade of a eucalyptus that rose to a massive height. Silvery-green leaves fluttered overhead. Below, the sidewalk was littered with those same leaves dried to a crisp shade of pink. Across the road, patriotic festivities were in full swing at a park. When Dr. Brooke motioned for them to keep walking, Rosie did, taking another taste of her ice cream.

He was quiet beside her for several paces. "Do you have a good life, Rosie?"

She peered down, then all around—giving herself time to truly search her heart. Finally she nodded. "I do have a good life." She got to live and work in a wonderful place. And she had Abner. For a good many years, she had Esther as well. Rosie did her best to explain that to the doctor. "Two people who loved me as if I were their own. I felt it every day and still do."

"Do you know the reason you were on their doorstep as a toddler?"

"I have my theories."

Dr. Brooke's expression was kind. "Certainly." His forgotten cone dripped. "And do you know of the reason that you were in the water the day you were rescued?"

Slowly, Rosie shook her head. "No. At least not precisely. But perhaps the two are connected. I think I was trying to get away from someone. But who—I don't know." Someone who had come to take her back? Wanting her after all? She didn't remember love or safety with whoever it was. Only fear and danger. She could only now recall being put into a boat in the night, then stroke upon stroke later, hitting the water hard and fast and sinking out of sight. Holding her breath. Swimming as far as she could. . .

Then blackness. Everything blank. Memories wiped clean away. Some of her limbs crippling.

Much of it now slowly, slowly being restored. But some—lost forever. They both knew it to be true. Because however long she'd stayed under, it had been more than her little mind had been able to handle without air.

The doctor paused and faced her, causing Rosie to halt. "Are you ready to be all right with that?" he asked. "To let the past be the past and, if God wills it to return to you in whole, to face it with a heart of courage? And in the meantime, to rest in knowing that there are many who love you and who are here to walk with you through any storm that may come."

Her eyes stung, and she nodded again. "Yes." The single word came out teary.

"And that you are worth a great deal, Rosie." Dr. Brooke smiled, and she could see how much he meant it.

She smiled back, feeling the joy of those words rise inside her.

"What do you think about letting go of the shadows?" he asked.

She pondered that, and it felt like freedom. "I like that idea." She thought of the lighthouse. Of the beaches she now combed looking for reminders of not being alone. She thought of Jonas's face and of the sunrise, and she knew what she needed to do. She looped her hand through the crook of the doctor's elbow when he offered it. "I like that very much indeed."

Chapter Fifteen

S un's about down. You coming out to see the fireworks?"

At his cousin's voice in the doorway, Jonas peered up from lacing a shoe. "I guess so. You?"

Oliver leaned against the jamb. "Yeah. The boys are saving us a spot in the gazebo. I told them I'd come find you."

Still needing another shoe and suspenders, Jonas nodded. "I'll be down."

Oliver patted a hand on the door frame. "See you."

He was gone, and Jonas tugged on his other shoe. He made quick work of the laces then dug through the wardrobe. He pulled out a pair of gray suspenders then clipped them to the waist of his pants. After sliding the suspenders onto his shoulders, he grabbed a waistcoat and pushed the three buttons into place. Finished, he checked his appearance in the mirror and shoved his hair into place with his fingertips. Never one for hats, he stepped out and into the sunroom.

Other vacationers already filled the area where the crack and pop of fireworks would be muffled by the glass and where night's chill would be softened. Jonas strode toward the exit, his eyes lifting to the evening sky.

"I bet she's gone mad," a woman said, her nose so close to one of the windows that it left a mark.

Then another woman spoke. "They say she's been out there for over an hour now and won't be coaxed from the water. She'll be fired, that one. Or frozen come morning."

Something in Jonas caused him to pause his mission toward the exit. He strode to the windows and peered down. With the sun now vanished, the dusky purple air was a haze he had to squint against. Below, crowds were clustered about, some on boats, some on blankets, all awaiting the Fourth of July spectacle to come. But a crowd of a different kind had gathered on the north side of the resort's beach, all watching the water. Many pointing, others chattering. Jonas squinted and peered past them to the sea. There in the crash stood a young woman with a mass of wild, white-blond curls. Rosie.

He didn't stop to think. Didn't pause to contemplate what this meant for her, or what it would mean for him, he was simply jogging toward the stairwell, down, and through the courtyard where he burst past the exit that freed him from the hotel. He was halfway across the sand before he realized he'd yanked his shoes off. He wove through the onlookers then was striding into the darkening water sloshing up to his knees.

The crowds murmurs rose, and he ignored them—his sights only on the young woman who stood up to her hips in the water. The skirt she wore was drenched, and her pale blue blouse soaked so that it clung to the shape of her corset. Jonas didn't call out to her. She spotted him and turned back toward the sea. He reached her, and still he didn't speak. Just wrapped a hand around her waist and angled his body so that the next wave crashed into it as a shield. Her hip braced against his, and he could feel her trembling.

She peered up at him with tear-filled eyes. Not of grieving, but of something different. "Everyone can see you, Jonas. You're going to get in trouble."

He shook his head. He was in trouble the moment she tugged that bottle from his grasp and he saw her face—knew her spirit. And it was a kind of trouble that he never wanted to break free of. So he gripped her other arm gently and dipped his face closer to hers, asking, "What can I do?"

A wash of emotions filtered through her expression, from gratitude to grief. It was the latter that lingered, her chin beginning to tremble. She peered longingly out to the sea, and he thought perhaps she meant to swim to kingdom come, but she just dipped her face and pressed her forehead against his chest.

"I'm letting it go," she whispered.

He lowered the side of his face into her wild curls and closed his eyes against the sensation. Her nearness and trust. All the tenderness she was feeling, be it sorrow or freedom. It seemed a blend of both. He wanted to ask what it was that she was letting go of, but he stayed quiet and simply wrapped an arm around her. He didn't dare glance at the crowd on the shore. Not for fear of their reaction, but because he really didn't care. Several stars were appearing in the sky, and he whispered words that he hoped would coax her toward shore, toward warmth. The tide was coming in. He could practically feel the water growing deeper around them. It was up to his own waist now.

A new wave crashed against them, trailed closely by another. Jonas braced her and she him.

The water retreated, the sea drawing in its breath for the next blow that he could already see coming. The air was crisp. He could feel her chill right through his shirt that was now as wet as she. "We need to get you warmed up," he said softly. Though night had settled, the hotel was lit up with a thousand bulbs, making it easy to see everything from the shoreline to her face.

"I'll. . .I'll be along." She glanced around. "But I—" Her eyes landed on something in the water and her expression turned puzzled. "It came back."

He glanced down to see the bronze bottle bobbing beside her.

"They're not supposed to come back when you throw them out to sea."

Jonas smiled, loving everything about her. "I think it's how the tide's moving just now."

"Oh."

He fetched it and was about to offer tossing it out again when a flash of color popped overhead. Bright red. Then blue, followed by shades of yellows and greens. At the burst of fireworks, the crowd let out a collective gasp, and every eye turned toward the sky. Jonas just watched Rosie. Watched the way the color tinted her pale skin—flashing it the same shifting colors as the water's surface with every pop and fizzle. Mouth parting, she glanced upward, toward the spectacle, and she looked peaceful.

"Did you ever look inside? The bottle, that is."

Her gaze shifted back to his face, and she nodded.

"May I ask what was in it?"

"There wasn't anything."

"Nothing?"

She shook her head, and he could tell she wasn't a bit disappointed. Because sometimes the good news was right there to be seen all along. It wasn't always etched in bronze, but it was as real and tangible as five curving letters. Ones that had traveled across lands and lifetimes to deliver the smallest—most profound of messages: hope.

A wave shoved him closer to her, and though she still looked chilled, her expression was so earnest, he dared not broach the notion again of getting her to shore. Instead, he thought of the night before and the words he wished to say to her. "Rosie, I'm sorry about last night—"

"No, please." She bumped against his chest when water pushed her into him. "*I'm* sorry," she whispered, struggling to right her footing.

Holding her arm, he helped steady her.

"Would you. . .would you be willing to try again?" she asked. "That is, if you haven't changed your mind."

She wanted him to. . .what?

"Rosie." He stepped closer, gently taking hold of her other arm, and the barriers that had been collapsing between them—those that society deemed necessary—dissolved into nothingness. "I'll try as many times as you wish." When she tipped her chin up, he dipped his head. A pair of fireworks burst overhead, so loud that he sensed her flinch. He glanced from her eyes then back down as he eased his lips to hers. It was a gentle kiss. A coaxing that he meant only in question. At eighteen, she was plenty old enough, but he knew in some ways she was still the girl who had been saved from the sea and he didn't wish to startle her.

He kissed her as he had meant to the night before. For her to know, to see. That he meant this. That it wasn't just a fleeting attraction or a stolen touch here or there. He wanted this. He wanted her. Oliver was right—he was in awfully deep.

The current pulsed, and her skirts swirled about them, brushing his leg, tangling them together. They stumbled as one when another wave struck, and he righted her best he could without breaking apart. She smiled against his mouth, and he felt it. Freedom.

Perhaps hers. Perhaps his. God help them, a little bit of both.

Jonas opened his eyes as another wave came, tugging her from him. This one the boldest yet now that the tide was rising higher. He caught her elbow as she nearly slipped beneath the surface. Her hair was wet ribbons that stuck to them both. Water swelled to his chest as her bare feet lifted from the ground for a moment, before the wave retreated. Before her footing had even returned, his mouth found hers once more.

He heard the crowd roar and, willing to lift only his gaze, saw that most who dotted the sand weren't cheering for the sky. A laugh built inside him, and he pulled away only for breath to fuel it.

Rosie did as well then glanced toward the commotion.

Knowing there was really no way to do this covertly, he slid a hand around her side and, when she didn't resist, urged her toward the shore. His pants clung to his legs, and she had to heft her skirts out of the way to keep from falling.

Fireworks continued to boom and fizzle overhead as the crowd parted some. A maid about Rosie's own age rushed forward with towels and a worried look. She draped one across Rosie's shoulders. Before he could take the towel offered him, Jonas spotted a familiar face beneath the brim of a derby hat. Babcock. Their sponsor.

One of the hotel's very owners.

Like a stone tossed into an eddy, Jonas's heart plummeted. He turned to speak to Rosie, but a frowning maid was drawing her from his side. With that stern look of disapproval, the woman had to be one of Rosie's authorities. Rosie glanced back and, despite everything, gave him a small smile. Jonas held it in his mind as she was escorted inside. Wishing he could do something, he scanned the crowd for the hotel owner. The one who could fire Rosie in the blink of an eye. The gentleman was leaning against a lamppost, adjusting his tie. Steeling his nerves, Jonas strode that way.

Chapter Sixteen

Walk with me," Mr. Babcock said—his voice holding a midwestern lilt. Though a middle-aged man, he used a glass-topped cane to point along the path.

Jonas strode with him up the walkway that led away from the beach and along the north side of the resort.

"How are you enjoying our hotel?" The gentleman wore a navy tailored suit and swiped at his mustache. He nodded to a gathering of patrons who watched the fireworks from the benches that lined the walkway.

More than a little nervous about what the man had just witnessed, Jonas pushed his hands into his pockets. "Very much, thank you."

Two valets, who looked to be on break, stood a little taller upon spotting the man at Jonas's side. Mr. Babcock dipped a friendly nod to them then spoke to Jonas. "And how is it going out on the bay? In the boat, that is. Have you made it around the point yet?"

It took an effort to keep his voice strong and steady. "We aim for it tomorrow."

"Good, good." He adjusted his bowler hat, and his cane made tapping sounds on the path. "I noticed you had the lighthouse keeper in your employ."

"He's come to our aid."

"Graham is a good man. Known him for years. Before this hotel was even built. His granddaughter. . .she's a fine young lady. It's been a privilege to have her on staff." He pointed with his cane up toward the maids' quarters, and Jonas forced his gaze to stay steady on where they were headed.

Finally, Jonas slowed to a stop. "About what happened back there. . ." He thumbed over his shoulder. "I owe you an explanation."

But Mr. Babcock simply said, "I see you lads out there on the water from my parlor window."

Were they going to discuss him and Rosie or not? Confused, Jonas nodded. Had Mr. Babcock not seen what had transpired in the water? Jonas had no doubt that it was against regulation for a staff member and a hotel guest to be found in that way. But if the man wanted to talk about boats. . .

"Every morning I say to my wife, 'Now that is what I would like to be doing.'"

Mr. Babcock adjusted his hat again. "You may recall that I'm an oarsman myself."

"Yes, sir." That's how they'd met. A day forever etched in Jonas's memory. The reason he was here and four boys' proof that hotel founders, Babcock and Story, had developed a love for this very island upon their many trips across the bay. Two tycoons in a small rowboat. Armed for both sport and leisure—off to hunt jackrabbits and birds on this island that once held nothing other than small game and native plants.

As if remembering as well, Mr. Babcock glanced around at the fine, sprawling resort. Every window was aglow, the sound of the fireworks faded, the tang of gunpowder and sulfur still in the air. "Those days are long gone now. But there are moments, often at dawn, when I remember what this land was like before we built. When it was just sagebrush. Waves on sand. Pesky seagulls. But this"—he waved a hand around them—"this I would not trade for the world. This is its own kind of paradise. A glory that few would see otherwise." He pointed toward the ocean.

Jonas tried to formulate a response to that.

"Oh, it's the young man!"

At a woman's shrill voice, he glanced over his shoulder.

A reed of a woman bustled up to him, her husband trailing a few steps behind. Jonas recognized them instantly as the couple from the observatory when Rosie had slipped away.

"I've been simply aflutter with wonder," the woman began. "Was that your young lady out there in the water? The two of you. . ." She pressed a thin hand to her heart. "So romantic!"

Babcock lifted his eyebrows, and Jonas had to force out the words. "Yes, ma'am." He said it without shame, for he felt none. Only pleasure in knowing Rosie returned his feelings. Yet it wasn't a conversation he meant to have in front of Babcock *just* now.

The woman whispered loudly behind her hand to Jonas. "Did she say yes?"

Mr. Babcock's smile said he was no stranger to mischief himself.

Jonas cleared his throat. "Still working on it."

The hotel owner chuckled, and when the curious woman scurried off with her tidbit, Jonas braved a glance up to the maids' quarters. He slanted a look back to Mr. Babcock. "Please don't discharge Rosie. Please hold me solely responsible. I'll leave. I'll leave now if that would help."

But the man only smiled. "You know what I think? And it's taken me a few minutes to come to a conclusion that sits right with me."

Jonas shook his head—waiting.

"It's come to mind that you and your friends have not been the only ones to wash ashore on this beach. The four of you taught me something about determination that day—as did Miss Graham, sometime later. I'll be forever grateful." Mr.

Babcock leaned his cane against a portion of low fencing that hemmed in a rose garden. "It's been a reminder for others—me included—to press on."

Overwhelmed, it was all Jonas could do not to pace.

"In regards to Miss Graham's fate. I view neither of you in any way but morally upright, and I'll be sure my head staff knows that, as well. Protocol would be to discharge her, and in truth, it will be out of my hands, but I'll do all I can for her. And with you. . .leaving would be wise, but I must ask you not to go too soon."

Jonas idly rubbed his palms together, trying to comprehend all of this.

"You make it around the point tomorrow, all right?"

Relief washed through him at the knowledge that he hadn't ruined this quest for Dexter, Oliver, and Oakes. "Certainly, sir." He'd give it everything he had tomorrow. And for tonight. . .there was a note he needed to leave for Rosie. The lobby would have something to jot the words on, and he'd find a maid to get it to her.

"Perseverance. That's the ticket, isn't it? And it's what I love about these waters." Mr. Babcock motioned back toward the sweeping, frothy bay that would have been fully dark were it not for the light of the hotel cloaking it in a man-made glow. "There's always the crash. But there's also the swell."

"The swell." Jonas said it with a hint of question.

"The rising. The returning of strength." Hefting up his cane, Mr. Babcock motioned toward Jonas with it. "It's that getting up again and pressing onward. It's the swell that always follows. Always."

"Yes, sir."

Mr. Babcock consulted a pocket watch then glanced to the nearest entrance, his destination, likely. He tipped his hat to Jonas and gave a final, friendly smile. "Here's to the swell."

Stepping back, Jonas thanked him. To the *again*.

Chapter Seventeen

To the what?" Oakes asked

"The *again*," Jonas said over his shoulder.

"What on earth does that mean?"

Oliver shifted in his seat to look back. He pointed first to Jonas. "It means you stop trying to be poetic. And you"—he pointed farther down the line to Oakes—"stop talking and put your oar in the water."

From the cox seat, Abner chuckled. "Any day now, boys."

Smiling, Jonas tipped his head from side to side. So much for his attempt at a motivational speech.

"I understood what you meant," Dexter said, and the skiff rocked as he pushed it farther from the beach before lunging in. A fading wave splashed against the bow, and Jonas drew in a slow, steady breath then adjusted his two-hand grip on the single oar. An unfamiliar sensation, but one that felt right all the same.

Behind them was the roar of the churning break.

They all looked to Abner and, at the man's nod, lowered oars. After a few steadying breaths, Jonas spoke for them to *set ready*. A few more breaths and, "Pull!"

Even as he dug in deep, his arms complained—muscles stretching to the difference of a single oar. They dipped and pulled a few more times until a wave slammed them. The rush of water jerked the boat to the right. Abner turned the rudder to match. Three more strokes and another wave crashed, yanking the whole vessel downward. They rowed ten meters, twenty. The next wave came with a roar, slamming everything forward. Jonas nearly collided into Oliver, but he braced himself. He gripped his oar tighter lest he lose it and dug in with every ounce of strength he had. It seemed they'd only gone a few meters when the next rush of salty foam collided into wood.

The boat soared upward, creaking as it crashed down on the other side. Jonas's leg smacked the side of the skiff, and Abner winced as he endured his own kind of pain. Cold seawater sprayed them, and Jonas dug in with his oar, giving three more strokes along with the rest. He braced himself when Abner called out for another wave. More cold water drenched them as they rushed over the churning swell, crashing back down. The boat creaked. A fierce slam sent Oliver to the floorboards and Jonas gripping the back of Dexter's collar to keep him from falling out. Again and again and again waves came, and it felt just as it had when they were boys. Like they were fighting a losing battle.

As another wave slammed the boat down, Jonas plunged his oar in and steadied himself for the next rush of seawater, but moments passed and nothing came. Just, gentle, rolling sea. He glanced over his shoulder to see the smooth bay. They'd made it past the break.

Abner nodded his pleasure and angled the rudder—directing them toward the far end of the point. *Nothing left to give.* It was the cry of his whole being, but Jonas dug in—dipping and heaving with the rest of his crew. Minutes past, tumbling into what felt like an hour as the pain became mind numbing.

It wasn't until he could no longer feel his hands that Jonas closed his eyes.

Suddenly the hands pulling the oars were just fourteen years old—the vessel beneath him, a borrowed rowboat. The panting of his teammates, that of lads and not men. All of them wondering what they had gotten themselves into as they plunged and heaved and plunged and heaved.

"I'm wondering if this was a good idea," Dexter had said as a rising wind whipped at them.

Then Oakes's young voice when a spray of salt water hit them all. *"Should we turn back?"*

Oliver's worried face tilted toward a churning, dark sea. *"These waters don't look so calm anymore."*

The crash of a wave. Last of all, Jonas saying, *"Just keep rowing. We can do this."*

But his chest was narrow, and his arms were thin, and his confidence was nothing more than words. So onward they had all rowed. Facing wave after relentless wave. The tide rising, the sea tossing around them as if to swallow them up. There they had sat, each of them as pairs to an oar, an awkward rhythm as they fought against nature.

Over and over, the sea shoved them down and turned them around, and by the time they knew they weren't getting out, a giant churning of froth and foam struck the rowboat, whipping it around, tipping it over. Down they all went.

Jonas had swallowed a chestful of salt water, and an oar struck him in the gut. He felt someone thrashing beside him and latched onto whoever it was, pushing off the bottom of the sand—desperate for air for both of them.

He surfaced with Oakes, and all of them fought the ripping of the tide that was trying to drag them back under. Pieces of shattered boat fanned about them—becoming foe instead of friend. A chunk slammed Oakes in the side of the jaw, leaving a gash.

It felt like an eternity that they fought their way back to shore, praying they would make it all the way. And when they did, it was to the sandy beach that was void of vacationers. Of any kind of hotel. The gray, sunless beach occupied by scarcely more than shrubs and jackrabbits.

As Jonas and his friends had dragged themselves out of the water, they'd spotted two men running toward them. Dressed in sporting coats, two fine gentlemen. Before Jonas could wonder why such men were on an uninhabited island, the strangers set shotguns aside and suddenly, a strong, sure hand was gripping him under the arm.

"This one's bleeding the worst, Babcock."

Oliver was shaking, Oakes and Dexter, too. Jonas would have noticed what the cold and fear was doing to his own limbs, but in that moment he was simply trying not to die. There was something about being that age and noticing the blood dripping into the sand that had him quite certain it was his last day on earth.

Then the second man was kneeling in front of him, grinning as he dabbed at Jonas's shoulder and arm with a handkerchief. At the deepest gash, he pressed the cloth down and held so firmly that Jonas fought a squirm. He peered up into the face of the man—trying to keep hold of his name—Babcock.

"What in Sam Hill are you boys doing?"

Jonas had tried to come up with an answer better than the truth—that they'd been bored—when Dexter spoke up.

"We wanted to see how far we could go."

"Young men on a mission, then."

"Yes, sir," Dexter admitted.

Jonas gripped the soiled cloth to his shoulder as the bleeding lessened. At the men's bidding, he rose and followed them to higher ground, where they settled near a boat and a picnic basket. The one man, Story, helped patch up Oliver and Oakes, while his comrade saw to the injuries of both Jonas and Dexter.

The men finished by asking them if they were hungry.

Not a one of them nodded, but Jonas had a hunch his friends were as starving as he.

"The next time you seamen scheme something as crazy as this, throw in a little more forethought, will you?" Mr. Story said with a jovial expression. "Lunch at the very least."

Within moments, sandwiches were brought forth and sliced into halves and then quarters, so that each of them—man and youth—had the same share. After sandwiches came huckleberry pie and the smell of cigars as the two men shared a match. It was a comforting smell, a calming smell, as it settled about them and their full bellies. A peaceful end to a wretched afternoon.

And as the boys climbed into the sportsmen's boat, they settled down, sobered and quiet, and the two men—the ones who would one day soon purchase that very island because of a dream and a plan—rowed them back to San Diego. Away from the desolate island named Coronado. The one that no one really visited because it was too hard a journey.

Jonas opened his eyes, and it was the hotel now in its red-and-white glory that had grown small on the horizon—a vast bay now separating them. His arms were that of a man's again. The gash in his shoulder but a memory. A sobering one. They were rounding the point. The farthest they'd ever gone before. But his lungs were closing up on him. And as his lungs tightened, his breathing growing more and more shallow, he knew what he had to do.

Jonas closed his eyes. Tipped his head back toward the hot light of the sun and pulled his oar in. "Way enough," he whispered to himself.

The boat powered forward. The oarsmen now three strong instead of four. As if feeling it, the others adjusted their rhythm—keeping the boat propelling straight. Jonas's blade sat still and steady above the water's surface. Dripping with what felt a lot like failure. That failure threatened to plunge him below, but Jonas just focused on keeping steady breaths. Breaths in time with the splash and rise of the oars. A slow, easy in and out and in and out and in. . .

He shoved off any feeling of failure, inviting humility to be what settled about him, instead. To bathe him in understanding, in respect for the men surrounding him. Jonas opened his eyes to see that Oliver's oar was tainted with palm prints of blood. Dexter's neck beaded with sweat. Even Oakes's breathing sounded like it was giving out.

Abner's words settled into an easy rhythm. A balm. Jonas breathed them in and plunged his oar again just as Abner was saying, "A few more meters, lads."

Pull. He grunted with the rest of the crew—a freedom bubbling up despite the pain.

Four blades dipped below the water for the catch, and when they feathered back after the drive, Jonas all but laughed aloud at the feel of the boat skimming past their finish point. Because there was Rosie, just overhead, waving to him. It was such a sight that Jonas wanted to remember it always. That's when he realized that a man stood beside her, waving a black derby hat. Babcock. Jonas grinned so wide it hurt. As if they all felt the finish at the same moment, oars went limp, clattering into the boat bottom, and his teammates doubled over. In front of him, Oliver lay back, crushing Jonas, and Jonas slapped a hand to his cousin's chest to return the sentiment that none of them could quite speak yet—they'd done it.

Abner took off his hat, tipped it to them. "Well done, lads. Well done."

"And that," Jonas panted, "is a record, my friends."

"We set a record." Reaching back, Dexter tapped Oliver's shoulder and then Jonas's knee. "We set a record."

"And we did it like Vikings!" Oakes hollered as he launched himself into the sea.

The boat lurched from the force, sending the rest of them tumbling out port side. Jonas collided with the water. Down he went, kicking back toward the surface, thinking about Abner. But when Jonas broke from the ocean's hold, he swiped a hand down his wet face and saw Rosie's grandfather with one arm gripping the boat, soaked through and laughing a laugh that set them all to join in.

Skirts hefted above her shoes, Rosie picked her way down the far side of the bluff, steps ginger, smile wide.

"So what are we going to tell them is on the other side?" Oliver asked, swiping a hand through his wet hair.

"Spero," Jonas said.

"Huh?" Oliver asked, climbing aboard.

"Spero." He looked to Abner, and the sparkle in the old man's eyes hinted at just who had thrown that bottle into the bay for Rosie. "Hope." With Rosie drawing nearer, Jonas swam that way. When he reached the base of the cliffs, he worked around a large boulder, clambering upon a pile of smaller stones.

She was there above him, crouching down on the boulder, skirt fanning about her.

Jonas reached up and grazed her fingers with his own. "I have to go now."

"They told me," she said.

He glanced back to his teammates, who worked to keep the skiff away from the rocky cliff base. They needed his help, so he spoke with this, his last chance to ask her. "Rosie. . .may I come back and call on you?"

She smiled, cheeks pink from her efforts down the bluff. "I would like that *very* much."

"Over the holiday? Christmastime?"

"I'll watch for you."

He squinted up at her. "Do you think the lighthouse keeper's granddaughter would quiz me for my final exams?"

Rosie smiled down at him. "I'd love to."

"And show me how to wrestle tubs of whale oil up the stairs."

She laughed.

Knowing his friends needed him, Jonas lowered himself back toward the water. "Did you get my note?"

"Oh, yes!" She reached into her skirt pocket then tossed down a little leather pouch, which he caught.

"And Rosie?"

The breeze stirred her hair, her hem.

"Stay a girl a while longer?" Sea sprayed around them. "Or I'll be the worse for missing you."

Her grin that bloomed was so sweet, so filled with joy, that the ache to be able to reach her ran deeper.

"I promise to."

It was a promise she kept.

Because when winter came, painting the California landscape in shades of brown and gold, and with Christmas just around the bend, Jonas boarded a train that all but brought him to their doorstep. In his pocket rested a gold band that held a small piece of sea glass, all surrounded by a wreath of tiny diamonds. And running across the bluffs to him was Rosie—all girl—and when she reached him, pressing the sweetest kiss to his mouth—all his. He felt it.

Epilogue

Present–Day California

Steering her rental SUV up the curving, seaside road, Alyssa ducked toward the steering wheel. She squinted against the shadows of eucalyptus trees that lined the road, stretched long by early morning. There. A sign up the way—was this it?

HISTORIC NATIONAL RESERVE.

Grinning, Alyssa tapped the steering wheel victoriously and let out a little shriek of joy. At the entrance to the reserve, she veered off the busy highway and onto a drive that meandered along the rocky bluffs of the point. The asphalt curved past a military cemetery where her heart pulsed with a bittersweet twinge at the sight of hundreds upon hundreds of white gravestones. With the naval base near, a helicopter hummed somewhere in the distance, and as she drove farther out toward the narrowing state park, so rose up the sound of waves to greet her.

When a welcome booth for the historic lighthouse came into view, Alyssa fetched her wallet. She paid the small entrance fee then turned her car into a spot near the front. No other vehicles were in the parking lot yet, and she began to second-guess her timing. She'd read online that on certain days, historians were on hand to open up the lower rooms of the lighthouse to visitors. If no one was in attendance, people could only view the parlor and kitchen through glass.

Alyssa said a prayer that somewhere in this beach town, a historian was getting ready to come to work today. "Please let it be so."

She climbed out and grabbed her camera case and notebook from the backseat. Even as trepidation wriggled through her calm, she reminded herself that early was best as the national monument wouldn't be crowded for a while yet.

Classical music began chiming from her purse as if the leather satchel housed a tiny orchestra. Alyssa pulled out her phone, and as much as she wanted to savor the brassy ringtone courtesy of composer George Frideric Handel, she saw that the caller was her brother, so a press of her thumb halted the symphony. She tucked the phone between her ear and shoulder to adjust the strap of her bag. "Hey, Neil. I just got here."

"Wow, you made good time."

"Right? My thanks to you for the direct flight."

"For this, anything. You find someone to talk to yet?"

"Not yet."

"Have you seen the bottle?"

She smiled. "I'm still in the parking lot and it seems rude to enter a hundred-year-old building while talking on the phone, so here I stand."

"The lighthouse is actually well over a hundred—"

"Neil."

"Yes."

"I will text you the moment I find the bottle, 'kay?"

"The split second you see it."

She chuckled. "I promise I'll call you if I find it. Talk to you on the other side."

"Have fun. And happy Saint Patty's Day. I hope you're wearing green, li'l sis."

He was gone, and she smirked down at her moss-hued blouse. She stashed her cell and wove around a dusty sign that welcomed visitors then strode up the sidewalk toward the quaint white building. Brush and sage swished gently, and wildflowers were just starting to let off their scent to the warming day. Slanting her gaze up to the tower that housed the great glass light flooded her with a thrill. After years of research and months of planning, how good it felt to finally be here.

Air off the salty bay tugged at her bangs, and Alyssa adjusted the hair clip on her auburn twist. When she reached the front door, the rusty handle was locked. She glanced at a nearby plaque that stated she had arrived fifteen minutes before opening. No wonder the parking lot was empty. With a gorgeous view of the water, she decided to walk out to the edge of the bluffs and snap some pictures. Freeing her camera from its case, Alyssa took a long look at the ocean that spread out to the edge of the sky then lifted it with a squint. "What a view." She took a few shots—one in each direction.

After slinging her camera over her shoulder, she mentally kicked herself for not stopping by a coffee shop for something to eat and instead, shuffled through her bag, glad for the apple she'd snatched from the continental buffet. Having left the hotel at first light, she'd been thinking to only scurry on her way. This was a quick breakfast, but a bite into the tart green apple confirmed it a tasty one.

A peek at her cell showed that it was a few minutes after opening. What if no one came? Would a maintenance man at least open the main door so she could peer inside the entryway? At the sound of footsteps on gravel, Alyssa angled away from the sea to see a silver-haired woman striding up to the whitewashed building. With keys in hand, she looked to be on a mission. A very working-at-the-lighthouse mission. Alyssa chewed her bite quickly and dug in for another as she started that way.

The woman climbed the steps to the door and slid a key into the antique-looking lock.

"Good morning. Might you be one of the historians?" Alyssa asked.

"Yes." The woman nearly dropped her purse. "And I'm so sorry that I'm late." Her keys rattled when she twisted the one in the lock. "My daughter just graduated with her doctorate, and to surprise her, I'm commissioning a portrait of her dachshund." She swiped at her slacks. "So if I have black fur on me, that's why." Her nose scrunched in a friendly way.

"You must be very proud."

"Terribly proud." The woman straightened, looking lost in thought and leaving her keys to dangle forgotten in the door. Then she snapped to attention and tugged them out. "Come on in! We're open, we're open." She motioned Alyssa forward. "Looks like just you and me so far. Oh, and happy Saint Patrick's Day."

"Thanks. You, too." Alyssa took two more bites of apple then pitched the core into the nearby can. Her sandals tapped up the steps, and she ducked into the cool, still air of the museum. A lighthouse that had once been in operation, it now sat quiet and still as if anticipating the people who would travel near and far to poke about in its tiny rooms—look up at the lamp that no longer burned now that a newer establishment had been built closer to the edge of the point.

The woman set about unlocking the glass-door barriers to the two lower sections, opening them up for visitors to actually step inside each time capsule. Alyssa glanced first into the tiny parlor where a fireplace stood sentry between two rocking chairs. Small tables were bedecked with antiques, and the view straight out overlooked the glittering blue in the distance. "Heavenly," she breathed.

The historian bustled about, unlatching a cupboard, turning on an overhead lamp. She fastened a name tag to a plaid scarf that wrapped around her shoulders.

"Love those colors, Suzanne," Alyssa said, noticing the woven reds and greens.

The woman smiled. "Ain't it darling? My husband got it for me last year when we visited Scotland. Little gift shop near Loch Fyne." She slid her hand fondly along the bright tartan then tapped a silver pin that was fashioned into a twig of heather.

"It's beautiful."

The friendly face lit with a dimpled smile as she strode to open another door.

Turning toward the warmth of sunlight that spilled through a window on her right, Alyssa stepped toward it, past the staircase and into the kitchen. She glanced around at the tidy shelves of homey wares. A stack of bowls and a crock of wooden spoons. A vase holding fresh flowers. Towels folded on the end of a quaint antique table.

On the wall was a cross-stitched sampler that read, EVEN THERE SHALL THY HAND LEAD ME, AND THY RIGHT HAND SHALL HOLD ME. Such a comforting thought that Alyssa read it once more. Beside that hung several black-and-white photos. Pictures of men and women from the nineteenth century. She stepped closer to a photograph of a man wearing a Civil War uniform. His hand lay clutched over his heart—expression both brave and tender. "Wow," she breathed. "Are all of these artifacts original to the house?" Alyssa glanced to the historian.

The older woman shook her head, setting her short curls to bounce. "Some are original to the family, but others are for decoration. All are carefully researched to be accurate for the 1800s. Even some directly from the area. This"—she strode over to one of the glass hutches that housed all sorts of dainty relics—"is from the Hotel del Coronado. . .just across the bay."

"That's where I'm staying. Gorgeous place." Squinting, Alyssa leaned closer to the protective glass and saw a ledger dated 1891.

Suzanne was beside her then. "If you look here," she said, pointing to the fifth row down, "you can see the reservation they made for their bridal week at the resort."

"They?"

"This was my grandmother and grandfather. She grew up here as a girl, and they met on that very beach."

Alyssa read the names carefully. "That's so romantic."

"I've always thought so."

"May I take a picture?"

"Certainly, but please no flash."

Alyssa uncapped the lens of her camera. "Of course." She adjusted the setting and snapped a photo of the open book then turned the camera to get a selfie of her in front of the case. Her thumbs-up was probably utterly cheesy, but she couldn't help it. This was so fun!

Which reminded her. . .

Having stalled enough, she cleared her throat. *You can do this, Alyssa.* What was the worst that could happen? The worst that could happen was that it wasn't here or that it didn't fit, and they would have to search some more. Or give up. Lay it all to rest. Peace could be found even amid that which was forever lost, couldn't it? She prepared her heart for any outcome and slowly braved the words. "I was wondering. . ." She wet her lips and motioned toward the cabinet. "If you happen to have an old bottle here somewhere. It would have been made of bronze. Very, very old."

Suzanne pursed her mouth. One earring hung crooked in a way that made Alyssa adore her all the more. "Oh yes, that's upstairs in the top bedroom." She reached up and fiddled with the piece of jewelry. "You'll have to peer at it through the glass, I'm sorry, as the room is closed to visitors."

Alyssa's jaw fell. "It's still *here*?"

"If we're talking about the same bottle." Suzanne held her palms open, one above the other. "About this tall? There's a pretty etching at the top, though it's awful hard to read."

Shooting out a sigh of delight, Alyssa reached into her purse for the gently wrapped bundle. Was this really happening? She pulled out the soft, acid-free cloth and, with her new friend looking on, gingerly freed the folds to reveal a brass topper.

"You see," she began. "This is an antique of my family's, starting way back with my grandfather, who bought it for a dime at an estate sale in Oregon. We've had it ever since, but no one has ever known what it went to. I did some research online and at the university near where I live, and to make a *really, really* long story short, we think it may belong to the bottle you have here. The one that was photographed in a 2006 edition of *Victorian Times* when they featured this museum."

"Oh, yes! We have that article here on file."

"Yes!" Her hopes rising, Alyssa cupped both hands under the cloth, holding the topper with great care. "Is there any way of getting inside that room just for one itsy-bitsy moment in time to see if this topper might fit to the bottle? If it might belong?"

Indecision warred in the woman's face, beginning first with a pinched brow that looked bent on following the rules. But then that brow softened and a spark of curiosity filled gray-blue eyes. "Well, now. . ." She pressed her mouth to the side then glanced at her wristwatch. "It is awfully quiet." She peered out the open door toward the parking lot, then back to Alyssa—finally dropping her gaze to the topper with a hint of wonder. "And perhaps if we were quick. . ." She was already starting for the stairs. "You'll promise not to touch anything?"

"Not a thing. You have my solemn vow."

"Then let's be stealthy." Suzanne winked.

Nervous energy rocketing through her, Alyssa followed her escort up the winding staircase that coiled upward. They climbed to the landing, where an antique-laden bedroom was walled off with glass. Another time capsule of sorts. Taking that moment to dig into her camera case, Alyssa pulled out the *Victorian Times* clipping and glanced to the picture of the bottle she'd looked at a thousand times before. The one she'd spent hours comparing to illustrations of the ninth century—learning more about monks and monasteries than she'd ever meant to. But it was research that had wedged into a special place in her heart. And now. . .

Key to lock, the woman had to shimmy the narrow, glass door open as if this hadn't occurred in quite some time. Alyssa drew a slow inhale—feeling the reverence of this moment.

"It's just across the way." She motioned Alyssa over a faded rug, toward the far window that had a perfect view of the sea.

Breath bated, Alyssa stepped slowly in. Her skin tingled. Face flushed. This was it. The air was musky, quiet, still. As if the scent and silence alone were stories waiting to be told. Beneath the window sat a small table that was draped with a lace cloth. Atop that rested a stack of books, an old pipe, and beside that. . .

Alyssa wet her lips, barely able to believe her eyes. Stepping nearer, she crouched down so she was eye level with the old vessel. "Hello, you," she whispered. Washing over her was the realization of just how old this treasure was. How many hands had touched it? How many lives had it passed through?

Her throat pinched with a tightness—a wash of joy that she didn't even know how to express. Eyes stinging, she unwrapped the topper. Alyssa looked up to the woman standing beside her. "May I check?"

"Ever so gently."

Nodding, Alyssa rose a little higher and, with trembling fingers, held the stopper over the bottle. It looked like the same size, but she wouldn't know for certain until she pressed one into the other. A joining. Might it be a homecoming?

With a gulp, she said a small prayer, and careful not to touch the bottle itself, she settled the topper down. It wedged in only a fraction. There it snagged. With a ginger touch, Alyssa turned the ornate cap slightly, trying to greet the two portions of dented metal as they might have once known each other. There. She felt it give—two halves becoming one—lining up just perfectly.

The historian gritted her teeth in anticipation, clutching both hands in front of her chest. "Let's hope," she said.

Alyssa grinned. "Yes." She nudged the topper down, and it settled in flush. "Hope indeed."